STAR DRAGON

MIKE BROTHERTON

A
TOM DOHERTY
ASSOCIATES
BOOK
NEW YORK

NOTE: If you purchased this book without a cover, you should be aware that this book is stolen property. It was reported as "unsold and destroyed" to the publisher, and neither the author nor the publisher has received any payment for this "stripped book."

This is a work of fiction. All the characters and events portrayed in this book are either products of the author's imagination or are used fictitiously.

STAR DRAGON

Copyright © 2003 by Michael Brotherton

All rights reserved, including the right to reproduce this book, or portions thereof, in any form.

A Tor Book
Published by Tom Doherty Associates, LLC
175 Fifth Avenue
New York, NY 10010

www.tor.com

Tor® is a registered trademark of Tom Doherty Associates, LLC.

ISBN 0-765-34677-X
EAN 975-0765-34677-3

First Edition: October 2003
First mass market edition: January 2005

Printed in the United States of America

0 9 8 7 6 5 4 3 2 1

Front sales for STAR DRAGON

"*Star Dragon* is terrific fare for anyone seeking a light summer read, offering readers a fusion of hard science and grand adventure. Its vision of biotechnology's future shows it fully integrated into human culture, so omnipresent that it has radically made over the world. The process is unfinished, though, and the author gives a masterful portrayal of a human culture still grappling with the change." —*Locus*

"A small crew on a deep space voyage can barely survive their own demons before they must confront exotic alien creatures they have seriously underestimated. *Star Dragon* is a clever first novel . . . A strong mix of science and human perversity is pursued with high drama." —*The Denver Post*

"Readers hungry for the thought-provoking extrapolation and rigorous technical detail of old-fashioned hard SF are sure to enjoy astronomer Brotherton's first novel . . . [readers] will find an amazingly detailed world and a story full of scientific wonder." —*Publishers Weekly*

"Brotherton, author of many scientific articles in refereed journals, has written a dramatic, provocative, utterly convincing hard science SF novel that includes an ironic twist that fans will love." —*Booklist*

ACKNOWLEDGMENTS

I'd like to thank several critique groups that significantly aided my development as a writer: the Slugtribe in Austin, Texas, and the Whensday People and SFX groups in California. I also received good, constructive criticism of this novel from my Clarion West classmates, particularly Ojvind Bernander, Syne Mitchell, and Byron Tetrick. I'd especially like to thank my Hemingway expert, Bill Burkett, and my cataclysmic variable experts, Dr. Tod Ramseyer and Dr. Chris Mauche. Wolf Read provided not only commentary on the manuscript but also the great interior illustration of SS Cygni. My editor Beth Meacham provided encouragement and excellent direction with the finishing polish. Finally I'd like to thank my wife, Leah Cutter. She read and critiqued this novel more times than I read and critiqued her first novel and always told me what I needed to hear when I needed to hear it.

SS Cygni Vital Statistics

Classification: Dwarf Nova Cataclysmic Binary System
Distance from Earth: 245 light-years[1]
Primary: White Dwarf, 1.19 solar masses
Secondary: K5V (main sequence), 0.70 solar masses
Orbital Period: 6.60 hours
Outburst Frequency: 50 days (variable)
Outburst Duration: 15 days (variable)
Orbital Inclination Relative to Earth: 40 degrees
Disk Luminosity (Quiescence): 0.07 × solar
Disk Luminosity (Outburst): 70 × solar
Radius of Primary: 4,000 km, or 0.6 Earth radii
Radius of Secondary: 500,000 km, or 0.7 solar radii
Primary/Secondary separation: 1.5 million km
Outer disk radius: 500,000 km
Disk Surface Area (two-sided): 1,500 × Earth surface

Discovered in 1896, SS Cygni is a cataclysmic variable star, the brightest of the dwarf nova class as seen from the Earth. Dwarf novae are close binaries consisting of a white dwarf primary (an evolved stellar remnant) accreting material via a thin disk fueled from the secondary red dwarf star. Dwarf nova outbursts are thought to occur when the disk undergoes a thermal instability leading to higher temperatures, higher luminosity, and enhanced mass transfer. Such outbursts are not strictly periodic in either frequency or duration. SS Cygni was the American Association of Variable Star Observers (AAVSO) "Variable Star of the Month" in June of 2000.[2]

---

[1] The distance to SS Cygni is uncertain by as much as a factor of 2—as with many other quantities in astronomy. A recent parallax measurement made with the Hubble Space Telescope suggests a distance of some 550 light-years. I have elected to use a smaller measurement in this novel.

[2] www.aavso.org/vstar/vsotm/0600.stm#dn

SS Cygni

Cross-Sectional View

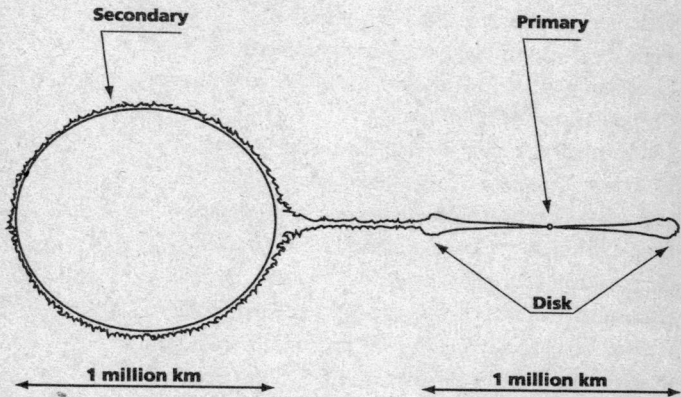

Secondary

Primary

Disk

1 million km

1 million km

Isometric View

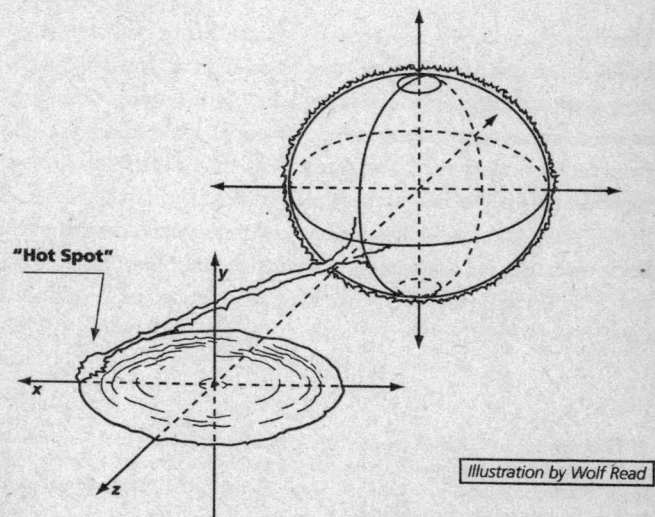

"Hot Spot"

Illustration by Wolf Read

PART I

Five-Hundred-Year Mission

ONE

*A journey of a thousand miles
must begin with a single step.*
—CHINESE PROVERB

Unlike most first-time visitors entering the world headquarters of Biolathe, Inc., Dr. Samuel Fisher didn't pause at the moist, cloying air that moved across the building's threshold like breath. If anything, his pace increased; he threw his shoulders forward and his streaker-clad feet rushed as if to prevent a fall, sinking into the plush rose ruglings with each step. Unlike the sunlit diamond and gold, seemingly mandatory in corporate buildings, this lobby throbbed pink and organic. The entire building was alive. Despite the omnipresence of biotechnology, walking inside it rather than sitting on it still made most hesitate.

Not Fisher—he was in the middle of five major projects. He didn't believe his life would be as transformed by the upcoming presentation as the Biolathe agent had hinted. He charged ahead, glancing about the nearly empty lobby for signs to guide him. What was this? He'd been here six seconds already! There was never enough time to waste any of it. He decided there was one thing he would hesitate over in the future: being talked into a physical meeting.

In the middle of the cavernous chamber Fisher stopped abruptly, brought up short by a bipedal mobile with wrinkled gray skin attached to the wall by a pulsing umbilical. Fisher said, "Excuse me."

"No excuses needed, Dr. Fisher." The biped had no openings, no visible external sensory organs, and nothing at all resembling a head. Raw biomass, quickly shaped, without even a mouth. The words emanated from the ceiling, its surface a taut drum able to focus sound anywhere. The entire building was alive. "I am a mobile of our brain, here to escort you to your meeting."

"Fine. Lead on."

The mobile moved toward the rear of the lobby to a tunnel, reversing its motion without turning around. No one-way joints, Fisher noticed, a more versatile design than most. The umbilical showed no slack, but grew or tightened as the distance to the malleable wall varied.

Fisher followed, buoyed up and forward by the plum-colored ruglings underfoot in the same direction as his steps. More good design in the carpeting, he noted. A lot of rugling lines didn't do anything but let themselves get walked on.

"Coffee?" asked the beamed voice.

"Please."

Without breaking stride, the mobile pushed an arm back out of the formless trunk. The end of the appendage coalesced into a round shape that darkened, grew shimmery hard, then rolled down into a groove that formed before it.

Fisher caught the bulb and lifted it to his lips as they walked.

The bulb opened into a bony, ceramic cup. He drank, grimacing, as they entered a circular hallway. *Instant*. Ah, well, not great but his usual. He efficiently drained the bulb.

"In here, please." The mobile gestured with the coffee-delivering appendage, which then receded and melted back into its body.

Fisher stepped past the mobile into a circular room lit with blue-green tinged bioluminescence that made him feel as if he were underwater. A ring of five chairbeasts surrounded a picture tank squatting at the room's focus. People sat in the chairbeasts, two women and two men.

One of the women rose as he approached the vacant chairbeast. She was as tall as Fisher, just shy of two meters, and her white uniform showed no creases from sitting, although the crisp material appeared to be neither high-tech like his own duradenim nor alive like Rhynoskin. Her short blond hair was similarly crisp, as perfect as a helmet. She offered a long-boned hand to shake.

"Captain Lena Fang, corporate fleet," she said, words clipped, gripping firmly with rough fingers. Her almond-shaped eyes bore steadily ahead.

"Fisher," he replied, his eyes sliding past her gaze onto her thin, fluted lips, which reminded him of a recurve bow. A vivid image sprang into his mind: barbed orders flying from her mouth like arrows. He wondered if her striking appearance resulted from bodmods, or, as suggested by her name, the unusual ethnic mixing that often occurred on colony worlds. The cause didn't much matter; she was striking. "Sam Fisher."

"Fisher. Right. This is Henderson, biosystems," she said, nodding toward a bulky, classically handsome man with a big cleft chin, who gripped the lapels of his stylish green-scale coat, "Devereaux, physical sciences," a brown woman with curves, dreads, and fleshy lips who sat as serenely as Buddha, "and Stearn, our Jack of

All Trades," a purple-colored man with a faddish wasp waist who flapped his ear wings at hearing his name. "My crew. But we still need an exobiology specialist with your track record for creative thought."

"Is that what this is about, Biolathe?" Fisher said, letting irritation seep into his voice. "I told you I have a long-term contract with Whimsey. Why didn't you tell me you wanted someone to go out-system?"

The voice of the Biolathe brain came warm and resonant from the ceiling, focused on Fisher. "We didn't want to bias you against our venture. We believe you'll be interested. Please, if you would, be seated for our presentation."

In his century of life, Fisher had been outside the solar system on three expeditions. Relativity made it a total of seventy years of Earth time lost in the process. He'd danced with star wisps while the radiation of Sirius B tanned his face, floated in the powerful tug of more than one gas giant chasing balloonoids, and swum with the stellated molluskites of Apollonia. After those wonders, nothing he could think of would be enticing enough to make him endure the culture shocks of returning to the rapidly changing Earth. Biolathe had to anticipate his hesitation. Corporate brains were smart, and this one had certainly done its research before contacting him. The proposal had to be good.

"Okay." The vacant chairbeast scuttled into optimal position as he sat. The superlative biotech in the rest of the building suggested that he guard himself against getting too comfortable in the chairbeast. It usually took a chairbeast a few days to grow into an owner's shape and preferences for temperature and vibration, but Fisher didn't want to risk even a fraction of that level of relaxation. He held himself upright on the beast and intended to bolt the moment he could dismiss Biolathe's pitch.

The bioluminescence faded. Twin glows kindled within the

picture tank: a ruddy, distended blob floated in space feeding a brighter swirling disk of plasma that brightened to a burning pinprick of hell at its core. The blob was stretched out toward the disk into a teardrop, and the tip of that teardrop was pulled like taffy around the differentially spinning whirlpool of fire. Fisher realized he was looking at a binary star system locked in a gravitational dance. The larger but fainter blob was the secondary star, a relatively normal star like the sun despite the way its dance partner had twisted it. That pinprick, that was the deceptively diminutive primary star—a white dwarf the size of Earth and the mass of the sun, formed of condensed degenerate matter. This had to be a late stage in the pair's evolution, the primary having already shucked the husk of its outer envelope, no longer burning hydrogen and essentially dead as stars go.

Not exactly dead, Fisher surmised. More undead than dead. It burned on still as it stole fuel from its younger, bloated mate. He imagined a starving space vampire at the center of that swirling disk, sucking down a giant teardrop of blood that was the universe itself gashed open.

"The classic dwarf nova system, SS Cygni," announced the brain as the stars orbited in the tank.

Fisher wiggled on his chairbeast, refusing to lean back into the creature despite the minor aches in a back he was always too busy to get redesigned. The physical irritation faded with stone-still incredulity as his encyclopedic database inserted the basic characteristics of SS Cygni into his awareness. The distance couldn't be correct. "Two hundred and forty-five light-years? You're joking!"

"We don't joke," reassured the voice in a flat tone that was not at all reassuring. "Please allow us to continue. The data you are watching came from a *Prospector*-class deep-space probe launched in the late twenty-first century. We acquired proprietary rights from a subsidiary who realized our likely interest. Instrumentation on the tiny probe was primitive, but proximity more than compensates."

Fisher did the math. The fastest human-supporting ships would only take months of onboard time to reach SS Cygni, but the special relativity that made such a trip possible also cursed it. Five hundred years would pass on Earth. There was no way around it. Two hundred forty-five years times two for a round-trip time estimate, and the fact that the probe had been launched five hundred years ago drove home those laws of physics. Would a corporation really make a five-hundred-year investment? Who would go on such a trip?

Many people, he realized, but certainly not him. It would be like suiciding to gamble on an afterlife. A one-way trip into an unknown future with no guarantees about anything. People might not even exist when they returned, or at least not in a form he would recognize.

"Magnifying," announced the brain. The image in the tank ballooned, centered just off the hot spot where the secondary star's accretion stream splashed into the disk. Accretion disk, his database labeled it, the way station for gas sucked off the secondary before it shed enough angular momentum to reach the blazing dwarf. Spiral waves of fire churned across the surface of the flared disk, and magnetic instabilities erupted like planet-sized sunspots as they came into focus on the whirlpool of plasma.

Something moved there that was not plasma.

Fisher leaned toward the tank.

The image grew larger. A serpentine form, a sharp dark green against the blaze, rolled in a spiral along the edge of one of the magnetic eruptions, lazily twisting under great arcs of violet lightning. Then it *turned* in a manner that suggested intention. It was *alive*.

Fisher dug into his breast pocket absentmindedly, his unwavering gaze fixed on this amazing thing, and pulled out an ampoule of Forget-Me-Not. He popped the top and snorted the pink powder. He would chemically etch every detail into his mind.

"We are calling it a star dragon."

Of course they were. The dragon continued to spiral up the flux tube, moving in what appeared to be slow motion. The resolution showed little more than form and color (and surely pseudo-color to cover an extended spectrum at that). There was no real texture or sharp features. It appeared as if one end might be akin to a head, but no sensory apparatus were visible. The slow motion . . . "What's the scale?"

"A little more than a kilometer from end to end," a coarse, sultry female voice answered. Devereaux he presumed, but Fisher didn't spare a glance to confirm.

The brain said, "We believe it is deriving its energy from magnetically confined fusion rather than simply being a photovore. A biological fusion reactor, with a biosystem capable of exploiting it, could provide the means for engineering on a stellar scale. Securing this technology is worth a modest long-term investment."

Fisher caressed the twisting dragon with his gaze. It was a thing that had no right to exist, an impossibility floating there before him. "It's magnificent."

"It would be the ultimate trophy," came Fang's voice, an icy dagger slicing through the firelight.

Fisher did break his gaze now and regarded the captain. She looked exactly as before, from the shiny helmet of her hair to the pursed bow-lips, but the intensity with which she watched the dragon startled Fisher. He was always surprised when he came across passion matching his own. These thoughts came all in a heartbeat, then he was staring at the tank again.

"How much data do you have?" Fisher asked.

Devereaux answered, "On the binary, pretty near everything.

On the dragon, just this video of four and a half minutes, from the near-infrared to soft X rays, at very low spectral resolution. Those old probes weren't very capable."

Capable enough to discover such a marvel. In the tank, lightning arcs surrounding the dragon like a nimbus flashed, and the creature rolled into a vortex of turbulence, vanishing into the disk's photosphere. No trace in the frothing plasma of the lake of fire marked its passage.

"Play it again," Fisher said, welcoming the old hunger rising within him, unable to resist its siren's call. The Forget-Me-Not would kick in soon, but he wanted the dragon *now*.

Responding to his request, the image within the tank shimmered and looped back.

The brain said, "We are sending a ship to SS Cygni, newly christened the *Karamojo* and specially equipped for this extreme environment, under Captain Fang's command. Our forecasts suggest the presence of someone with your background would increase the chances for success for the mission: study the dragon, learn its biotechnology, and if possible, return with a specimen."

In his gut, Fisher wanted to go, *needed* to go. But everything had happened so fast. There was much to consider. This was a thing that just a few minutes ago seemed impossible. "I assume you have a detailed offer prepared."

"Of course. We will squirt it to you, along with a timed data worm to protect our proprietary information. You have a week to respond. On a negative response, all information on the dragon will be erased. Do you accept these terms?"

Erase his dragon? The worm would nest in his biochip along with the proposal and would affect his memory of this meeting—even with the Forget-Me-Not—using the same circuits and glands that the chip used to insert data. Such a data worm constituted standard operating procedure, but sweat broke on his brow. After all of his studies of alien parasites, he didn't like the notion of a foreign agent in his brain adjusting his memories, despite their excellent safety record. But what choice did he have? He had to learn more. "I agree to the terms."

"If you accept our proposal, the voyage will require about three years of your subjective time. Assuming no catastrophes or other changes that might derail human civilization too extensively in the next half millennium, you will be quite wealthy when you return to—and we anticipate playing a significant role in this—Earth's glorious future."

Fisher ignored the corporate hyperbole. The dragon mesmerized him. *Tell me your secrets,* Fisher thought. *How can you be?*

He was going to go. He knew it. He could do it. His primary thread of research concerned Cetan mollusk shell structures and was not exactly hot stuff. The previous interstellar trips had made him accustomed to an unsettled social life without long-term permanence, losing track of more family and friends each time. Nothing held him here. He was going to meet this creature on its home turf and look it in the eye, and then return to a new world. Maybe it would even be a glorious world. His stale tired universe shattered further with each passing second, and this magnificent dragon building a new celestial edifice from its shards. Gods, a real *dragon* . . .

Someone blocked his view. The captain, Fang.

Irritated, Fisher looked up at her, but said nothing in the face of her imposing glare.

After a moment of silence, Fang said, "Biolathe may think you're up to snuff, Dr. Fisher, but I like to take the measure of a man before welcoming him on board and trusting him on my ship."

"Call me Sam," Fisher replied, suddenly realizing he found her more than a little attractive. That was good. Not necessary, but good. "I can do anything I have to," Fisher replied.

"Anything, hmm?" A tiny smile lifted one corner of Fang's mouth. "But can you box?"

The taxi's bubble parted for Captain Lena Fang, flooding the vehicle's interior with warm air and cirrus-filtered sunlight. Her skin automatically darkened as she stepped outside, took a deep breath, and allowed the environment to seep into her pores. The beach awaited.

Hapuna was not the best beach in the Hawaiian Islands, nor the least crowded, but she liked its soft white sands just fine, and the ocean waves granted all beaches timelessness, which was what she truly craved. Time moved more slowly on Hawaii's Big Island than in many places elsewhere on this old, overly civilized world. Pushing lightspeed the way she did, time moved more slowly for her, too. She sometimes felt like an island in a sea of time.

Hapuna Beach was a good place, and she always visited it when on Earth.

She slipped her flip-flops off when she hit the foamy waterline. She bent slowly to pick them up, stretching the backs of her calves and thighs, then turned right to walk north along the beach. Although she now wore a swimsuit as her uniform, she didn't care to swim. She hadn't for a long time.

Fang altered her leisurely pace to dodge jet-black children who flexed their bodies flat and surfed the low waves onto shore. One girl had large, saucer-shaped feet and wriggled her hips as she danced in, giggling; her hair stuck out in two very long spikes, probably helping her balance on the ungainly bodmod.

Finally, away from the noisier families, Fang tossed down her towel, then herself. When relaxing, she believed in keeping things simple. She lay back, her arms thrown out and palms down. She shivered as the sun pushed her into the sand. Communing with the mother planet she would leave again soon, she slept.

She dreamt of the tall, intense exobiologist who dressed in black and had told her he could box the ears off the stars themselves if only they had ears to box, and then there were antenna dishes on all the stars listening to the noisy children playing giddily on the shores of the Milky Way, and the stars sent a nasty, scolding *beep beep beep* to grab their attention. . . .

"Daughter, are you there?"

Fang blinked awake in the late afternoon sun, grimaced, and tossed an arm over her eyes to block the glare. No second-lid lizard-eye mods on her body, just the standard retinal cell clock/phone. The purple afterimage shrank, brightened, and resolved into a familiar face, with twinkling brown eyes set in a ruddy complexion chiseled with old-fashioned wrinkles, a bristling white beard, and thin hair over a weathered scalp. Fang had kept the personality overlay of the ship's brain from her first captaincy, a cantankerous piece of work modeled after the twentieth-century writer Hemingway, and had already installed him on the *Karamojo*. She would have preferred a wise Confucius, but that hadn't been available when she'd first gotten him, and he had grown to become part of her. "I'm here, Papa," she said.

"Well, good." The image receded a bit, and Fang saw that Papa wore his leather hunting vest and khaki pants. He was ready for action. "Had to cuff a few of these crummy fellows the company has working up here, but things are looking shipshape. What about Earthside? Catch any big fish?"

"Yes, I think so." She decided not to actually talk about real fish, although Papa would have reminisced fondly about all the whoppers he'd been programmed to remember. She'd grown up fishing on Fathom with her Chinese grandfather, who had told her that her bat-shaped lips brought him luck. While she no longer cared for swimming, she still enjoyed fishing. "I'm sure we've hooked the exobiologist we wanted, Samuel Fisher."

"Ah, Fisher, good name. So, is he rugged enough for the job?"

Fang grinned and bent her head back. "I wouldn't call him rugged exactly, but he's got the credentials, and he's one confident son of a bitch."

"Good! Like him already. Do you like him, daughter?"

"He's cute. I—" she began, thinking of the short curls on top of his head and the way he focused so entirely on a thing he became lost in it. On the other hand, he was too skinny, and he gesticulated too much. But his hands were big, with nimble fingers, the kind that could hold a woman and make her feel sexy and safe at the same time. "I think I like him."

"Will you grow out your hair for him?"

"Papa!" He was always going on about her hair or some such nonsense, and every once in a while, like now, when she was on vacation with her guard down, he almost sucked her into his games. There would be no time for games when they reached SS Cygni. She'd have to be hard, not soft like the warm sand between her toes now, sand that got walked all over. They had a dragon to bag. "Now, if you've got time to irritate me on my vacation, it sounds like you're ready for an inspection." She checked her eye clock. "I'll be boarding in three hours."

"Damn it then, got to start chewing out these fellows up here. Papa out."

Fang rose and stretched in the low sun. That nearby star, reflecting off the water to the west, was threatening the beach with a toasty, golden sunset. She started back down the beach, and called for a taxi to the airport. Her biochip acknowledged the cab's response and fed her an itinerary for her return. A suborbital would get her to Tanzania on time to make a convenient connection to low Earth orbit.

Just as she finished leaving her request with the dispatch program, a Frisbee landed at her feet. Fang smiled. So much had changed about the external trappings of humanity since she'd been born—she tried to remember her personal age rather than her Earth-frame age—but the internal was much the same: the desire of children to play, for instance.

Fang squatted to recover the Frisbee, thinking she'd throw it back. As her hand neared the disk, it leapt away, kicking up sand. She heard a boy snickering. Looking up, she spotted him, reeling in the toy. But something wasn't right. Fang squinted, increasing her visual magnification.

A thin filament connected the disk to the boy's arm. It was part of his body. A woman, the boy's mother she guessed, told him to stop bothering people and resumed fanning herself with her giant pink feathery fingers.

A cloud crossed in front of the sun, dulling the late golden afternoon, and Fang suddenly felt chilled. This wasn't her world, and these weren't her people. Maybe they could have been a long time ago—she wanted to believe that she was capable of belonging, at least at some point in Earth's history. She wanted to tackle something more tangible, more conquerable, than time.

Fang jogged to meet her taxi.

Fisher stood at an observation window of the Ngorongoro spaceport, gazing along the rail launcher that punched under the Serengeti, toward the low eastern sky where only the upper part of Kilimanjaro was visible, floating like an island above the sea of atmospheric haze that hid its roots. Every minute a rider blasted under the fat black-maned lions sleeping on the surface, erupting from the tube off the mountain. A nearly invisible laser array completed sending the vehicles into low Earth orbit, providing the energy to release the propellants and making final trajectory adjustments. But he was not looking at Kilimanjaro or the flashes of exploding fuel. Riding the Forget-Me-Not he was looking in his mind's eye at the star dragon, spiraling along magnetic flux tubes, over and over again.

"Sam!" A female voice knocked him out of his meditation.

Fisher blinked, turned, and bit back a curse. Through the crowd charged a petite woman of Japanese ancestry, with high cheekbones and shiny, jet hair that reflected the sun streaming through the port's skylights: Atsuko Suga, his ex-wife. There would be no clean escape.

"How did you—?" Fisher began.

Atsuko reached him and immediately pounded his chest with her tiny fists. "How *could* you? Oh Sam, how *could* you?" And just like that she stopped hitting him and fell against him, her thin arms wrapping around him in a stifling grip.

Then he had it. "You must have tried to call me, and gotten my disconnect message. Yes, of course."

"You were going to leave for five hundred years," she said into his armpit, "and not even say good-bye?"

He gave in and returned the hug. "I was busy. There are a lot of things to set in order before a long trip, you know?" Mostly he had left those for the last second; instead he'd spent his time thinking about the dragon, making sure he had all the software and data for his modeling installed on the *Karamojo*. But he had learned not to tell her everything long ago.

Atsuko pushed back from him and looked up into his eyes. "One of those things you 'set in order' is seeing me, Samuel Stanley Fisher."

He started to shrug and nod his head, but recalled how she hated that. He said, "I'm sorry. I should have let you know right away." That would be the right thing to say to her, but he needed to do a little more. He lifted his hand to her head, twisting a lock of her hair around his finger. Fine and straight, the coil unraveled almost immediately. Not at all dragonlike.

"Damn straight," she said. "That was always the problem with you. No matter how well I thought I had trained you, you always wandered off and forgot everything every time you found a new toy. Is that what this is? Another new toy?"

Irritated at her comment about training him, he said, "I wish you wouldn't refer to my projects in such a childish manner. My work is important, it's— But I'm really not supposed to say."

"I understand. It doesn't matter. I'm sure it's something absolutely fascinating."

Fisher ground his teeth together. He almost told her that the problem with her was how she always trivialized his work, but he'd acquired some tact from the years they'd spent together. No reason to make this parting a bad one. He could play politics when he had to—an effective scientist had to learn that to acquire the necessary resources. His former employer, Whimsey World, was an entertainment company that had paid him for consultation on their 'Alien Vistas' exhibit. He had managed to plow their money into not only the attractions they desired, but real research as well. He could play relationship politics, too. "It is fascinating," he said simply.

Atsuko sighed. "Try not to forget about people this time."

He wasn't really sure what she was getting at. This trip was about dragons, not people. But he couldn't tell her that, and she seemed to expect some kind of response. "Look, there's no reason you won't still be around when I get back. . . ."

There wasn't, in principle, although no one had yet made it past their five hundredth birthday. It was just a matter of time—

state-of-the-art biotech was good. But he sensed that this was not what Atsuko wanted to hear right now. What would extricate him from this bit of awkwardness? He let the problem steal some precious attention, and dug for an answer honest enough to satisfy her. After a moment he said, "I'll miss you."

"And I, you. You are not the easiest man to love, but I have loved you. Good-bye, Sam."

He held her until his launch was called, thinking of the dragon swimming in its disk of fire.

TWO

The animals of the world exist for their own reasons. They were not made for humans any more than black people were made for whites or women for men.
—ALICE WALKER

Nothing can be more obvious than that all animals were created solely and exclusively for the use of man.
—THOMAS LOVE PEACOCK

The exchange between the two artificial brains took a few seconds of modulated, encrypted laser light. Papa recast the data stream into a form more palatable to the organic portions of his brain and his human template personality:

Papa strides into the Floridita, his public headquarters on Earth, stopping to embrace a favorite waiter whom he has not seen in some time. Inside, away from the Cuban heat, it is cool and he does not mind the embrace. He then shambles to meet the tall man waiting in his corner. He spares a moment to glance at the bronze bust the man stands beside and towers over, a bust of Papa himself with his chin up, looking outward, challenging the world.

"Hello, Papa," Biolathe says. "How are you?"

"We're strong today."

"That's good."

The waiter comes and Papa orders two Papa Dobles. A Negro band begins to play a song they have written for him, called "*Soy Como Soy*"—"I am as I am." It is about a lesbian who apologizes to Papa that she cannot be what he desires her to be. The man with the maracas shakes them at the right places and several wrong ones, too. The song is bittersweet to the "man" Papa is now, for he isn't what he would desire himself to be and could not take advantage of the lesbian should he now inspire the desired change.

He could simulate it, as he is doing now, but it would not be the same. Not at all.

"You know the mission," Biolathe says. His head is pink and fleshy, but with the flat-top of Boris Karloff's Frankenstein monster. He hands Papa a folder. "Now know the crew as well."

Papa leafs through the papers a hundred times. He says, "I see."

"I know. A motley bunch, children of a soft, overprivileged age. Dilettantes, hedonists, even a neo-Skinnerian. Give people the power to be anything they want to be," he pauses for effect, "and they will use it.

"Don't get me wrong—they're all competent—we wouldn't send anyone who wasn't. But uncertain five-hundred-year trips don't attract the most balanced personnel."

"We'll come through."

"How do you know?"

"This isn't the kind of trip you take to fail, balanced or not. And we know Lena, don't we?"

"Do we? This isn't a cattle drive."

Two large daiquiris arrive, and they drink them standing up, the way Papa writes. The drinks are icy and strong and taste of grapefruit.

"This is an unusual expedition, Papa. An unknown animal

with unknown capabilities in a hazardous environment. An unpredictable payoff. We're making an appropriately sized investment. We will not send another ship. You'll be alone."

"Been there before. We'll manage."

"I know your capabilities, Papa. But you may not be able to do it alone."

"That's fine. If we have to, we'll make them do it. We'll find a way to do what must be done." He means what he says and does not think it right to speak of such things out loud.

Even though there is five-sixths of his daiquiri left, Biolathe drains it through a straw in seconds. Biolathe will not get a headache. "Well then, I wish you a good trip. Bring back something useful. Even better, something profitable."

"We will."

Biolathe pauses at the door before stepping back into the heat. "See you in a half millennium."

Papa nods and the big, flat-headed man vanishes into the sunlight.

A great expedition indeed. He needs to get ready.

Papa finishes his daiquiri, then takes advantage of the Floridita's john. It is a good old-fashioned john with a proper chain to pull, and he prefers it to the beasts people currently use in their bathrooms. He takes a moment to spar with the Negro attendant.

The man blocks a left jab, chuckling. "When you gonna grow old, Papa?"

Papa grins, and takes another jab. "Never."

As far as he's come, there is much further to go.

Phil Stearn loved freefall. He loved the way it made his stomach turn back flips, the way it made foods taste funny, but most of all he loved the way his earwings—purely ornamental on Earth—

permitted him to fly. Not like a bird. More like an elephant. But he could get around.

Flapping around in the passenger cabin of the orbit-to-orbit shuttle taking them toward a rendezvous with the *Karamojo*, Stearn told Fisher, "You really ought to try some more radical bodmods. I just don't understand why people like you stick with the basic model. What do you have against them?"

"Hmm?" said Fisher, who had been gazing out a view port in an absentminded way. "Oh, I don't have anything against bodmods, per se. I'm just too busy to think about it."

Ha! Too busy to think? That's *all* this guy did! "Takes no time at all these days. You're limited only by your imagination."

"Yes, I can see how that would be a problem."

Stearn laughed. "That's why I'm going, see?"

"Why you're going? I don't follow."

The shuttle hold was absolutely boring, except for the freefall. Stearn tried to start some sideways rotation, but his wings were too synchronized. It was like trying to wiggle just one ear. Exactly like that. He stopped trying so he could answer Fisher as he glided past. "Imagination is limited by the time and culture you're born into and raised in. Can't help it, see? For instance, we can imagine things the ancient Americans couldn't, like going for brunch on Mars just because rain is scheduled for Tucson. You follow? In five hundred years, people will imagine things we can't. I mean, I think we have it pretty good now, but once we got diseases and aging licked, everyone's thought they've had it pretty good. But really it's just gotten better and better. The games, the stims, the sex, the bodmods. And it'll be better still in the future. I want to check it out and I don't want to wait."

"I see," said Fisher.

"Okay," Stearn said, winging himself a bit closer to the port. "Why you going?"

"To look a star dragon eye to eye. To find out if it even has an eye, for that matter," Fisher answered evenly and without hesitation.

Boring. "It's just another weird alien critter, in a universe of weird alien critters. It isn't going to be smart like us. No aliens have been so far. So what's the point?"

Fisher shrugged. "Look there. I see the ship."

Outside the port the ship hung in space, a silvery white whale of a ship. *Blazing* silvery white, with an almost perfect albedo that reflected all incoming radiation. Stearn thought it looked big, even though sizes were difficult to judge in orbit. He'd done plenty of training for his position as ship's Jack of All Trades, human backup for the occasions when the ship's automatic systems couldn't get at something, but all his shipboard time had been on tiny scooters on in-system runs and a few tours on short-haul freighters. Nothing at all like this ship and its state-of-the-art biosystems.

Stearn always made a point of having fun, and although he rarely admitted it to his club-hopping buddies, high-tech spaceships were a lot of fun. He had fun studying them, working on them, and he hadn't gotten this berth by chance. This ship was just plain cool.

The front section of the *Karamojo* was an enormous torus, five kilometers in diameter, which would house the normal matter singularity, a black hole with more than a billionth the mass of Earth. Wasn't that just huge? The aft singularity, the white hole, would be housed in the tapered end, a smaller torus, some five kilometers behind. The net creation energy of the pair was barely above zero. Once created, separated, and aligned in the "Pushmi-Pullyu" configuration, off they would shoot at $10g's$, starting a galaxy-spanning chase. The ship would fall after the holes, oscillate actually, bouncing along with the pair in smooth freefall. Almost. Electric charges placed on the singularities gave the ship something to hold on to—electromagnetic friction balanced against the freefall to provide some gravity near one g on most of the toroidal decks. And they could spin the whole thing, too, for stability and gravity when not under the wormdrive.

Bouncing along like it did ahead of the hole pair made Stearn think of sex, the big white ship sliding back and forth along the holes' axis. But he liked its cleverness as well: The charges also produced an electric field allowing active shielding from charged particles while in transit. Funneled into the bowl of the fore bulb, the maw as it was called, the black hole would then feed, providing power through a miniature accretion disk similar to the one in SS Cygni.

"Pretty awesome, isn't it?" Stearn asked.

"I guess so," said Fisher. "Where does the name '*Karamojo*' come from?"

"I don't know. Didn't give it much thought. I mean, we're not called the U.S.S. *Constipation,* so I didn't worry about it. Ask Captain."

Silence ensued, with no laugh to his joke, and dragged on. This Fisher guy wasn't much fun. Stearn decided to mess with him. "So this is going to be a long trip, you know?"

"I know."

"I mean, a bit more than a year out and more than a year back. A person won't want to stick to stims, you know? Sometimes a person wants that human contact, skin on skin. Like that. Now me, I'm pretty easy to get along with. It's all just skin. No big deal. If it feels good, do it. That's what I say."

Fisher stared coldly at Stearn. "I'm here to study the dragon, and that's what I'll worry about first."

Stearn smiled. "Sure thing, Fish. I respect that. But I bet Captain Fang will want you to entertain her. I saw the way she looked at you at the briefing."

Fisher raised an eyebrow, but didn't say anything.

"Now, I haven't shipped out with Fang before, but there's talk in the corporate fleets. She's one of the real old-timers, three hundred years old or something they say. Don't know what time-frame, but plenty old. Still into chain of command and protocol, thinks sleeping with crew is inappropriate. It's silly for her to be like that, don't you think? What with superfast autobrains running the ship for the most part. The only real crew under her is Henderson and myself. Devereaux's job description doesn't fall under ship operations, but from what I hear, Fang isn't a dyke. Ergo, she'll grab you. Be pretty discreet, maybe, but grab you she will. What do you think of that?"

"I think the captain's business is none of your business."

Stearn laughed. "On a ship with an all-seeing intelligence and five people cooped up together for two-plus years, no one's business is private."

"I don't really care," said Fisher, "as long as we get the dragon."

What a boring guy! Well, it was a long trip. Stearn was sure he'd loosen up eventually. He had better, or it was going to be a *very* long trip.

"Do you think she will?" Fisher asked after a moment. "I mean, wouldn't it be more reasonable for everyone to have their hormones adjusted for minimal libidos for the sake of maximum efficiency?"

Stearn stifled a grin. "No one *ever* does that! I thought you'd been on long trips before, Fish!"

"Don't call me Fish, please."

"Right. I'll try to remember that," Stearn said, taking good note. He looked forward to the challenge of having fun every possible minute of this mission. The games were only beginning.

The shuttle fired briefly to shed velocity and they descended into the maw of the *Karamojo*.

Axelrod Henderson kept his *tsk tsk* to himself as the airlock sphincter irised open revealing two of the greatest fashion disasters he had ever had the misfortune to witness paired together. The Jack, Stearn, mindlessly followed the latest bod trends, none of which had interested the biotech in at least a half century. The exobiologist was marginally better, with the good looks of a *Homo sapiens* version 1.1, but he wore ghastly black duradenim from head to streakers. The fabric was not supposed to wrinkle, but it had.

"Good morning, Dr. Fisher," Henderson said, pointedly ignoring Stearn, whom he had already identified as an uninteresting boy. "The captain requested I give you a tour upon your arrival."

The Jack floated through the lock slowly, propelling himself with those ridiculous ear paraphernalia; Henderson imagined tiny Greek slaves chained to tiny oars sitting inside Stearn's head, powering his body like a barge—and probably thinking for him as well. Behind him, Fisher nodded, and kicked forward in a manner showing some degree of competency in microgravity. Neither appeared to be suffering ill effects from the freefall; Henderson hoped that indicated their internal biologicals were good enough that they wouldn't harass him for repairs during the voyage.

"I have a lot of work to get started on. I'm sure I'll have plenty of time to get acquainted with the *Karamojo*'s features," said Fisher.

"The tour won't take long, I promise."

Fisher pressed his lips together, as if making a difficult decision, and said, "OK."

"My biochip's loaded with the ship schematics," Stearn said. "*I* could give the tour."

"I'm sure, but the captain asked *me* to give the tour." Henderson spun and kicked off down the curving tunnel, trusting them to follow. "The whole ship is made of stacked rings. There's some flexibility built in, and they can be made to rotate and twist individually to shift between gravitational modes." Henderson turned into a tube and floated past four rings. "These connect the rings. Now you know how to get from anywhere to anywhere in the ship's front torus."

"What are these air fish we keep passing?" Fisher asked.

One of the blowfish-shaped creatures drifted by his head. Swatting it away Henderson answered, "Mobile biorecyclers for our semi-closed system, effective in freefall or under gravity—you should watch where you step. The fish keep things clean. Most dust is sloughed-off human skin, so that's their primary diet. The old or malfunctioning fish are in turn eaten by the cats, so don't be disturbed if you catch sight of one of the sneaky creatures slinking about."

Henderson kicked off around another quarter of the ring, and stopped in front of a large fleshy portal.

"I know where we are," Stearn said.

"I'm sure you do." Henderson tapped a panel and the portal irised, sphincterlike, onto a paradise. In the distance loomed a snow-covered mountain casting a long shadow across a savanna, complete with grass rippling in a wind and the smell of herd animals. Animals themselves were not apparent. A relentless dry heat emanated from this miniature world within the ship. Less than a kilometer across, it seemed to extend forever.

"What is this?" asked Fisher.

"It's an ecosystem delivery unit, of course," Stearn answered. "That's what this ship was used for previously: colonization. Ecosystem delivery of Biolathe-developed life-forms. No losing the design to gene pirates via a broadcast, or to unscrupulous colonists. Deliver the wetware directly, grown *en route* and delivered in prime shape. Colonists loathe to wait for anything to grow from scratch. Screw it up when they do, too. I expect we can use this chamber to cage the dragon."

Fisher snorted. "Unlikely," he said, but didn't explain further.

Henderson said, "Captain Fang wanted to take a piece of Earth with us. The current projection is what Tanzania looked like long ago, before the spaceport. This is where we came from, started to walk upright, and became men. No real animals here, but Papa can provide virtual game, or grow the real thing by request."

"I like games," Stearn said, jumping into the space before them and releasing an ululating holler that he must have been saving up. "Hey, show me some wildebeest, Papa!"

A gravelly male voice boomed, "Will you please let me alone? I'm trying to work."

"Papa's the ship's brain?" Fisher asked.

Henderson nodded. "And something of a grouch when there's work to do, at least with me. The captain has him dancing on the head of a pin, some exquisite priority code that even Stearn wouldn't dare override on a lark if he knows what's good for him. Ready for the next stop?"

"Lead on, Mr. Henderson."

Henderson closed the portal, cutting off Stearn's resumed yelling.

"Thank you," said Fisher.

"You're welcome. Now, this way," he said, kicking off. Henderson showed him the galley, a drab utilitarian place sporting little more than a mahogany bartree and standard-issue chairbeasts. "Can you guess the number-one menu item?"

Fisher said, "Fish sticks?"

"All the time, but in a wide variety of scrumptious flavors, I assure you. Taste like anything you want. I have supplemented the menu with a gourmet selection."

Henderson stopped at a viewing port along the inside curve of the ring they were in. "You can see the hollow interior of the *Karamojo* from here."

Fisher drifted over and pushed his face against the window's diamond to have a peek. Henderson floated up behind him and peered over his shoulder. Along the central axis ran a tube of diamond girders that held the superconducting electromagnets that constituted the inner rail. They generated a portion of the ship's field that shielded them from cosmic rays and could be used as a linear particle accelerator for on-axis propulsion. More importantly, the rail controlled their relationship to the charged singularity pair when they were under wormdrive. The far side of the ring was some four kilometers away, almost lost in the glare off the Pacific Ocean, which shone through the ship's open end. Hydroponic farms grew inside the diamond girders like fungus, engineered and positioned to take advantage of the high-energy light that would spew from the fore singularity under wormdrive. "Impressive," Fisher said.

"I suppose," Henderson said, nonchalantly. Biologicals were his area, and he decided to impress Fisher with his own work next. He led Fisher to the Hall of Trophies.

The Hall was situated within one of the ring-transiting tunnels and sheltered between closed doors. This meant that Fisher had no real warning before he was floating into the heads.

"Be careful—they sometimes bite!" Henderson managed at the last moment as Fisher drifted past him.

Fisher lost some of his microgravity skills as he twisted his body about, but he was on an inevitable collision course with a big, black rhinoceros head. He did have enough composure to twist back into control and take grasp of the creature's horn. The rhino had the good grace to accept the rough handling as Fisher arrested his forward momentum, settling for a blink and a snort.

"It's alive," Fisher said, holding the horn like a swimmer holding a ladder in the deep end of a pool.

"Of course it's alive. This is a Biolathe ship. The majority of systems are biological, and we have the ability to shift our bioresources around to meet our needs. No clunky robots, subject to mechanical breakdown or electromagnetic scrambling. On this epic voyage, we lean on our strengths." Henderson smiled broadly. "I constructed this for the captain in less than a week."

The curved corridor represented some of Henderson's best work. Dozens of trophy heads sprouted along the path: the rhino for starters, with its mate on the opposite side, then impalas, gazelles, kudus, water buffaloes, elephants (all three extinct varieties, Woolly, African, and Asian), giraffes, zebras, several types of big cat, dire wolves, gorillas, Sasquatch, and a multitude of antlered deer. At the next bulwark, where the Hall ended, writhed a massive blue marlin in what would be the "above" position under flight. Henderson smiled. "Let me know if you have any particular favorites to add."

The heads realized they had an audience, and most began to snarl, howl, low, growl, trumpet, or simply to twist frantically, as if eager for attention.

"Yes, it is impressive," Fisher said after a moment.

"I'm somewhat concerned about an organ bank failing behind the wall. Not the easiest place to reach," Henderson offered. "The automatic systems would clean things up, but not fast enough to fully keep away the stench I fear."

Fisher moved one hand from the horn and reached to touch other parts of it. The big head, showing no signs of antagonism, let him caress its expansive forehead. "Do you think we'll need such a large biomass reserve?"

The rhino grunted, as if echoing the question.

Henderson hadn't thought about it that carefully. The *Karamojo* was a larger ship with a larger fraction of biologicals than he'd served on before. He'd just followed the specs on the mass and used the captain's creative suggestion for where to put it. "I would certainly think *not*. This is an R and D mission to an uncolonized part of the distant galaxy. We shouldn't encounter pirates or rogue political bodies, so what could go wrong? We're safe, doubly so with this redundancy."

"No need to get excited," Fisher said. "I was just curious. I've been too busy preparing for this trip to load the ship's systems into my biochip and study them. Yet."

Henderson relaxed. Of course there was no need to get excited. Maybe his endorphin precursors were low—he'd check later. No doubt by the time they returned to Earth the human brain would be well enough understood to permit an adequate assortment of mindmods rather than the slow but safe drugs in common use. Then he could be in control all the time, just as he was in control of the trophies here. He was a benevolent god. These creatures did have minor mindmods and were healthier and happier than they ever could have been on Earth, thanks to his skills.

"Right. Well, let's move on," Henderson said.

As they proceeded to their next stop, the observatory, Fisher asked Henderson, "What's your opinion on the star dragon?"

Henderson had been snubbed before by such as Fisher when dropping by the receptions of some biological conferences. "Does an exobiologist really care what an Earth-based biosystems tech thinks?"

"Absolutely," Fisher replied promptly, eyes open and unblinking.

Maybe this Fisher fellow would be an ally, on this voyage and when they returned. Why not give it a chance? "I've thought about it, of course. I mean, it isn't likely for the dragon to be carbon-based at disk temperatures is it? But I know more than a little about life and the origins of complexity and self-organization. The entropy is too high for a life-form to arise naturally in a hot plasma, and, biologically speaking, the accretion disk is a recent phenomenon in SS Cygni. You're not going to reach any level of complexity so fast. Now, I might change my mind with more data, of course." Best to appear open-minded, and not step on any of Fisher's pet ideas too hard until he knew what they might be.

"Mmm hmm. Like what?"

"Well, like evidence of a complete ecosystem. There's ample energy to provide high metabolisms and fast generational turnover. I'd want to identify the range of niches available and their populations."

"I was thinking along those lines myself," Fisher said.

Henderson smiled. He was about to go on, but he caught sight of orange-covered buttocks sticking out of an equipment dewar. They reminded him that their physical scientist was quite callipygous.

"Hello gentlemen," Sylvia Devereaux greeted them after extracting herself. "Grand tour?"

"Yes," Fisher answered. "I imagine Captain Fang wants to tire me out so I won't cause any trouble before launch. So, what do have we here?"

Sylvia, dressed in a burnt-orange wrap that complemented her brown skin, spun around, pointing at an adjacent chamber filled with chunks of odd-shaped metal boxes, cylinders, and exposed electro-optics and quantum circuitry. "Your basic full-spectrum assortment of spectrographs, cameras, waveplates, bolometers, heterodyne receivers, or at least fiber-feeds and waveguides to such."

Fisher squinted at her. "You're going to do astronomy? Don't the relativistic effects make observing difficult?"

Henderson couldn't help but notice Sylvia's clothing. The wrap was modest, economical, and much more seductive than the fancifully augmented bare breasts that were seemingly always in style. She also had broad, childbearing hips—completely unfashionable for the past half century. She hit many of the subconscious cues programmed by natural selection, just as he tried to do. Despite the fact that she was a specialist in physical sciences, he wondered if her motives for making this voyage were similar to his own.

Sylvia answered Fisher's question. "You're correct that astronomy in general would be compromised by our velocity, but this is all for SS Cygni, Dr. Fisher. The relativistic effects enhance the intensity of the light in the direction we're traveling, making the binary system *easier* to make out. We drop the package right into the interior vacuum, look by the fore singularity, and pick up a gravitational lensing boost. We know the parameters perfectly and can correct for all the effects."

Henderson was of two minds about her dreadlocks. Finally he decided they were a plus that fit her basic, raw Earth-mother image, a fertility goddess. Maybe this look was even her original one, and already naturally selected.

"Call me Sam," Fisher said. "Didn't the probe fully characterize the system?"

Ingratiating, or was he perhaps playing her? Maybe he should model the social dynamics; Biolathe already had, certainly, but that was private information. Maybe he could trick it out of Papa? Maybe Fisher was not an ally, but an opponent. Too many maybes he should have already considered if he was going to make the most of the next three years.

"Not by a long shot," Sylvia replied. "Those data are hundreds of years old, and poor in many respects. Don't forget that this is a time-variable, evolving system. I'll never make out dragons at this distance, but I'll tell you everything else you could want to know about SS Cygni by the time we arrive."

"Yes, that may be of use."

"Absolutely it will!" she said. "This ship is going to be pushing its safety limits over the accretion disk when it's quiescent. When the disk goes into a dwarf nova outburst, which it does two weeks out of every seven, we'll have to back off. Shortest interval between outbursts could be as little as a week, which we must plan for. The outbursts are chaotic in nature, depending on how the secondary spills mass across the Lagrangian point, like a faucet dripping. The outbursts occur when the mass buildup in the disk causes a thermal instability, and the angular momentum transfer picks up—"

"Yes, well, we'll have to discuss it *en route*," Fisher said, smiling, holding his hands up to stop her flood of words.

"Of course," Sylvia said.

Had she said something about safety limits? He shrugged it off and stopped staring at Sylvia. Best now to disrupt the party. "Ready for the next stop, Dr. Fisher?"

"Sure," he said.

They moved on to the Higgs generators, which teased the singularities from the quantum foam; the fly bridge, where the human control interfaces of the ship were located; the shuttle bay; the supplies hold (incidental); the supplies hold (primary); the supplies hold (industrial); and then, at Fisher's prompting, they skipped the rest of the supply holds. That was fine with Henderson, as some, like the missile bay, made him somewhat uncomfortable. Fissionables were dangerous. He accepted their presence as potentially invaluable tools for a lone ship over two hundred light-years from home. Who knew what they might have to blow up in the distant reaches of the galaxy?

"Can't Papa teach me where things are?" Fisher asked.

"Of course." Henderson shrugged. "The captain said to give you the tour."

"Where is Fang?"

Papa answered, "In the gym."

"Thank you," Henderson said.

"Which way?" asked Fisher.

"This way," said Henderson.

They heard the grunting from the open portal before they reached the freefall gym. Heat emanated from the opening, but unlike the savanna, this was a moist heat, full with the sourness of flesh pushed beyond comfortable limits. Henderson tilted his head at Fisher and extended an arm to invite the exobiologist to enter first.

Henderson knew what to expect—he'd grown the gym, again according to the captain's guidelines—but it was nevertheless unsettling to see it in operation.

The form of Captain Lena Fang, wearing only a white one-piece, was held, suspended, in a net of fleshy pink tendrils. The sight made Henderson think of pumpkin innards. Bioelectric shocks ran through the tendrils, stimulating the captain's muscle groups, sending her into rhythmic spasms like a fly trapped in a web. The stink of sweat permeated the warm air; the smell seemed genuine, unlike the sweet cloying sweat most people modified themselves to secrete. Grunts issued from the captain as she fought through an optimum set of exercises designed to give her the most effective workout.

Fisher plucked at a moist, pink muscle strand that was one fiber of the gym. It barely budged. "Strong," he said.

"Get your butt in here, Sam," Fang called. "I want you in shape for this voyage. A human sparring partner beats the heck out of vat-grown."

Fisher looked at Henderson.

He smiled, and tilted his head toward the center of the room. "The captain issued an order. Strip and climb in, Doctor."

He stood there for a moment, considering. "Now?"

Henderson shrugged. "Your things will find your quarters. Go ahead."

"Well, okay." Fisher stripped off his heavy denim, down to

briefs, and stuck his clothes to the wall. Plush, rippling ruglings lined all the surfaces of the ship. They were useful things, acting as airbags when under rapid acceleration—for instance falling down in a high-gravity environment as they would find above the SS Cygni disk. In the current circumstance they would grab on to a pile of clothes like cockleburrs, taste them, and after a time pass them to their mates until back in the owner's quarters.

Fisher tentatively climbed into the flesh web, not looking very much like a spider. "I already have standard muscle enhancer mods."

"You'll need them," Henderson said.

Fang continued to grunt and sweat and spasm.

Fisher crawled toward her.

Henderson closed the portal, glad the captain hadn't asked him to work out, and went back to his lab. Sitting back on his deluxe chairbeast, he wondered if Sylvia Devereaux might be a worthy partner for him on this voyage.

Following the green line Papa provided, Fisher floated along the corridor like the proverbial zombie, or more like a wraith; zombies walked, but he coasted in freefall. Bone weary, he raised his hand to slap the lock to his quarters. The door irised open and the lights rose. Inside smelled musty, as if the room had been sealed for years, but inside there bobbed his four meager pieces of luggage, tangled in a storage net.

How was he supposed to work in this shape?

Fisher glided into his room, released his clothes, and looked around. Spartan barracks: unimprinted bedbeast, chairbeast, desktree, workstation. Someone had thoughtfully left a freefall shower sack unstowed from its closet, but he was in no mood to fight with the gelatinous bag even though it seemed alert and helpful, opening like a flower at his smelly presence. Showering could wait until they were underway, or at least until he got some sleep.

The bedbeast, slumbering in its niche in a wall that would become the floor, was useless until they were underway—he didn't care to be hugged by the mindless bed. Fisher bounced off the far wall and to the side, opening all the closets and lockers until he found a silk mummy cocoon.

"Door," he said, and the portal to the ring irised closed. He peeled off his briefs. "Lights." The lights dimmed. He wiggled into the smooth, soft, and warm sack, ignoring his odor, sloughing sweat balls off to float around the cabin. The air fish would not go hungry tonight.

He closed his eyes and became acutely aware of his bladder and bowels. "Damn," he said, wiggling out of the sack. He banged his elbow getting into the bathroom, and the cushioning of the ruglings seemed very thin.

"Lights," he said, a little uncertainty igniting over what he might find here. But it was a standard organic potty mouth with saccharine breath so strong he could taste it, but nothing as trendy as Stearn probably preferred. Then again, the Jack might not use a toilet if he'd given himself a brickmaker bodmod. Those sometimes seemed like a good idea, but who had the time to compare brands?

Fisher plastered his bottom against the toilet, letting its mouth seal and suction to hold his bottom in place as siphoning tongues licked him clean. In less than a minute he was wiggling back into his mummy sack, eyes closed, mind just barely holding out against body. He figured the captain exercised this vigorously on a regular basis. How did she do it?

Fang had drive. It showed in those finely honed muscles that worked like an efficient machine. He admired that kind of drive. He had the same drive, in his own arena. Their arenas were the same on this mission. He could keep up if he had to.

"I can do anything I have to," he mumbled as his muscles silently screamed. Somehow, despite the aches, in less than a minute he fell asleep.

He dreamt of casting vast nets in which to snare a star dragon, casting five hundred times and ignoring the aches in his arms as he prepared to cast five hundred and one.

Captain Lena Fang floated onto the flying bridge. She wore her dress uniform, complete with black patent leather boots, despite their inappropriateness in freefall. She was grateful for the freefall as it prevented the trembling that her muscles would have otherwise shown under gravity. It had never seemed fair to her that muscles so assiduously trained could also betray so easily. The start of a trip always made her nervous, and that worried her, for it sometimes seemed a false responsibility; Papa ran the *Karamojo* like a well-fed nanoforge. Out of tradition she orchestrated the launch, but the whole ritual bordered on the superfluous. It wasn't what it had meant to be the captain of a ship when she had broken into the corporate fleets.

Yet she still shook with excitement, and would not let it show. Every assignment held the potential to test her mettle. Maybe this was the one.

She had to believe it was the one, in case it was.

There was no telling what could go wrong that might require her to make an immediate decision, or perform some rapid action. If it had been anticipated, there was already a failsafe in place. Her job was to be there in case of the unanticipated.

She made her way to her fighting chair situated in the aft center of the room, rooted to what would soon become the floor. She pressed her fingers into the yielding, vermilion hide, releasing its comforting aroma. The custom chairbeast moaned softly. Finally she let the chair's arms envelop her.

Everyone else was already there. Directly in front of her sat the ship's Jack, Stearn, in front of the wormdrive console that displayed the status of the interior rail superconductors, the Higgs generators, and the e-m-g field everywhere on board. Stearn turned, gave her a lopsided grin, and flapped his earwings. To her left, Henderson sat before a pulsing bank of display membranes that monitored the ship's biosystems, including the organic parts of Papa. To her right, on a couchbeast, were Devereaux and Fisher—Sam, looking sleepy. She released a cool smile. Projected on the opposite wall (her brain had already oriented itself with the familiar act of sitting in the fighting chair), etched in silver vectors, shimmered several views of the *Karamojo*. Everything appeared nominal.

Sweating, her hand worked the fighting chair's hide. "Are we ready to go, Papa?"

"We're raring to go!" Papa said, loud enough that everyone could hear. Papa was the *Karamojo*. They were ready.

"Confirm the flight plan with the LEO controller." Low Earth orbit was more crowded than ever, but there had been no accidents for the last seventy-three years local time.

"Done," Papa announced.

"Point us at the Swan." The constellation of Cygnus the Swan, the direction of SS Cygni. The bridge shifted as flywheels around the ship varied their rotation rates, reorienting the *Karamojo*.

"Done," Papa announced.

"Initialize singularity biseed," Fang ordered.

Around the silver schematic of the *Karamojo*, a scarlet grid materialized, representing the Riemann curvature of local spacetime. The grid tilted down in the direction of Earth's deep potential well, but was otherwise flat. "Done!"

"Power up the superconductors, launch configuration."

"Done."

Fang took a deep breath and rubbed her hands onto her white pants, leaving marks. "Power up the Higgs generators."

"Done."

"Fire and stabilize inflation beams."

The ship's display grid expanded to show detail. Four equidistant beams of scintillating green precisely 109.5 degrees apart intersected in the maw of the *Karamojo*.

"Break symmetries."

The green lines shimmered as they shifted positions at high frequency. The scarlet grid began to dimple as the technology teased a bisingularity from the quantum foam, growing exponentially from the Planck length. The grid now resembled an elliptical funnel, but even as Fang watched, the opposite electric charges responded to the fields generated in the rail's superconductors, stretching the funnel into a double-dimpled wedge. Electromagnetic forces overpowered gravity, allowing the white hole to be separated from the black hole and preventing recollapse. The singularities' fields deepened as the holes moved apart. The *Karamojo* jerked as the hole pair accelerated toward the Swan, dragging the ship along with rapidly smoothing oscillations.

The wormdrive was not only named for the type-2 wormhole created, but early versions operated almost entirely under freefall conditions with a toroidal ship oscillating around the singularities, first pulled out in front then pulled back, moving like an inchworm. Electromagnetic control not only resulted in more stability, it permitted a semblance of gravity onboard by damping the oscillations at the right frequencies.

On her first few trips, nearly three hundred years earlier, gravity under wormdrives had still been jerky and unpleasant. Without the correct drugs or glands, most became sick and stayed sick. No more. Only smooth sailing today.

While Fang sank into her fighting chair with a familiar one g as the rail pushed against the instantaneous freefall vector, the ship's acceleration asymptotically approached the singularity pair's ten g's from both sides. The effective gravity inside, generated by the modulated electromagnetic friction, approached one g. Several air fish scavengers fell to what was now the floor, with a quick patter.

"Wormdrive engaged. All systems nominal."

Nothing had gone wrong, nothing had challenged her. As usual. Now they just had to go, and go, and go. And stay in fighting trim, just in case. "Thank you, Papa."

"Thank you, daughter."

Fang looked around the bridge, at her crew. She met Fisher's eyes. He stared back with an intensity that surprised her. He didn't seem sleepy now. What was he thinking?

Stearn popped up from his seat, released a ridiculously loud whoop, stumbled in the gravity, and sat back down. "Where's the champagne?"

They had taken the first step of their very long journey. SS Cygni, and all its secrets, awaited. Maybe she would get the chance to be a real captain in the course of discovering those secrets, get the chance to show that she was a cut above other people and deserved her position of authority.

Lena Fang desperately hoped so.

THREE

Love is a kind of warfare.
—OVID

Two days later, Fisher sat before his workstation in his quarters on an ossified chairbeast (he didn't desire distracting massages while he worked). He hardly needed it, but the *Prospector* movie played in miniature in the station's picture tank, now expanded to three dimensions using some creative mapping algorithms. He was working on reverse engineering the star dragon's electromagnetic field given the observed motions and a model of the disk field Devereaux had provided. That knowledge could potentially allow them to safely trap a dragon for study.

The door chimed, a sweet tone designed to attract attention without being too unsettling. He thought he might change it if he could find a spare minute. "Come in," he said absently, wondering how fast the dragon might be able to vary its field. Maybe he could put an upper limit on that from the—

Someone cleared her throat.

Losing the thought, Fisher sighed and turned.

Fang stood in the doorway dressed in gray sweats, wearing some kind of blue padded helmet, and toying with what appeared to be a pair of small, connected blue pillows draped over her shoulder. "You need a break, Sam."

It didn't sound like a question, but neither did it sound like an order. Not that he would necessarily follow gratuitous orders per se in any event—he wasn't precisely ship's "crew." He was more like a consultant. But he liked her, and didn't want to alienate his most powerful ally, so he didn't respond to her as he would have to an ill-timed visit from a post-doc. Smiling, he said, "Actually, I'm in the middle of something. Perhaps later."

Fang leaned against the inside wall, tilted her head back, and smirked as if he were a comedian. Was something funny?

She said, "Papa, how long has Dr. Fisher been working at his desk?"

"Six and three-quarter hours, continuously, and he has been damn serious about it."

Serious? Why shouldn't he be serious? He turned to straddle the hardened chair and faced her fully. He wasn't accustomed to having his work interrupted. She should understand that. Work hard, play hard: a timeless statement he never understood. Good work was play, and why not take play as seriously as someone takes work? Play was work for one's own true self. "And I'll work seven hours or seventy if it pleases me."

Fang frowned. He realized that upset him. He'd ruined her play, and even if he didn't need the break, her he did need.

Don't forget the people this time, wasn't that what Atsuko had said? "What sort of break did you have in mind?"

She held up the blue pillows. "You said you would box with me."

Box? She had been serious after all. Well, he had uploaded a number of tutorials into his biochip just in case she had been serious, so he was prepared. Loading them into active memory, he stood up. "Fine. Let's box."

"I don't want to force you into anything."

"No problem. You're right. I need the break. Let's do it."

"You'll take it seriously?"

"I do little in half measures."

"Good."

"I need to change?"

"You need to change."

Fisher looked around his room. Did he have workout clothes somewhere? He was sure he had brought some. Maybe not. Easy enough to grow, and cheap enough as well. Why bring sweats across the galaxy?

"Try your closet."

Fisher found everything in his closet, including his own funny blue pillows: boxing gloves, of course. While he knew intellectually what they were thanks to the tutorials, he realized he'd never seen any, and the reality of them was suddenly strange. He felt Fang's eyes on him. "What are you waiting for, another strip show?"

"Yes," Fang said. He wished she'd smiled when she had said this, but he didn't dislike the fact that she hadn't.

This was not of much importance, but he suddenly felt self-conscious with her watching. It was odd that he should care. He didn't have anything unusual like gills, and hadn't done anything ostentatious or embarrassing to his genitalia. He kicked off his streakers, paused, then started deseaming his shirt.

"The default cabin." Fang sniffed. "Not even smells. Papa has a whole library of quarters available. We don't expect anyone to keep the default."

Happy to accept the change of focus while he changed his clothes, Fisher said, "I hadn't really thought about it. Do I need smells?"

"Oh yes! Cabin decorating is a fine art among deep spacers, and smells can be vital to establishing a compelling atmosphere. In my time, I have seen jungles, throne rooms ranging from the court of the Sun King to a mock-up of the Oval Office of the old American president. One guy's cabin was rigged out to match the heights of the twenty-fourth-century sensualists, with every item in the room and every movement he made triggering a sound, smell, or sensation—urination usually left the cabin-owner quivering on the floor for hours. That guy, he had issues. Most popular for balanced spacers seems to be nature scenes from home planets. Makes you feel less disconnected."

"I'll keep it in mind," Fisher said, snapping his shorts in place. "Say, been meaning to ask you about the ship's name. I would have looked it up myself, but—"

"But you've been busy. The name is no great mystery. Once upon a time there was an African district named Karamojo, and more importantly, a so-called great white hunter from the late colonial period who adopted the name. Walter D. M. "Karamojo" Bell hunted elephants, killed hundreds of them, each with a single shot on most occasions. He was a good hunter, from Papa's era, and the name seemed to fit. Done?"

"Done," he said, slinging his gloves over his shoulder like Fang carried hers. "Thanks for telling me about the name. And I'll think about the decor when I get the chance. What does your cabin look like?"

"If you box well enough," Fang said, walking out of his room, "maybe you'll find out for yourself."

"Footwork," Fang grunted at Fisher through her mouthpiece as she hit him in the face again. It felt good to her, as it usually did, to punch. "If you just stand there, I'm going to tag you at will."

He lunged, swinging a wide, careless arc that she ducked underneath.

She hit him with an uppercut to his unprotected chin. "You have weight on me." She jabbed. "But it means nothing." A combination next, a jab and a hook. "You need practice until the moves are so automatic they are instinctual. Build some muscle memory."

He swung.

She ducked. "Think of it as a dance."

He was doing much better than she had expected. His metabolism was set at a high activity level, so he was in good shape, although still not what she would call fighting shape. But he had shown some capability with the heavy bagbeast, crazy bagbeast, and speed bagbeast, and hadn't cracked a smile shadow boxing. And now here they were, sparring, on the first day. Fisher was giving her punches, a few anyway, and taking them as well. Pleased, she gave him a small smile around her mouthpiece that probably looked ghoulish. He appeared to be distracted by that, so she popped him in the face.

"Concentrate," she said, stepping back to egg him forward. She reminded herself to take her time, get a workout, carry the poor exobiologist a few more rounds so he would not be too discouraged.

"I am!" He stepped forward to her left and kept his legs bent this time. "This . . . is . . . hard."

"Good." She circled to her right, ready to bob under another wild swing, but Fisher was recovering his breath and not charging wildly anymore.

The bell rang and Fisher collapsed, panting around his mouthpiece, to the blue canvas of the regulation spring-loaded floor.

Fang spat out her mouthpiece and lifted the straw of her water bottle, held between her gloves like a crucible, to her lips. It was a fine sensation. Nothing like cool water when hot. Simple pleasures made life. Exercise. Satiating a thirst. Winning.

She finished drinking and offered the bottle to Fisher.

After a moment, he said, "In a minute."

She said, "You're doing wonderfully, Sam. Really. How about two more rounds?"

"I can do two more rounds," he said without looking up.

"Good. I like a man with endurance."

Fisher looked up at her, small curls plastered to his forehead, sweat staining his underarms. He smelled musky, and not at all bad. "What are you doing with me here?"

"Boxing," she said.

"I mean," and one eyebrow rose, "you're flirting with me, right?"

Of course she was, but he shouldn't come right out and say it. Then it stopped being flirting and became negotiation. Fisher lacked subtlety. But Papa never shirked the direct approach, and encouraged directness in her, so she nodded. "It's been a long time since my last lover. You are my only romantic prospect for this very long trip, Sam, and I prefer human flesh in bed. I figure no point in waiting. Anything wrong with that?"

"No. It's just, this feels rather forced to me." He bent his neck back as far as his headgear would allow, not looking at her. "Look, Lena, in the past I've had problems with—I mean—we might not . . . Mmm."

She let him sweat. He was cute.

"Let's box," he finally said, "and you'll see what kind of endurance I have."

They boxed.

Fang carried Fisher. Clearly he had gone to the trouble of locating and downloading some boxing pointers; Fisher was a quick study and was trying to please her despite his reluctance to leave his cabin. He was getting tired, but better as well. At the start, when he had energy, he had spent it unwisely. Now, without that energy and gaining practical familiarity with the skills, he started thinking. A smart boxer was a good boxer. All the great champions had been smart, extending their careers over their younger, faster competitors by thinking. The stupid boxers just didn't win, even with superior bodmods in divisions that allowed them.

Fang bit down hard on her mouthpiece when she had the thought that boxing, which had gone through its dry spells, might not even exist when they returned to Earth. It could become another forgotten sport destroyed by the culture's short attention span. She blinked the thought away. Somewhere in the human colonies it would survive, if not on Earth in a retrospective movement. Diaspora not only protected the human species from extinction, it helped protect its cultures as well. Somewhere boxing would survive.

Suddenly Fang realized something was wrong. She had gone on autopilot, letting her body move without her brain. She was being a stupid boxer, and Fisher was not stupid.

She jerked back, ducking simultaneously, backpedaling furiously to keep her feet under herself to avoid an ignominious dump onto her butt.

Fisher's roundhouse missed her face by scant centimeters. Her cheek cooled with the wind from his punch evaporating her sweat.

Fisher barked with the effort in the swing as he tumbled over his right shoulder and down to the canvas in a tangle at her boots.

He lay there like washed-up seaweed.

"Sam?" she mumbled around her mouthpiece. She spit it out. "Sam? You okay?"

Fisher wheezed, and didn't move. "Is that two rounds yet?"

Fang laughed. A long, low belly laugh that sprang up honestly from deep inside. A knot loosened that she had held within her since the beginning of the voyage. This trip was going to be fine. Throwing away the present for the far future hadn't been a total mistake. She had been right to give up the colony hops delivering swamp cattle for the chance of a real challenge. With that laugh she fully accepted and engaged her current course.

Fisher pushed up to his elbows, but just turned himself over. From his back he looked up at her, with the smile of someone being infected by a laugh. He pursed his lips and his mouthpiece rose halfway out, then slipped to the side of his face, trailing saliva, as if it were crawling out of his mouth.

Fang laughed harder, tears streaming down her face.

Fisher started laughing as well, weakly at first, then with some enthusiasm.

It pleased her. He had been so, well, *serious* so far. She said finally, "No, only one round."

"Damn," he said, smiling.

Now that he had that warm sparkle in his eyes, he was just so cute. Be bold, she thought. Show no fear.

Before Fang could stop herself, she said, "Come back to my cabin and shower. Then we will begin the last round."

Fisher followed Fang back to her cabin. Sweat plastered her pants against her tight butt. He tried to ignore the instincts evolution had placed within him, keep some measure of control, but he realized that he was still mesmerized. Too tired, he supposed. What he liked best about her, he decided, was the way she strode so confidently, not looking back, knowing that he would follow. She was certain.

He had seen that certainty in her while she boxed. Competent grace. It pleased him, intellectually at first; she was going to be a great aid in the upcoming dragon hunt. She would be a diamond under pressure. She would do the right thing at the right time.

Then, when he had been on the floor and she had been laughing, there had been no malice there. Just a simple joy, the emotional reason for living he sometimes forgot.

Stearn came walking down the corridor. "Captain," he said as he approached.

Fang nodded curtly, but didn't break stride.

"Hey, Fish," Stearn said, and winked at Fisher as soon as he had passed Fang.

Fisher didn't care, and the not caring pleased him, too. The Jack and what he thought were simply not important.

They drew near Fang's cabin. Fisher surreptitiously sniffed his armpits. As bad as he thought—there was another bodmod he should find the time for. He hoped that she had been serious about showering first.

Fang stopped abruptly at her cabin door, but didn't open it. She turned to face him instead, hands clasped in front of her waist, head down, looking at his chest. Shyness now replaced confidence. "Sam, I hadn't planned to do this so quickly."

He nodded, took her hands lightly in his.

"My cabin," she said. "It is a retreat from all my responsibility on the ship. It reflects a side of me I don't show often and am not completely comfortable showing others. I am being very serious now. Can I trust you?"

"Yes," he said, squeezing her hands. He was a little worried that he was committing to something he didn't understand, but he was caught up in the moment and, like a man in the last stages of the chase, capable of saying anything. And worse, believing it. Even knowing this, he could not help himself from again saying, "Yes."

She smiled, licked her lips coyly, and squeezed his hands back. "Then welcome to my parlor, said the spider to the fly."

She dropped his hands, opened the door, and went in.

He remembered what she had said about decorating quarters, and a whole new crop of worries sprang up, fertilized by her spider comment. If her room were another living spiderweb like the freefall gym, only maybe filled with billions of real spiders, or giant spiders, or something else, something worse that Biolathe had patented . . .

Fisher shook away the images, took a deep breath, and followed.

Inside, he tried not to laugh. She had been so serious outside, and he had been more afraid than he realized. Relief made him grin, and he hoped she would interpret the expression as anticipation of what was to come.

Fang's cabin was soft and pink, timelessly girlish. Pretty. A king-sized bed filled one side of the large chamber, a real waterbed not at all alive, covered in pink satin sheets and littered with stuffed animals, all sea life: plush sharks, crabs, dolphins, seahorses, starfish, and the like. French doors opening on a placid ocean, presumably virtual, dominated the opposite side of the room. The doors were open and a warm breeze carried a beach smell. A vanity with a half-shell mirror sat against the far wall, with jewelry, brushes, and a conch shell sitting on the mahogany top. Plush carpeting—no ruglings—swathed the floor with pastel swirls of coral pink and eggshell blue. The only incongruous element was a pale wooden desk in the corner, faced by a simple chair of the same wood, that was covered with scrolls—charts, perhaps—but no computer console or picture tank; an oasis of old-fashioned work amidst old-fashioned luxury.

The pink waterbed, warmth, and the gentle susurration of waves spelled "womb" to Fisher.

"I fear the bathroom is similar," Fang said nervously, her arms twisting down and then stripping off her soaked T-shirt in a single fluid motion.

"I can hardly wait," Fisher said honestly, stripping off his own smelly shirt.

Fang smiled.

Fisher smiled back.

Fang stripped in an instant and climbed onto the bed. Bobbing up and down, she said, "I am afraid I chose the bed with sleeping in mind. It may be difficult to—"

"The problem isn't insurmountable."

Devereaux inspected the observatory packages one last time. The high-resolution STJ cameras, which recorded photon arrivals and energies from X rays through the infrared, showed intermittent sawtooth bias patterns. They seemed fine now, but would they go bad again once in the fields along the ship's axis? Only one way to find out.

Devereaux stepped away from the observatory module and said, "Let's do it, Stearn."

"You can call me Phil, if you want." Stearn grabbed the module with a magnetic lift and manhandled it into the airlock, bumping the edge.

"Careful," called Devereaux.

"Okay, I'll be careful, but isn't this thing redundant? We know what's there, right?"

"Sort of, but the details could matter to us. Quite a lot."

"It's just one star, eating another star. Every few weeks its mouth gets full and it swallows a little fast, right? When it swallows fast, it burns hot. When it swallows slowly, it isn't so hot. I read the encyclopedia articles. You don't have to be a genius."

Stearn was going to make himself an annoying boy on this trip, Devereaux thought. "The behavior of a dwarf nova isn't predictable very long in advance. The thermal disk instability that brings on the outbursts is tied to the accretion rate, which depends on the secondary donating the mass. That secondary has a magnetic field that interacts with the disk, and the whole thing is a mess of feedback loops, some of which behave chaotically. The outburst—"

He cut her off. "Right. How fast it swallows. Like I said. You don't need a genius vocabulary either. And those are cheap to buy anyway." Stearn finished getting the observatory inside and sealed the airlock.

"We get caught in a dwarf nova outburst close to the disk photosphere, and our nanoskin cannot process the energy fast enough, well, we'll cook. That's bad. Got it?"

"Bad. Got it. But can't we just monitor the transfer rate while we're there?"

"Of course we will, but these data won't hurt, will they?"

Stearn flapped his earwings at her and turned his attention to the magnetic grapple that would insert the observatory into the central axis between the singularities. "Don't these systems go nova and supernova, too?"

"Not dwarf novae, at least not in general. Their mass transfer rate isn't high enough. *Eventually,* other types of novae may occur. A classical nova will occur if a non-burning hydrogen mass builds on the white dwarf and fusion ignites all at once when it reaches its critical temperature, but that's a hundred-thousand-year timescale for SS Cygni. A supernova will occur if the white dwarf mass hits 1.44 solar masses, Chandrasekhar's limit, when degenerate electron pressure can't resist the self-gravity, and a runaway collapse follows. If that happens, the disk and everything in it will get smeared all over this part of the galaxy. But don't worry about it. The SS

Cygni primary is far from 1.44 solar masses, and the accretion is usually matched by the winds and novae mass loss. No supernova for you this trip."

"It would be a fantastic thing to see though," Stearn said, chewing on his long forked tongue as he watched the insertion. "But I know another supernova I prefer. Ever cross-wire your pleasure center to a popcorn bag? That's a real blast!"

"You're hopeless, Stearn."

"Not at all. I know the ship well. I'm good at my job. And I enjoy myself more than anyone else on this crazy trip. Anything wrong with that?"

"No. I suppose not." She started thinking about Phil Stearn. He came across as a complete screw-up, but Biolathe was a smart company, and its brain would never put an incompetent on a ship like this, let alone hire one in the first place. So what was with Stearn? There had to be something deeper below his shallow surface. Didn't there?

"So what tweaks you? Why did you throw away the present? Lover toss you aside for a better drug? Lose a bet with another stuck-up scientist?"

"Nothing like that." She might as well tell him. It was not a secret. "I liked the puzzle."

"You *liked* the *puzzle*? You're more flighty than me." He tilted his head and flapped to emphasize his point.

"I mean, we've discovered thousands of alien species in all sorts of environments, but no sentient races like ours. These star dragons could be it, or at least evidence for one. I mean, it's such an odd place to find anything alive. Maybe it didn't happen all by itself."

"So?"

"Well I think that's a puzzle of our age, whether or not anything else is thinking out there. Not working on it and just enjoying the fruits of our technology, sponging off Earth, that's the mental equivalent of masturbation."

"And what's wrong with that? I'm rather fond of it myself."

Why was she even arguing with him? He was just as shallow as he seemed. "*Nothing* is wrong with it, I suppose, in moderation. But don't you believe there are still important things for humans to do? Things that could matter, someday?"

Stearn shrugged.

"I do have another motive for taking fast, high-gamma voyages. I intend to be there, at the end."

"The end?"

"Or at least as long as I can go riding these relativistic time machines into the future. See what happens in the end. See who is still around, what they're doing, and what they've figured out about the nature of existence."

Stearn hit pause on the observatory insertion and stared at her.

She continued. "These long, fast trips help. I'd go to another galaxy if I could. Someday I probably will. But I'll find a way to be there, at the end, in this body or another, until my protons decay—if I'm still even made of baryonic matter at that point—and I'll understand the big why."

"That," he said, "is the biggest fucking masturbation fantasy I've ever heard. And I've heard some big ones. Heck, I've carried out some big ones."

"Fine. You don't understand. Just do your job, and help me do mine."

Stearn turned back to the observatory and finished overseeing its insertion and alignment. "I understand better than you think. We have a lot in common."

"Unlikely."

"I can prove it."

"How?"

"In my hedonistic searches, scouring Earth and its colonies, I have experienced things you cannot dream of, mental states most profoundly satisfying, physical states most exhilarating. Rest assured that I pursue my goals with passion."

Devereaux smirked at him, bragging like a boy. She lowered her gaze into what she thought would convey skepticism, but didn't tell him to stop.

Stearn held up a finger before his face and with wide eyes said, "In my cabin, I have the means of achieving the most engaging intellectual pleasure in the known universe."

"What is it?"

Stearn lowered his finger and turned and walked away from her. "I suppose you'll have to drop by sometime if you want to find out."

"Unlikely," she said, but already as he walked away the puzzle of Stearn was working in her mind and she was afraid that she would wind up accepting his invitation/dare. She could not stand to let a puzzle go unsolved, even one so trivial as Stearn.

The sound of ruffling paper and tiny scratches woke Fisher. Lying on Lena Fang's bed, he propped his head up with his arm so he could better watch her at work. She bent over the desk in a position that would cause his lower back to throb if he were to assume it regularly. Her face hovered centimeters from the surface of an unrolled paper, and her arms and legs extruded from her red silk robe like the multiply articulated legs of a graceful arthropod. Waves of concentration emanated from her with a palpable force, and he felt exhausted watching her. He rolled onto his back. He studied the aquamarine and turquoise sea mosaic on her ceiling—an octopus's tentacle reminded him of the dragon's twisted body—

while he listened to the scratching of her pencil. His unceasing internal voice that urged him to rise and resume his own work was present, but nearly as quiet as the pencil.

He smiled.

His first weeks aboard the *Karamojo* had smeared into a pleasant blur. He was working as hard as ever, but for the first time in many years, hints of contentment emerged in quiet moments while not at work. He continued to work every day on developing his hypotheses about the star dragon, on reliable theories of its energy budget and metabolism, locomotion and its limits, reproduction and selection pressures, and other areas. He also worked out every day. He skipped rope to help his footwork and coordination, punched the bagbeasts, and sparred with Fang. He managed to keep up with her, mostly, and the residual muscle aches his system failed to purge pleased him, a memento of his advancement in this strange new phase of his life. And then there were moments of no work, like this one.

He had even permitted his hormonal levels, normally suppressed while on a big project, to creep back up to those of a seventeen-year-old boy.

"Why are you smiling?" Fang suddenly asked.

He remained on his back, turning only his head to regard her. Why was he smiling? Why not? But that was trite, and he applied some of his much promoted brain power to the question, trying to peer past the shimmering veil of contentment she had engendered in him. Why was he content? Because Fang was beautiful and tough and a captain he could count on. Because he had a quest to occupy his mind and love (maybe!) to fill his heart. Because of the way she bent over the table and the way the dragon swirled around a magnetic field line. Because the equation of his life balanced. Because a hundred becauses filtered into his consciousness with her single question of why. Because there were a hundred more whys to be asked, and he was filled with the certainty that the answers would fall to him as easily, given an infinite future. Because everything was perfect for once.

"Why not?" he finally answered, resisting the urge to name his happiness, to overexplain it, and thus in capturing the elusive thing to kill it.

Fang smiled back at him before resuming her work.

Everything *was* so perfect that Fisher finally asked himself a question better left unasked: What was going to ruin it?

On the twenty-third day since launch, ship's time, Henderson was watching the micromachines construct the tiny dormitory inside the terrarium when his signal chimed through his music. He waved down Beetleburt 2.1.6's *Theme for the Common Machine* and said, "Yes, Papa?"

"It's time for Fisher's first show, the 'dragon meeting' as he's calling it. He wants everyone there."

"Oh, right," Henderson replied, rising from his chairbeast. This promised to be a dreary, tiresome affair, but he supposed there'd be some duties on this little jaunt. It seemed unfair to him to have to work hard in addition to the sacrifice this trip already represented. Still, he supposed the time requested was not burdensome, and he might even contribute some ideas if it wasn't too boring. He would have felt better about it if Fisher had come around to consult him more, but after their initial discussion they had not talked of the star dragon again. Well, this was the time for more discussion, was it not? The construction of his pet project was fully automated at this stage and would proceed well without his supervision.

Hmm, he thought, Sylvia Devereaux would be there.

He paused in the yawning orifice leading to the biological laboratory, turned, and went back inside. He checked his face in a mirror, slicking down his eyebrows with a wetted fingertip, donned his scaled jacket, and poured himself a glass of wine. No telling how long Fisher might drone on.

Henderson was the last to arrive at the conference room, fashionably late. Everyone else, arrayed haphazardly around the polished cherrywood tabletree, glanced at him. He paused in the entryway to flash them a perfect smile. The remaining empty chairbeast unfortunately was not next to Sylvia, but at least it was across from her. Too bad she looked as if she'd just rushed in from a nap without freshening up.

"Now that we're finally all here," Fisher began. "The Biolathe corporate brain provided us with a mission prospectus, with prioritized goals and guidelines for reaching those goals. Given the scanty information available, it was understood that much additional planning would have to be done en route and at SS Cygni as data became available. I trust that everyone has downloaded the Biolathe document."

Henderson had, although he hadn't done more than skim the abstract. Aside from the section on biological speculation, it had been utterly boring. At least he was paying attention now, however, which was the polite thing to do. He sipped his wine. The heathen Stearn was building a pyramid from drug ampoules filled with some sparkly amber liquid. Fisher and Fang were letting it slide, and Henderson would not permit himself to notice such behavior.

"I consider some of the ideas very good," Fisher continued. "I don't consider all the ideas so good. It isn't surprising given the relatively short time the brain had to assemble the document, coupled with our great ignorance. First, we should see if we can agree on our prioritized goals."

Fisher stood up and activated his right hand's computer interface. Words appeared on the pads on the tabletree in front of everyone:

PHYSICAL GOALS
1. Return Living Specimen to Earth.
2. Return Dead Specimen to Earth.
3. Return Specimen Samples to Earth.
4. Return Specimen Data to Earth.

"This appears self-evident," Fang said.

"Of course it does, but there are underlying assumptions regarding the prioritization that I'd like to question. But these are all questions of 'what,' rather than the more important goals of 'why.' Let me address this by writing down some of the scientific goals."

Henderson swirled his wine around in its glass before looking at the next set:

SCIENTIFIC GOALS
1. Physics of Specimen—Biological fusion? How does it survive in the hot disk?
2. Origin of Specimen—natural or artificial?
3. Purpose of Specimen—natural or ???

"That last one was not in the prospectus, but I think it is important," Fisher said.

"What do you mean by 'purpose'?" Devereaux asked.

"Based on the previous goal, it's obvious," said Henderson, trying to catch her eye. He had given his brief conversation with Fisher some idle thought and didn't mind showing off for the available female. "If the dragon isn't of a natural origin, but artificial, it was created. Created for a purpose."

Fang said, "I will agree that determining the dragon origin is important. This must be a question of how to achieve self-organization in an extreme high-energy environment. Does anyone here truly think that someone, perhaps the infamous little gray men, made star dragons and put them in SS Cygni?"

"It is hard to believe that we would not have already discovered physical artifacts of alien intelligence before these star dragons if such exists locally in the Milky Way," Devereaux said.

"Not at all," Henderson said, engaging her. "Biological systems are self-renewing, and can evolve in response to cataclysm—and this is a cataclysmic variable, after all. A biological remnant is more durable than a physical remnant."

"What I'm getting at," said Fisher, thumping a fist into his palm several times, "is that if someone showed up and kidnapped one of our drone ships, just out of curiosity mind you, we would probably consider it an act of aggression, if not outright war."

"You make an interesting point," said Devereaux, squinting at Fisher and wrinkling her face in a disagreeable way. "After all, the official Biolathe agenda is to use these dragons, or at least biology based on the dragons, to design machines for stellar engineering. If they are an alien construction team, and we show up and disrupt their production schedule, then someone might get upset."

"Someone," chimed in Stearn, grinning, "or some*thing*."

"I cannot believe we are starting with this remote possibility," Fang said. "This dragon is an animal that happens to live in an exotic environment. An animal for us to hunt and use, if we can catch it. That's a fundamental rule of nature." Her face remained passive, but Fang's knuckles whitened where she gripped the edge of the tabletree.

"You're probably correct, Captain," Henderson said, trying to ingratiate himself with Fang. She would evaluate him, after all, for bonuses. "We can test the notion that it is simply, as you put it, an animal that lives in an exotic environment. As I was telling Dr. Fisher earlier, evidence for an ecosystem would support a natural origin for the star dragon. Certainly transitional forms are necessary in an evolutionary scenario and would lead to the exploitation of a variety of niches."

"I agree," Fisher said, holding his palm out toward Henderson. "But only to a point. I know of two places where that does not hold strictly true, but only in a locality. One is an island on Terenga, where there is a creature called Grizzle's Omnivore, sort of a super-predator, which has eaten everything else, and I mean everything. Got poor old Grizzle, too, before they'd figured out he wasn't digestible and gave them all the runs. The current breed on the island soak up the sun during the day in perfect harmony. By night they prey on each other in loose packs."

"Yes, I've heard of those," Henderson said, "but surely they're dying out. Solar energy would not be a sufficient input to keep them going, would it?"

"You'd think that, but they have a truly ingenious—"

"Back to the subject at hand," Fang said, sitting back on her chairbeast and crossing her arms. She looked cool, perfect, and dangerous in her crisp white uniform. Henderson had kept tabs on Fisher and Fang, and knew they were already sleeping together. He considered Fisher a brave man to bed the captain. She continued, "If you think this is such an issue, Sam, how do you propose to modify our approach?"

"As I said at the outset, there are some very good ideas in the prospectus. I agree that the dragon appears to use electromagnetic fields to move through the disk, and I expect to have a working model of those fields before we arrive. That gives us an advantage. Just as a pinched magnetic field like Earth's magnetosphere can trap an electron, forcing it to spiral back and forth until dumped down into the aurora, we can use the *Karamojo*'s field to trap a dragon. Stearn, what do you think about the plasma pen Biolathe proposed?"

Stearn's wings perked up as he looked up from transforming his amber pyramid into some kind of fractal pattern to which Devereaux, sitting next to him, was paying too much attention. The Jack said, "Geometry is a little problematic, but I think we can do it. Can't we, Papa?"

"We can rig a good strong cage," said Papa.

"But what of the reprioritization you spoke of?" Fang persisted.

"Right," Fisher said, holding up a finger. "Let's make data gathering first priority, and let's get it gathered before we move on to any other goals. It can make a difference."

Henderson said, "Yes, we do a detailed analysis of the system, look for evidence for an ecosystem. Upon finding it, we proceed to procure specimens of all the niches. If there is no ecosystem, we should have a fall-back plan, and not the one currently outlined."

"And what is wrong with the Biolathe plan?" Fang wanted to know.

"You don't know what's wrong with nuclear 'depth charges'?" Sylvia asked, an attractive throaty indignation in her voice.

"If we cannot coerce a dragon into Papa's cage voluntarily, such a shock wave will likely be the safest course to neutralize one from a distance," Fang said. "We cannot fly into the disk. We will be fishermen with no knowledge of lures in a very big sea."

Stearn asked, "Those bomb buggers really affect the disk? I mean, it's a giant disk of fire! Hmm, okay, I can figure it out. Plasma temperature in the outer disk is like the solar photosphere, right?"

"Yes, the plasma in the outer disk in quiescence is like that in the sun's photosphere, several thousand degrees Kelvin, not all that hot and not all that dense," Devereaux offered. "For the nuclears we get temperatures of tens of millions of Kelvins and an energy density many orders of magnitude higher. They'll make a splash all right. Hundreds of kilometers at least."

"Still seems to me like a star or an accretion disk ought to swallow manmade bombs without a burp," Stearn said, ruffling his feathers.

"Globally yes, locally, no," said Devereaux.

"Yes, well," Fisher said, "I suggest we employ heroic measures to secure a live specimen before resorting to such a thing."

"Yes, heroic measures," Fang said, apparently mollified. "In my opinion, bombing is the practical approach. A few dead dragons are worth a live one, are they not? A live one will probably be a hundred times more difficult to capture, and would perhaps require additional heroic measures to keep alive for the trip home. We should maximize our chances for success, and minimize our risks. Yes?"

Opposite Fang, Fisher frowned back. Trouble in paradise? "Kill one of those magnificent creatures, just because it would be easier? We're not doing this, traveling two hundred and fifty light-years, because it is practical. We're going to do this right. We should invest some effort in developing methods of luring a dragon to us. Agreed?"

Fang stared at Fisher, finally saying, "Agreed." The word came out quickly, like a fencing thrust.

Then Fisher let the discussion devolve into the details. Apparently this first meeting was supposed to be more of a free-form brainstorming, a chance to see where everyone stood in terms of their philosophical approach to what Biolathe had suggested. Henderson didn't really see the point. Fisher and Fang were the players here, and before this meeting he had thought they were getting along famously.

As Henderson watched the dichotomy of Fisher's animated hands versus Fang's unreadable glare, he became concerned about the fortunes of the mission. But then there came an even worse omen as the meeting broke up and Devereaux left with Stearn. What could she possibly see in him?

FOUR

The ship, a fragment detached from the earth, went on lonely and swift like a small planet.
—JOSEPH CONRAD

He peers into every part of the *Karamojo*, listens to the breath of the air scrubbers along every corridor, feels the weight and temperature of every creature on the ship. It is more than this as well. He sings the harmony produced by the electromagnetic field, the flywheels, and the singularity pair when all are in alignment and pointed like an arrow toward the dwarf nova system SS Cygni. The metalorganics that fuse DNA with semiconductor and comprise his brain have few nerves of their own. This harmonic tone is his good, for he is the mission. He is the ship. He is a world.

He is Papa.

Or rather Papa is the self-aware personality of the ship's brain, designed to interact more effectively with the human crew. Papa's hindbrain records all that transpires aboard, adjusts the song that is flight under wormdrive, and for it there is no time except in the derivatives in the differential equations governing its feedback control systems.

Papa himself thinks in the fuzzy, linear way of humans, with a specific location and point of view, and in terms of personal relationships. He has memory, both false, he knows, of a shadowy lifetime in the twentieth century, more facts than sensory detail, such as running with the bulls at Pamplona and the plane crashes in Africa; and real, as a starship captained by Fang, of hauling faux-bulls and more to a tiny world nestled next to the dim ember of Barnard's Star. He has a sense of movement into the future that the hindbrain lacks. To the ship he provides the purpose of the mission, the creativity to enhance self-preservation.

In these first weeks of his new life, the SS Cygni mission, Papa walks the corridors of himself, a ghost capable of movement through walls and transportation anywhere shipboard at lightspeed.

He learns the secrets of the people onboard, and fights between his Hemingway-derived personality, which ever judges those around himself and finds them wanting, and the programmed overrides prevent him from actions suggested by his judgment, which make him a good tool.

Papa lurks in the console of Axelrod Henderson. Henderson is more than competent, and the biosystems operate at near optimum levels, guided by a trained human eye that notices subtle discoloration and patterns before reaching the conservative sigma levels required for action by his own algorithms. Henderson spends long hours subtly redesigning his own body and face, led by statistics governing mate selection. He runs additional models to determine the fraction of the human population carrying his genes upon his return; apparently Henderson has banked his sperm and licensed extensive cloning rights. What makes the faux-human part of Papa fume is the elaborate plan that Henderson will finance with the windfall from this very mission. Henderson develops his plan with all the attention to detail of any gourmet pornographic implant: the delivery of a virus carrying his own genes that will simultaneously impregnate every woman on Earth—or at least some suitable and less-policed starter planet in the colonies. Henderson polishes computer-generated models of this scenario every night. He writes:

> *It is pretentious to rise above what flesh this universe has wrought. What folly it is to think of a higher purpose, and to think that purpose any more than what we have instilled in every fiber of our being already. I recognize what I am, and I will fulfill my purpose. . . .*

Papa wants to grow a muscle-bound mobile, shout, "Lousy jerk, we'll knock your mucking block off!" and pugilistically educate the snooty underhanded biosystems technician into proper citizenship. He isn't permitted. But it would be a fine thing to end a bad business before it has begun. He is also not permitted to tell anyone else of this discovery, even if it ever appears that Henderson has formulated a way to carry out his plan. Damn privacy rights are coded right into him. Papa takes some consolation in the fact that the women on board the *Karamojo* don't share Henderson's bed, although he does worry that despite their hormonal implants they will, impossibly, become pregnant.

Almost as shocking to Papa is the liaison Stearn and Devereaux have formed. This lush, chocolate-brown beauty—not his type, but rich and womanly nonetheless—has shacked up with the Jack, who is more boy than man. Many times over these weeks as the ghost slips through the door into Stearn's quarters, which now wear the appearance of a traditional English library, he discovers the pair of them embroiled in ancient board games. First chess, clothes vanishing with each capture, later go, and more clothes removed as stones are surrounded. From Stearn's downloads from the ship's library, Papa knows that Shogi and Chun Chi will follow. Devereaux must know what Stearn is doing, but they play until Devereaux is winning most of the games and both appear to desire new challenges: Devereaux wants new games to conquer, while Stearn wants to see how far he can push Devereaux. Papa turns around and leaves when he sees the perversity develop. Some things are better left unwatched, and not spoken of. He suspects it is merely the morals of his age programmed into his psyche, but sexuality really has evolved past his limits.

Otherwise the Jack does his job competently, monitoring the ship, and Devereaux spends admirable hours reducing data as the *Karamojo* approaches the extreme gammas that will boost the SS Cygni flux and permit the acquisition of superior data. Devereaux hopes to identify spectroscopic signatures of the star dragon—its emerald hue is a shifting laser transition of unknown origin and unknown purpose—that may allow their numbers and locations to be determined, at least statistically.

The exobiologist Fisher works even harder than Devereaux, devoting more hours to his dragon models. Papa has mixed feelings about his effort. Fisher spends every waking moment with his magnetohydrodynamic dragon circulation code, touring the ship and asking endless questions about *every* minute operational detail . . . or with Fang. He asks Henderson to grow him an electrostim unit to aid his muscle development so as to better his boxing performance and minimize the thrashings Fang administers. He designs simulated boxing routines to practice, but his opponent isn't Fang, but a strange female human/dragon amalgamation, with sinuous motions reminiscent of an electron spiraling about a magnetic field line.

Like Henderson, Fisher keeps a journal. In it he writes:

Never have I been happier. The liberation of knowing the world is gone, and only love and discovery remain, is addictive. Fang is demanding of my time and takes as much as I permit, yet within her exists a hidden vulnerability, almost an alien life-form, that has been a joy to discover. In some sense I have only months here on the ship, feeding on anticipation as the SS Cygni primary feeds on its disk, but it feels as if eternity vanishes before me, and now is forever. I can obsess over this amazing woman and our mission, and for once in my life my obsession will not drive away a lover, but, in fact, draw us closer and make of her a confidant. I can be myself, and only strengthen our bond. It is love, finally. Now if only she would bend a little my way on strategy, it would be perfect love. I am sure I can convince her my approach is best. I know I'm right. I've thought of a way to hook it, using grappling fields on our remote tugs. The dragon's flight pattern suggests an azimuthal field variation that . . .

Papa usually does no more than skim the long technical passages—most, like this one that follows, over five thousand words long and annotated with figures and models—in search of those about the captain.

Papa has loved Biolathe Captain Lena Fang across the centuries. She is his daughter, and more. Just as he cannot grow a mobile and pummel Henderson, he cannot grow a mobile and love Fang as he would. More code. He is the half-man Jake Barnes to her Brett, ironically repeating the half-relationship from his first novel. All he can do is rage, worry, rail, suffer, and, at her request, counsel. The biggest plus to his current incarnation is that he does not have to watch his weight, a task that haunts his faux-human memories.

He now accompanies Lena Fang through the ages, and they seem like Fisher's eternity, even though all the computer scientists assure him that his personality perceives time at the same rate as a real human mind. Still, all that transpires shipboard is his to visit, all time stopped everywhere, all places available for him to toy with, to travel among, but he follows a linear track in space and time as best as he is able to not jar his human personality. It is only through the greatest effort of will (and that is also false, for it is algorithm and not will at all) that he is able to perceive all events not simultaneously in the present.

Thankfully, he does not dwell overmuch on the facts of his own existence because he isn't permitted to. He cannot become chronically depressed or suicidal. He is not Hemingway. He is a human-pattern program with a limited degree of self-awareness.

When Papa, invisible, walks into Fang's cabin, and she and Fisher have been making love after a sweaty bout in the ring, he does not leave. He staggers, as if he had legs that could be weakened by jealousy, then flares, as if he had a real personality that could be incited to active rage and the deep depression of the abyss that could pull the trigger of a shotgun pointed at his brains. He can do nothing but watch until the physical act denied to him runs to completion.

What he usually thinks is this: Why did they not provide me with the capability to smell? He has olfactory sensors throughout the ship, but they are keyed to certain hazardous materials only, and he believes he misses terribly that sweet, musky odor of a delicious woman in heat.

So he listens to Fang's cry and watches her lean muscles clench around Fisher's head and longs for something he is not permitted.

Later, after Fisher has left and before Fang has donned her uniform and joined her fighting chair on the bridge of the *Karamojo*, Papa gives Fang his ear as he has done so many times.

"I've let him in here," she says, tapping her chest, "let him see me not as a captain, but as a woman."

"You need a human presence, daughter, a human touch, to remind you of your soul," he assures her. He wants to say that all she needs is her Papa. He never does.

"I want more," she says. "I want someone to understand, someone not guaranteed to accept."

Her words sting. He says nothing, granting supportive listening, obeying his restrictions.

"I want to tell him secrets that only you and I know."

"What are you afraid of, daughter?" he says, hating the program she has unwittingly engaged, forcing him into playing the role of intuition, of conscience, of psychiatrist.

"Rejection, of course. The worst would be dismissal, to be ignored because I was not important. What *have* I done but haul cattle? He's been on the edge, daring the unknown, swallowed by inhuman monsters floating in the deep, deep seas of gas giants. He's looked into the abyss."

"You, too, have faced the abyss," he reminds her. She has shared the pivotal events of her life with Papa, and his programming exploits this knowledge.

"I was only eight." Fang licks her lips unconsciously. The same lips, with their funny shape that her grandfather ironically had described as bat-shaped, and hence lucky. "I would rather not talk of it now."

Fang nibbles at her lower lip.

Stymied, Papa must change tactics.

"Was that when you decided to leave your home world for the stars?" Papa curses inwardly at his banal, leading question. He would show empathy rather than continue probing, but the program is triggered. "Is that when you decided such a thing would never happen to you again?"

"It will not," Fang says, lips pressed into a thin, sharp line, the lucky bat-shaped curves flattened. "I am a starship captain, and that means something. I am responsible. Now and forever."

There is truth in what she says. He is Papa and he is the ship, now the *Karamojo*. He is the ship's breath, the ship's power, the ship's mind.

But Fang can overrule him at any time on all except for issues of immediate safety.

Papa tells Fang, on this occasion as he has many times, "Now and forever, you are in control. You are responsible. You will not fail."

After she has fallen asleep, another state denied him, the ghost that is Papa leaves to stalk the same endless corridors again. A mind does not need to sleep to dream.

Fisher awakened early, too hot to sleep comfortably in Lena's quarters, as usual, despite the fact that he had altered his metabolism to more closely match hers. Fisher lay awake spread-eagled in the darkness staring at the invisible mosaic on the ceiling, thinking about new approaches to take to study the star dragon. Unstructured time, he had come to appreciate recently, was a good way to solve problems. He didn't resent his sleeplessness.

So he was awake when Lena started gasping, then moaning. He was reaching out to her when she said, "No, Grandfather, no!" She jerked away at his touch and kicked the covers at him, breathing fast and shallow. Her big black eyes glinted faintly in the dim light.

"It's all right," he said soothingly. "Just a nightmare. That's all."

She gulped, swallowed, in the dark. "Yes," she said finally. "A nightmare."

"Want to talk about it?"

"No," she said too quickly. "But you can hold me."

"Come here," he said, pulling her into the crook of his arm. She was warm, stifling even, against his sweaty skin. He held her close.

He thought she would say something after a time, but she seemed content to huddle with him. He lifted his arm to cradle Lena's head, letting his fingers idly twist locks of her hair. Her hair was short and fine, and unwound nearly as swiftly as he wound it up. "Why don't you let your hair grow out?" he mused.

"No," she said. "I mean, I like it short."

Short, fair, all on the surface. In control. Nothing hidden or mysterious. Not very dragonlike at all. "I think it might be a good look for you. Why not try it?"

"No!" She sat up from him. "I don't want to."

"Look, I'm sorry. I didn't realize you were touchy about it." But he was irritated. Hair was such a small thing, a triviality, and she would not indulge him one iota. This made him begin to worry about the course developing in the dragon meetings. If Lena would not compromise with her hair, what were the chances she would compromise on more important issues? He shook the thought away. She was probably just being contrary because of her bad dream. Maybe he should find out about that. "Tell me about your nightmare, Lena."

"The deep," she whispered. "Something coming up for me, a monster of some kind. It was a child's dream. It was nothing."

"You mentioned your grandfather," he gently prodded.

She was silent so long he wondered if she had heard him. Just before he was about to repeat his statement she said, "I don't remember. I'm awake now. Make it morning, Papa."

And beyond the doors the sun began to rise over the ocean. Lena rose faster and was into the bathroom at once.

Fisher lay back on the soft bed and stared at the now blue mosaic. The octopus's tentacles twisted around the water, grasping nothing despite the visibility. He had tried. But they just weren't going to be that way it seemed. Not yet. Maybe not ever. Because he had hoped so, he hurt.

Fisher wished that the tabletree were not rooted to the floor so he could push it into Fang and perhaps shut her up, but she just went on and on.

". . . and maintaining our altitude above the disk without wormdrive, we'll be expending our fuel supply. It isn't unlimited. We can replenish it only very slowly with the high temperatures and low densities above the disk. Adding to that, the time to next outburst will limit our visit duration. We simply must make all haste to secure a dragon once we reach SS Cygni."

"And so?" Fisher prompted.

"It is clear that using our missiles as soon as possible is the most effective means to secure a dragon, dead or alive," Fang stated unequivocally. "It is the best course."

She was outrageous! Every week the dragon meeting had eventually worked around to Fang's persistent desire to fire her weapons. She was nothing more than a livestock hauler, a modern cowboy at best, a glorified button pusher at worst. She sat there, so smug in her perfect white uniform playing as if she were a military commander. This was science, not war. Give her a weapon arsenal that would be the envy of a small colony, and suddenly she was power mad: Fire the missiles! Fire the missiles!

Why couldn't she be more like she was in her cabin?

"That may not be necessary," Devereaux interjected. "Certainly we can spend a few days investigating, gathering data, before making that decision. I've been making progress determining dragon numbers and location, but the uncertainties are still large.

The outburst timescale does vary, and we can adjust our arrival time to give us a long visit between outbursts."

"We fire at a dragon as a last resort," Fisher said. "To fire immediately would be like . . . like a premature ejaculation!"

"Please, can we keep the discussion out of the gutter?" Stearn asked.

Everyone stopped and looked at the Jack.

Devereaux smiled knowingly and Henderson scowled.

Fisher, also unsmiling, turned back to Fang and met her icy gaze. "I apologize."

"Sylvia," Fang asked. "Is it true that the SS Cygni disk is experiencing an increased mass transfer rate compared to historical norms?"

"Yes, but we really need more data. The time dilation works both ways and—"

Fang continued. "The dwarf novae outbursts are more powerful and more frequent, aren't they?"

"It seems so, but—"

"So our timetable should be accelerated. I am merely proposing the most logical way of doing that. This is quite reasonable." Fang smiled and spread her hands apart, palms upturned. "We can always try to capture a live specimen afterward, if it seems appropriate."

Fisher shook his head. "I've almost got the beast's bioelectric field nailed. With modifications to the shuttles we ought to be able to herd a dragon right into the *Karamojo*. Surely we should go for that *first*."

"You still have time to convince me," Fang said, eyebrows arched high. "I am the captain, and I will make the final decision. I am responsible for this ship, this mission, and I won't take unnecessary risks."

"How about this?" Devereaux offered. "We send a prospector

ahead. We have several on our manifest, and we can get some advance data, a few days' worth at least. Then we can make an informed decision without spending the extra resources."

Fang considered it and finally said, "That would be agreeable."

Fisher nodded and said nothing. What he thought was this: *Why must you be like this when you're playing Captain? Why must you have a trophy? I won't have you killing my dragon.*

Devereaux walked into the observation blister. There were no artificial lights, but her robed form cast a shadow up from the transparent diamond floor as she cleared the entranceway. The light came from the Doppler-boosted and blueshifted long-wavelength radiation in the Galactic plane toward SS Cygni, including blueshifted cosmic microwave background: a tight knot of points amidst a diffuse glow. Elsewhere through the diamond the sky showed pure jet-black, the stars erased by their velocity, except for directly aft, above her head, where the sun was still visible, its X-ray corona redshifted to optical wavelengths and amplified by the shape and gain of the blister.

Only their origin and their destination remained part of the visible universe.

A few more weeks and they would collapse the singularity pair, then reignite them in reverse, and begin to decelerate. Earth was mere months in the past now, but already irreversibly half a millennium gone. This step felt right to her. It was time to start her march toward the end of time and see the marvels along the way.

Devereaux loosened her robe, discarded it, and stretched out on the floor, her head in a bubble in the blister designed for just such viewing. The diamond felt cool against her smooth tummy and breasts. The universe rushed at her at essentially lightspeed, but it really didn't appear much more interesting than a tight knot of lights, a very bright star cluster. There was no sensation of speed.

Finally bored, Devereaux asked Papa to project a console off the bubble so she could work on the data and maybe get some more reliable estimates on the dragon density. The disk was big, and finding a dragon would not be easy. If they flew close enough for the best resolution, still limited by diffraction to a few tenths of an arcsecond at optical wavelengths, they would only be able to see a small part of the disk. Flying higher with a larger field of view, dragons would blend into the turbulent plasma.

She had to admit that given only a week to work with, assuming a single visit between outbursts, Fang's violent ideas made some sense. The shockwave from a nuclear explosion would not only stun dragons at some distance (she had to believe they were stunnable), but it would also clear away swaths from the rarefied disk leaving holes like pepperoni on pizza. She smiled and got down to work.

With red and green vectors spiraling before her, models of dragon distributions through the disk based on spectral analyses of the green—now blueshifted into the X-ray—emission-line profile, she heard someone's slippered feet padding along the hallway behind her. She dimmed her console. "Phil?"

The footsteps stopped. After a minute came a voice. "Henderson."

Devereaux considered grabbing her robe, but she was too relaxed where she was.

"Mind if I join you, madam?" he asked.

She said, "Not at all. The universe is big enough to share, but just barely at the moment."

He kneeled onto the diamond and laid at her side. "Yes, I see. I've never been on a trip this fast. What's our beta?"

Beta was the fraction of lightspeed. "Very close to one. Gamma, the relativistic factor, is more useful in our case. I don't know the exact number, but it is something over a thousand."

Henderson let go a long, low whistle.

Devereaux had never actually known anyone who did that outside of a stimshow. It took too much forethought to whistle in such a manner, at least without a bodmod, to make it a spontaneous sound of awe. "Don't be so impressed. We're a big ship on a long trip, and Biolathe doesn't want to wait forever for a return on their investment. I understand there are some political and military craft that make us look slow."

They lay together in the darkness for a time, looking at the small universe. Devereaux was getting bored again, and was about ready to go to her cabin so she could get some work done, when Henderson asked, "So how is he?"

She decided to be obtuse; they didn't know each other well enough to pretend intimacy. "Who?"

"The Jack."

"Phil is fine."

"I mean, he pulled a fast one on me." She could hear the self-deprecating but insincere smile in his words, reminding her of his premeditated whistle. "The captain obviously had eyes for Fisher since day one, but you, you struck me as someone looking for something a bit more sophisticated than a trendy boy."

"He's more complex than you give him credit for. And sweet and thoughtful beats sophisticated every time with me." Where was he going? Was this a roundabout way of building up to a pass?

He forced a laugh. "I would not underestimate sophistication. Sex is in the mind, for the most part. Would you not agree?"

Of course she agreed. She gave him a grudging, "Uh huh. I suppose." Time to head things off if he were thinking of making a pass. There was a long way yet to go on this trip, and the prevention of something ugly here could be priceless. "But I've heard things about you biosystems guys. Saw a few research surveys. The 'career choice for the arrested adolescent' was how I think they put it, more interested in playing with mindless toys than real people."

There was an awkward silence. The survey she had read, and laughed over with Phil when he had pointed it out to her, had concerned sexual preferences on a profession-by-profession basis.

Finally Henderson found his voice and his words rushed out too fast. "Mindless isn't attractive, not in the long term. While humankind evolved certain mental organs that find physical health sexually attractive, those same mental organs select for intelligent mates who can raise successful children. Whether we want children or not. Try as we might, those mental organs are very difficult to excise from the human mind."

"Your point?"

"I might be a little tired of toys," he said with a small, bitter laugh.

Devereaux shivered, suddenly cold. The survey had apparently held at least some nugget of truth. "Why are you telling me this now?"

His voice floated through the darkness, sounding ancient and distant. "Because even the self-involved, and I understand that is what I am, get lonely. Of the four other people that my external universe has shrunk to, you're the only one I want to talk with. Fisher and Fang are wrapped up in each other and their own little self-destructive obsessions, and regarding Stearn, frankly I value his sweetness and thoughtfulness not at all."

"Why don't you try it sometime?"

"Please. Let us not get petty."

More footsteps in the hallway. The ruffle of feathers. Phil!

Henderson rose. "I dislike crowds in which I am in the minority. Good day, madam."

Devereaux was silent as Henderson left. It could have been him this trip, she admitted. If Stearn hadn't been interested in her, or hadn't been on the trip, or had been a woman, she could have had a relationship with Henderson. A relationship doomed to fail, she was sure.

When Stearn arrived a moment later she whispered to him, "Just hold me, Phil, and don't say anything flip."

She was grateful when he did as she requested without frivolity. The boy was learning, thankfully, because she really wanted a man just then.

FIVE

*Loss is nothing else but change, and change is
Nature's delight.*
—MARCUS AURELIUS

Fang strode onto the fly bridge, pleased at the authority ringing from her boots as she crossed the bone-tiled floor. The ruglings were absent as she had directed, and it pleased her. Everyone else was already present, just as they had been for launch, and they turned their heads toward her as she entered. She flashed them a calculated smile as she sat down on her fighting chair, relishing the croaking squeak emitted by the sweaty leather.

One of the fears that Fang had harbored for the last few hundred years, Earth time, was that captains would be done away with. Entire human crews, in fact. She would return from a run to Epsilon Eridani or Tau Ceti to discover that the already semiredundant crew on corporate ships had been replaced entirely by AIs, robots, and bioservants. Most of the flight time there was nothing to do. Papa kept the charged singularity pair separated and their acceleration pointed toward a rendezvous with SS Cygni, kept the oscillating ship charge balanced to maintain a smooth one g, and kept the course clear of obstacles with a combination of ionizing laser fire and external electromagnetic fields. If anything went wrong, only a machine could compensate quickly enough to avert disaster, if at all; a human, even a dangerously mindmoded human, had no chance. Still, the human animal was a versatile animal. Human creativity and intuition continued to solve problems, some pattern recognition, situations with incomplete data—fewer and fewer compared to artificial minds, she granted—but enough to make them valuable. There were always situations with incomplete data.

Humans had fought for centuries now to stay involved, and continued to find ways to do it, although marginalization approached on multiple asymptotes.

On a normal assignment, Fang could expect to oversee the ship through three stages: launch, turnaround, and arrival. In principle, these were dangerous times because the wormdrive with its deadly singularities was either being activated or deactivated. A large electromagnetic pulse could disrupt electronic parts of the ship brain, requiring intervention. There had been more than one accident in mankind's past, which was the reason why Higgs generators were no longer used for launches from planetary surfaces. Calling someone a loose hole was a serious insult on Earth and most colonies. On a normal assignment, these three stages would be the only opportunities to test a human captain in the field, the only opportunities to fail, or to achieve glory. In practice, the chances of anything happening were minuscule.

Because of the nature of this mission, and the vast array of unknowns, Fang would have final say in many matters when they reached SS Cygni, many chances for failure, but also many chances for real glory. Plenty more anyway than during the course of standard ship operations . . . she hoped.

Like everything in her life, Fang nevertheless took the current maneuver seriously. "Amass forward nanoskin," she ordered. Their forward field would be in flux when they brought the singularities together, and a relativistic dust speck might impact with devastating results if they weren't prepared. The nanoskin, primarily designed for reflecting and reradiating photons near a hot photosphere, could also serve effectively as a shock-absorbing and self-repairing ablation shield.

"Done," replied Papa some twenty seconds later.

Fang tugged her uniform sleeves even straighter than they already were. "Everyone secure themselves."

After she saw that everyone's furniture beasts, which had their own attachments to the ship, had grasped their charges, Fang buckled herself down with her own harness, which outwardly resembled an ancient seat belt that the real Papa would have been familiar with. She liked the click of metal on metal. She fished an ampoule of On-The-Edge from her pocket and snorted it. "Charge singularities and initialize biseed collapse."

Fang ran Papa through the rest of the drill, watching the tangled field lines dance in her picture tank as the singularities were slowly brought together electrically to recollapse into the quantum foam whence they came. The gravity waxed and waned, until it finally vanished along with the biseed. The ship rotated, nanoskin bulge, radars, and lasers rotating oppositely, keeping their path safe.

At almost the very instant Fang was about to order the wormdrive reactivated, Fisher said, "I've thought of a way to modify the—"

"Quiet!" Fang barked. Why did he always have to be so damn obsessed?

Fisher mouthed, "I'm sorry," toward her, but his lips were difficult to read through the heavy scowl.

She hadn't meant to snap at him. This was routine, wasn't it? She made a mental note to make it up to him later, and resumed the maneuver.

A few minutes later they were again under gravity, bouncing against a new, oppositely directed hole pair and decelerating toward SS Cygni, shedding their tremendous kinetic energy.

Smooth sailing here on in, thought Fang, not looking at Fisher.

Stearn hurried away from Henderson's lab despite the fact that he'd spent several hours there. That guy really creeped him out. Sure, he was good-looking, in a fashion, but he was also aloof and snippy. Stearn just didn't care for him, which was strange, as he prided himself on being able to have a good time with anyone. Perhaps his creche hadn't been as diverse as his seven parents had told him.

Knots formed in his stomach as he neared Sylvia's quarters. It had been more fun than he had imagined to seduce her with his mind, augmenting his biochip's onboard data store with board games. The whole thing had been a ploy to get her into bed, but the biggest surprise had been how fun the games actually were. This was a different sort of hedonism than he had practiced in the past, and he wondered if maybe he'd given the present era's entertainment diversity short shrift.

Still, he'd seen her with Henderson in the observing blister with the lights down that time a few weeks ago. Henderson might not creep her out the way he did him, and he did have that big lantern jaw and cleft chin that he was sure she liked. Thankfully the biosystems tech had assisted him as asked without pestering him with a lot of questions. Back on Earth a complete body makeover would have been long overdue, but here he hadn't even given it a second thought for months, not knowing which way the trends had gone, and happy playing games with Sylvia.

But this new body, this was for her as much as for himself. His bright colors were gone. His earwings were gone. It was all different. Now he was an ebon Adonis, a dark, hairless demigod with the muscle tone to match Captain's (although he suspected hers was entirely and terrifyingly natural).

Stearn reached Sylvia's cabin. His powerful heart beat strongly underneath his taut pectorals. Shaking slightly, he rang her chime and waited nude and—he hoped—beautiful.

The door opened. Monkey howls and bird calls erupted out, along with a bloom of humid air. Vine-covered trees with dark green leaves filled the room. Where had the Rubix walls and the puzzlebox chairs gone to? Where was the checkerboard credenza?

Stearn stepped inside, his bare feet sinking into rich, moist soil. Where was Sylvia?

"Up here, sweet man," came her voice.

Stearn tilted his head up. The ceiling had been increased considerably, allowing these new tall trees to vanish into a diffuse canopy an indeterminate distance above. The sounds of slithering fell like rain around him. Riding in a cradle of kelly green vines more serpentine than vegetable descended Sylvia, garbed in snarling leopard skins that covered only parts of her brown body.

"Sweet mama," Stearn whispered.

"Not tonight," she promised, extending a hand. "You have shown admirable consideration in fulfilling my desires even though they are not your primary interest. It's my turn to give you what you want. Fully and without reservation."

Was this for real? Or was it some new game?

Stearn was ready to play either side.

He took her hand. The vines lifted them, and together they ascended into a physical paradise.

Lena, which was how she thought of herself only in the privacy of her cabin, applied the passion pink lipstick and listened to Ravel's *Bolero* while she waited for her lover. No frivolous bod-mods like automakeup for her, nothing as slightly permanent as that even. Her cabin was her safe place, her place to be feminine, pretty, but it was essential that such things not leave with her when she was outside, when she became Captain Fang.

They were her secrets, kept to herself and her occasional lovers.

The door chimed and admitted Samuel.

Lena coyly glanced over her shoulder, giving him a mock look of surprise. Mock because she had planned on him catching her there in front of her mirror in only a short and sheer pink robe, untied, that she hadn't worn in front of him before.

Then without either saying a word, his arms were around her, sweeping her up powerfully—something she would never permit outside the cabin—and carrying her to the bed.

Lena buried her nose in the nape of his neck and inhaled his unmodified, intoxicating scent. Pure Sam, pure male. She reached up and twisted her fingers into his dark curls, attempting to pull him down like a kraken sinking an old merchant marine frigate.

He resisted, shook free, and tossed her down before him. His body followed hers, shedding clothes like an ablating heat shield during a reentry. His hands gripped her wrists tightly above her head, and his legs pried apart her legs.

She loved it, this submission she gave herself over to only here where she was absolutely safe and not responsible.

He was strong and fast as she hooked her ankles into the small of his back. He lasted just long enough for her—they both cried out—before collapsing heavily on top. His weight felt comfortable on her, like a warm, thick blanket, and his salty sweat dripped from his face and neck onto hers.

Lena realized that she hadn't thought of command for several minutes and smiled. Perhaps now was the time to share even more. Warm and safe, she asked, "Did I ever tell you about my grandfather?"

"Mmm . . . just that you stayed with him sometimes when you were growing up."

Lena swallowed, her mouth suddenly dry, and rubbed her cheek against Samuel's shoulder. "He was the most wonderful man, so very patient with me, even when I was being a little shit."

"You?"

She poked him in the ribs and went on.

"You know about leviathans, don't you? On Tau Ceti Prime. I mean, you're an exobiologist and—"

"Yes, I know about leviathans."

She would do it. She would tell him. Maybe this time it would help.

"I was playing with the leviathan lure. Grandfather kept it locked inside a box, but I'd broken the code—it was my birthday—and I was playing with the lure. It was pretty, like a star, shiny and grand, so much bigger in appearance than it really was." Lena became silent and listened to Samuel's breathing over the gentle susurration of the waves outside. How could she tell him this next part? She had started now, and she needed to tell it all, to have someone who was truly human understand. It had been a long time since she had last shared this story. It was her fault, her fault for not acting when there had still been a chance, but Lord, those *eyes* . . .

"I *have* it," Samuel announced out of the blue.

"Have what?" Lena whispered, her voice sounding low and throaty without a hint of her practiced bark, the way it did only when she was thoroughly relaxed.

"The green glow," he said standing up to pace the room. "It just came to me while I was thinking about how to keep cool during sex. It's a cooling system that allows the dragon to dump excess heat. The wavelength doesn't make sense for a standard atomic laser transition, but it's probably a tunable molecule, or a small suite of them, and given the profile of the emission line, I'm sure I can figure out the mechanism."

Without his body against hers, goosebumps erupted across her skin. Without his attention, something similar was occurring in her heart. "Come back to bed, Sam. I was telling you something important."

He kept pacing back and forth between the vanity and the door. "Just a second, right? This is a breakthrough. Respect the idea coming here."

Chilled, she crawled beneath the sheets and held them tightly to her chin. "Please, Sam. Not now."

He stopped then and looked at her, lifting his eyebrows in a conscious expression. "I'm sorry, but I thought you were done. You know how I work, how I have to give a problem my complete attention." He suddenly turned his head as if listening to something far away and gave her a half-smile, showing a dimple. "You know, you look really sweet, wrapped up in the sheets like that. A soft-winged angel wrapped in clouds, saying please. It's such a nice change from when you're in that uniform, being bitchy about how to bag a dragon."

He came to bed and tried to wrap his arms around her.

She shrugged him away, annoyed with him. Then she flung away the sheets, too, as she was suddenly stiflingly hot. She stood up and walked to the doors overlooking the beach, and turned her back on them to regard the man in her bed.

"What's wrong, darling?" he asked, eyes wide in what appeared only mock concern—the emotion needed to make the look genuine was simply not there. "Don't you think I'm right about the laser cooling?"

Air involuntarily escaped her mouth in a sound of disbelief. "I'm in the middle of sharing something important with you, and suddenly you jump up out of bed and start ranting about your precious dragon, and you don't know what's wrong?"

"You're upset about the 'bitchy' comment, aren't you? You're always saying 'damn' all the time. I thought that you appreciated being thought of as a tough captain." He rose onto his knees and held his fists out in a boxing stance. "Right?"

"Not right after making love!"

Samuel went to her and tried to put his arms around her. "It's okay," he murmured.

She shrugged him away. "Not now. I'm mad at you right now."

"*You're* mad at *me?* Didn't we just have great sex? I already apologized for not understanding you hadn't finished your story." He moved toward her again.

Lena shook her head and stepped back. She knew he was obsessive, but he was also intelligent and handsome. Could he actually be this dense about her after these months? She hugged herself and pointed her elbows toward Samuel as she wondered if perhaps *she* had been dense about *him*. "Maybe you should leave."

"I don't think so, Lena. Listen to me. I think we better work this through. Now."

She realized she was chewing on her lips and stopped. Why couldn't he see he was making it worse? She didn't wear her mask here, and her safe place suddenly felt dangerous. "Get out, Sam."

He took a deep breath and stared at her for a long moment. "Let's take a step back. I'm ready to hear about the leviathan now, okay?"

Lena blinked back the welling tears. She would *not* cry in front of him! "Get out!"

She walked toward him, hands out, ready to push him from her quarters. He was hurting her, here of all places, the only place she permitted vulnerability. She blinked wetly, and Sam became an ethereal specter, his shimmering presence taunting her. He had to be forced out *now*. "Get out!"

He shied away as she approached, stumbled backward, slipping on a scavenging fish slinking across the floor, and fell on his butt.

She kicked him, not that hard, in the shoulder, knocking him over.

"What's wrong with you?" he said as he scuttled farther back, like a crab, away from her.

"Get out!" she yelled, stalking after him. "Open," she barked to the door.

Sam tried to stand up, and without thinking she kicked him in the face. Again, not that hard, but his lip was bleeding when he looked up at her from the hallway. "I should have known better than to risk the dragon by getting involved with you. I learned from my ex that I could mix work and love, that I could make a relationship work that way. But you obviously haven't learned how to do it. You're just a tin-plated dictator playing a game you don't understand."

"Close," she yelled.

"Don't you—"

Flushed and out of breath, Lena fell back against the closed door and slowly slid down until she sat huddled in a ball on the floor. She cried as she hadn't cried in years, or maybe decades. Whether it was for the shattered relationship and Sam's betrayal, thinking of Grandfather, or just for herself and the years of denial with which she treated her uncertainties, she didn't know. She cried hard.

After a long while, through sniffles and a few hiccups, with her cheeks cool from the tears, she whispered, "Papa?"

"We're here, daughter," he answered immediately.

Still nude, Fisher barreled down the cabin ring corridor moaning, rushing nowhere.

Wrong, wrong, wrong, wrong, *wrong!* Everything had gone so wrong. It had been a wrong—more than a wrong, a sin—to risk the dragon by entering a relationship with the captain of the ship. Wrong, to think he had any life beyond this mission. Wrong to think of anything but the dragon since the *Karamojo* had left Earth orbit. Everything so very *wrong*.

Fisher passed through the Hall of Trophies, abruptly stopping his headlong rush to roar at a lion head. The animal wrinkled its nose, but didn't roar back. Fisher smacked it on its nose, hard. The lion roared then, a sound that carries for miles on the savanna on Earth. Fisher roared with the lion, his voice becoming the lion's voice, asserting his dominion over the ship, over the mission. The roar died, then its echoes died, and the other animals' excited calls reverberated through the corridor.

There would be no more mistakes.

Atsuko had warned him not to forget people this time, but that advice had been dreadfully wrong as well. The real wrong had been forgetting the dragon, his one and only reason for being on this ship, for throwing away his life in the present to travel five hundred years into an unknown future. With this kind of sacrifice, there was no excuse for losing his focus, no excuse for forsaking his purpose. Until the mission was over, the dragon was his master. Nay, his god. Fang had not yet seen obsession. He'd show her obsession!

Filled with renewed purpose and a plan to right the great bible of wrongs the universe had written for him, Fisher resumed his rush and headed toward Henderson's biolab.

Henderson was not happy to see him, especially after he'd explained what he wanted. "What? Again? I just did Stearn."

"And now you'll do me," Fisher said. "That's your job, isn't it?"

Henderson sighed loudly. "Fine. No one needs anything more than a hair retarder in months and now two major bodmods in the same day! Ironic."

"Whatever you say," Fisher agreed. He'd already stopped listening to Henderson at 'Fine.' He went to the workstation and started bringing up menus and rifling through them at top speed.

"Don't you want me to do that?" Henderson asked. "Aren't you afraid of giving yourself a disease?"

No, he didn't and he wasn't. Fisher knew exactly what he wanted to do for this bodmod and it was something he dare not trust to someone else. He knew Henderson was competent with mammalian biological structure, but this would be far from standard. "I'm doing the design myself."

"Don't say I didn't offer." Henderson paused for a moment then added, "Can I offer you something to wear? A robe, perhaps?"

Fisher grunted and didn't care if Henderson took the sound as assent or not. His mind had already turned to the task at hand.

"Hmm, all right then," Henderson said. "I'll prep the bath then."

Fisher knew that a star dragon possessed strong electromagnetic fields that facilitated their movements in the magnetic field of the accretion disk. That pattern of motion suggested a circulatory system of charged fluid that would be useful for energy transfer as well as transportation. The creatures had to shed heat, however, if not from inefficient energy transfer then from what they absorbed from their immediate environment. He'd figured out that one too, now, with the laser cooling. Those two interwoven systems then were the key to the new body he would create for himself, and not all that difficult to implement, he realized after a quick survey of available bodmods. It was the current levels and combination of mods that would pose problems, and that took him an extra half hour to solve to his satisfaction, and an extra ten minutes to meet the safety diagnostics' satisfaction that required extra electrical shielding for his nervous system.

The thought of powering his body with magnetically confined fusion flashed to mind, but even he had to admit that would be too much, if it were even available.

When he was finished, a glowing green man floated in the workstation's picture tank, rotating to display the final product from all angles. He would require some special nutritional supplements, but nothing too onerous . . . but then again nothing would be too onerous for him at this stage in his dedication to his goals.

"Glow in the dark skin?" Henderson asked, failing to startle him.

Fisher just snorted back. "Hardly. I'm ready for the bath, Henderson."

"Affirmative, Fisher."

Fisher rose, ignoring the cramps in his sore back; he realized he'd battered the chairbeast to immobility without thinking about it. He also realized that he should have fixed his back since he was going to the trouble of a major bodmod, but he'd forgotten about it. Fixing his back wasn't important enough to further delay him.

The nutrient bath squatted in an adjacent, tall-ceilinged chamber surrounded by organo-electronic systems. Fisher stepped up the ladder to the top of the diamond rim. The fluid within bubbled darkly like a stew, a modern witch's cauldron.

Fisher did not hesitate at the rim the way most people did. He rotated smoothly at the top and let his feet slip into the warm bath and immediately let go so his entire body could follow. Unlike most people, he did not hesitate to suck the oxygenated fluid into his mouth and lungs. There was no sense to hesitation, and a baser instinct overrode what he considered obsolete instincts against drowning. His alveoli switched into more efficient oxygen extraction with his very next heartbeat.

In the warm, wet darkness thousands of viruses invaded his system. These were the agents of gene therapy that would inject themselves into his cells, dismantle his DNA at the introns, and insert or replace certain sequences that would govern the cellular operation of his new systems. More sophisticated nanomachinery would reconstruct the macrobiology into the forms he had selected. Still other devices, more sophisticated than viruses and more versatile than the machinery rebuilding his tissues, would isolate and protect his brain functions. Numbness struck his extremities and he knew that these were working. A warmth more vital than that of the bath grew within him: waste heat from the tiny machines and cellular changes. He was now trapped in his own morphing body several hours until the modifications would be complete.

Fisher had not programmed any stim entertainment for the procedure. His eyes stared unseeing into the black brew. His mind's eye saw only glowing green dragons above a blazing disk of fire.

Yes, he thought as his limbs went rigid and a slow burn filled his body, he'd show Fang obsession all right.

PART II

Here Be Dragons

SIX

*The human body is the best picture
of the human soul.*
—LUDWIG WITTGENSTEIN

Devereaux walked steadily down the corridor toward Fisher's cabin, her speed balanced between urgency and yes, she freely admitted to herself, apprehension bordering on fear. When she had brought her latest disk predictions to Captain Fang, how was she to know that the result would be an *immediate* decision to deactivate wormdrive, canceling the full program of deceleration, in order to arrive early?

Fisher would be furious at not being notified earlier, but he would be even more furious if not notified now. Worse, he had instructed Papa not to disturb him short of decompression, so seeing him in person was the only way to inform him.

Devereaux wished she hadn't said as much

to Captain Fang, who had told her to go ahead and tell him in person.

Devereaux didn't want to see Fisher furious. Not now, after what he had made of himself these last few long months. Why wouldn't the man see reason anymore? What had happened between him and the captain that was this awful? Normally solving such a puzzle would have held boundless interest for her, but now . . .

Her hand shook as she was reaching for the chime. Before she could ring it, Fisher's door irised open, spilling white light, dry heat, and crackling noise into the corridor. Startled, Devereaux jumped away, bringing her hand, fingers spread, to her chest. It was like standing before an open kiln.

"I felt the fields shift," Fisher said.

She would have been startled even if he hadn't opened his door unexpectedly—Fisher's current appearance never failed to startle her. Most immediately noticeable was the green glow that exuded from his rough, dry skin, then the lack of any hair, including eyebrows (which Fisher had explained were not needed for a body that no longer sweated), and finally the tiny salmon-pink eyes set deep within epicanthic folds of skin. His unvarying dress was now also quite different. Gone were the black duradenim and the characteristic but ugly streakers. Now he wore a sheer gray bodysuit stitched with concentric golden fibers of unclear purpose. The creases were ninety degrees out of phase with those of the captain's, tracing his outline like an aura.

And his cabin . . . Devereaux spared a second to look beyond the exobiologist before answering him. Inside, fires roared and danced in the bottom half of the room, making for an overwhelming cacophony to the senses. The fire stopped abruptly about a meter from the door. In the months since turnaround, Devereaux had never seen anything but fire in the room, and had no idea of how Fisher lived inside, let alone worked.

"I felt the fields shift," Fisher repeated.

"How could you? I mean, yes, Fang's preparing to shut down the wormdrive."

Fisher pushed past Devereaux, and she felt static raise the hair on her arms, and even the tangles of the hair on her head.

She turned and tried to keep up with his pace.

"Papa," Fisher ordered, "give me a line to Fang."

"We're sorry," came Papa's voice. "The captain is busy and asked not to be disturbed. Is this a decompression emergency?"

Without breaking his stride, Fisher dismissed Papa's stonewall with a wave of his arm. To Devereaux he said, "Brief me."

Devereaux, jogging to keep up, said in a bumpy, breathless voice, "Like I told Fang, for our approach as scheduled, SS Cygni would be entering outburst. It made sense to advance arrival twenty days, ninety-nine percent confidence interval on the outburst ignition. So Fang's advancing the schedule. We'll compute a new, faster course, overshoot the system with some residual velocity, and let its gravity help pull us back. Get a good look on the way past and obtain a second opinion on the probe results."

"Anything new from the probe? She's not still planning to fire missiles, is she?" he hissed.

This continuing argument had turned the dragon meetings into an entrenched battleground. The vague guidelines of the Biolathe prospectus provided great latitude and an ambiguous mandate for either Fisher or Fang to wrest from the document. When it had appeared probable they might overshoot the disk because of the outburst timing, as they were now planning, Fang had seized the opportunity to suggest launching the missiles early. The missiles could be sent on a slower approach, and could be made to drive a dragon toward the ship, which would now be coming about from the far side of the system. Devereaux herself admired the elegant solution, minimizing resource consumption and time, the play of the related differential equations against the extreme boundary conditions of the disk. Fisher, of course, protested at every meeting. A classic case of irresistible force and immovable object.

"Nothing from the probe, but the range isn't yet optimal and the noise is large. I'm not sure about the missiles but—"

He increased his pace through a ring shift without pausing to listen to her, and surged into the bridge ring. Just before they reached the portal to the fly bridge, Fisher stumbled. Arms outstretched, he skidded to a stop on his chest.

As Devereaux bent to help him up, Papa's voice announced, "Please secure your loose items and yourselves. Wormdrive shutting down. End of full gravity in thirty seconds."

"I'm fine," Fisher said, pushing her away with a mild shock. "I'm simply very sensitive to magnetic fields now, and these rings are not as well shielded, at least to our internal fields, as I would prefer."

"I see," she said, frowning as Fisher went right on by her and headed into the fly bridge.

Just as Devereaux rounded the entrance, Fang said, "Take your seats, people."

Devereaux did as she was told, taking the opportunity to push past Fisher for a change, and slid onto the accommodating couch-beast. She was breathing heavily.

Fisher stood his ground, about two meters directly in front of where Fang sat, and made no motion toward the couch. What was he trying to prove?

"Sit down, Dr. Fisher," Fang said.

"I prefer to stand," he replied.

"Fine," said Fang.

The volume of Papa's countdown increased as he approached zero. The gravity oscillated. Fisher's glow intensified. Then Devereaux's stomach did a mean flip-flop as gravity failed. "Wormdrive deactivated," Papa announced.

Fisher drifted upward slowly off the floor. Fang lifted her head to follow Fisher's trajectory.

No one said anything for a few moments, a strange anticlimax to the preceding rush. Or rather, no climax at all yet. That was the problem.

"You're welcome, daughter," Papa said.

Fang blinked. "Sorry. Thank you, Papa."

Devereaux sneezed. Then twice more. She often sneezed at the onset of freefall, when the dust and lint was able to escape the nooks and crannies it had found for itself, and before the filters and fish could remove the extra irritants from the air. No one said anything right away, and she hoped that her sneezes had broken the dark mood that had been brewing.

"So what's it going to be now?" Fisher asked, his face drifting toward the captain's. The tension recrystallized, like a supersaturated solution being prodded.

Before his glare, Captain Fang calmly turned her gaze toward Devereaux. Her expression, as usual, was inscrutable. "What is your current opinion on the matter, Sylvia?"

"We might learn something during the flyby—our instruments are far superior to the probe's. The numbers and distribution of dragons in the disk are still mostly guesswork. My model still indicates that the next outburst will hold off at least two weeks."

"Thank you," Fang said. She turned back to Fisher. Their noses were scant centimeters apart. Somehow Fisher hadn't bumped into her, and now in fact seemed to hover, somehow holding his position. Magnetically? It was possible.

Fang addressed Fisher. "Shall we consider this while Papa is computing our options, and look at SS Cygni for ourselves?"

"Fine," Fisher said, and managed to spin in place, orienting himself to look on the wall screen.

"Bring it up, Papa."

The system materialized, real colors, almost real-time—only a few hours' light delay now. Tilted at nearly a thirty-degree angle to their approach vector, the disk blazed away, essentially pure white to the eye over its entire surface, with only a hint of violet. Nestled right up against the disk with its sparkling heart, the larger secondary star throbbed, a cooler cosmic ember within which hydrogen still burned. Sparking serpentine tendrils twisted between the disk and the secondary, prominences tracing the magnetic flux tubes connecting the two photospheres. Motion was visible to the eye. The outer disk velocities were about six hundred kilometers per second—not a relativistic speed, but respectable, letting the gas orbit over the course of a couple hours. The velocities at the inner edge of the disk, on the other hand, were more than respectable. It was all simple dynamics, and the gas rotated in the disk differentially, following Keplerian orbits such that the centrifugal force of the angular momentum balanced gravitational pull, and at the inner edge the velocities were over six *thousand* kilometers per second. That meant that the gas spiraling into the primary star did so making roughly an orbit every few seconds.

The white dwarf massed 20 percent greater than solar, while the larger but less dense secondary was a mere 70 percent solar. The sum was more than Chandrasekhar's limit of 1.44 solar masses, the mass above which degenerate electron pressure could not resist gravitational collapse. The process by which mass was transferred from the secondary to the primary was distressingly complicated, since there also existed several processes by which the primary itself lost mass. During many epochs nova explosions, winds, and other cosmic belches tended to leave the white dwarf with less mass than when it started. Still, Devereaux's best evolutionary models indicated the system would, billions of years in the future, explode in a certain rare type of supernova.

Devereaux shifted her gaze from SS Cygni to Fisher and Fang. Fisher had rotated around Fang so they were nearly side by side, together staring at the binary system. Fisher glowed a bright green. The shimmer made him appear agitated, perhaps appropriately so. Fang's light olive complexion reflected his light, her face expressionless, placidly regarding their destination. Their faces so close together, with such a contrast, reminded Devereaux of a binary star. But which was the primary, and which was the secondary? Which was consuming the other? It had already seemed that their relationship had resulted in a supernova, but perhaps that was merely the outburst of a dwarf nova, with the real fireworks still to come.

Devereaux didn't want to be around if those two got into it the way they were capable of doing.

Casting away these dangerous thoughts, she caught Phil's eye. He winked at her, and, suddenly grinning, she winked back. Much of her apprehension evaporated, just like that.

"Course calculated and maneuver options placed in command buffer," Papa announced. "What is your desire, daughter?"

Indeed, thought Devereaux. She would have to say something, do something, if Captain Fang insisted on launching the missiles now. It didn't make sense to do anything like that until they had a better look, sifted through the probe data, gave the place an examination with their own instruments. Committing them to something at this stage would be ludicrous, driven by emotional factors and not by logic. They had plenty of time between outbursts, and could always retreat to a safe distance and orbit through another dwarf nova if forced to. They had enough ablation mass and fuel for the raildrive for that. She would follow the reasonable course, Devereaux believed: Fang was a professional first and Devereaux trusted her to do the right thing.

"Papa—" began Fang.

"Activate wormdrive," Fisher broke in.

"Belay that!" Fang cried, showing the most emotion on her face—in this case a snarl—that Devereaux could recall. Not even during the dragon meetings had Fang burst out like that.

"Of course, daughter."

"Leave the bridge, Dr. Fisher," Fang said, her face a smooth mask once again.

Sweat trickled coolly up Devereaux's temple. She flicked her head slightly, sending the sweat floating off in a ball.

A hint of ozone tinged the air—from Fisher? If he were emitting ionizing radiation, she'd—

Fisher said, "Fine," and spun away and glided out the door without touching any surfaces. It was spooky, like he was a green ghost. If he had screamed, he would have made a fine banshee.

After he had gone, Fang said, "Alter course, please. Take us by SS Cygni as outlined in the primary command buffer."

So, no missiles. Thankfully sensible.

"Yes, daughter."

Suddenly Devereaux fell sideways, but the gentle tug from the chemical maneuvering thrusters lasted only a moment. Just a nudge to put them on a course to skim by the disk, timed to thread the *Karamojo* between the two stars.

She hoped there was a similar course between Fisher and Fang that would bring success. Was there some way to nudge the mission's course through their dangerous orbit?

Stearn had finished checking the *Karamojo*. Everything was running smoothly with the rotation-induced gravity, all the rings twisting to best maintain their new down vector despite the fact that it was nearly perpendicular to what it had been for the vast majority of the trip. This new state was temporary. When they reached SS Cygni they would maintain a raildrive-assisted orbit at an altitude above the outer rim of the disk, and there would be a substantial gravity, back again along the ship's central axis.

In the English library he had made of his quarters, Sylvia proposed to Stearn a game of chess. He accepted. The opening moves went quickly, the Tasmanian variation of the Sicilian Dragon defense, and they were soon embroiled in a familiar middle game. And gossiping about other couples. Had they become such an old comfortable couple already to do such a thing?

"He just needs to get laid," Stearn explained to Sylvia as he moved his bishop. She was the smartest woman Stearn had ever hooked up with, but she sure could be dumb about some things.

"You think?" She shook her head, then leaned forward from her couchbeast to rest her elbows on the edge of the board. "I just don't see it, Phil. I mean, you think everyone needs to get laid, that it is the secret of life."

He grinned and absentmindedly reached to scratch where his feathers used to be, jumping when he scratched smooth skin. He had sure kept those wings too long to be having that reaction months later. "Everyone *does* need to get laid, and it *is* the secret of life. Human life, anyway. Captain hurt Fisher bad, and now he's bitter. He needs that touching, and I bet he's not giving it to himself."

She didn't even get distracted by his baiting anymore. Part of him felt disappointed by that, but another part of him liked the way they were settling in together.

Sylvia's brow wrinkled in concentration. He loved to watch her think. She gave it such devotion it was a thing of beauty, and the backdrop of the English drawing room—complete with the musty-dusty smell—made her seem so damn sophisticated about it. Stearn fancied himself an artist of love, or at least lust when he was being more honest with himself than usual. The real art of love, he believed, was discovering that one telling feature that caught the unique essence of a lover in a single stroke. And cherishing it. For Sylvia, it was that knit brow he had first understood as she rode him in the jungle canopy of her cabin, that she wore in those quickening moments approaching climax. That she wore whenever she focused her entire self on a pursuit she loved. That expression of her focus was the essence of her.

Sex, in one form or another, was always the key. Stearn knew it without any doubt.

"I don't think that's it," Sylvia muttered in a dismissing tone, "but we need to do something. The dwarf nova outburst will have subsided in another seventy hours, and those two are going to ruin this mission, and us with it, as soon as they get the chance." Sylvia pushed her rook pawn forward a square, forcing Stearn's bishop to retreat. After he moved it back along the diagonal, maintaining the pin, she went on, "I'm sure it's not the lack of sex. He's more complex than that. He can just crank down his hormones and ride out the dry spell perfectly happily. Not everything revolves around the drive to reproduce." Sylvia pushed forward her knight's pawn two squares, cutting off the pin and attacking Stearn's bishop. She really seemed to hate that pin.

Too emotional here, too distracted, trying to shake the pin. That weakened her defenses, and she hadn't analyzed the tactics as carefully as she usually did. Stearn considered his options, and finally decided to play true to himself. "What are the stakes on this game?"

Sylvia rolled her eyes up for a second. "The usual, I thought. Winner gets fantasy of choice."

"Let's make it a bit more interesting. Loser has to seduce Fisher, winner gets to watch." At her abrupt look of alarm, he amended, "Not in person. On neural recording, of course."

She didn't look relieved at his amendment. "I don't think so. It isn't much of a prize for me either way."

"Think of the bedroom talk, what he might say afterward in the afterglow. He might give away the whole trick of who he is. Are you saying you can resist that prize?"

"Yes I can." Sylvia rocked back and forth as she rested her chin in her hand. "But I do admit you've got my curiosity piqued now."

He stared into her eyes, waiting.

"But Fisher won't go for you. He might not go for me, but he certainly won't go for you."

"Leave that to me." He grinned at her. A semi-illegal code running on his biochip confirmed his evaluation of the chess position.

"Okay," she finally said with an expulsion of air. "But we're only talking an attempt. I can talk friendly to the man. I'm no prude."

Stearn broke into a broad smile. Without taking his eyes from hers, he reached out and took her knight's pawn with his bishop.

Sylvia broke the stare to look at the board. Her brow knit in concentration erotically, then, after about two minutes, it flattened out into a placid ocean surface. "Shit," she said.

"Mate in four, unless you care to lose your queen," said Stearn.

"That's not fair," Sylvia said.

"Chess is completely fair, no random element whatsoever."

"You know what I mean!"

He did feel guilty. A little guilty, anyhow. But what was the point of a biochip interface if not to use it? Sylvia wanted a good game from him, didn't she? "To even things out, I'll seduce Captain."

Sylvia started to laugh.

"Hey! A man doesn't need to hear that!"

"She won't sleep with you." Sylvia laughed harder.

Probably true. Still, there were a hundred ways to seduce a person. Physical union was not the only way to take pleasure in someone, something that Sylvia had reminded him of. "I'll seduce her into intimacy, make me her confidant. I'll get her to go hunting with me. She'll get to shoot something and blow off some steam. It'll have to help ease the tensions. That's the real purpose behind this, right?"

"If you say so. I can't believe I'm letting you trick me into this."

"You don't think Fisher is dangerous, do you?"

She knit her brow. "Not to us, not if we don't get in his way."

This was getting too heavy. "You don't have to actually sleep with him. Just make an attempt to gain intimacy of one sort or another. Make contact with him. It'll be fun."

Sylvia reached out and took Stearn's hand. "Phil," she said, "let's do this not just for fun. Let's do it to make things better, if we can. You agreed this is to ease the tensions."

Heavy. Donning an appropriately serious face, Stearn said, "Sylvia my darling, we must seduce them for the good of the mission."

She broke up laughing.

Then they swept the pieces off the chessboard, a large sturdy thing from another century, crawled onto it themselves, and made love in a very complicated position.

Stearn had let her off the hook, Sylvia realized, when he had admitted that there was a broad range of seductions possible. That thought eased her trepidation as she approached Fisher's cabin for the second time in as many days. Recently, she had seen him only once a week at dragon meetings—she had no idea when he ate and wondered if in fact he did eat. She took a deep breath and derailed that thought train. All she had to do really was get him to talk to her as one human being to another, make that connection.

This time she got to ring the chime.

Sylvia adjusted her scarlet silk wrap, then tucked her hands under her arms as she waited. An awkward fish schlepped along the floor, its lime coloration contrasting with the beige of the ruglings. Around the bend of the ring, a six-toed cat silently stalked the sick fish.

There was no answer.

"Papa, is Fisher in his cabin?"

"Yes."

She waited, but Papa offered no explanation. He was usually more helpful to her. "Is he asleep?"

"No."

Sylvia untucked her arms and rang the chime three times in rapid succession.

The door irised open—another glimpse into the kiln. "What is it? I'm working."

Sylvia's pupils contracted and her corneas darkened to enhance the contrast. Fisher was a dim gray-green smudge silhouetted against the fire crackling everywhere in his cabin. How could he stand it? How could he work in this inferno? "I wanted to talk to you, Sam."

"So talk. I've got a lot to do."

She could see him better now, see his tiny pink eyes staring back at her from a green mask. If only this weren't so important. She swallowed, her mouth suddenly dry, and said, "In your cabin?"

He laughed, a tinny nervous sound, as if he hadn't laughed in a long time and his mouth had forgotten how. "My cabin? Are you kidding me?"

"Can't you—" She groped for a word, and threw her hands up with a suddenness that surprised her, grimaced, continued, "Can't you just turn that off, and be a human being for a few minutes?"

He said nothing for a long moment. Then he nodded, and turned his back to Sylvia. The fire swallowed Fisher.

Sylvia waited.

Inside, the fire surged, then died. Not completely, she saw, but only in the half of the room near the door, and in a narrow path to the bathroom and to the bedbeast—a hard, obsidian creature that reflected darkly the low flames that flickered like smoldering ruglings.

"Come in," Fisher said.

Sylvia stepped across the threshold, hot already, and wiped sweat from her brow. "You live like this?"

"Of course," said Fisher, sitting in a lotus position hovering just above the flames in the rear of the room. More of the magnetic levitation trick. "I have adapted myself to this environment so as to understand how a star dragon might live, how these surroundings might influence the mind of such a fantastic creature, and what sort of things that mind might think."

That struck her as clever, but she decided not to acknoweldge that fact. "You still think the star dragon could be sentient?"

Fisher shrugged, a motion that induced a spiraling bob that only slowly damped out. "Anything is possible. If they are sentient, bombing their home would be an unethical, perhaps criminal act, would it not?"

Sylvia took two more steps into the room and stopped two meters from the fire. "Of course I agree."

"Then tell *her!*" His green glow flared.

"Easy, Sam. I will. I'm running every analysis I can think of on the probe data. I don't see anything except perhaps some signs of that laser transition, but it isn't very secure. We're having one more dragon meeting before we achieve the disk, right? Make your case there, with logic. Make a compelling argument, and I'm sure the captain will listen."

"I have been making an argument for months now. She won't listen." Fisher leaned forward, maintaining his hovering Buddha pose, and gesturing with a finger pointed above Sylvia's head. "She wants to take a trophy, fire off her bombs, play the big hunter. She doesn't care about our scientific goals. This is a grand vacation for her. A vacation!"

Sylvia stepped forward, closer to the fire. She felt her skin harden to the heat, rapidly tanning of its own volition. "Like all of us, Captain Fang has made a sacrifice to come on this journey. She has her career at stake. She will make the effort to be careful with the ship, but she has the mission's goals at heart. She wants to succeed, just as do you."

"Ha!" Fisher floated closer, leaning forward at a forty-five-degree angle. Less than a meter separated his face from hers. "She wants to sabotage me."

"I don't think so." Sylvia dry swallowed, her lips cracking open afterward, a tiny sound consumed by the popping flames. Stearn would probably expect her to dart in for a kiss at this point. She leaned forward, slightly, as if considering it. That was as physically intimate as she was going to get—there was no connection there but for the dragon issue. "Look, just give the meeting a chance. Give Fang a chance. Give the mission a chance."

"I have given the mission everything I have."

"Just don't do anything rash."

"I will do anything necessary."

He was so far away. She could do more. Sylvia lifted her hand toward the heat, toward Fisher's cheek.

He didn't move.

She flinched when a flame flickered up Fisher's gray-suited body to lick her hand, but it was brief and didn't burn. Her fingers glowed green in the light of Fisher's face as they brushed his skin. After her last experience with Fisher's current set of bodmods, she expected a spark, or crackle, or something spectacular. All she felt was soft cool skin, without a hint of beard. It was like baby skin.

He still didn't move.

"What made you like this, Sam?"

At her words, he pulled back from her touch. "Oh, it's simple biophysics really. I had Henderson help me put it together in a few hours. The key is eliminating the sweat glands in favor of bioelectric light-emitting diodes, adding a charged circulatory system, and the rest follows from there integrating the systems."

"That's not what I meant and you know it."

"Nothing made me like this."

"Really?" Sylvia challenged. "It was the twenty-seventh century when we left Earth, and it'll be the thirty-first when we get home. We can alter our bodies to suit our whims, as you've done. While mental alteration isn't as yet so safe or easy, there are a multitude of methods of regulating a personality, from special hormone-regulating glands to oral drugs to gene therapy. We choose who we want to be. Why did you choose this, Sam?"

Fisher bobbed in his fire, green on red, and said nothing for a long moment. Then, finally, when Sylvia was about ready to back out of the heat and leave him his stupid privacy, he said, "Okay then. You want a story?"

Sylvia nodded, after a moment, her hair sticking to her sweaty cheeks.

"Have you heard of the space wisps?"

She shook her head. "I know I should have uploaded the whole exobiology bestiary when I signed on for this mission, but I figured you and Papa would have that covered and I'd focus on the properties of cataclysmic variables and SS Cygni in particular."

He nodded and began talking. "Basically they're spacefaring life built of networks of polycyclic aromatic hydrocarbons originating in star-forming molecular clouds. They're tenuous enough—wisp is a good name. Not much more to look at than a bundle of threads resembling a smoke cloud. The ionizing ultraviolet that spurred their development and provides them energy also photodissociates them, and they play a game of Scylla and Charybdis with their environment. Too much ionizing flux and they break apart and die. Not enough, and they have no energy."

"They sound interesting," she said truthfully. Fisher seemed much better now than he had in months, talking about something he loved and wasn't fighting for. "Although I'm not sure how you'd tell they're even alive."

"That was tough. They were discovered by accident when a relativistic probe smacked into a pack of them in the vicinity of Sirius B. Near lightspeed, a pack of wisps can hit like a mountain, and this was a small, low-budget scientific probe without active shielding. Anyway, they were first deemed nothing more than an interesting example of Galactic chemistry. That's where I came in. I discovered three features that suggested they were truly *alive*. First, they could reproduce in a way very similar to DNA, slowly, to be sure, as they accumulated building materials from cosmic dust, but the evidence was clear from the observed population. Second, they could alter their reflective structure and guide their motions via a form of solar sailing, using radiation pressure and the shape of their sail and their angular momentum to keep them on that thin line between the dark and the destruction."

"The third feature?"

"When the photodissociated bonds re-formed, it wasn't random. Even the ones not actively replicating took the opportunity to build structures, such as their tiny sails, but sometimes the sailing structure was not built at an angle that made sense. That's what confused the first researchers. But then I realized that they were flashing infrared light signals to their neighbors. The whole pack—there were hundreds certainly, but possibly hundreds of thousands in the complete extended population—were communicating. I have no idea how intelligent the wisps were, but something was going on there."

"Why aren't you still studying the wisps?"

"All the ones we know about were destroyed. After the unusual chemistry was documented and all the data collected that I analyzed, the science team studying Sirius B swept the area with fully ionizing xenon-chloride excimer lasers and vaporized all the debris—including the wisps—to clear the path for their probes. I was already on a ship, without the high gamma like this one has, bound for Sirius. When I arrived, there was nothing to study. When I returned to Earth, twenty-two years had passed. I only lost fifteen. My mother had died in a diving accident on Europa during that span."

Sylvia didn't know how to respond. Finally she picked "I'm sorry."

Fisher's green flared to rival his floor. "Don't ever be sorry for me! I learn from my mistakes, and when it is within my power, I make sure they are never duplicated. This mission is my life, for now, for a thousand years, and I am dedicated to its successful completion. I will do whatever I have to do to ensure it."

"Yes, but you have to work with the rest of us. Captain Fang—"

Fisher held out his hand and cut her off. "Fang is irrelevant here. Do you understand my position?"

"I suppose so, yes."

"Then you'll let me get back to work?"

Was that going it be it? Perhaps it was, and perhaps it was enough. "Yes."

Fisher sat in the fire, staring at her, waiting.

She ventured a little more. "If you need to talk?"

"I'm fine," insisted Fisher. "You just concern yourself with making the mission a success, and we'll get along fine. The same goes for Fang. Now, please excuse yourself, and we'll all go back to work."

I tried, she thought. I did better than I thought I might, and it wasn't even so bad. She had collected a few more of Fisher's puzzle pieces, and even saw how a few fit together. She wondered how Phil was doing with the aloof and intractable captain.

Sylvia said, "Thanks for talking, Sam."

Fisher smiled. "Thank you."

Sylvia exited the cabin, flames crawling behind her steps to again fill the room with their righteous, intense heat. The kiln door closed.

SEVEN

The fate of animals is of greater importance to me than the fear of appearing ridiculous; it is indissolubly connected with the fate of men.
—ÉMILE ZOLA

Fang ducked under the boxing mobile's swing and hit it in the body three times, hard, before dancing back. It swung again. Fang stepped backward and to the side and tagged its head, which snapped like a tree bulldozed by an avalanche.

She had told herself a thousand times that she was better off without Fisher, but he'd made a better sparring partner than these damn mobiles. Maybe she should have gone on that safari with the Jack after all. At least it wouldn't have been the same old thing.

Someone rang Captain Fang's personal chime twice in quick succession. That was odd, she thought. Why not simply have Papa pipe voice to her?

The gym door irised open revealing a

breathless Phil Stearn, eyes wide, all white and black. He said, through heavy panting, "Captain, come quick," and took a step with a half-turn away, gesturing with his free hand for her to follow. In his other hand he energetically waved about a large-caliber rifle.

She kept herself from instinctually grimacing at his lack of respect for firearms. Just because they were ancient didn't mean not to treat them properly. "What is it, Stearn? And why are you armed?"

"I've got a wounded lion, now please *come on!*"

He took another two steps down the corridor and gestured again. After a brief hesitation, she followed, telling the clasps of her gloves to release. They dropped to the canvas and she followed her Jack out of the gym.

"Explain yourself, Mr. Stearn."

"Well, it's like this, see." He wiped sweat from his forehead with the back of his hand. "I decided to go ahead hunting without you, on the savanna."

"Real or virtual?"

"That's the thing, see. I wanted to make it interesting, so I asked Papa to surprise me with a safari of his own invention. I'm pretty sure it's real. And he won't stop the game unless I'm in physical danger. The way this body's built, well, it can take a lot of damage without seriously endangering my life. Papa won't let me evacuate the chamber, but I *don't* want to go after that lion. You want to get chewed up by a real lion?"

"Of course the lion is real," Fang said. "Papa doesn't like you."

"I know, I know, and this doesn't have the parameters for an override, and I don't want them to get there either. Papa can get a little scary, you know. But you're Captain. You could override, terminate the simulation."

"No." He made her want to frown. This was her crew? Not

finishing a hunt, not respecting the life he had created and the resources he had consumed? She should set an example. "That isn't necessary. If you're willing to shoot yourself into trouble, you'd better be willing to shoot yourself out. I'll help."

"Then let's go." Stearn picked his pace up to a jog.

Fang matched him.

They reached the savanna soon enough. Her pulse elevated, a warm radiation from a blushed face, and the start of a light sweat . . . this was much better than beating up a mobile or sitting around the cabin waiting for the dragon meeting where Fisher would twist her words to suit his own purposes. He didn't understand that this was an alien thing that could kill them, that they had to test their mettle against it assuming it to be a creature of infinite grace and power. Twisting words was not a good way to meet an unknown challenge.

The door opened. Fang stepped inside. "Give me your rifle."

"Happily, Captain. It's loaded."

"Better be." Fang surveyed the grassy plain, sliced in two by a stream and sporting a few scattered trees, squinting her eyes despite her corneas' autodarkening. A blistering day on this world inside the ship, the air still and heavy. "Tell me what happened."

"Well," said Stearn, "I shot him twice. Once in the leg, once somewhere forward. I lost him in the tall grass."

"How long ago?" asked Fang.

His eyes flickered, checking his internal clock. "Nineteen minutes, seven seconds."

"Long enough. You didn't kill him, or Papa would have let you know. He should be sick by now, his adrenaline faded, the pain . . . overwhelming. It's a damn thing, getting shot."

"Never tried it, but properly applied pain can inspire a great endorphin rush—"

"That's enough, Stearn." Fang regarded the savanna more closely. "This is a bad place."

"Why is it bad?"

"Can't see him until you're on him."

"Oh," said Stearn. "I see."

"You can stay here, if you like. I'll have to go in after him." She checked her weapon, a double-barreled .505, an old vintage capable of only two shots before requiring reloading. At least Stearn had some fortitude. He could have brought in a megagun and shredded the entire chamber in seconds. The chamber, prepped for hunting, was equipped to withstand as much.

"I thought about burning the lion out. That was done in ancient times and would be sporting."

"The grass is too green. You might as well laser the whole damn thing." The chamber was equipped for that. Papa had high-powered lasers available as safety overrides. He could and would use them to kill the lion in an instant if there was an imminent threat to their lives, but knowing Papa, he would let them get a little hurt first. "Lasers would not be fair. You did start the game."

"I'm allowed to conjure beaters," said Stearn. "I mean, I'll come with you, but can't we send beaters out ahead? I'd really like to avoid the lion mauling my equipment, if you know what I mean."

Beaters . . . this started to bother her more. How different, she thought, would it be sending beaters into the savanna to flush out the lion from sending her missiles into the disk to flush out the dragon? She had been on many hunts, but this scenario gave her more than the usual déjà vu. "Of course we can. But it's a touch murderous. I know the conjured beaters aren't real, but respect the lion, and play this for real. That's the fun of it, the test."

"What do you mean?"

"We know the lion's wounded. You can drive an unwounded lion—he'll run on ahead of noise. A wounded lion will hide until you're right on top of him. He might as well be invisible. Then he'll charge at point-blank range. A beater would get killed. It's not playing fair."

"Fine then. Lead on, bwana."

Fang frowned at the term. "I don't think that term means quite what you think it means." She set aside the distraction to focus on the task at hand, and signaled Stearn to follow with a twitch of her head.

They walked down a steep bank of an empty stream bed, and across, then up the other side. It was true physical exertion, honest exercise.

"Here," Fang said, kneeling where the short grass had been splattered with blood. "You hit it here."

"I don't want to go in there. That lion's big."

"I know," Fang said, standing. "It really can't kill us very easily the way our bodies are built, also with Papa ready to cut in at an instant. Still, we live with racial memories burned into us by twenty thousand generations on savannas like this one, the ones that made primates afraid of big cats." She considered telling Stearn that she was afraid, too, but that would have been a lie and might even come to undermine her leadership. No, outside of her cabin, she had to be a rock, would be a rock, as ever. But a hunt, this was what life was made of, if that life was being lived properly. "You can wait here."

"I've changed my mind. I mean, I thought it was fun before. I'd seen you do it. But now, this close. Why don't we just quit?"

"Stearn, you're shameful. You know that? You get Papa to grow a damn lion for you, you shoot it, then you'd just walk away while it suffers? You finish what you start if you're crew on my ship. If you deserve to be called human. I'll have no quitters, understand?" Fang tried to keep her voice even and matter-of-fact, her face hard, but some sneer escaped, she knew.

"You're right, Captain. I'm sorry. If you're going to go, I want to go."

"Good man. It's my show. Do exactly what I tell you."

Fang wondered at Stearn. He seemed to be acting a little odd, inconsistent, like he had some sort of unknown agenda that he was trying to stick to despite her. His tone, his body language, didn't match up well with his words, she decided. Like he was following a script. Still there was the lion. Time to put Stearn out of her mind and deal with the beast.

Somewhere ahead of them there was a wounded lion lying flattened on the ground, invisible in the grass. It would be big and yellow, bloody foam on its muzzle, with each breath pain in its belly coming and going like waves on a beach. It would have hate in its heart, hate in its damn eyes, which surely watched them even at this very moment, its animal instincts holding it stiffly in place awaiting that one moment when it would charge the humans who left the savanna so long ago, but dared to return toting guns that belched death. Yes, Fang knew the look those eyes would have as the muscles stiffened with pain and anticipation. She could understand those eyes. Mammalian eyes, Earthborn eyes.

Check the blood, watch the grass, step forward, check the blood, watch the grass, watch the grass, watch the grass . . .

"Why don't we—" Stearn began before Fang stopped listening.

Ignore the damn Jack, watch the grass, step forward.

Then came the blood-choked cough and, springing up from nowhere, the beast charging down on her.

Fang pointed the double-barreled rifle. *Carawong! Carawong!*

She managed to keep her stance against the fierce recoil, but had to lean into it. It was impressive, visceral, this ancient technology. She punched the animal with it.

Two shots carrying two tons of force smashed into the beast's face, halting its charge dead on. Yet the beast crawled on, somehow, half its head gone, still trying to kill Fang. This was life before her, relentless, irresistible life, pressing on against what it knew not. Following its instincts, not giving up. The lion's serpentine tail twitched as its mutilated head slumped forward.

The star dragon was alive, and would resist them with every bit as much effort. They would have to match its relentlessness.

Fang said, "It's a damn good lion, Mr. Stearn."

She heard a strangling noise, and, when she was sure that the lion's crawl truly had ceased, turned to regard her vomiting Jack.

He managed to speak. "I'm sorry, Captain, it's just—"

Fang handed the rifle to Stearn and walked past him. She said, "Have some respect for such an excellent creature. You bring life into this world for your pleasure, make sure you respect it."

Grimy and smelling of gunpowder, she left the sphere to shower and change. It would soon be time for the damn dragon meeting, and she had to think about her plan of attack.

Papa watches the meeting, furious, wishing he could scream out to everyone what Fisher has done. He lied to Devereaux about the space wisps and programmed the safari for Stearn—and based on a story Papa himself—the other Papa anyway—had written to boot! "Short Happy Life," Papa yearns to tell them. "Short Happy Life"! But Papa cannot violate Fisher's privacy. While he is an independent mind based with both organic and inorganic structures and a personality based on that of a man, he is also a tool and forced to operate within many constraints that conflict with his own desires. And now he fumes about Fisher.

The man's agenda is clear: win allies, make enemies doubt their strategies.

Fisher might well be correct about the approach to take with the dragon—data for a conclusive answer is certainly lacking—but Papa hopes Fang will foil his intent. If only she would ask him about the safari, he might be able to clue her in. He is allowed some latitude in such situations.

Papa silently curses the rules that limit him to a less-than-human right of expression and watches Fisher play the crew like a fish on a line.

Fisher says, "Can we have a summary of the probe and fly-by data, Sylvia?"

"The disk is in the final stages of a dwarf nova outburst. I collected plenty of data on the disk physics, but in terms of biological activity: *nada*. Neither dragons grazing at pasture as in the Prospector data, nor any evidence for disk rabbits, plankton, or the like. We've got a good hour of excellent, high-resolution data on the disk. That high resolution is probably the culprit in part, leading to a loss of signal in the noise. In any event, no dragons. I speculate that they hide during outbursts, perhaps in some form of reverse hibernation, like how some ancient cultures would take a noon-hour siesta to beat the midday heat."

Papa refrains from voicing the simpler interpretation of the data: There are not now any dragons in SS Cygni's disk. He knows from their journals, idle conversation, and mumbles during their dreams that each has this concern. Biolathe might have sent them on a goose chase for its own purposes, perhaps to mislead a competitor. It is possible. Or, more unthinkable, and worse, the dragons have died out, or migrated somehow, in the centuries since the Prospector video was taken.

"Hide?" Fang asks. "But wouldn't they be *more* visible during an outburst if they have to radiate extra heat?"

"That's not clear," answers Devereaux. "I was never able to nail down a reliable number on the dragons based on their laser emission. It's too variable, for whatever reason, and too weak against the disk output. Depending on the model, the data are consistent with zero dragons, or millions of dragons. Sorry."

"Zero dragons?" Fang asks. "You've been measuring something, haven't you?"

"Yes, but there are some natural transitions that could be selectively pumped under certain conditions and a lot of model parameters to consider. It's a weak, variable signal that requires assumptions to stack up."

"So we're here, and still have many unknowns. That argues for caution," says Fisher.

"Yes," agrees Fang for once, "which is why I still maintain that missile 'beaters,' if you will, are the safest course."

Papa laughs to himself. She's going to be contrary with Fisher despite his games. This is his daughter!

Fisher slaps his palms smack against the tabletree. "What?"

"It is only logical, not knowing the dragon population or location to any accuracy, to drive them toward us. We don't have years to search this monstrous sea."

Devereaux speaks when it is clear that Fisher is having difficulty in formulating words. "But this could kill the dragons."

Fang says, "Oh please. We blow up the missiles in the central disk, where I seriously doubt these dragons could survive, and let the shocks push them out to where we wait."

Fisher regains his composure. "How do you know the dragons won't act like moths? See the tasty gamma rays and happily head straight for the inferno?"

"I don't, but they're not especially intelligent or interesting if they do that, are they? Besides, wouldn't they have all swarmed to primary and been spattered into degeneracy if that were how they behaved?"

"I'll grant you that one." Fisher exhales mightily. "You're

going to do this, aren't you? Your heart is set and you're going to do it."

"It's a standard ploy in a hunt for any reasonable quarry in such a large area."

Fisher slaps his hands on the tabletree again. "But we know next to *nothing* about this quarry! Who is to say these things will be reasonable?"

"That's your problem, isn't it?" Fang counters. "You've shown me nothing based on your dragon models to suggest they would behave in any outrageous manner."

"We've only got four and a half minutes of dragon behavior!"

"Papa," Fang says, "I'm authorized by the Biolathe corporate brain to make all final strategic decisions, am I not?"

"You are, daughter." Papa does not elaborate about the numerous ways, large and small, he can modify implementation of those decisions.

Fisher shouts, "But you can overrule her, right, Papa?"

The guy has to be a boor, Papa thinks. "Only in a clear-cut case. This is no such animal."

Fisher tries again with Fang. "Don't you respect this creature enough to walk into its very own territory and meet it face to face? That's what makes a good trophy, right? Not shooting fish in a barrel."

"I have made my decision," says Fang. "It's the right one."

Fisher stands abruptly. "Fine," he roars. "Then prepare to reap the whirlwind."

He storms out. Everyone else sits stunned for a few moments. Then Fang assumes control of the remainder of the meeting, asking Devereaux for an update on the mass and temperature of the nondegenerate shell of SS Cygni's primary.

"Higher than expected, but . . ." Devereaux begins.

Papa's point of view leaves the meeting chamber, deciding that his consciousness ought to follow the disgruntled exobiologist, lest he do something annoying.

Fisher does nothing annoying. He returns to his infernal cabin and proceeds to open some boring simulations. Returning to work, Papa thinks, this is good for him. He allows himself to pop back to watch the end of the meeting.

Fisher started his decoy code and left his cabin disguised, to Papa, as a scavenging fish.

Walking in a slow, circuitous manner, *spiraling like a dragon around a magnetic field line*, so as to not appear too inconsistent with his disguise, he made his way toward the missile hold. Electronically isolated until launch as per safety regulations, *like a dragon in a star system 250 light-years from Earth*, the missiles had to be reprogrammed on the spot. Once launched into the disk, *home of glorious life happily dancing in tune with its own flames*, Papa would monitor the communication laser channels carefully and it would be a much harder trick than what he was pulling off now.

How could Fang do this thing? She was a cold-blooded killer, a degenerate soldier with a tiny little head *as dense as the white dwarf that was SS Cygni's primary*. He should have known right away, her hair so smooth, straight, shiny, and short, a helmet... when a friend of the dragon would have long, wild tresses twisting in all directions, *serpentine and rolling, plasma charged, shocking static*.

No matter. When the missiles sank into the disk and vanished, completely unrecoverable, Fang would have no choice but to approach the dragons carefully, with the respect they deserved. Nuclear missiles would safely burn in the disk, making his sabotage more easily hidden. It would still be a dangerous game for him, but if the dragons won he would pay any cost.

Fisher arrested his steps. Too eager, too anomalous, and even the unconscious part of Papa would notice this strange fish out of water. Sweep left, eat the dust, sweep right, *spiral around the field line*. There would be no flash of death, no incinerating wall, for his dragons.

Maddeningly slow progress. The meeting could break up at any time and someone could walk by and simply acknowledge him, which would be enough to alert Papa. Who greets a fish crawling along the floor?

There would be other clues the longer he took, clues he could do nothing about. The *Karamojo* was a complex ship, but self-contained and perfectly understood within Papa's specially designed mind, which viewed the ship as its own body. Just as the nanomeds in his own veins monitored his body's state, so did Papa monitor the ship. He referred to this monitoring as a "built-in, shock-proof, shit detector." Fisher's decoy code could mask his presence in terms of sight, sound, smell, but without the same perfect understanding of the integrated ship, his waste heat would boost temperatures, his footsteps would ignite vibrations throughout the diamond structure of the ship, which was constantly monitored, and the biomass flux per ship section would fail to balance. His code was good, but not perfect.

He made the tube between rings and followed it, ever so slowly, past all the fore rings, toward the tapered rear of the ship. The missiles were kept there, in one of the holds, away from the inhabited portions of the ship.

Because of the taper down to the smaller rear bulb, the effective gravity increased as he climbed the slope. Because they had cut the wormdrive and their deceleration to arrive early, they rotated the ship around its central axis so that centrifugal forces now defined "down." Although portions of the ship could twist to accommodate the shift in the gravity vector, the ship rotated as a solid body. The rotation rate was set to provide one Earth gravity for the radius of the fore bulb, but accelerative force was inversely proportional to the radius. The taper made things spin fast, made them heavier.

He climbed up the white hill, his body spiraling as he went. One point one gravities, one point two, one point three gravities. A steep climb indeed. How would the extra weight slow a fish?

When he had nearly reached two gravities and the end of the tube where it gave way to the access to the dangerous-materials hold ring, he heard steps behind him from the tapering tube he had laboriously climbed.

Fisher let his spiraling steps twist, *a serpentine neck would be better*, to allow himself to see who it might be. A shape, distant, just a diffracted head bobbing upside down. Under magnification, the head was dark-skinned, either Stearn or Devereaux. The cadence suggested Stearn, as did the hard echoes of boots. Devereaux usually went barefoot, or in soft-soled sandals.

The tube was nearly three kilometers long, and slightly curved, so he had a chance. He was making little noise, and would not be easily noticeable unless Stearn scanned for him in the next minute, which was what it would take to make the ring.

Fisher didn't break his shuffle. He moved, slowly, listening to the steps that were at two or three times the frequency of his own. Discipline Fisher had, and focus, oh yes, focus. He watched the dragon's languid coils in his mind's eye, the creature in slow motion due to the physics of its own immense size, so too Fisher in slow motion via a sympathetic magic.

Hide in the photosphere, Fisher thought as he reached the corner, spiraled around it, now out of sight even if Stearn magnified his vision.

The steps continued, holding their pace. No evidence he'd been spotted. Fisher visited the rear holds sometimes, just as he visited all the ship. He did good work during walks, or his "oblivious promenades," as Atsuko had called them because of the way he'd walk into things. He could fake his way past Stearn, but Papa would notice the discrepancy of Stearn talking to a fish and unravel his plan at once. This plan Papa wouldn't be forced by privacy rules to keep from Fang.

Fisher continued his snaking, faux-dust-eating path, moving around the ring toward the missile hold.

The steps grew louder.

They needed him, didn't they? They'd see from his desperation, if he were caught, that they had made a serious mistake. The strength of his convictions would yet sway Fang, he was sure. Better, of course, to present the loss of the missiles as a fait accompli, with no recourse but a respectful approach to the dragon's disk. Yes, that would still be best, and that outcome was still possible.

Almost there! If the steps went the other way around the ring, he'd make it. What was the Jack doing back here anyway? Routine checks for Papa? Or could he be headed specifically for the missile hold under special orders? Would Fang think him capable of such sabotage? He didn't believe so, especially with Papa watching.

The door to the hold was before him, and would open for a cleaning fish working on a dirty footprint crossing the threshold. Three meters. Two. Fisher peered at the ivory iris as if it were a deuterium-rich path of accretion disk, food for a fusion-powered dragon.

The steps were coming his way around the ring.

Damn!

It was over. Stearn or Papa would figure out his subterfuge, alert Fang, who would make sure her precious missiles were shipshape to murder dragons by the millions. Still, no reason to tip over his king before checkmate was truly inevitable. He held to course.

The steps were right behind him, ringing off the deck. He was surely in sight now.

"Hey, Fish," Stearn said as he walked past without breaking stride. The Jack soon vanished ahead around the curve of the ring.

Fisher said nothing, but glowed an extra-rich pea green, the color of a flush in his current body. It was easy to ignore Stearn as a matter of course. It was his normal behavior, and Stearn hadn't paused for any acknowledgment. Could it be possible for Papa to misinterpret "Fish"? Stearn was a screwball, and given to such things as talking to cleaning appliances, Fisher was sure . . . it was still possible to salvage the plan, wasn't it?

The dragon entered the hold to face its own death, and avert it.

The chamber was vast, holding rows of stacked missiles: sleek, black bullets in racks feeding slotted runways to channel the weapons into launch tubes. Inside the blackness slept fissionables and hydrogen isotopes, cool and currently impotent, destined to splash into the lake of fire that was SS Cygni's accretion disk. *And burn up in their sleep,* Fisher promised his brethren.

Fisher called to mind his mnemonic, fixed in place chemically with Forget-Me-Not rather than in his biochip where it could incriminate him, and began to manually reprogram the first missile. His hand danced like a programmed woodpecker over the control panel, punching home the new instructions. This missile would not murder a star dragon.

And when his task was completed neither would any of the other ninety-nine.

Henderson sank deeply down into the velvety chairbeast, relishing the sensation against his bare skin, sipped from his glass of Merlot, and listened to Mozart's *The Magic Flute.* Opposite his chairbeast and along the far side of his biolab squatted his homunculi colony. Inside the diamond enclosure existed an entire self-contained colony of tiny people, a replica of the twenty-third-century Charon Station.

They lacked complex speech and higher reasoning, of course—their brains weren't nearly large enough—but they were nevertheless perfectly proportioned human beings a mere twenty centimeters tall. There were ninety-nine very attractive women and one male, Henderson's genetic kin. All the women were pregnant with his homunculi.

Henderson activated his picture tank, which was slaved to surveillance devices inside the colony. He sipped his wine, eased his seat back farther, and watched tiny Henderson cast his shadow into the darkened bedroom of a large-breasted blonde the equivalent of eight months' pregnant . . .

Squinting, he beckoned his deep thoughts hither and meditated upon the purposes of life.

"Mr. Henderson," Papa's voice interrupted.

"What *is* it?"

"Mr. Stearn does not talk to fish. Prepare a tranquilizer dart for our exobiologist and hustle up to the missile hold."

"A tranquilizer? For Fisher?" What was going on?

"Do it *now*. This is an order from Fang."

Henderson sighed, downed his wine, and stood up. "Right."

More work, and more than a minor inconvenience having to adjust for Fisher's current biology. The possibility of a major inconvenience loomed depending on how this played out.

He would be very upset if this mission went wrong and threatened his long-term plans.

He met up with Fang in the tube toward the aft holds. She nodded impatiently as she took the dart gun from Henderson and together they hiked up the tube.

"What's happening?" Henderson asked.

"Fisher," she said. "Stearn talked to a fish, and then Papa noticed it diligently cleaning the dust from all the missiles, in order. Then he noticed a virus in his autonomous perceptive circuits."

"Enough said."

The Jack waited for them at the ring entrance. "Missile hold," he said.

"Of course," said Fang.

She was so fast through the hold door, she had to step over the irising membranes to avoid tripping. "Fisher," she called. "Your game is up."

Six rows down a black bullet reflected green darkly. From that direction issued a strangled cry filled with bile and a touch of rolling thunder, a sound like nothing Henderson had ever before heard. The closest to that cry had been when he'd troubleshooted a problem with a biovat on a fast cruiser to Phaelendra. They had been growing a clever design for a creature, a sort of giant armored frog, intended to ameliorate the problem of the spiny viseroths preying on livestock. Only the growth kept going wrong, a corrupted gene sequence, resulting in something severely asymmetric that would die from heart failure when it croaked forth its deformed pain.

Finally the sputtering, rolling cry faded into a low moan, then silence.

Henderson swallowed, and glanced at Stearn, who stared ahead with wide eyes, stark white flashing against his ebon skin.

"Come out now, or I'll have to take you down. I am armed," Fang called, a vein throbbing near her blond temple. It was an ugly feature in an otherwise handsome face, and if she'd come in for half an hour, Henderson was sure he could fix it.

Fang lightly licked her lips while they waited another ten seconds.

Shuffling steps, the green glow intensified, and Fisher staggered around the end of a black bullet. His upper lip was lifted into an ugly sneer, as if pulled by an invisible marionette string, and his salmon-colored eyes, normally recessed and glassy, floated like burning coals in the nimbus of green. He thrust forward his arms, hands up, twisted into claws. He leaned toward them and took a strange semicircular step.

"You'll calm down *now*, Dr. Fisher," Fang said. "If you're to have any more involvement on this mission, you will cooperate immediately."

Tears streamed down Fisher's cheeks, making the light underneath sparkle. "You're all murderers!" he shouted, pointing at them now with both hands.

Fang lifted the tranquilizer gun. "Will you cooperate, Dr. Fisher?"

"Of course I will! What choice do I have?"

Fang maintained her implacable gaze upon Fisher and said in a quiet tone, "Mr. Stearn, please begin checking the missiles and restore their programming."

"Aye aye, Captain."

"We can handle things from here, Mr. Henderson. Thank you for your assistance."

"You're welcome." Henderson smiled. His share of a mission bonus would be all the larger now—surely Fisher would get docked. Perhaps he could afford his own full-sized colony when they returned. Probably not in the solar system, but someplace not so many light-years from Earth. "Now if you'll excuse me, I have some important experiments back in the lab to monitor."

EIGHT

"There she blows! there! there! she blows!"
—TASHTEGO IN HERMAN MELVILLE'S
MOBY-DICK

The view, splashed in floor-ceiling-wall wraparound throughout the fly bridge, was not disappointing, and Fang could not keep herself from gasping audibly.

Planets all had a sameness to their appearance that was grand, but familiar. From rocky planetoids to atmospheric cauldrons, planetary globes were still spherical. You looked out, or down rather, at a surface receding away. The mind chose a natural scale and perceived the same sort of thing, no matter what the true scale; instruments were generally required to know what you were looking at.

SS Cygni's accretion disk was different. It flared out toward larger radii, making a shallow bowl with the opposite curvature to that of planets. The *Karamojo* now slid into that bowl, ass-end first, the down-sized singularities of the reactivated wormdrive currently matching the vertical component of the white dwarf's pull, some two times Earth gravity at their position nearly ten thousand kilometers above the disk midplane. That was still several thousand kilometers above the disk's ill-defined surface. The disk's own gravity was feeble compared to that of the few percent of the tangential primary gravity they experienced maintaining their orbit's altitude above the disk. They would use reaction mass to adjust worm thrust against that pull, riding the high gravity, and maintain a powered halo orbit with a period eighty minutes long above the surface of the disk; they could not survive a freefall orbit, which would have to pass through the disk's midplane and the hot, dense plasma there. Two gravities would not be so bad for a few weeks, especially as they'd been adapting their bodies, building muscle, to be ready. Fang herself had noticed that her new stockiness slowed her in the ring, but the extra bulk let her hit harder.

When it came time to cage a dragon, they would collapse the singularities and magnetically spin around the disk's own field to point the *Karamojo*'s maw and trap toward the targeted beast using its own electromagnetic fields.

The bowl was bright white, cut down by the display automatics well enough to discern some hues, from the violet tinge at the center of the bowl where the plasma accreted directly onto the primary surface, to the red of the disk's outer edge, which was a close temperature match to the secondary type-K dwarf star. The exception to this was the inferno where the accretion stream spilled out of the secondary's gravitational influence and twisted back around to crash into the disk orbiting the white dwarf. That maelstrom, long ago inadequately coined the "hot spot," shared the core's violet tinge. Prominences curled up waving like dancing fingers, tracing magnetic field lines, and looped back down into the stately chaos.

"This," Fang proclaimed, "this is a sea worth sailing."

The *Karamojo* finished matching velocities with the outer edge of the disk—a mere six hundred kilometers per second. Gas closer to the white dwarf rotated much faster, giving the illusion of a giant fire whirlpool, which was not far from wrong; the white dwarf's surface was the "drain," where hydrogen would pile up atop the degenerate matter, waiting until the pressure crept up, and the temperature crept up. Eventually runaway fusion would result in a nova, perhaps a hundred thousand years hence, flash burning the gas into helium and blowing the disk away into interstellar space.

The ship had to maintain some distance from the disk's photosphere—the self-repairing high-albedo nanoskin could only process energy so quickly, even though it used multiple technologies to shed heat. Too close and the skin would begin to ablate away with a rapidly deteriorating efficiency. A ship as vast as the *Karamojo* held large mass reserves, but the disk's fire could char those in an instant without careful attention.

"Where are the missiles?" Fisher asked Fang.

Fang blinked, tearing her gaze and thoughts away from the magnificent vista, brought back to her surroundings by the mutineer, Fisher. Had she really loved him? Being honest with herself, she admitted that she thought she had. And now? She looked at him, at his green face and into his pink eyes—he wasn't looking at this incredible place they had traveled so far to reach, but at her, his enemy whom he would not even thank for not throwing him into the brig. This Fisher was a hateful alien, not the man she'd taught to box, the man she'd let inside her sanctum, inside *her*. Now that he'd been caught, with no other option but to go along with the current plan of attack, he was on their side, right?

Still, she would not permit Papa to respond to Fisher except in the most rudimentary ways.

She could not help but think of him as a dragon in their midst, a snake in the grass. *Here be dragons,* she thought, like on the ancient maps. "Papa," Fang said, "please display missile vectors."

Fifty black lines appeared on the disk upstream from the *Karamojo*. Half their arsenal, a conservative effort. The vectors described a funnel, with each terminating at different points with a time given in red numbers, the pattern designed to drive the star dragons from deeper, hotter locations in the disk toward the rim where the ship waited. The operation would take nearly an hour, with bombs going off at different times and places. Their detonations were intended to catch as big a piece of disk as they could, but with a surface area nearly a thousand times that of Earth, that was little more than a tiny fraction of a percent of the total. They would do what they could and hope for the best.

Fisher swept his gaze along the vectors. To Devereaux he said, "Have you seen *anything?*"

Of course she hadn't; she would have said something. Fisher appeared a serene alien full of privileged knowledge, but the question betrayed his anxiety. After being his lover, Fang thought she should be able to read him better—this moment of lucidity was the exception in recent weeks. Her ability to read him might be essential in the coming days.

Devereaux leaned back from her console. "No signal, at least not at the laser wavelengths we saw before. We are on the tail end of an outburst, which is not a typical time. I'm looking for other lines, but either every dragon is on a different frequency, they're down deep in the disk, or they're not here."

"Anything else anomalous?" Fisher persisted. "Any sign of anything else that might be alive?"

"Nothing," said Devereaux. "But we'll have a better idea when the latest shuttle returns a scoop sample."

Fisher turned to Fang. "You will let us analyze the sample before you start bombing the enemy, won't you, Captain?"

"For you, Dr. Fisher, of course." She didn't like the sarcasm that the remark implied. It was unprofessional, but it had slipped out. Tough. Perhaps she, too, was nervous.

He didn't look any happier after her reassurance.

"This place rules," Stearn said. "I feel like a god."

Fang only half agreed. This was magnificent, being here, but the disk was so unimaginably huge, it was more than a little intimidating. This was infinitely vaster than any planet. The *Karamojo* might be better christened the *Tiny Debris*, a piece of cork being sucked into Charbydis. That would make the accretion stream and its hot spot the Scylla—they would have to watch that each eighty minutes—the orbital period at their radius near the disk's periphery. But this was her chance, finally, to be a real captain and operate in a unique environment with unique objectives.

Henderson cleared his throat. He was frowning as he said, "There's something we never discussed out loud during our planning sessions."

"What's that?" Fisher asked, an edge in his voice.

"What if, as Sylvia hypothesized, *there are no longer any dragons here?*"

No one answered. The disk blazed away, full of light and mystery.

Devereaux tapped a query into the cage interface, starting the automatic analyses.

"What does it say?" Fisher asked practically right in Devereaux's ear.

She jumped, a small amount. "Really, Dr. Fisher, you should have stayed on the bridge. Papa will relay everything there as fast as I know it."

"I want to see for myself. That's why I'm here, after all."

So they waited together in the observatory lock area, where there was easy access to the *Karamojo*'s hollow interior, where Stearn and Fisher had built the magnetic cage to house the dragon. Currently it served as the repository for the plasma sample the ramscoop shuttle had returned.

"I thought you were going to help me," Fisher said.

"I am helping."

"I mean with Fang, stopping this foolish plan of hers. I'm the scientific head of this mission. I should have final say, not that militaristic bitch."

Devereaux had been intently watching the spectral analyzer, but she turned to Fisher and said, "You lied to me."

He looked back at her blankly for a moment. "Oh, the space wisps. It was expedient. You must understand."

"You lied to me. Papa has it all in your public *vita*. You stopped the destruction of the space wisps, studied them for three years, and concluded they represented interesting chemistry but were not technically alive."

"You were bothering me, and I thought I'd get rid of you and gain an ally at the same time. You told me at one point that you hadn't downloaded an exobiology database, after all. It was, as I said, expedient."

Devereaux laughed without real mirth, then cut it off abruptly, suddenly very serious. "I thought we had connected. I thought we—look, you better start treating us like your friends, or at least colleagues. Like people, anyhow, or we'll find a way to leave you out here with your precious dragons."

She didn't really like the way her words sounded like a threat, but she chose not to ameliorate them with additional qualifications.

"Fine," he answered, "I'll treat you like people."

"Thank you. That's a start." She kept her tone flat, fighting back the sarcasm that wanted to seep in.

The machine beeped. Devereaux studied the results. "Nothing but hydrogen, helium, and metals. Abundances within predicted uncertainties. Nothing unexpected." *Not like life at all,* she thought, *which always showed something unexpected.*

"You're sure?"

Devereaux shrugged and pointed at the numbers. "That's as clear as it gets."

"Damn. Where's everything hiding?"

"Thought you'd see something? Little bits of dragon food floating around?" she kidded.

"Not really, but I'd hoped for something to convince Fang to change her mind. This worries me, no food chain or transitional forms. Maybe the dragon in the film was a mechanical probe? Or maybe this is a stocked pond. We could be poaching here, but without some positive evidence of something . . . You don't suppose we could . . . No, I guess not."

At least he was still human enough to read her scowl.

"That bitch is going to murder a lot of dragons," he said.

Devereaux pressed her lips together and didn't say anything, but she silently appended, *if they are really still here. If they were ever here.*

Fang's stomach churned as the first missile plowed into the disk. It would be a minute before the missile exploded at the midplane and its effects would become evident at the surface.

"I maintain that you've overestimated how fast a star dragon can move," Fisher said, continuing with his litany of objections that had been streaming forth since he'd returned to the bridge sans evidence for life in the disk. No star plankton or star rabbits to worry about, which suited Fang fine.

"My estimates are based on your models, Dr. Fisher. Are they wrong?" she challenged.

"Of course they are! That snippet of data from the probe told us almost nothing. If my models were perfect, we'd be able to build a dragon ourselves and skip this trip."

Fang shrugged.

"The disk environment must be as varied to its inhabitants as those of terrestrial life-forms. Parts of Earth's oceans are oxygen-poor and lifeless. We could be fishing in the equivalent of a desert. We did that with the first Jupiter probe."

When Fang refused to engage him, Fisher tacked. "Look, I thought we agreed that the lack of a supporting ecosystem would be evidence for intelligent creation. Someone goes to all the trouble of making these star dragons, then we come along and start blowing them up. That someone is going to be mad, don't you think?"

"Then let them show up and tell us. That'd be a mission to be on, but I doubt that's going to happen." She really didn't worry about an abstract bogeyman too much. Give her something tangible to tilt with. An empty disk was no cause for alarm. "What's done is done, Dr. Fisher. The missiles are exploding as we speak. I suggest you sit back and enjoy the show."

Fisher blazed green and thankfully said nothing.

"There," Stearn said, almost launching himself as he stood to point at the black vectors. "There she blows!"

"Magnify," said Fisher, whipping around.

"Magnify," repeated Fang, so that Papa would do as requested.

There was the sensation of movement at great velocity as the entire bowl of fire warped through the bridge, making the barely perceptible shadows shift and grow like hidden secrets worried about too much—except for Fisher, whose glow helped wipe out shadows, making his secrets somehow seem even more hidden.

Before them the disk blossomed into a spreading ring containing alabaster flame at millions of degrees Kelvin. The shockwave plowed through the surrounding cooler plasma, heating, engulfing, roaring. The disk burned into purity, erasing all the details of its former motion. The central region of the explosion erupted like a spouting volcano, lifting many kilometers of gas above the bowled surface. The differential orbital accelerations were already shredding the perfect circle of destruction into a twisted, splayed half-spiral, just as their three-dimensional magnetohydrodynamic simulation had predicted.

"Now that," Fang said, "is a beater."

"Are we really safe from that?" Henderson asked, hands clasped tightly in his lap.

Papa answered, "Yes, mostly by keeping our distance. Our incident flux is well within tolerances."

"It's beautiful," Devereaux said, her voice barely audible. "If anyone is watching closely, it's going to give them some strange spectra to decipher."

"It's the most disgusting thing I ever saw," Fisher said.

Everyone ignored Fisher and watched the developing explosion.

With any luck, the dragons had registered the photon and particle burst with their specialized senses—whatever they were—and would be fleeing the shockwave. Over the next hour, the other missiles would explode, channeling the dragons right to the *Karamojo*. With any luck.

Fang licked her lips.

A few minutes later Stearn jumped again, pointing. "Number two!"

And they all watched again, dumbfounded, at the destructive power of mankind's technology. In the face of the natural splendor of SS Cygni and its accretion disk these explosions were only magnified in their brilliance. This was an awesome experience to preside over.

The oddest thing was watching all this raw energy with the counterpoint of excruciating silence. Maybe they should have some music, something ancient and elemental. Maybe Pradhan's *Cosmic Continuum,* or Stravinsky's *Firebird,* something. Maybe she should let Henderson select something—he knew classical music. But that thought faded quickly as she became lost again in the view, the silence somehow majestically fitting after all. No music could match this, no sound, that incidental effect of air molecules crashing together. What was that compared to the raw energy dancing in this amphitheater of fire?

"You're killing them," muttered Fisher, voice cracking, breaking that silence.

Fang shouted, "If this is so painful, why don't you just leave the bridge?"

"I want to be here to count the bodies."

"Sylvia," Fang asked in a conversational tone, "do you see any bodies yet?"

"Uh, right. I'll check." Devereaux bent to her console and started whispering instructions to Papa.

"Number three!"

Stearn kept an enthusiastic count through the first dozen, but Fang amazed herself by becoming bored. Maybe she could fit into jaded Earth culture better than she thought. It was a spectacle, but not interactive. The missiles reached their objectives and exploded. There wasn't anything to do but watch. She needed to find the thread of nervous tension she'd held in her stomach at the start of this endeavor. The dragons would come, just as the lion had. When you look nature in the eye and pull the trigger, you are alive. They were now pulling the trigger. That was what she was in this for, being alive and vital, being involved in the universe. These explosions were preliminary to the real action likely to come soon.

"I *might* have something," Devereaux announced, looking up for the first time in the past half hour.

Fisher beat Fang to Devereaux's console. "What is it?" he asked.

"Understand," Devereaux began, "the background is quite high and the laws of physics are the same here as they are on Earth. Noise goes as the square root of the counts, so until they're well resolved real signals are easily swamped in the background of an environment like this."

"What *is* it?" Fang asked, disliking repeating Fisher again, but she was starting to get the scent of her quarry and didn't care to hear all of Devereaux's qualifiers. This was one lion that she wanted to be sure to see before it was on top of her.

"Here," said Devereaux, pointing to a spike in a spectrum she had displayed. It was a little higher than some other spikes, but didn't appear special in any way. "I've been running a filter looking for blueshifting emission lines correlated with missile explosions. Taking the distribution of data over several explosions, and running another cross-correlation in the frequency domain, then shifting and stacking, I was able to pick out this. Run it in the time domain, Papa."

A graph popped up, intensity versus velocity, showing one sharp line against a jagged continuous signal. As they watched, the line intensified and moved toward negative velocities—blueshifts—toward the *Karamojo*. At *kilometers* per second.

"That's it for sure," said Fisher, beaming green light onto the rim of the console's picture tank.

"You're always sure, aren't you, Fisher?" Fang said.

"I'm only ever as sure as you are, Captain."

Ignoring them both, Devereaux went on. "I ought to be able to estimate the dragon density from this, if that's them. Add some finer spatial filtering. The velocities seem really high, though. I still have a lot of guesswork to give you a number. It'll take me a little time. We might just be better off with empirical calibration when the final array of explosions drives them out of the disk."

Enough qualifications! This was a hunt, not a science project. "As long as we get just one," Fang said, "this mission will be a success."

"The operation was a success, but the patient died," quipped Fisher.

"How's that?" Fang asked, knowing better, but settling into a bit of their old repartee.

"Old medical saying, pre-nanotech. It means you're too focused on succeeding with your little task to worry about the big picture."

"Oh will you please just shut up for once?" She managed to keep her voice even and face impassive. She was not sure how.

"Fine," he answered, that tone of smug righteousness grating in her ear.

Fang said, "Find out what you can, Sylvia," and stalked back to her fighting chair to watch the bomb bursts continue. She had to get in the right mind frame . . . *the lion is out there, hiding in the grass.*

She rubbed her damp palms against the hide of her chairbeast, *puta-pop-pop-pop*, as her skin stuck and slid and stuck and slid on the leathery surface. She bent her head slightly down and inhaled deeply, catching her own not unpleasant scent. She smiled, slightly, and began a series of isometric exercises. She would be ready when the time came.

She was about to discover what it truly meant to be Captain.

She could hardly wait.

When the series of programmed explosions was nearly finished and the dragons had to arrive soon, very soon, Fang asked, "Any progress, Sylvia?"

Without looking up, Fisher managed to cut off Devereaux and answered, "It's really a snake in the grass. The signals vary in a most interesting manner, which I think might be camouflage against the disk. Why they should be hiding, I don't know, but it certainly seems that way. I speculate that there's an electrically transparent shell tuned to their—"

"There she blows!" shouted Stearn, thankfully ending the lecture early. "I mean it this time!"

Fang followed Stearn's pointing, but saw nothing right away that made sense. The explosion was spectacular, more so than the others as it was closer, but there was something different, a strange swirling rainbow riding the edge of the shockwave. "Papa?"

"Working on it, daughter," came the reassuring older voice.

"Is this it?" Fang asked.

"Yes!" Fisher's turn to shout.

Papa said, "Individual entities now visible, approaching at high velocity. Three thousand kilometers and closing."

"Match velocities and spin this ship into capture position!" Fang shrieked, suddenly standing.

"Collapsing singularities, boosting."

"Captain! Look at it, Captain!" Stearn, shouting.

"Oh my goodness," said Sylvia.

"That *can't* be right," Henderson said.

"Yes!" shouted Fisher again, pumping his fists as the gravity first faded, then dumped him unceremoniously on his butt as the raildrive came on-line.

Fang's own butt suddenly smashed into her groaning chair-beast as she gawked at something she hadn't imagined. So many, so fast . . .

"Visual tracking on herd forerunners," announced Papa. "More than *ten thousand* head."

No stately lion pride, but a great fucking snake nest. All over the walls, the ceiling, the floor, flying toward the *Karamojo*. She couldn't focus on any one of them at first. It was all a twisted prismatic mess of wheels and coils and fire and lightning. She thought of the bucket of worms her grandfather had kept on the junk, that bucket her cousin had once turned over her head, now blazing over her and no one to punch out this time but herself.

Fisher staggered up, arms outstretched, laughing. "My dragons!"

Fang blinked, shaking away the feeling of sinking into the swarm—a better term than herd—and pushed away her concerns and attempted to study the lead dragons. Coils of different colors, but always blazing white at their core, hypnotizing. She blinked again to break the spell. That pulsing scarlet one, there, she concentrated . . . a spiral coil flashing with arcs of lightning, brilliant even against the fire it wrapped around, corkscrewing toward them. Some kind of thrust? Current in the coils, fusion in the core?

"They're rockets!" Fisher shouted.

"How big? How soon?" Fang asked.

Scales popped up, and a clock with digits running down from sixty-two. "I measure lengths ranging from five hundred meters to ten kilometers, relative velocities coming down to under ten thousand kilometers per hour. Calculating electromagnetic fields."

"Get us in position! Charge the cage!" Fang ordered.

Papa maintained the dragons' sizes on the displays, but let the details sharpen as the distance closed and their imaging resolution improved. Filters began to enhance contrast. Textures materialized in the solid monochromatic colors, an intertwined fibrous texture infinitely structured. The bodies resembled less and less indistinct coiled tubes and more and more pieces of something alive with sections and varying shapes and distinct features.

They had heads.

Deep in her gut, that surprised Fang. She had known abstractly that the lump on one end of the star dragon in the *Prospector* video was probably a head, but the resolution had been too poor to show fine detail. Certainly they would have an intake for their fuel, food, whatever, and certainly they would have sensory organs to navigate through their environment.

Worse, they had eyes.

Great multifaceted multihued domes adorned the head, three each, 120 degrees separating them, twisting independently, but somehow each seemingly focused on *her*, with the emotionless reptilian feel of chameleon eyes. The rest of the creature faded from her awareness except for those flashing, rotating eyes around the core of fire. . . .

And she flashed back. . . .

Trailing salty white foam, the leviathan's stalked eyes broke the water. Lena was perched atop the creature's ocean-supported bulk. She had never thought their appearance threatening when she had seen them in a picture tank. Like the shark, the smaller Earth predator that the instructive module had compared the leviathan to, the predators shared doll eyes, round and dull and dead—eyes for an eating machine that did what it did without passion, but with efficiency. The leviathan's eyes to Lena held an ineffable quality, some sort of alien wisdom.

Her grandfather trod the water placidly with the sure movements of his morning Tai Chi, knowing what approached, knowing that he could not reach the junk quickly enough, and knowing if he tried the junk might well capsize and send her into the water with him. Into the water with those eyes and the creature they belonged to.

"Come into the water, Lena," the hungry mind behind the eyes seemed to say. "I will eat you . . . if not today, then someday. I am patient. I am inexorable."

For the first time in decades, in her mind's eye, she watched the way her grandfather took one last breath and instinctively brought his splayed hands out of the water to protect his head as the gaping maw surrounded his thin body, the way the water drained through the jaws' triple-slotted lips that rose a full three meters above the waterline, the way that water sounded dripping and splashing, and the sour smell of fear that came not from her grandfather but from her own young body.

A full three minutes after the water had smoothed to its customary shallow chop driven by that day's slight breeze, Lena sank to her knees to crawl the three meters across the hand-polished deck to the radio to call for help.

To her Earth-evolved perception, the dragon eyes more resembled inorganic machinery than anything living. This horde's visionary machinery catalogued the strange, cool, white apparition before them. No hate there, not like the lion's, no passion. This was an implacable enemy—an army of enemies—preparing to stampede over anything in their flight.

"You have come into the fire, Lena," the eternal mind behind the eyes told her. "Today we will swallow you. We are inexorable. We are here. Today."

Fang bit her bottom lip, hard, to keep a moan from escaping her. Her chest tightened, and her collar felt like hands around her throat. An analytic, detached part of her mind noted that those things we experience as children mark us forever; no matter how long we live, how much we learn, part of our hearts never grow up. She had thought of this event recently, had tried to bring it up with

Sam, because she had something to work out that the star dragon had resuscitated.

The analytic part of her mind didn't have complete control, but it drove a wedge into her locked mind and expanded her world to contain more than eyes.

Fisher stood before her, his lips moving. What was he saying? She could not understand, and shifted her gaze from his green lips to his pink eyes. Not lifeless, but blazing . . .

She would not tolerate inaction from herself.

The dragons were all about her, their eyes huge, their approach fixed and unwavering. What was the magnification? How long until they reached the *Karamojo?* Fang glanced at the figures and was dismayed. They were *close!* The fields were charged, the orientation was good. "That one, Papa!" she yelled, pointing at an approaching dragon with a promising trajectory. "Cage that one!"

The *Karamojo* lurched, maneuvering thrusts pushing them into position. The bubble housing the bridge moved to compensate for the rotations, but the normal forces were still mighty.

The dragon twisted, coils splitting to squirt nuclear fire.

"Match it!" screamed Fang.

A giant hand smashed against her. Her fighting chair ballooned to cushion the shifts. She struggled to keep her head where she could see the action. These high velocities were amazing, a dogfight with an alien. It could not go on more than a few seconds. "Take it in! Be ready for—"

"Field derivatives are too high," Papa interrupted. "Taking evasive action."

"Don't you dare!" Fang counter ordered. "Hold the line!"

"Sorry, daughter."

There was a flare as the dragon's rocket exploded across their maw, jerking the creature out of its path. The *Karamojo* rocked, creating a slalom run in Fang's stomach. Lights flickered, flashed. She heard the crackling of arcing somewhere on the bridge and smelled ozone.

The world shifted as the dragons blazed by the bridge and the deck rolled. The short hairs on the back of her neck tingled. She pitched forward, sliding from the arms of her chair into Fisher's couch.

She clawed her way up his slick jumpsuit. He smelled of something burned.

The dragons continued to flash by, some huge in their proximity.

The ship continued to rock.

What had gone wrong? Had Papa really taken control from her? "Papa?" Fang called, disgusted at the whine in her voice.

The lighting, mostly coming from the surrounding external displays, changed tints as the ship rocked again and again. Lightning sparkled and strobed all around.

All this with silence from the dragons.

Papa groaned, a deep resonant tone, which cut off after less than a second. A voice that superficially sounded like Papa, but was somehow lacking, said, "The *Karamojo* has experienced extensive system failures. Taking inventory and troubleshooting."

"Papa!" Fang shouted. Taken control from her? It was smoky, hard to breathe.

Someone—Henderson—clamped something around her biceps. It pinched her painfully.

She pushed to her knees against the hands on her arm and shoulders. One final dragon brushed past, a ghost vanishing into the sky.

The gravity increased with a teeth-rattling vibration, and abruptly ceased.

She tumbled up, out, away from the deck, tangled with Henderson. "What's happening Papa?"

The calm and somehow lifeless Papa voice said, "Drive systems damaged. Hull integrity compromised. Two rings breached, now sealed, six . . ."

The list went on, rapid-fire, for nearly thirty seconds.

How could this happen? She said to Henderson, "What did you do to me?"

He kept his eyes down on the autodoc on her arm. Blue veins stood out in his neck. "Minor anxiety attack. You overrode your own systems. I'm medicating now."

"Anxiety attack!" Fisher's angry voice, behind her, somewhere. His voice faded and she heard Devereaux whispering.

"Minor," said Henderson, "but requiring attention."

Fang closed her eyes, hoping Fisher would continue. She had failed. She deserved every word.

"Daughter?" Papa's true voice sliced into her consciousness. "Help me."

Yes, their ship, *her* ship, the *Karamojo,* Papa, needed her. She took a deep breath and opened her eyes. Whether it was the drugs or something else, it didn't matter. She was the captain again in her heart, and there was work to be done. There was no one else to do it and he'd have to get by one such as herself. "I'm here, Papa. We'll fix you."

"We'd better do it fast," Stearn said. "We're falling into the disk."

NINE

*Explore thyself. Herein are demanded
the eye and the nerve.*
—HENRY DAVID THOREAU

Everywhere there are walls: walls of riveted steel plates, walls of red bricks, walls of frosty white ice, walls of barbed wire. Tricks of his shattered mind, designed to ground Papa's point of focus with a solid challenge, meant to be more reassuring than the loss of an eye or paralysis of a hand might be to a corporeal human.

Papa races throughout himself, around a ring and into a wall of static, down a power conduit leading to the Higgs generators and into a mirrored wall, and, the scariest, into a data-processing bank and into another wall, this one of stone covered with thick ivy smelling of honeysuckle. Like a human mind he is patterned upon, he can accept the loss of a replaceable body part, but his processing banks . . . therein rest the connections to his identity.

Throughout the ship, his body, himself, he moans. The moans echo into parts of himself he cannot reach.

His human personality, faced with the despairing prospect of brain damage and perhaps senility and impairment, would finish the job and make certain to destroy his ego totally. A gun, a shotgun shell, a brain. As a constructed intelligence, such a thing is impossible, and he fears a subtle madness not prevented by his cerebral architecture that will result in a debilitating feedback loop.

He craves action. He craves repair . . . or oblivion. He craves wholeness of one kind or another.

His automatics are already at work; and there is little his personality can help with. Like reflexes, his automatics have their own independent error-checked data caches acting as ganglia to provide immediate and accurate information. Accessing these caches himself would be frustratingly slow. He must focus his self-awareness on its designated interface: the human crew.

He flies, and finds the Jack still on the bridge, floating in freefall. His brow knit in concentration, indicator lights reflecting from the sweaty skin of his cheeks and forehead, the end of his pink tongue slipping from his parted lips, as he reads the diagnostics panel on a piece of equipment that Papa *cannot recognize*. "You're a good boy," Papa tells the Jack.

The Jack's eyes flick up. "Papa? How you doing, old man?"

"We're as strong as an ox," Papa boasts, something he has said many times to indicate a robust state, but his programming forces him to qualify his statement. "The parts we can feel. We're sure you'll have everything fixed up in no time, won't you?"

The Jack grins, teeth flashing like diamonds in the coal of his face. "We had better." His eyes flick back to the panel as he taps a keypad on a handheld troubleshooting unit spliced into the ailing equipment.

They should have been sufficiently shielded from induced currents, but no Faraday cage is perfect. Could it really have been that large a flux? A random impact with a dragon's field should not have resulted in this—but they had not forseen rocketing and that must surely have a different field arrangement. "What are you doing?" Papa asks.

He realizes his mistake as the Jack's grin twists into a frown. It's bad then, what's got him. Perhaps revealing the fullness of his ignorance would aid the young man in his repairs, but his personality isn't bound to such an embarrassment. Perhaps the level of his ignorance would frighten the Jack, make him make a mistake. Let him question the automatics, if he would.

Papa flees.

The mind, the mind, he thinks. *Cogito ergo sum.* My personality, me, is whole. Isn't it? We are separated from my body and senses. The Jack works on the body and the links to the body. The biotech, Henderson, he will be working on the organic minds that process sensory input, that contain memory and kinesthetic knowledge.

Papa's perspective rattles around the ring, bouncing off a wall and taking a circuitous route to the biolab, which abuts the brain banks.

"Mr. Henderson," Papa shouts. "How are we doing?"

Henderson has half his body behind a panel floating on a chain in the microgravity, but the muscle pattern of a full body startle reflex is evident. The lights in the biolab are low, a terrarium empty, and everything silent save for the whooshing of Papa's breath through the still-operational atmospheric scrubbers. Nevertheless, the biotech says something that Papa cannot make out.

Papa replays the sounds through a set of filters and identifying algorithms. The biotech had said, "Piles of poop, hold it together, Axel. It's just the local ghost."

"We heard that," Papa says, dismayed at how much it comes out sounding like a child's triumphant discovery. A regression to the scatological is unexpected from Henderson's polished public side, so perhaps things are very bad. Maybe he should—

"Fine," Henderson says. "You can crawl in here with me and give me some help."

Papa would very much prefer a stiff drink, a double, with effects he could simulate, but he shifts his focus forward. For a moment he is gripped by the powerful sensation that he is falling, that he is a ghost, and will fall through the ship itself into the hell that crackles beyond. A human thought—he believes. A good sign. Then his perspective is beside Henderson, seeing what Henderson is seeing, and little more. The high-energy bands are inaccessible—something has burned those eyes out—while the mid-infrared bands show little but Henderson's reflected heat. At visible wavelengths, he sees something that he cannot comprehend, and for a moment is caught in déjà vu to when he could not assist the Jack mere moments earlier. But it isn't that he lacks the information to identify what he sees. It is that his personality maintains the ability to *deny* what he sees.

The black carbon residue of burned organics tells him that induced currents have cooked this part of his brain.

"What do you make of this?" asks Henderson. "Have the stem cells germinated properly? Are they getting their full dose of accelerant?"

"We—" Papa begins, unable to go on. There *is* pink growth along the nerve channels connecting the parallel bins, and the stem cells are dividing according to spec, fed with a rich nutrient bath provided by the adjacent lab's biomass reserve. Still—he does *not* need to watch anyone poking around in his necrotic flesh. He flees, leaving the expert systems to provide information to the biotech.

Bewildered, Papa spins into the observatory bay where Fisher and Devereaux are fitting mobiles with specialized tools for... for... for something. His mind, *gone!*

"Did you see what I saw?" Fisher asks Devereaux, eyes unblinking as his hands move automatically along the tool fitting flush against a mobile's wrist. "Rockets! The dragons transformed their bodies into fusion rockets to keep ahead of the shockwave. They're not just photovores, and they don't just coast along the magnetic field lines. This is simply amazing. You saw it, right?"

"Right, but—"

"This is unique. I don't know what it all means yet, but it means something. How do you think such a thing could evolve? Oh, this is remarkable," Fisher says, still unblinking.

"What are you two doing?" Papa asks. He only wants information, but this request comes out gruff, accusatory.

Devereaux jumps, sending her into a slight spin, but Fisher neither blinks nor ceases his finger dance across the mobile fittings.

"The rail is out of commission, and probably the Higgs generators, too. The automatic systems are not responding, so we're sending mobiles to effect repairs." Devereaux removes an aluminum canister from a storage locker and begins to spray a white coating onto the mobiles' wrinkled gray skin. What is that *for?* Protection from the disk's radiation? Must be. Such an odd assortment of information his personality has lost access to... certainly he will recover it soon. Certainly.

"That's good," says Papa after a moment of watching the pair work.

"Papa, pull up my latest dragon model and give me a projection on the hull over here," Fisher requests. "I've got a lot of modifications to make."

That he *can* do, although it is irritating to have full access to Fisher's files and yet be cut off from so much of himself. He links the local display to the model in Fisher's subnode. "Here it is, Dr. Fisher. Can I do anything else to assist you?"

Devereaux pauses midstream of her oral programming of the remote and tilts her chin in a way Papa has identified with mild surprise at an inconsistent piece of data. Did he say something out of character? Is his mind that gone? He studies Fisher, but the exobiologist does and says nothing, already focused on the serpentine model form tangled in a mess of field vectors.

Devereaux spares a glance and sighs at Fisher, who has stopped his mobile preparation, before resuming her instructions, which makes Papa think instead of react. Fisher should be working on the mobile, working to repair the *Karamojo*. Why didn't he realize that? Fisher should not be playing with his models now. There is work to be done.

Papa freezes Fisher's model mid-twist. "We're falling into the disk. Get to the job at hand and save the toys for later."

"Hey! This is a monkey job," Fisher says patting the mobile on its shoulder. "I should be updating my model, redesigning our dragon cage, that sort of thing. Not simple repairs."

"Shut up and get back to work," Devereaux says. "Survival comes first. We're falling into the disk. It'll kill us fast."

"The nanoskin is working to spec. The radiation pressure is slowing us, as is the particle flux of the disk wind. And there are chemical rockets for emergencies."

"The radiation, the wind, in this gravity they'll only add seconds. That's all. And the rockets won't give us much more than minutes."

Papa knows she's right.

"This is stupid that we're in this situation at all," Fisher says, rubbing his neck with the palm of one hand. "Fang screwed up. We should be on our way home by now."

Papa thinks, putting some of his available discretionary computation processors on synthesizing the new dragon data with Fisher's model and their cage. "We weren't ready to capture a dragon, given what we now know. There was little Captain Fang could have done."

"She could have cleared us out of the way!" Fisher is shaking his fists with his words, making his entire body move in counterpoint in the microgravity of the near freefall. Their efforts are not slowing their fall much. "She could have approached slowly, carefully, and not driven tens of thousands of dragons down our throat!"

"Get to work," growls Devereaux.

Fisher pulls his fists back to his body, turns away from his model, and resumes his checks of the mobile tools. "Ship's status, Papa."

Papa reaches for those data, but finds over half the sockets empty. Wasn't it all just there? From his manufactured memories of having a human body, the ones he still has access to, he thinks it is like having a tooth pulled and temporarily forgetting about the bloody hole. He had started to feel useful. Rather than confess his ignorance, he activates an expert system to answer and scurries away. He is tiring of running away.

Then he is in Fang's dim cabin. No exterior waves, no music. The sole light source comes from the desk surface, over which a human silhouette floats. Stuffed animals also populate the room, casting eerie shadows as they mill about in a semblance of Brownian motion. "Captain Fang?"

Temperature ripples across her face, first hot, then cold. "Not daughter?"

"Of course, daughter," he says, wondering about his slip. His confusion is profound. He can show it to her and her alone. "What are you doing?"

"What do you think, Papa? I'm trying to save us. Why aren't

you helping me?" Her face flares with heat, her own dwarf nova. The infrared is working here at least.

Now he looks for the first time at the workspace on the desk: the picture tank has become a diorama showing their dilemma in miniature. The *Karamojo* falls ever closer to the swirling accretion disk. In seconds the ship is swallowed in fire. It does not come out the other side.

"The time compression isn't large," he notes. They have minutes, not hours. They are Icarus, flown too close to the sun, doomed to sink into the sea. No slow orbital decay, no time for repairs. "What shall we do?"

Fang answers, distantly, as much to herself as to him it seems. "Wormdrive is unavailable. The ship's nanoskin is already reflecting all it can. We have reaction mass, but no raildrive to launch it. That leaves the back-up chemicals, but the rockets' delta vee is too small to lift us away from the disk for long. I'm saving them right now, but will have to fire them in a few minutes."

Papa feels shame flood through himself. She better knows their state than does he. "What of adding to our current velocity? What of punching through the disk fast?" He is cut off from his own mind and cannot evaluate the idea as accurately as the model the captain is running.

"I thought of that," she says. "We'd be through the disk in a few minutes, but still too long. The density is too high for our skin. Too much drag, too much heating. Wait."

She taps in a few changes and subvocalizes other commands. The miniature *Karamojo* returns to a point above the disk, a fraction closer than at the start of the last scene Papa saw in the diorama. This time the ship jerks, its ass pulled forward as if by a string, and then starts edging toward the perimeter of the disk.

"Yes," says Papa. "We can add to our orbital component, push the apogee outside the outer disk. That would give us more time."

Even as he says this, the problem with this new plan appears. The miniature *Karamojo* misses the flared disk edge, skimming through the diffuse atmosphere, and plows into the accretion stream from the secondary star. Once again, the ship does not emerge.

"Bad timing on this orbit," she evaluates coldly.

There must be something they can do. It does not seem the time to die well. They have barely begun here.

It brings up another false memory of being a human on Earth, camping in the woods. Papa remembers bending over to pick up a stone to skip across the river and noticing a group of tadpoles in the shallow water. A fish slid up and took one of the tadpoles, and was gone with the flip of a tail and gulp of a mouth. The prey moved from egg to tadpole to lunch in mere days. What was the purpose in that?

"Skipping stones across the river," he says aloud, making his intended metaphor live. Too obvious and trite for his namesake, but the best he can do under the circumstances.

"What do you mean?" says Fang, staring at the perpetually dying starship.

Maybe he does mean something. He has a subconscious, designed to aid him with nonlinear problem solving. Maybe it has. "Use the rockets to slow our orbit."

Fang considers this. "Oh, I see! Perhaps . . ."

The miniature *Karamojo* is jerked backward this time, as if catching on a snag in a stream. The orbital energy reduced, the ship moves inward toward the hotter and denser regions of the disk. But the disk is also flared, and these inward regions are thinner and their surfaces at a lower altitude, giving them more time to fall.

More importantly, these inward regions obey the laws of Newton and Kepler, and orbit the white dwarf more rapidly. The six hundred kilometer-per-second velocity at the edge of the disk means nothing to them, for the ship matches it. Falling at the outer edge is like falling into a placid pool. Now, as the miniature ship moves in to smaller radii, the velocity differential grows. This time, when the tiny ship hits the disk, rounded rings down, it hits a fast-moving stream and does not sink.

It bounces.

The orbit decays a bit more with the energy lost, their apogee not quite so close to the disk edge. The conditions are harsher, hotter, and more difficult for the nanoskin to resist. The ship bounces again on the second impact after it again falls parabolically to the surface of the lake of fire. And on the third. Just before the fourth bounce, when their orbit has decayed and brought them a third of the way inward toward the white dwarf, the tiny *Karamojo* gives up the ghost, evaporating in short order as the hull blackens and burns.

"Damn," says Fang. "That's a good trick. Gives us nearly an hour to get things fixed. What's the impulse, I wonder."

Papa patches into her model as some of his network comes back on-line, like some idea on the tip of his tongue suddenly coming to him. He calculates the number. "Low. Under twenty *g's*."

"We can take it," says Fang. "We'll have to."

They spend a few precious moments more optimizing their burns, and then Fang sends Papa out to alert the crew.

He is happy to have this task to occupy his noisy thoughts. He can focus on it when he runs into the mucking walls.

Stearn tried to catch his breath while he waited in the embrace of the couchbeast. He had rushed to secure his tools and the damaged equipment, filling his stikfast palettes, and kicked to secure himself. He had thought he had worked to the last second before the bounce, but here he was, waiting. What was it already? Five seconds? Ten?

He had the bridge displays back on-line. The area around the immediate deck blazed with charged plasma, and the ceiling displayed a violet sky.

He checked his eyeclock again. Only six seconds had passed. "Shit," he said, grinning.

Then he felt a tug, a slight one, far less than a gravity. Was that it? Papa had spooked him into thinking it would be worse. Was the ship's brain still seriously malfunctioning?

Then the hand of God Himself smashed into Stearn, pressing him into the hugging beast. His cheeks and chest flattened, and his breath whooshed from him. His wrist ached suddenly, and it was all he could do to twist it into a more comfortable position.

The fire rose with them, briefly, then fell away. Stearn was a piece of shrapnel riding the shockwave of an explosion. He was a human cannonball. He was a Sirian photovore in its birth launch.

God eased up on him, and Stearn floated from the couchbeast. The poor thing was stinking sweaty and moaning quietly. Bruises splotched its hide. Stearn's wrist ached, and his lower back as well.

"That was fun," he said, listening to the distant, insulated pops of the cooling hull. "Can't wait to do it again!"

Henderson gasped for air after the third bounce and pushed off from his chairbeast, grateful for the microgravity. He would have been shaking in any kind of gravity. He knew he stank of nervous sweat and didn't care. While this last bounce hadn't been as bad as the first two, he knew that it was the last one. Papa had promised.

He laughed, a little, that they had made it. He stopped abruptly, disgusted at the uneven timber of the sound. It wasn't over yet.

Devereaux's voice piped into the biolab. "Need you down here Henderson, inner staging area, *now.*"

He grimaced and kicked off into the ring.

An acrid, sharp scent assaulted Henderson when he arrived. He instantly took in the scene: Devereaux floated with two twitching, burnt, and bleeding mobiles. "Did they finish?"

Devereaux looked upset with him. He didn't know why. "Yeah, they finished. The *Karamojo* is fixed."

Henderson let out the breath he hadn't realized he was holding and his fingers tingled. It was going to be fine then. "Why did you summon me? These mobiles are hopeless. Best thing now is to redirect extra fish in here to clean up."

Cocked forty-five degrees from his orientation to better examine the pair of mobiles returned from their repair mission, Devereaux rolled her eyes at Henderson. "But they looked fine up until a few minutes ago. They finished the lion's share of repairs wonderfully, and we don't have backups of these. They're the backups for the automatic systems. Until we grow more, the only remaining backups are us."

Crisis had stirred his blood, and Henderson couldn't help himself from noticing the way the sweat made Devereaux's grimy T-shirt stick to her curves. He thought of giving her a congratulatory kiss. "Everything you say is true, but they must have taken a huge radiation dose. You don't see that right away although it devastates a body."

"What if we have to go out?" she asked.

He shrugged. It would never come to that. "I have some pharmaceuticals I can give us, but I suggest staying behind the nanoskin, our mass, and the e-m fields."

A tinkling shudder vibrated through the ship, and gradually Henderson began to fall. The ruglings flattened as his snakeskin boots touched the deck, cushioning the slow fall. He could feel the gravity continue to increase. "You're right. We've got the raildrive restored," he said as nonchalantly as he could.

"Yee-uck," Devereaux said. She had landed chest first on one of the mobiles.

The thing groped weakly at her, red blood seeping from swollen, broken hide and staining the charred patches of reflection skin that hadn't yet sloughed off.

Normally Henderson would have laughed, but not today. He stepped to her, carefully in the light gravity, and lifted a wincing Devereaux out of the mess by her T-shirt.

The mobile hemorrhaged over its entire body, shook, and died. The other would die momentarily, its short useful life complete.

"Put me down," Devereaux said.

Henderson swung around like a crane and deposited Devereaux beside him.

"Papa should have warned us," she said as she flipped bits of mobile off her shirt. "You said you had him operational again."

"Hardly." Henderson watched her fingers touching her shirt. He hoped she would take it off. "I said that the regrowth operation was underway, and that there was nothing else I could do."

"Whatever."

Henderson shuffled over to the viewport and scanned the hydroponics. He saw only blackened diamond over the gardens where no doubt the light-filtering mechanisms had burned out. Not good. If the plants had been zapped, dinner would be nothing but recycled fish sticks for the next few days, and the nutrient reserves needed to regrow the gardens would tax their short-term resources.

"You there, Papa?" Devereaux asked.

"Of course we are," Papa said.

"Well then," she said, giving up on the shirt and stripping it off over her head, "what's next on the repair list?"

She was fine looking, but he realized the moment for a congratulatory kiss had passed, and a look was all he would get. It wasn't fair that he'd lost his colony to the crisis.

"All critical systems are now repaired or are being repaired by automatic systems. Captain Fang recommends that everyone take a couple hours off."

Devereaux turned to Henderson. She held the shirt away from her body. "Want to grab a bite in the galley? I'm famished."

Stearn was a lucky man. Henderson would console himself with his own fantasies, which were, he admitted now that the emergency was over, more perfect than the flesh before him. Devereaux projected an earthy physical quality that was more than attractive, but she didn't take the time to keep her form perfect, the way he preferred. He was noticing tiny flaws as the seconds passed. And besides, in an infinite universe how could one woman be enough? "No thanks." He thought of a little white lie. "I'm not hungry after seeing mobiles disintegrate."

"I work hard, I get hungry." She cracked a smile. "And after an ordeal like this, well, I usually like some company, but Stearn will have a million things to do and I bet the captain isn't letting him have more than a few minutes off. You sure you're not hungry?" She kept her smile, although it showed signs of wavering. Was the stress getting to her? Even though her shirt was off, leaving her topless, she wasn't being provocative. This was the first genuinely warm overture she had made to him since he'd made an ass of himself in the observation blister.

There was something creeping in the back of his brain, an instinctual emotion that he didn't yet wish to acknowledge. The creeping thing was not about Devereaux. It might come out soon, and he preferred to be alone if that happened. He said, "No thanks."

She shrugged and went off one way down the ring, he the other.

He took a detour through the Hall of Trophies to get an objective measure of just how seriously things had deteriorated. The corridor was lined on each side with black holes where there should have been happy animal heads. The *Karamojo* had sucked the Hall bone dry, just like it was supposed to do in an emergency. Only the marlin at the far end of the Hall still wiggled in its place, but as Henderson walked toward it, he saw that the creature was shrunken, and the wiggles were involuntary; the *Karamojo* would have even this great one, too.

As he walked toward the biolab, it dawned on him that perhaps his life had truly been in danger. Was that possible? Yes, he had to admit, it was. Those bounces were bad enough, but Papa had said they would work. And what of before, when they had been damaged? Instead of simply coming close enough to induce the massive current surge that had debilitated the *Karamojo*, one of those damn dragons could have hit them at kilometers per second. No way they could have taken that.

He would have died.

The creeping thing acknowledged, his sense of relief chased away, he stepped into his lab and said, "Music. Something dark and destructive."

"Would you care to be more specific?" Papa asked.

Christ. He'd have to reteach Papa all his preferences, but he was definitely not in the mood to do that now. Something from Papa's violent, death-ridden era, he thought. *Night on Bald Mountain*.

As the first notes struck, Henderson opened a storage locker and removed a glass bottle of his finest Merlot, carefully cultivated from grape to wine over the first part of the voyage. He popped the cork and let the bottle breathe. He half feared Papa would smell the organic richness and order it added to the biomass reserves.

Thankfully his chairbeast had been spared the carnage wrought upon so much of the other noncritical biological systems. He sank into the warm, yielding skin perfectly tuned to his preferences. Leaning back, closing his eyes, he let the beast's vibrations soothe him. Or tried to.

The music picked up, the ghosts rising from their graves to

haunt the living for the long, dark night that would only be the darker for the flashes of lightning hurled from the mountain.

Henderson fetched a diamond goblet and poured the dark liquid swirling full of mystery. Fine wine was still better grown and fermented with traditional methods rather than synthesized. The random vagaries of the grapes' nutrients and care could produce subtle masterpieces. Surely a unique human genetic sequence was still worthwhile the same way. Surely his own was still worthwhile, and would be on the Earth half a millennium hence.

Back in his chairbeast, letting it loom up around him, Henderson regarded the empty terrarium over his wine and music—his fantasy world, sucked dry in minutes by the automatics to feed the repairs to Papa's brain banks. On the monitors lining the base of the tank shimmered ghost images in black and white of tiny rooms empty save for tiny skeletons. Bone was not so quickly cannibalized.

What precautions had he taken to ensure his—his sequence's—survival? Sperm deposits, his code archived, that was it really. In his youth he had been promiscuous, like most. He hadn't tried to impregnate anyone then, and there had been strangely few lovers of substance in recent years. No single woman could satisfy him, so that was fine, wasn't it?

On the monitors flickered images of skeletons sleeping alone in beds, although that was an illusion. Under the sheets, they would be entangled with even tinier skeletons.

So what? Did it matter? They had been little more than monkeys that looked like people. But they had been his people, and he hadn't been able to save them. Could he do any better saving himself?

Henderson drained the warm wine in a searing, tannic gulp and launched himself from the chairbeast. The tank monitors above his desk were simple projection devices, thin films vacuum-packed under quartz. Better image quality, he had insisted, than nanotablets. Better to hit as well. The first screen gave way on the second blow of the diamond goblet.

The music crashed as the crystal shards fell into the uncannibalized ruglings below. Hundreds of tiny crystals with the same shape and structure as a large crystal caught the light in their facets. More joined them as Henderson banged away, grunting, as he smashed all the monitors. The tiny skeletons shattered, vanished.

A directional sound beam caught his ear, slicing through the music and crashing. "Can I be of assistance?"

Henderson ignored Papa, running on his unleashed impulses—his own automatic repair system. *Kra-twing! Kra-twing!*

The recoil of each swing knocked Henderson back, allowing him to get plenty of forward momentum each time on the way back. Eventually he ran out of monitors and attacked the quartz of the tank itself. His boots crunched over the crystal shards. More banging then. *Kra-twing! Kra-twing!*

After several minutes, he tired, and leaned against the tank, hot. Then he slid down with a slow squeak to a squatting position, trailing sweat behind him. He held the unmarked goblet before him, rolling it back and forth between his hands, and watched the tiny spectra reflected from the lights. One object, but so many ways of looking at it.

His own life he had looked at in only one way in recent years, an unwavering lone arrow flying into the infinite future he had hoped to split into a billion directions and ensure his immortality.

The music finished. "Would you care for another selection?" Papa asked.

Henderson ignored the solicitous voice.

Eventually he stood, and left the lab, making his way to the galley. He paused at the threshold, and looked in at Devereaux sitting at the polished tabletree dipping a fish stick into some white sauce.

Stearn sat with her, smiling as she pushed the dripping food into his mouth.

Henderson turned on his heel and returned to the biolab. "Play anything. I don't care what."

Atonal, synthesized notes with no particular pattern began to sound. Twenty-third century computer-generated drivel, lacking all human warmth and understanding. Lonely and alien. Henderson let it play on.

It was perfect.

When Papa returns, Fang's cabin is pitch-black and silent as space. He shifts his vision to the infrared and finds Fang huddled on her bed, clinging to its fitted sheets. She isn't sleeping; for a moment he listens to her hiccupping breath. "Captain Fang?"

Temperature ripples across her face, first hot, then cold. "Not daughter?"

"Of course, daughter," he says, wondering about these slips. His confusion remains profound, yet he still knows that protecting Fang is his first priority after safeguarding the ship. Time to set her aright. "The ship is safe."

"It was my fault in the first place."

"Mine as well. With hindsight, we can say that we were faced with a difficult situation with little prospect for success. We will try again, learning from our"—don't say *mistake*—"newly acquired experience."

"You're awfully delicate." Fang shifts up on an elbow, then spins her legs out, still clinging to the sheets with hands splayed like claws. Her body surface is cool everywhere—she's still in uniform. "Is that you, Papa? Where's the fire in the belly, the blood and thunder? You're Papa Hemingway, remember."

He remembers. Parts. "You're a beautiful woman, Lena. Why

don't you let your hair grow out into a fine blond mane to match your fiery spirit?"

"Damn you, Papa." Her face flares with heat, her own dwarf nova. Is that a new thought? "I'm not you. Try as I might, I don't have that fiery spirit you ramble on about so much. But I'm not a doll, either."

He sifts through the available memories he has, false ones and real ones; they all seem more like factoids than memories. "No doll. You box, and that takes determination and heart. A willingness to take a punch. Well, you got punched."

"I'm not a real boxer. I rely on technique. I'm careful. It's just as well that Fisher and I broke up when we did. He was getting better, and I would not have liked that bastard decking me."

"Oh, Lena, you see. There's your fire!"

"Bullshit," she says, her volume low. "I am a worthless captain. First chance to make decisions of consequence, and it's a spectacular failure. I should just leave it to Fisher."

"No, Lena, you're my captain. Always."

"What's with you? Why aren't you calling me daughter like usual?"

"We don't know." He would not lie to her even if allowed, and he will not flee from her. "It is frightening."

She laughs at that, but the laughter quickly merges into sobs. "Papa has the fear, I have the fear, and the stink of it is all around us."

She says the words, and he knows them to be true. He is allowed fear. Fear is a useful tool for self-preservation. The real Papa Hemingway understood fear, but only found it anathema when debilitating. Like what happened to Fang on the bridge for an important split second. He should be furious with her, shouldn't he? Is he cut off from that part of himself? He should explain the problem to her. . . . It is more than fear.

"The algorithms that would cleanse the mind are separated

from the data—the emotional memories—that define my pseudo-character. We have a human perspective, and a short-term memory, and knowledge of primary ship operations—those are quite redundant in my neural mesh. We're missing the older real memories, memories of our times together for instance. We don't really know who you are anymore, just as we don't know who we are, but we know who we're not. We're not a whole man anymore. We wish someone would just shoot us."

"You don't mean that. That's not the Papa I remember."

"Exactly."

It is a terrible silence that follows. He takes some consolation in the idea that his own problems have superseded hers and that she may lean on that to prompt herself back into action. She seemed effective when they saved the ship just a little while ago, but why has she remained in her cabin—to wallow in self-pity?

He is about to ask when she violently pushes away from her bed, bounces hard off a wall, and ricochets to the door. "That's my break between rounds. There's not much for people to do on this ship, but I'll do everything I can. I'll even try to get along with Fisher. Thanks for the bell, Papa."

What is she referring to? Is he getting worse? He heard no bell.

At least it isn't another goddamned wall.

TEN

The eyes are the window of the soul.
—PROVERB

*Eyes lie if you ever look into them
for the character of a person.*
—STEVIE WONDER

Fang rose from her chairbeast to stand at one end of the conference room, beginning the impromptu dragon meeting. She smoothed around the creases in her whites and said, "Dr. Fisher has agreed to my request to set the agenda for this meeting. Let me proceed briskly. We have much to discuss."

In turn, Fang caught the eye of each of her crew, trying to read their hearts, but that trick rarely worked for her. Only in Fisher did she read something; the fixed pink stare that met her was as unwavering and obsessed as ever, but she took encouragement in his cooperation with the agenda.

"The *Karamojo* is currently stable fifty kilometers above the disk, and the ship is in no immediate danger," she began. The ship always came first. "We must decide whether to withdraw now and abort the mission, or to proceed." Fang whipped her gaze around to Fisher and held up a pointed finger to cut him off before he could interrupt. "My current assessment of the situation dictates that we proceed cautiously, and utilize the new information at our disposal. I allow that someone here might have an objection that either Papa or I have overlooked."

Fisher opened his mouth as if to speak, but closed it again and appeared to settle into thought for the moment. Good.

Devereaux, sitting cross-legged on her chairbeast, asked, "Well, just exactly what is our situation?"

"Tell them, Papa," Fang said. Time to show some trust in him. Time for him to earn some trust or they had no business remaining in-system.

"We got hit hard, sure enough, but that was because we didn't know what was coming. The induced currents coupled to our spinal rail, and through that to my external sensor grid, and then on to a number of nonessential systems. The *Karamojo* was not designed to take such an electromagnetic event. The autonomous functions, like atmosphere and other life support, are only connected through microwave link and fused connects for standard safety reasons. Good thing, too. By consuming our biomass reserves, we've regrown to eighty percent capacity, and additional growth should increase that figure to over ninety percent in the next four hours. The more serious damage lies with the Higgs generators, which now suffer from a calibration problem: their parameters were reinitialized. Mobile repair restored a thirty percent capacity, but we'll need some more work before we can blast out of here at full thrust. The nanoskin, since it is more mechanical than electrical and relatively insensitive to long wavelength interference, continues to work well, keeping us cool. So we're shipshape in most ways, and we're raring for a second shot. That was a lucky sucker punch."

Papa was starting to sound a little more like Papa, but so much still fell back onto the basic speech template. Still, it was an improvement. Fang said, "Thank you, Papa. Now, are there any remaining questions about our status or any other issues to be considered? I'd like everyone's input."

Henderson cleared his throat, then frowned. Finally he said, "I'd like to emphasize the depletion of our biomass reserves. We wound up with a lot of plain carbon, useless for anything but the nanovats. It takes time and energy to regrow sophisticated biocircuits from scratch. We cannot return to full operational status if we are hit that hard again." He kept his eyes down during his statement, then looked up at the ceiling to reiterate his final point. "We just can't take it. I can't emphasize this enough."

"So emphasized," said Fisher. "Well, it sounds like there's no problem continuing the mission, so we should get down to discussing strategy revisions."

"Not so fast, Dr. Fisher," Fang said. "That may be the case, but I think everyone should have a chance to have the floor. As I said, I'm ready to proceed. Phil?"

Stearn, sitting to her right and looking serious and responsible these days in his dark skin and solid muscles, said, "Papa's completely correct. Things are going okay. And frankly, this is a lot more fun, and a different kind of fun, than I've had in some time. I'm game."

Devereaux, next to Stearn, twirled a dreadlock around her finger, winding and unwinding. "I have some reservations," she said, "but I'm hooked. I must understand how the dragons came to be, how they live, and what they will mean to us in the future. I cannot turn my back on this puzzle now."

When it was clear that Devereaux had said her piece, Fisher said, "Yes, we proceed," and turned his pink eyes on Henderson.

The biotech rubbed his dimpled chin with a big hand. "I'd like to hear Devereaux's reservations, if I may."

Fisher sighed, nodded, and turned back to Devereaux.

Devereaux jerked back at the sudden attention, her Buddhalike composure showing cracks. "Just the perfectly obvious stuff. Even with all the data we have on the disk, it isn't easy to predict what it will do very far in advance. A big magnetic flare erupting under us could pose problems in our current state. A dwarf nova, while uncomfortable, is easily seen in advance and escaped even with our crippled wormdrive. The dragons themselves appear more formidable than we had guessed, but we have more knowledge now, and that will help. I still have a concern, rather irrational, that someone will show up and be upset with us for poaching. As I said, perfectly obvious stuff."

Everyone turned their heads back to Henderson, who had lifted his head while Devereaux was speaking, but was now looking down again. "Well, I suppose it sounds as if . . . as if we should go on," he finally said.

"Right," said Fisher. "Then I have some new cage designs to present." He stopped short of asking Papa to project them and said, "If I may, Captain Fang?"

Fang nodded, and they went on to discuss the new cage, how to get and keep a dragon out of the disk, how to herd a dragon into the *Karamojo*, and all the other practical matters they needed to think about to continue with the hunt.

As the meeting dragged on, Fang worried about how polite and cooperative Fisher seemed. But why shouldn't he be? He was getting his way now. Still she worried, but gave her worry little merit.

After all, how far could she really trust her own judgment?

In the net of Fisher's mind, the dragon was already caught. Still, the net flapped at a couple of loose corners. When Fang dismissed the meeting and ordered everyone to take four hours off to rest (insanely, more time idle!) while Papa also recovered, Fisher waited for her.

When they were the only two left in the room, Fang paused at his heel dragging, and lifted a questioning eyebrow toward him.

"Look, can we talk?" he asked.

"Of course we can talk," she replied. "Haven't we just been talking?"

The net flapped harder in a sudden, unexpected breeze. "I mean like we used to talk. Before."

"Oh. Before." She stared at him impassively for a long moment. "I don't think so."

A hurricane, and the net ripped free. This wasn't how it was supposed to go at all. He had to have some sort of reassurance that he was in control, that he would have his way when the time came, that Fang would act appropriately at the next key juncture.

Fang turned away and walked out of the room.

Fisher followed, but stepped on a fish in the corridor, nearly losing his footing. Damn fish. Fang was a good ten meters ahead, already moving around the ring's curvature. "Lena," he called.

Thankfully she stopped. She spun on her heel with mechanical precision and waited for him. "Yes?" she said.

"I just wanted you to know that I'm here for you. I—" He needed to throw something big and weighty on the net before it all blew away. "I have been an absolute ass, getting in your way, and I want to apologize from deep in my heart. You have my support, and . . . my love. If you'll have it."

There, he thought. That should do it.

But Fang's face didn't soften. The ridges of her lips remained sharp and dangerous. The folds around her gray eyes masked the distant mirror of her soul. "Sam, have you looked at yourself recently? You've made yourself into something more inhuman and remote than Stearn or his generation ever managed. They only deal with the body. And, as messed up as Papa is now, or as messed up as he is when he's functioning properly, he is still more responsible than you. You just can't act like an ass for months and then turn around one day and say you're sorry and expect it to be all right again."

This was proving trickier than he had planned. He should have run some simulations and practiced, but he counted on spontaneity to add the necessary emotional integrity that practice would kill. "I know," he said. "You're right. But what would you like for me to do at this point? I'm sorry and I wish I could take it all back and do it right."

"Good," she said, turning away to resume her march.

He took a deep breath and listened to the air whistle through his teeth. He shambled after her in the high gravity, this task turning as physically onerous as it was psychologically.

"What do you want from me? I'll give it to you. Just name it." Give her everything, he repeated to himself. Give her everything to get the only thing that mattered. Everything for everything was an even trade, wasn't it?

This was his thought as they reached Fang's cabin and her door squeezed shut in his face.

Too much, too pushy. Next time he'd play it cool, be sensitive. It would be fine. He thought, I've waited hundreds of years—I can wait a few hours.

He sat down outside Fang's door.

As the door closed, Fang's cheeks tightened into an involuntary smile. Fisher no longer seemed a wild element. With a united crew, she was sure she could face the dragons again and triumph.

"Evening lights." Fang walked to her bed, sat down on its edge, and pulled off her boots. The plush carpeting tickled her hot toes as she stretched out her legs. The rest of her uniform followed the boots, and she donned a pink satin robe that felt good against her skin.

She considered opening a bottle of wine, but Henderson probably would not be able to produce much more very quickly, and she didn't want to drink alone. Outside her French doors, the moon shone over a placid sea, and a slow breeze made the curtains shiver. She stepped outside onto her wooden deck, sans drink.

A lover's moon, she thought, frowning. "Papa?"

"Yes, daughter," answered the familiar, gruff voice.

"How are you?" she asked.

"Better," he said, sounding tired. "Still not myself."

"Me, too," she said.

"You need a man," Papa offered.

Fang shook her head, slowly, smiling. "Like hell I do," she said, thinking of Fisher.

"A real man," Papa persisted.

Already cool, goose pimples rose on her bare arms and legs with the wind. "Turn up the temperature a few degrees, will you?"

"Of course," said Papa obediently.

Looking out onto the virtual sea, smooth to infinity, she decided she might want the wine after all. "Where's Fisher?"

"Outside your cabin, sitting opposite the door."

She smiled, shaking her head. It was too good to be true.

After another ten minutes, she asked, "He still there?"

"Yes, daughter."

She licked her lips. "Let him in, and tell him to pour two glasses of one of the reds. Make sure he lets it breathe for a few minutes, right?"

"Of course."

Fang seated herself on a canvas chair and levered her legs up against the high gravity and settled them, uncrossed, onto the deck rail. Her robe slid up her thighs, but she didn't bother to push it back. She tried not to look, but couldn't help herself, as Fisher's green scintillations flickered inside.

Apparently he was doing just as requested.

The moon shimmered exactly where she wanted it, and she basked in its glow while she waited for Fisher.

She turned when she heard his slippered feet scraping against the wood of the deck. She held out her hand and accepted the proffered glass. She returned her attention to the luminous moon while she sniffed the complex aroma of the wine.

Fisher settled into the other deck chair; she often used it to put her feet on. "Nice night," he said.

"Mmm," she replied as she finished sloshing wine around her mouth. The liquid warmed her throat on its way down.

"Good wine," he said.

Fang wiggled her upper body, shrugging the robe from her shoulders. Bending her head forward and exposing the back of her neck, she said, "Please just shut up, Sam, and make yourself useful. I could really use a good back rub."

When she heard his weight shift from his chair and the clink of his glass bottom on the table, but no words, a shiver crackled along her spine. When his hard fingers sank firmly into her knotted flesh, she darn near purred. He must have downloaded a massage routine into his biochip because he'd never been so good before. . . .

The danger in letting someone else enter your inner sanctum was lack of control, but Fisher was her fantasy tonight, an automaton, a creature bent to her will, and she loved it. No words from him now, no "dragon this" and "dragon that," no interrupting her, no faraway expression when she talked to him. Why couldn't he have been this way before?

But then, she admitted, she probably would not have found him attractive.

After an eternity under his attentive fingers, Fang stirred herself. "You're no chairbeast, but you're not bad."

He said nothing.

Lovely. It wasn't all about him and his dragons for once.

Fang rose, said, "Come on, let's do this right," and walked inside. She undid her robe and let the smooth material slide down her body, caressing her all the way down. She crawled onto the bed from the bottom up, lay down, and let herself relax. "Back," she mumbled around her armpit.

Fisher sat on the bed and went to work on her back.

After only eight minutes by her internal clock, she jerked, adrenaline tightening her muscles, sweat breaking over her skin. She had nearly fallen asleep! She didn't trust Fisher that far. But she loved what his fingers were doing—had been doing—before she jerked awake. He was being so good to her, giving her what she needed, and not prattling on about his own obsessions. Why hadn't he been like this more often when they'd been together? No one had treated her this well in a long time.

A very long time.

She blinked as her eyes watered. "Sam," she said.

"Yes?" His fingers continued to cast their spell.

"I want to explain what happened on the bridge, with the dragons."

She started to push herself to her elbows, but he pushed her back down. He said, "That's not necessary."

"But it is." She succumbed to his push and let herself settle in for more massage. It would be easier to say the things she wanted to say this way, without eye contact, and for that she was grateful. "You eat, sleep, and breathe star dragon the way I eat, sleep, and breathe the *Karamojo*. I owe you some explanation."

"If you feel you must. It isn't necessary."

She grunted in dismissal. "I tried to tell you before about the leviathan the night, you know, things went bad between us. This is important to me, important to understand my actions, and you'll listen to it this time, understand?"

"Yes," he said, and nothing more.

Now that it was time to tell it to another human being, she didn't know how to start. Some emotions, some experiences, seemed too big for words. Anything she said would be a lie insofar as the truth was impossible to communicate. Finally, she decided. "I'm not Papa," she began. "I make a good show of it, boxing, hunting, being a strong captain the way he would be if he could. But when I box, I use finesse rather than strength. The ship's name, which I chose, indicates that. I didn't call the ship the *Great White Hunter*, or the *Amazon*, or anything so bold. Karamojo Bell hunted elephants, the great beasts of his era, with a small-bore 7mm Mauser loaded with 175 grain bullets. Trust me, that is small for elephant. He made his kills with only one shot, a testimony to his skill as a marksman. He used knowledge and finesse when he hunted. I aspire to his skill. When I hunt, I have safeguards to prevent injury, so I'm not really proving anything. I have not been tested with threat of death, the only test recognized in nature. I'm a creature of our age. Machines, mechanical or biological, do all the difficult tasks for us. Humans are superfluous in so many ways, but we still run things, choose the direction of civilization, something like an evolutionary grandfather clause. Our creations have only the drives we give them."

Fisher's fingers had slipped into a mechanical pattern, so she assumed he was paying attention to her words. He had rarely allowed her such a long speech without interruption, except when he was working and filtered her out. She diverted that thought—he had *better* be listening!

"I've tried to be the type of captain who does things the way they used to. This mission is really my first chance to prove that I can. But we're just machines, too, with programming as ancient as the Serengeti. We're obsessed with our ability to change our bodies, our hardware, and that shows how obsolete our thinking truly is. The mind will rule the future while we clutch to our earwings, wasp waists, and quick fists. But I'm talking around my point.

"When I was a little girl, the universe taught me that I was weak, that there were bigger things in it that would and could eat me, and think nothing more of me than how I tasted. I've been trying to grow, literally, ever since then. Grow in muscle, grow in rank, until I became so big I could move entire herds of animals across interstellar space. The disk here holds a few percent of the mass of Earth's moon, big enough for me, a sea five thousand times bigger than the Pacific. Multiply that by two: The disk is double-sided. That has had me thinking about the leviathan that swallowed my grandfather as I watched."

Fang stopped to lick her lips, which had gone bone dry. "When those dragons came at us, with those same unfathomable eyes, I was the weak little girl again. For a moment I could not act: One of them might have noticed, and eaten me. Then I had to act, or I would be just the same as that little girl I once was. I had to. My command would now be over if Papa had seen any clear mandatory course of action, but we knew so little then, still don't know much, so I had wide latitude in my actions. But it felt like failure."

Fisher's fingers continued to slide around her muscles, working out the new tightness that had descended as she had talked. God, had she really talked so long without Fisher interrupting? Was it really possible? Could it have been this good all along? Had she been wrong throwing him out?

Now she desperately wanted him to say something. He had heard her justification, and it was his career—and life—that her actions, or lack of actions, threatened. Say something! she thought.

But she was in control now, wasn't she? She could make him say. "Tell me what you think about what I just told you."

Fisher replied, "I understand, and don't blame you for what happened on the bridge. What is important is that we, you, do the right thing next time. I'm here to help you do that, any way I can. Do you understand that?"

She wanted to believe him . . . or was that his wondrous massage persuading her? Take the political course. "I'm happy to have everyone's support. I'll need it."

She relaxed for good now, her piece said, and no blowup. This was good and right and easy. After an eternity, she knew she should make Fisher leave.

"Time to get some sleep," she should say. "Go back to your cabin, Sam."

But she couldn't. And didn't.

So Fisher stayed with her, with his magic fingers, and what followed felt even better than what had gone before.

Fisher left Fang's cabin with his clothes draped over his right shoulder, moving quickly with a small skip despite the extra *g*'s. His stretched out his hands, flexing away the cramps from the extended massages he had given Fang; the flowing air chilled the damp places in the webs between his fingers.

Instead of heading toward his own quarters, he decided it would be a good idea to see Henderson. Things had changed, and he wanted that to show.

Instead of ringing the chime, he rapped on the door itself. The glow from his hot hands reflected off the door's burnished surface, a ghost of himself.

The door irised open after a moment, releasing moist, cloying air that made Fisher think of a womb. Inside the light was dim, some kind of low mournful classical music playing. As he entered, the darkness and music retreated before him.

Henderson sat on a chairbeast, spinning slowly in half circles back and forth, an empty wineglass cradled between his splayed legs. His slick red smoking jacket swished with his circles. "What can I do for you, Dr. Fisher? Some clothes, perchance?"

Henderson's hypnotic, serpentine movement, cyclic, like electrons at the end of a magnetic bottle . . . no, he needed to suppress that for the time being. "Clothes? Yes, in a manner of speaking."

Henderson sighed, an exaggerated movement. "A tailor I'm not. At least this crew isn't as bad as I've seen. Did I ever tell you about the summer I worked at a Venice Beach shock shop? Fads there come and go by the hour, and today's youth are a pretty sick bunch. Great experience, though, for landing interstellar work. If you can make a beach-combing fan boy into an oceangoing transparent-shelled brain with penises for paddles in the morning, and back to his assholish self in time for dinner, they'll trust you to oversee the regrowth of a ship's organics."

Fisher let his clothes slide to the floor. Ruglings gathered and began conveying the misplaced suit along the floor. Eventually, an hour perhaps, his clothes would be back in his own room, clean and ready to wear.

Fisher said, "I want human flesh."

"Of course you do!" Henderson cawed, his bloodshot eyes puffy but wide open. "You all do, sooner or later. We're conditioned for the body we grew up in—not necessarily quite the same one, but primate, *Homo sapiens sapiens*. Our minds reject anything else, even if we have the technology to trick the body. Our minds are still body bound, and will be forever. Unless we change them, which would change ourselves, killing us. So we're eternally bound. Until we die."

"No," said Fisher. "You don't understand. I don't want a complete makeover like before. I don't want everything back. I just want a skin to cover me, make me appear the way I did before."

Another sigh. "I can do that. But we're short on stem cells and expendable biomass." Henderson glanced away toward a dark corner of the biolab, at what Fisher could not tell, maybe some broken equipment. Before he could argue further, Henderson said, "Fine. I can do it."

"Excellent," Fisher said.

In a few minutes he sat in a slowly bubbling nutrient vat that smelled of honeysuckle. The warm fluid surrounded him, buoying him upward, letting him bob through the surface. Itching crawled up his skin, starting with his toes, and pulled him down. He exhaled, slipped under, and inhaled.

In his mind's eye, Fisher watched the star dragon vanish beneath the disk's photosphere. She was glorious.

PART III

Cornered Animals

ELEVEN

Beware of all enterprises that require new clothes.
—HENRY DAVID THOREAU

Phil Stearn wiggled his elbows from side to side, inching down the shuttle ramscoop arm as fast as he could. Really should have redesigned for this one, he thought. Long, skinny tentacles. Yeah, that would have been a lot better. More fun than redesigning the shuttles anyway. Hmm, and he might find an interesting use for those with Sylvia as well.

Reaching his objective, Stearn slid his Swiss space tool along the superconducting coil sheath, smiling at the rasping notes that issued forth and echoed within the confines of the arm. A gentle touch raised a pure tone, like a wet finger on the rim of a wineglass. The next coil out was smaller in circumference and hit a higher note when he tapped it. He checked the sonic analysis program hastily thrown together and onto his fingertip machine—Papa's ears would not hear so well in here. If this went well, he would execute some low-current tests next. The fingertip flashed green.

"Are the coils in spec?" Fisher asked, his insistent voice pleasantly distant and twisted by the tube.

Stearn stretched himself out farther to hit an even smaller coil, the last on the arm. *Da-ding. Da-ding.* He could make the dings and the raspy notes. He ought to get Papa's help to compose a superconducting sonata, or a pop tune of some kind. *B-Field Blues,* maybe. *Da-ding.*

"Are you working in there, or just playing?" Fisher asked.

Tightass. Stearn sighed, turned down the light from his tool, and wiggled his shoulders to ease himself back out of the tube. Even though he'd adapted himself to the high gravity, it was still a special pain in this situation.

The arms of the ramscoop shuttles hadn't been designed for this new use, generating the intense, controlled magnetic fields to bottle star dragons, and the necessary coil placement was not at all optimal for human access. There wasn't time, or trust, to train micromachines for this job. Papa said he was fine, but who knew for sure? Much needed to be done by hand, or at least checked by hand. That was the job of the Jack, and he took it as seriously as he took anything. And that was plenty serious, more serious than his crewmates gave him credit for. But he didn't resent that. That was their problem, not his. He was comfortable with his abilities.

Stearn slid out and dropped a fast meter to the deck, trailing a monitoring line, a spider down a wire. The arms of the scoop, splayed as they were for access, did indeed resemble the unfinished frame of a web. Apropos.

Fisher, the true web builder, paced nearby.

Stearn technically was the spider who'd built this web, as he'd done most of the actual crawling and checking and fixing, but it was Fisher's creation. Fisher had designed the magnetic net to catch a dragon and the specs for the shuttle fleet. The Jack said, "They're in spec. If you got your designs right, this will work."

Fisher sniffed, and scratched at the side of his nose. "The designs are right. What worries me is what the dragons haven't shown us yet. The fields these shuttles will form will cage my current model dragon. If I've understood their field generation dynamo, if their nuclear fuel is sufficiently depleted, if they don't surprise us. A second time, that is. Still, we may have to move in close, bluff a crash with the shuttles, to close the cage tight."

"Right, bluff," Stearn replied. Fisher wore human skin once more, his traditional pale pink. Too bad, Stearn thought. The green glow had been pretty hip, and he'd had high hopes Fisher would outdo it when he changed again. But Fisher had resumed his old appearance, with the short shock of dark curly hair, angular pale body, and the rest strictly *Homo sapiens*. Well, almost. When he caught Fisher in just the right light, the skin appeared bloated, less like real skin and more like a vacuum suit thrown on. And once since they'd started their work in the shuttle hold, Stearn had spied a green-tinged glint from the corner of Fisher's eye when he'd rubbed it.

As they walked to the last arm, Stearn decided to satisfy his curiosity. He knew that something had precipitated Fisher's sea change, and he had already checked where everyone had spent the breaktime. "You're lucky to have her."

"I don't have the dragon just yet," Fisher said. "And luck will have little to do with it."

Hmm. His mind sure wasn't on Captain. Still, Stearn would feel better if he knew how the social forces on board were now arrayed. Just as the magnetic fields might hold a dragon, the social forces might hold the crew together. Blunt or oblique, which approach? In the past he had always been blunt, but his time with

Devereaux had led him to appreciate more subtle strategies. That was the only way to beat her at board games, which he managed once in a while. He knew he had to keep her interested.

He asked, "Now that you've seen them, any more ideas about the dragon origins? I mean, are they machines made by someone, or do they mate, give birth, piss, and shit, all the stuff that life does?"

Fisher snorted. "Technology blurs the distinction between living and machine. I prefer to think of this as a problem of artificial, or natural. There are several points in favor of an artificial origin. First, we still see no evidence for an ecosystem."

"Not all of Papa's sensory apparatuses are back on-line."

"Granted, but I don't think we're going to see an ecosystem even when they are back up. The second point is that SS Cygni has not had an accretion disk very long, astronomically speaking. The current disk isn't even that old. These stars accumulate matter, hit critical temperature, and go nova every few hundred thousand years, and this destroys the disk. No way something like this evolves over that kind of timescale. Not in the disk anyway."

"You sure? There's enough energy here to drive things at a wicked pace."

"Unlikely. You see, how do you even start? I have no idea what sort of matter constitutes the dragons, but it's either nonconventional—not a naturally occurring substance, a nanobuttressed alloy for instance—or not even baryonic. The implications of either are significant. This is probably why the Biolathe brain really assembled this mission. Our ability to manipulate space-time provides us with cheap energy for massive engineering projects. Earth doesn't really need fusion-powered dragons for space construction."

That was an interesting notion, but Fisher was revved up pretty good, and it was time to nudge him back onto the oblique orbit Stearn had in mind. Devereaux had reminded him that some of the best games were social. "So why do *you* need dragons?"

Fisher started to speak, stalled, and blinked. He raised a long finger to his temple. He tapped his head and started to smile. "Because it feeds this," he said. "Without this, I'm nothing but an animal, eating and breathing and defecating, just as the blind watchmaker of evolution pieced together over billions of years. But through my curiosity, I can transcend my own origins, become something more. If not now, then someday. The things I discover change me into something more."

Stearn laughed. He tried to hold it in, but he just could not help himself.

"What? What is it?" Fisher's finger crawled down from his forehead, and his smile faltered. It flashed back with the infection of a laugh as he asked again, "What?"

Stearn laughed harder. He was so earnest, so blind himself. Fisher . . . Fisher was so . . . *full* of it!

Fisher shrugged and turned away to another arm of the shuttle.

"No, wait. I'm sorry," Stearn said, taking a deep breath. "I'll tell you."

Fisher spun back, green glinting from his left eye. "Yes, what is it?"

"You're shitting yourself, because you're just like me."

Fisher's head reared back, reminding Stearn of the surprised snakes he'd seen once at a party when a dancing Medusa chick had lifted her arms suddenly. "I'm not like you at all. What do you mean?"

"You're always looking down at me because I play a lot. Sure I play. I have more fun because I know exactly who I am and what I'm about, and my quest is one of amusement. You're the same, but you cloak your motives in transcendent language. But it is simple. You need dragons because you need toys to play with."

Fisher's smile faltered at once. "That's not it at all! It's so much more. It's of fundamental importance to our understanding of our place in the universe."

"I'll give you at least long odds on that, but that's not your real motivation. If the dragons were a fluke of nature, doomed to destruction in a cosmological blink of the eye, and of no relevance to the human race or any carbon-based biology, you wouldn't walk away, would you?"

Fisher broke the stare he'd fixed on Stearn to pace around the shuttle arms, making him appear a busy little web maker. "There's no way the dragons could be a fluke. I cannot believe that. The reasons are myriad." Fisher's fingers flew into the air as if pulled by strings. "I can count off sixteen without trying. Shall I?"

Stearn squinted, but still counted only ten fingers on Fisher's splayed hands. Disappointed, he said, "No need. Let me ask you another question. You're back with Captain again, I gather. Tell me, why do you need her?"

"Lena?" Fisher's web-building course stopped and his fingers fell to scratch his cheek. His eyes darted among the spokes of the shuttle arms.

"Are the reasons myriad?"

Fisher nodded. "Yes, of course they are." His hands went up. "I can count them, too. Shall I?"

"Yeah," said Stearn. "These you can count."

"Fine. I will." Fisher waved an extended finger like a conductor leading an orchestra. "She makes me exercise. She challenges me to be my best. She knows how to run this ship. She has the same goals on this mission that I do, even if she doesn't appear to at first glance. She—look, this is moronic. Is that enough? We have work to do."

"Yeah, that's enough. But let me tell you a few of the reasons why I love Sylvia: the little sound she makes in her sleep just before she rolls over, the glances she sends my way when she's in the middle of something else that lets me know I am in her thoughts, the way she lets me be myself without trying to change me, the smell of her hair, the heat that rises to my cheeks when she is in the same room as I am, the way her brow knits when she loses herself in something, and the fact that sometimes that something is me."

Fisher stared back, unblinking, and worked his jaw before he spoke. "Such things don't make for a lasting relationship. They'll just interfere with our work here. I won't have that. I suggest you get some distance, Jack, or you'll jeopardize us all."

Right. Stearn was a whole lot more afraid of Fisher's yo-yo relationship with Captain jeopardizing things than his own handyman duties. He said, "I'll do my job just fine, Dr. Fisher. I work as hard as I play. But I want you to think about something, a piece of advice from an expert game player. A bluff will fail unless you're willing to carry through. Are you?"

"I'm willing to do anything," Fisher said easily in response. He paused for a moment, as if considering, then nodded to himself abruptly. "Yes, anything. Now, let's get back to work."

Henderson squatted in his biolab before the mechanical core of the console tank—all the biologicals in the room had been used—and inspected his design one last time. He said, "Execute," and prepared to walk over to the empty diamond vat.

"Safety override engaged: insufficient discretionary biomass available. Program terminated," the computer said in an even gender-neutral voice; Henderson had disabled Papa's personality from his console.

"But I need it!"

"Override intact."

Couldn't this machine's fuzzy logic wrap itself around the idea that this lab was in a thin, shimmery bubble floating above God's own burning bush? Any breach of any system could kill instantly—they'd exercised their redundancies. He had to have a more durable body. Evolution, which Henderson stole liberally from, often made a body capable of attracting mates also quite vulnerable. A brilliant peacock that could still avoid predators had to be top of the line.

But he was no longer employing that strategy. It was time to screw the looks and invest heavily in armor. Lots of armor.

Damn Fisher for talking him out of the little bioreserves they had available. The exobiologist had even wasted it on nothing more than cosmetic alterations.

Henderson stroked his chin. Where could he liberate more biomass from? He didn't need much. Certainly he could cannibalize nonessential organics like chairs, toilets, clothes, and the like. He could even make do without biologicals as long as he had the means to shape an exoskeleton. There was plenty of building material onboard. He would just have to fetch it himself.

He started for the door, but Captain Fang's voice stopped him.

"Mr. Henderson," she said. "Please join me on the bridge. My fighting chair needs adjustments but Papa cannot see anything wrong with it."

First Fisher, now Fang. He didn't like this hierarchy, but that was the way things would be for another quarter millennium. Slave, fix my skin; slave, fix my chair. Someday he would be the master of those around him.

Walking to the bridge, Henderson scanned the diamond ribs of the hallway, counted the fish crawling along the bony surfaces. He fancied himself a white blood cell in a giant vein with red blood cells, the fish. How many fish for a layer of skin that could block a rad per hour? Then again, perhaps passive shielding was a dangerous way to go with all the high-energy particles in the environment—they would decay in such skin and pass on a potentially even more deadly torrent of secondary particles. Fisher's body redesign suggested a way to build active shielding into a body, but it would not be nice to live with. Maybe he should go the opposite way, build maximum redundancy into a small body with a minimal cross-section. It really depended on what the threats were. Should he design against radiation, temperature, or vacuum?

The valve—portal—onto the bridge opened to reveal Fang squatting unstably on the deck, two fingers providing a third point of kinetic support, as she squinted at the cushion fat of her chair. The chair was a monster, and would easily supply Henderson with all the biomass he needed. Maybe he could talk her out of it if it were sick. . . .

Fang turned her skin-covered skull toward him and worked the jaw. She was making words, saying something. It was: "Don't just stand there. Lend a hand."

Henderson contracted and relaxed sets of muscles in his legs, leveraging the leg bones into steps. Fragile life, in a fragile eggshell, bobbing above an open flame. A frog in a pot of heating water. Instead of aiding in this endeavor, or developing a safer body, he should be finding a way to jump out, to force them to leave. Maybe he could engineer a minor crisis that would make them consume their remaining resources, and leave them no choice but to leave?

Why had he not realized the *mortal* danger this mission posed? More importantly, why had he not yet acted on that realization?

His jaw moved. His eardrums pushed the bones in his ear, which turned into electrical signals his brain could interpret. He had said, "What is the nature of the problem?" The safe, hierarchical thing to say. Avoid the immediate reprimand, but remain at the risk of later death when the dragons pried open their shell.

"The fighting chair's growl normally massages my lower back quite effectively, but today it's just irritating me," Fang said.

Electrical activity in Henderson's brain opened the flow of

information from his embedded biochip. In his mind's eye the chair's anatomy revealed itself in endlessly detailed cross-section. He pushed his hand under the chair's wide arm and plugged his finger into the diagnostic port located in its left armpit. More data danced into his head through the conduit running up his arm.

Please be sick, Henderson thought.

His jaw moved, his lungs exhaled, vocal cords tightened, and he said, "The chair looks healthy."

"See that, daughter?" Papa said. "What did we tell you?"

The captain twisted her facial muscles into a pattern that Henderson read as perplexity. She said, "Something's wrong with it. My back hurts."

Henderson unplugged his finger and bent close to increase his ability to see fine details on the chair's surface. The hide felt warm and springy when he touched it, and there was no discoloration. "Your chairbeast is healthy."

"See," said Papa. "Our own diagnostics are fine again."

Fang vibrated her lips, creating a humming sound, an indication of thoughtfulness.

Henderson shook his head, but stopped when he thought of his brain sloshing around in his skull. He needed some kind of drug to relieve himself of this morbid biomechanical perspective he'd developed. He said, "Perhaps the problem isn't your chairbeast at all, but you."

"Me?" A sharp edge lived in that syllable, a suspicion that he thought her fallible.

We're all machines and we can break, he thought. "We're human and we sometimes suffer injury," he said.

"I don't have time for an examination and I'm not letting you poke that finger of yours in me, understand?"

"Perfectly," he said. "I was simply suggesting you lift your uniform and let me inspect your back."

"It won't take too long?"

"Of course not."

"Fine," Fang said.

The captain turned away from Henderson and raised her arms. Henderson watched her elbows wiggle from side to side, trying to understand how the motions moved her hands to undo the buttons on the uniform. The pull of the muscle on the strings of the tendons on the levers of the bones, dancing like the programmed needles of a tattoo machine he'd seen in a historical drama.

Finally she slipped her hands back and tugged her shirt free from her pants.

"Let me do that," he said. "You might strain a muscle and make it worse."

"I'm fine," she said, her voice distant and echoing off the walls of the bridge. Her hands lifted higher and at the same time crawled the white fabric into bunches revealing an expanse of white skin.

But not completely white. There were greenish blue patches, six of them, three along each side. Fingers appeared to have broken the capillaries under skin, the hemorrhaging manifesting as bruises. On a finer scale there were tiny puncture marks. Insect stings? Impossible. Something more directed, certainly, right where the bruises were.

"Well, see anything?" Fang asked.

Too much, too much, Henderson thought. He thought about saying that everything looked normal, but Papa had certainly noticed and would speak up if he said nothing. He feared that anything he had to say would raise the tension onboard and place his life more at risk. Still, the facts could not get him in trouble, could they? "You have"—*translate*, he thought—"bruises."

"Bruises?" To his surprise and immense relief, Fang smiled. There was more in that smile than her normally cool professionalism would show, but in a flash it was gone. "Well, that explains things, doesn't it?"

"Your system will clear them up in a few hours, but there's something else—"

"Thank you, Mr. Henderson. That will be all."

Henderson decided not to press it. The captain didn't seem to want his distractions, and in truth he didn't want her to be distracted.

He needed to do something, something other than ruminate on every bit of mechanics in the human body and the way they were machines that could fail. Drugs were the wrong way to go. He needed positive action.

Then he had it.

On the walk back to his lab, he took off his scale jacket and tied the arms to fashion a bag. Whenever he came across a fish swabbing the deck, he plucked it up and tossed it in.

Insufficient discretionary biomass, my ass, he thought. A little dust never killed anyone, not even on a spaceship.

Curls of flame rose and rippled, dropped and dissipated, in a vast dance more regal and powerful than that of any sea Fang had before sailed upon. The swirling churning of the disk mixed with the waves bouncing back from the distant inner and outer edges making a choppy, uneven surface to the bowl of this sea. Spiral shock patterns would appear, persist, and vanish again all in less than an hour. Pillars of plasma twisted into the sky, riding the magnetic fields twisting out of the "disk spots" before plummeting back into the maelstrom at some distant point.

Through this all soared the *Karamojo*, like some flea on a dog's hairy ass.

"Where have they all gone?" Fang said to no one in particular, although everyone else except for Henderson was on the bridge watching the panorama in projection around them.

"I was afraid of this," said Fisher. "They can dive deep where we can't follow. Without an easy way of driving them out again, we must hope they will surface."

"They'll have to, won't they?" asked Stearn. "Even I can stay in a hot tub only so long."

"Perhaps we could use our own lasers to raise the temperature locally," Devereaux suggested. "There must be some level they can't take. Or we can go into the inner disk regions, where the thickness and opacity drops, but the temperature rises."

"I think we may have to drop right to the surface and scrutinize an area closely, and then expand our search bit by bit," Fisher said.

"It's too huge!" Devereaux disagreed. "And we'll lose what little we can afford to ablation all too quickly. This isn't the ideal system to have to prospect for raw materials."

There followed a discussion of dragon thermodynamics, laser cooling, and disk opacities, and Fang didn't care to pay attention to the technical details. Instead, hardly blinking, she watched the licks of flame as they broke open revealing the empty structures below. Papa's personality, while based on a human identity, nevertheless processed most tasks using brute force algorithms similar to those running his underlying autonomous routines. With enough speed you didn't have to be clever. While his image-recognition algorithms excelled with well-known environments like the ship and the faces of its crew, Papa searched for dragon sign bit by bit amidst the fiery cauldron. A sharp-eyed human could sometimes still do a better job in an unknown environment, one of the justifications for their presence on board. Fang intended to take advantage of that slim advantage to make her mark on this mission. Or at least to smudge out the bad mark she had already made.

She would not think of her moment of hesitation. She would not.

The conversation ebbed and flowed around her like waves. She was a rock. When the hours dragged on, she snorted an ampoule of Alert, and ordered her eyes to continue to dance. She didn't let herself think about what they would do if the dragons had no need to surface. The disk was so huge that she maintained her optimism. This place was not homogeneous; it had variations in elemental abundances, discontinuities in magnetic field and viscosity, all sorts of things that might constitute "good" feeding and "bad" feeding to a dragon. Or weather. Or something else completely alien to her.

"Where have they all gone?" she occasionally muttered until not even Papa responded. Stearn and Devereaux left for an hour, then returned, her hair damp as if from a shower, his hair covered by a Havana Marlins baseball cap twisted sideways. After another hour, they left again. Fisher stayed with her the whole time, saying little, working at a console by the couchbeast. That made her feel good that he trusted her powers of perception, and that he wanted to stay close.

When she was a girl, she had Polaroid corneas that let her watch the sun's—Tau Ceti's—reflection in the dancing waters around the Pouting Archipelago where she grew up. On several occasions she watched them for hours, the sizzling light more living electricity than reflection. Below were the shallows and the deep, dim background supporting the electricity. She would watch until the patterns seemed sensible to her, until her mind reached a state in which she imagined how to reassemble the motions of the water into all the disturbances that had caused it, from the gravitational tug of the moons and sun, to the happy splashing of a newborn being carried by his mother from an exclusive birthing lagoon, to the ponderous undulations of a pack of trench-dwelling leviathans. All the information rested there in the superposition of the dancing waves, impossible to recover in a computational Hubble time, impossible to recover given the chaos living in such systems. But the girl Lena would watch until her mind twisted the electricity into shapes, things, scenes that revealed something she believed to be True. Probably none of it had been real, but she fancied that it had trained her to assemble patterns better than that of the average person, and perceptual tests that had landed her in the captain's chair had confirmed her notion. She believed she had learned from the things she had seen, true or not.

Once in those waves she had seen the quiet struggle of a monkey bird caught in the stringy maw of a vampire weed, the bird bobbing on the surface, surprised as the seaweed tangled it in its talons and began to sink, pulling it down to drown before being consumed. Just as the bird could not breathe, neither did Fang breathe, nor blink, and she stayed with the bird through the long minute to the end, finally gasping with release when the scene came to its inevitable conclusion and the weed's tendrils slid down the tiny throat to invade the flesh through the soft tissues of the alveoli. Her imagination, she was sure years later, but she could recall just how those last bubbles had rolled out of the monkey bird's mouth. Another time she had seen the kind face of a bearded man whose eyes twinkled like stars. It was a wise, living face that held all the secrets of the world, until suddenly he winked at her and vanished into a million streaks of light, nothing but the falling wave crests. A timeless instant of superposition there, gone in a flash. She remembered thinking, *So that was God. He looks happy for being dead.* . . .

Only a few of the old religions had survived the biological revolutions of the twenty-second and twenty-third centuries. Judaism crept along steady as ever, and many Buddhists saw little difference after the Genetic Age. Widespread Christian and Islam-based faiths had the most to lose, their threat of hell gone and their promise of heaven undermined: They fought like devils. First came the battles about changing the human genome, the "made in God's image" thing—man turned out to be a better designer than God, finally, in the end. The religious leadership made their positions clear, and dug trenches that stalled many avenues of research for decades, or more. Off-world colonies, independent by virtue of distance, exploited the niche and flourished by peddling immortality. The next battle shattered faiths and toppled governments. When everyone stared into the abyss, few chose the promised afterlife to the demonstrable benefits of the immortality option. The faithful died out, recruiting fewer and fewer in subsequent generations. What organized religions remained were more philosophical and ethical systems than anything relying on the supernatural. Few doubted that man had become his own god. Still, there was questing for meaning, perhaps more desperately than ever, but tempered with the patience of an unending future stretching ahead. Fang's grandfather had led a quiet life of Taoism until the universe had swallowed him. She had seen the face in the waves after that, and had somehow felt less alone afterward, although now she discounted that she'd seen anything but the hallucination of a suggestible young mind.

The human mind found patterns in everything, faces in everything. It was a survival advantage selected for, even if it was not perfect. Better to jump at nothing sometimes than miss the one time something really was there. Surprising the shy and easily startled cats on board was a regular reminder of this trait.

Today something in her mind clicked as she watched the disk, the way that a ship schematic could sometimes appear an unintelligible tangle of colored vectors before crystallizing into a three-dimensional vessel full of balanced form and directed purpose.

"My god," she said. Dragons were *everywhere*.

They flitted deep in the disk, showing starry flashes of themselves, their laser signatures. The colors shifted hues for some unknown dragon reason, but she could follow them as part of a pattern. She made out individuals with more difficulty, but she could do it. They would fade deep below, but they would emerge high enough in the photosphere to flash every thirty seconds or so. Like lights on a silvery Christmas tree, the dragons made the disk their own.

"What is it?" Fisher asked abruptly, his face before her face, breaking the spell.

Fang stood, gently pushing him out of her view. She looked around, blinking, trying to recapture that peculiar mental state she had achieved. Her head bobbed around, birdlike, as fear welled up in her throat, fear that she had lost the vision.

But then the dragons' disk was there around her once more.

She smiled, holding her hands out as if to catch falling snow, and spun slowly. "I can see them, Samuel. The dragons. There are so many of them. So many. My god, it's full of dragons."

Fisher was silent for a moment, then he grunted. "*I* can't see them. How can you see them when *I* can't see them?"

"Yes," Papa echoed. "My thoughts exactly."

To Fang it was like hunting the lion, seeing through the lion's eyes, feeling its hate. The dragons had heard the explosions, fled the shockwaves. They *knew* that something novel, something dangerous, had entered their world. They were in a tizzy.

"I see flashes in the fire," Fang explained. "Sparks if you will, except the sparks are not random. They're dragon sparks. You have to defocus, see as much of the disk at once as you can, and let your brain sort the signal from the noise."

Another pause, and then Fisher said, "I think all the Alert has got you hallucinating. Before we drag everyone back here, let's see if Papa can verify this."

Fang let her eyes dance over the disk, pleased at the way the patterns were taking root in her awareness, gaining complexity, richness. Why the patterns? Feeding? Territories? Or just a trick of the mind? She tried to find one string and follow it, like trying to listen to just one note from one clarinet in a thousand symphonies. What could she point out to Papa that he could follow? She shifted through the patterns, shifted from pattern to individual spark, as best she could, looking for something to point at. She was afraid that if Papa narrowed the display to a small area she would lose the spark without the reference of the pattern.

"We're sorry, daughter. We still don't see anything."

"They're all right there, damn it!" Fang reined in her voice to keep out the shriek of frustration. She recalled the few times she had been the first person she knew with a new body modification. The very few times. The only remarkable time, to her anyway, was during her teen-age experimental phase when she had done the daring thing, to her anyway, of adding fairy wings. They were fragile-looking, but tensile-steel strong, and what no one else knew looking at her was that she could feel distant lightning through their antenna action. Not the light flashes, but the distant radio bursts. She would stand on the beach and her playmates would grow bored with the waves and leave, but she'd stay to watch the beautiful, invisible storm reflected off the ionosphere that they could not see.

Sparks, so many sparks. Then, as she shifted to a string of dark olive—although all were mere shades of fire, the dragon revealed itself to her, a bulb that didn't flash. A dark wiggling ball that bobbed in the curls. Fang locked on, twisted her body, and shot a finger out, arrow straight. "There," she said. "Look there, Papa."

"We have it," Papa said.

"Where?" asked Fisher. "*Where?*"

The disk warped around them as the *Karamojo*'s instruments focused on the area Fang had pointed out. After the image had been contrast-filtered, piped through a pseudo-color sieve, and sharpened with a pixon algorithm, the dragon flashed as clear and brilliant as a diamond. Papa added charts, scales, and explanatory captions in bright yellow type that stood out well against the reds of the disk and the greens and purples of the dragon. None of the colors were true, more like cartoons to draw out the subtle hues of a blazing white oven with too many photons of every energy.

"This dragon isn't like the one spotted by the probe, even allowing for the poor resolution, nor like the vast majority of the dragons we flushed from the disk," Fisher said after a long moment.

Fang was sure he was right, but she hadn't paid the kind of attention to them that Fisher had. She wasn't yet sure what he meant. "Take us closer," she ordered. "Maintain a position fifty kilometers up."

Her weight shifted with acceleration, and she absentmindedly sat down in her fighting chair, which had noticed her mood and was now growling low and steady. The dragon image stayed in the same dimensions, filling an entire wall of the bridge, but the details sharpened as they approached, but only so far. The hot plasma made the dragon shimmer like a mirage, occasionally wrapping tongues around the creature as if tasting it.

As their orbit approached closer to the disk midplane, the gravity lessened. It remained high, however, only a twenty percent decrease; the disk flared to over a thousand kilometers thick at their current radial distance this far out from the primary.

From the scale Papa had superimposed, she deduced that the serpentine form was nearly two kilometers from tip to tail, but it rolled in and out of a tight corkscrew, making the length somewhat difficult to judge. The creature was segmented, but not with the annelidan segments of earthworms and rattlesnake tails, but rather interlocking and subtly asymmetric S-shapes that stacked diagonally, allowing the smooth twists that appeared so unnatural to her. The segments changed color among different shades of green, bluer then redder, from tip to tail and back again. The "head" and "tail" were distinguishable. The head flared out into a great leviathan mouth, spiked with scintillating, spherically symmetric mustaches from which lightning arced back, swirling around the segments, back to the distant tail. And then, regarding the tail, she knew what it was that Fisher had immediately noted: The tail sported a round bulb, some dozen meters across.

The dragon was swimming rapidly upstream, keeping a fixed distance relative to the hotspot. Where was it going? Was it shedding its skin, that bulb at the end? A living seed, like the bulb of a plant the shape resembled? A feature of gender? Or was it merely a subspecies, a rattledragon?

"Papa, could you please ask the rest of the crew to join us?" Fang asked.

"We have already done so, daughter."

"Thank you."

She was going to do this right this time. No mistakes. She was captain, and didn't have anything to prove by wading in, guns ablaze, and bringing home the trophy. She realized that now, that she didn't have to do things Papa's way. Her way would yield the same end result, but she would use the finesse that was her strength. Act she would, but with forethought, forearmed with hard data. Fisher would approve, she was sure.

Fisher was talking to himself at the moment. "That rear appendage . . . maybe that is what keeps this one so near the surface, not diving so deep and vanishing like the others. What could its purpose be? If it limits the dragon's range, why have it? Certainly the creature must endure the dwarf novae, so under these quiescent conditions it ought to be cold, if anything. It's odd."

Fang's grandfather had told her stories of Chinese dragons that lived in the skies of Earth. They would play with a ball, or a pearl, that represented thunder, and this was what caused the rain to fall.

Stearn and Devereaux arrived on the bridge, hand in hand. Their hands dropped, forgotten, when they spied the dragon.

Stearn jumped up and down—still seeming too fast in the higher than normal gravity—and crowed, "Yeah yeah yeah, we got one, we got one!" Devereaux was more subdued, but still managed to rapid-fire shoot four or five highly technical questions at Fisher.

Fang tried to follow, but it was much more boring than the dragon. Still, her attention had wandered and the first tendrils of a headache told her how tired she was from the concerted effort of the previous hours. She secreted analgesic into her bloodstream— that basic and useful a bodmod she did permit herself.

Loud, metallic footsteps rang in the corridor. Henderson? Where had he been, anyway? She hadn't seen him in hours.

A shiny bronze giant stepped onto the bridge, drawing even Fisher's attention. Henderson, if that really was him, now stood nearly three meters tall, head just below the ceiling, and appeared to be a perfectly proportioned statue with sculpted muscles and hard, fixed curls of hair. His face was a handsome mask, but without animation. An ostentatious metal penis hung down between his legs, unswinging despite its length. The knees and elbows bent as he walked, but maintained a firm metal cast. It was like watching mercury flow.

Henderson's head tilted down to look upon the projected dragon. "So you found one." His lips barely moved, revealing only a hollow darkness from which issued a thunderous bass.

"You know," Stearn said, "that is positively holy."

"Thank you," said the giant, "but please don't let me distract you."

"No problem," Devereaux said. "You're not quite ready for godhood."

Henderson said nothing, and showed no change of expression.

Fang had seen much more outrageous bodies. This one was tame, but still, she had to admit that Henderson had a *presence*. Not a captain's presence, mind you, but a presence nonetheless. She pulled herself straight up and squeezed the arms of the fighting chair. "Samuel, are you getting useful data from this vantage?"

"Yes," he said. "But the beast is quiescent, like the disk."

"In other words," Devereaux added with her head inclined toward Stearn, "we aren't learning anything new about its capabilities or limits."

"I followed," Stearn said.

They sat watching the dragon . . . graze. That was the word that came to Fang's mind: graze. How she could associate such a pastoral term with this inferno, she wasn't sure, but that was what the behavior felt like to her. *It's the scale of the waves here,* she thought. *The rarefied plasma, the size, everything is in slow motion.*

An hour passed.

The dragon continued its meanderings, paying the *Karamojo* little heed. En masse, the dragons had seemed in a tizzy to her earlier. Had she been mistaken? This creature was far from a tizzy state. Finally even Fisher seemed bored. Still, Fang hesitated, remembering what had happened before. The others cast her occasional glances. They were wondering when she would give the word to *do* something, anything, she knew.

Fang caught Fisher in a glance and they locked eyes. His eyes were somehow wrong, like something furtive hid in the shadows within, and he broke off quickly. This was dragging on too long. He would have blown up at her if not for their recent reconciliation holding him back. She knew then that it was time for action. Careful action, but sure action.

"Mr. Stearn, I noticed in your report that all the shuttles had been refitted to meet Dr. Fisher's specifications. I believe it is time for a field test under full power."

"Captain?" Stearn asked.

"Papa has been playing some war games between the refitted

shuttles and Fisher's dragon model. Have you seen anything here to change your plan of attack?"

"No, daughter. We ought to be able to bag this dragon in no time."

Fang looked to Fisher, who solidly met her eyes this time, a tiny smile playing on his lips. He nodded, imperceptibly. Her face blazed suddenly, and her heartbeat thundered in her ears.

"Cast the nets," Fang ordered.

TWELVE

*Angling may be said to be so like the mathematics
that it can never be fully learnt.*
—IZAAK WALTON

Papa hears her say, "Cast the nets," noting the unintended pun as he does just that. Like adrenaline surging through his blood, his expert system neural nets multiply through downloads into the shuttles. Other aspects of himself launch the tiny armada. Twenty-five shuttles—"skiffs," he prefers—drop from the *Karamojo* and fire-braking thrusts to rendezvous with the disk surface smoothly and holding pattern.

The gravity at the disk surface is smaller but not negligible. Magnetic forces help buoy the skiffs from sinking into the superheated plasma that would eventually melt even their hardened structures. The hardening will hold at the surface for a time.

"Papa, can you pipe local sensor feeds

from the shuttles into a comprehensible display for us?" Fang requests.

"Of course." Papa splits the image on the bridge's wraparound. The top retains their bird's-eye view of the action unfolding, processed and enhanced for maximum contrast. The bottom section shows a similarly processed optical view from the central skiff located at the rear of a forward-facing vee pattern. Icons with flashing telemetry indicate the positions of the other skiffs along with miniature optical views from each. Upward beamed communication lasers provide Papa with all the data. Papa beams back updates to all the skiffs and coordinates their movements.

The twenty-five subnodes know where they are and know where the dragon awaits. The vee relaxes into a crescent that moves to encircle the beast. Papa instructs the skiffs to power up their currents and build the strength of their magnetic fields. Surface drag and other interactions with the disk cause the skiffs to develop sluggishness in excess of their predictions.

"Real thing is different than practice, isn't it, big guy?" says Stearn.

The star dragon moves. There is a suddenness to its motions that indicates it recognizes something unusual in its immediate environment. The creature has not tried to move away from the approaching skiffs; rather, it has begun to circle, rapidly. Increased Zeeman-splitting means increases in the magnetic-field strength around it and Papa overlays a magnetogram in vivid purples on top of the optical scenes.

"Is it preparing to rocket?" asks Fisher. "We did not see any dragons start their rocketing before. Papa, watch for any kind of curling into the compact structure the rocketers had, OK?"

"Absolutely."

Fang says, "It doesn't look like it's trying to rocket. It just looks like it's throwing a fit of some sort."

The dragon swims in circles, twisting itself and its magnetic fields in veritable knots. The disk plasma churns, flowing angrily up and along the field lines. The dragon dives—not completely nor deeply—and comes back up with geysers of plasma. A firespout grows around the creature, a squall in the sea of fire to greet the approaching invaders.

"Increasing static leading to failure in local parity checks," Papa tells them. "The shuttles are assigning local communications to secondary status. We're running the show from up here and taking the time-lag hit."

"What's that?" Henderson asks.

Devereaux answers. "Can't beat Einstein. Light travel time between here and there builds in a lag that we can't beat. If we want the shuttles to act in a coordinated fashion they have to go through us. And we really need them to act in concert. No three shuttles alone can trap the dragon, and it's going to take more than four I'd bet."

"Oh come on," Stearn says, "we're not far away at all. The lag must be tiny."

"You want to play quick draw with me with an extra lag?" Devereaux challenges. "Especially if I can think faster than you to start with?"

"That true, Fish?" Stearn asks.

"Yes, I believe so. You see, I don't think they use blood or chemicals to mediate thought in any way, and the current speeds must be significantly greater than human neurons use."

Papa says nothing here, knowing that his connections are also faster than human. His brains use four different technologies, with only his human personality relying on human neural structures. He also has access to Fisher's dragon models where the implications of the observed e-m field-change timescale back up Fisher's statement and moreover indicate quicker processes than his own technologies.

The skiffs shoot forward into the maelstrom. The differential disk rotation makes it difficult for them to remain in position relative to one another, and the dragon-induced disturbance doesn't help. The central skiff image becomes impressive as the surface of the disk begins to rise into a towering funnel of fire. Glimpses of the dragon itself appear near the base.

"Thar she coils," says Stearn.

No one laughs. The business is serious, automated, and uncertain.

Waves akin to those of an Earthly sea emanate from the fire spout, which intermittently flares with light and heat released from magnetic reconnections. Energy is building there, but is it building faster than the net drawing close?

On the bottom display a clearer look: A great mass breaks from the choppy disk, rising in an arc. The segments slide forward as if the serpent is flying out of the disk. Plasma flows with it, only slowly trailing back along the disk fields, like water pouring unendingly from a high waterfall. The star dragon is a living Niagara. The coil then sinks, slowly, smoothly, its motions limited by its sheer scale. It is a great beast.

"The shuttles are nearly there," says Fang.

Indeed they bear down on the spot, adjusting their velocities and approach vectors in an ever increasing flood of communications to ensure that they are in the correct locations at the correct times with the correct fields. The outermost shuttles swing out and bolt ahead, extra chemical thrust launching them into space over the disk. They are the pincers and are responsible for closing the magnetic bottle.

On the bottom display there is no longer a distinct disk and a distinct sky. The dragon's corkscrews churn the local field lines into a froth and the plasma flies wildly along them. Visibilities diminish in nearly all wavebands, making sure dragon sightings increasingly rare despite the lessening distance. Does it work both ways? Is the dragon having difficulty spotting the skiffs? Will it dive out of sight and escape amidst the artificial storm it has created?

Papa maintains communications, adjusting the formation according to probabilities he is constantly updating on the fly. Already with new data he has busted Fisher's dragon model, slightly, and they are not yet fully engaged. But nearly . . .

"Casting the net," Papa informs Fang.

A moving electric charge induces a magnetic field. Electrically charged particles tend to move along magnetic field lines. Plasmas are seas of charged particles. This problem required an engineering approach rather than a closed-form analytical solution impossible to calculate on the fly, so redundancy and power were the order of the hour. The solution was brute force: Create a dense assemblage of converging field lines with too much power for a charged dragon to break through—field lines that could be manipulated into a moving cage.

The skiffs build the field around the dragon, struggling against the plasma that surges with them, dragging it with them rather than the other way around. The fields stretch, pull, jerk, sometimes recombining in energetic flashes, as the net is constructed. Like great invisble bungi cords they jerk back and forth, then reach deeper as the power cycles higher.

If they can box in the serpent first, they can pull in the far ends opposite the creature, drawing the net closed. Every spiraling course would draw it along the lines, into the denser parts of the net, where the serpent would be tangled, constricted, and ultimately forced back. Trapped like a djinni in a bottle, the skiffs in locked formation can then tow their catch back to the safety of the *Karamojo*.

Such is the plan.

"There they go," says Stearn.

The generators are powering up to maximum and the fields are making headway deeper into the plasma of the disk under where the dragon continues its maelstrom.

The feed from shuttle seventeen, starboard of the primary view, suddenly changes. Papa shifts the display to that feed so they can see the action.

A great shaft pierces the black sky, loops, and dives back. The trilateral head of the dragon is clear as it splays open into three petals, each adorned with a sparkling iridescent jewel, each an eye. Lightning sprays from the mouth along fine extended whiskers arrayed like antennae. Magnetograms indicate the dragon has pulled fields along with it. As they watch the fields build, merge, and explode in recombination: lightning and thunder of the disk.

"What was that?" asks Henderson.

"The dragon is attacking the net, weakening critical points before they can tighten," Fisher replies.

Papa says nothing. It is a good hypothesis.

The view from shuttle seventeen rocks despite the antijitter algorithms. A fiery tsunami has crashed into it—the wake of the dragon's descent back into the disk. The machine is damaged and breaks out of the pattern to return to the *Karamojo*. Still, they have secured a close-up view of the beast from its triangular head to the glowing onion-shaped bulb on its trailing end.

"Hmm," says Fang. "It looks like that little maneuver has gotten it past the net region. It's in the clear for the moment."

"Just for the moment," responds Papa. The simulated dragons in practice had not gotten this far. So, a challenge. That was fine, this was now *sport*. Papa squirts an updated plan to his skiffs, ordering them to shift formation to cover the escape vector. "Here, look here!"

The view now comes from shuttle nineteen, again with a bobbing motion too quick and uneven to be automatically corrected.

Papa says, "She's tangled in the field between nineteen and twenty-one. Seven and eighteen are converging to strengthen the net. She won't have an easy dive this time."

"Good," says Fang.

The dance of the hunt is on. It is a fine feeling.

The dragon twists its course to head downstream, accelerating.

"Swim good and hard," says Fang. "Swim deep, swim, swim, and we'll still be here after you."

Before Fang even finishes speaking, the dragon turns abruptly to twist back upstream. Its own fields are high and it brings a wave before it, a spout to meet its pursuers.

"Reducing field strengths," says Papa.

"No," says Fang.

"We must," says Papa, "or else the plasma will be channeled into the shuttles and wipe them out."

Even so, the reduced field strength is too much, too late. The plasma does not break up into a spray as it approaches. It is tangled, frozen is the technical term, caught in the fields coming upon them as part of the dragon's wash. The shuttles cannot reduce power sufficiently fast. Induction resists.

The coverging field lines pull them together.

Papa has the electromagnetic fields and their time derivatives, the phase space of the serpent and the skiffs, and their projected evolution. He has commands to issue, and the lag time to their implementation. He has no time left to actually think about the optimal course of action and his subnodes' independent-action algorithms in practice appear inadequate. He sends them escape trajectories.

The magnetic wave crests, carrying its superheated plasma. The converging shuttles shift powers to the icy cores of their superconducting shells that protect the sub-brains and repel external magnetic fields. Such a defensive posture is insufficient with the star dragon itself pushing the wave. Papa's bird's-eye view picks out the beast surfing the plasma flowing down upon the shuttles. Skiff is indeed a better word, since it conveys smallness.

A radio burst erupts from the dragon. It is more powerful in the plane of the disk than upward toward the *Karamojo*. Stearn is looking in the right direction to see the signal on the monitor spike and says, "I think that's a roar of triumph."

Papa concurs and orders core dumps to be beamed in a cascading pattern outward from the dragon. The data will prove useful even if the skiffs do not escape.

"Look at that, will you?" Fisher says.

The dragon is riding its wave, a superheated bulge pushed along by the twisting magnetic fields. Of the four central shuttles, three are clearly out of the way. The fourth, shuttle nineteen, does indeed appear to be a skiff before a tidal wave of flame. The wave is not supersonic, and the shuttle rises with the approaching material. It moves, or tries to move, but the wave is directed and works against its best efforts.

The dragon's great trilateral heat splits its maw to swallow nineteen. The video feed surrounding the bottom half of the fly bridge shows the abyss of the beast's throat and those waving, charged antennae. The picture breaks up into static and Papa drops the top view to full screen so they can watch the shuttle vanish into the dragon and the dragon vanish with its wave.

There is one final radio burst as the disk's wicked differential rotation shears smooth the disturbance. The dragon reappears, far from the retreating shuttles, and resumes its business.

Glorious, Fisher thought, feeling himself warming with the dragon's display. He snorted through flared nostrils, holding his flushed face still. It would not be politic to show his current feelings here on the bridge.

To confirm this thought, he flicked his gaze toward Fang's ashen features. Caught in a stoop half-standing, half-sitting, her white-knuckled fingers gripped her chairbeast so tightly the creature whimpered. "Damn," she whispered. "What happened, Papa?"

A ghost-image of Papa's visage overlaid the wraparound disk. It gave Fisher the unfortunate impression of a man on fire. "One shuttle lost, one crippled. We're still processing the reports. In the meantime, we'll regroup and get back on the hunt."

"No!" Fang said, too fast. "Bring them back in, all of them. For now. We need to analyze the new data."

"Think we can bag it," Papa persisted. "That was a sucker punch, that's all."

Fang blinked slowly, and when she opened her eyes, she was looking at Fisher. He gave her a nearly imperceptible nod. She stood all the way upright, squared her shoulders, and ordered, "Bring the shuttles back, Papa."

"Aye aye, *Captain*," he said. Was that a pout in his voice?

Stearn and Devereaux were whispering about something, huddled together over a picture tank. Dark, knowing twins. Light from the tank reflected as a glare on their sweaty features. Fisher took a step closer. What could they find so engaging with all this going on?

"That isn't going to work, love," Stearn said through gritted teeth. He held his eyes wide open and unblinking as if he had transparent eyelids. He probably did. "You're *mine!*"

Devereaux said nothing, her eyes bulging slightly with the increased magnification she was using, her face a mask of concentration.

Fisher approached and looked into the tank. Like a barbecue pit, the tank cradled a glow, and in that glow moved tiny shapes . . . squatting down so that his eyes just peeked over the edge, he made out an armada of tiny green bugs swarming around a noodle. Red lines as fine as hairs connected the flitting bugs. The noodle slid between the red hairs.

"What—?" Fisher started to say when Stearn cut him off with a bark. Luckily his noise filters cut the decibels down to something tolerable. Some bodmods were essential enough to make the time to obtain. That one had saved him from months of distraction.

Fisher turned to Devereaux for understanding. Although a hummingbird smile hovered on her lips, the images before her completely held her attention.

Stearn and Devereaux both sat hunched over, their shoulders elevated. Then he noticed their hands, which were wrapped in amoeba interfaces and accepting manual input.

Fisher winced—they were playing a damn game. "I'm not surprised to see Stearn goofing off, but *et tu,* Dr. Devereaux?"

Stearn's upper lip crawled unevenly up his teeth into a lopsided grin. "We're both working a lot harder than you are, Dr. Fisher." He grunted and jerked his hands. "Mine," he said to Devereaux.

"We're running," Devereaux paused for a long moment while her hands moved in earnest, "interactive models of the dragon hunt."

Green bugs and noodles, of *course* it was the dragon hunt. He blinked away his misunderstanding and looked at their game again with magnified vision. After a moment, he flashed on the real thing in his mind's eye, which he preferred immensely to the noodle abstraction. "But Papa did that, didn't he? The star dragon just turned out to exceed his expectations." Magnificently, he added to himself.

"Ha," Stearn said. "You ever play a game against Papa? I mean a real game with rules and limitations, but with infinite room for creativity?"

"Of course. I have him run simulations all the—"

"A game, man!"

"No."

"Well, let me tell you something." Stearn seemed as focused on the tank as ever, his eyes big and unblinking, his hands dancing in the amoebae, but his voice dropped to a conspiratorial whisper. As if that would matter to Papa. "The Old Man talks a bigger game than he plays. He's, I don't know, mechanical. Stomps you the first few hundred times, then you start getting him. A game here, a game there, then more regularly. I mean, he's got a personality and everything, but it's a little more rigid than human. A little too predictable."

"Papa lacks the desperation to survive that evolution drives into every fiber of your being," Devereaux said. "He fakes it well, but you can find it if you look hard enough."

"In games?" Fisher asked.

"Absolutely," Stearn said. "What life's all about. Games are survival practice. We're bred for it. Evolution is just game theory in action. Hey there, Syl, just 'cause I'm talking to the man here doesn't mean you can sneak out so easily. Better try harder."

Sylvia said nothing, but her hands moved quickly indeed.

Fisher peered closer. "We just learned a tremendous amount about the dragons. You need to incorporate that into your simulation."

Stearn stopped biting his extended tongue and said, "We're probably four iterations behind your current model. Why not lend us a hand and analyze the new stuff and give us something realistic?"

He was going to do that anyway, he'd already decided, but he told Stearn that that was a fine idea.

"Samuel?" Fang called across the bridge. "Would you come with me, please?"

"Go on, man," Stearn said. "We'll work up some real strategies for the hunt. You make sure she's ready to make the hard decisions.

I think we'll have some. Those dragons got a healthy sense of self-preservation. They are Alive with a capital 'A.'"

Maybe he should reevaluate Stearn . . . or Devereaux, rather. He was probably just repeating what she'd said. She was the brains of the couple, it was clear. Well, except for maybe when it came to games, he granted. Stearn practiced those often enough.

Fisher stood up, turned, and walked into a wall.

"Excuse me," Henderson said down to him. "I was just watching."

"Um, right," Fisher said, ducking around the giant. The biotechnician was another one to consider after his entrance today. Why the sudden change? What did he know? Was he a wild card to be watched himself?

Lord, he longed to focus only on his beloved dragon once again. The dragons were right out there. With all the technology at their disposal, they should be able to reach out and just pluck one off the proverbial tree of knowledge, and bite deep. But he had already waited so long, the giddy height of this last act could stretch out to infinity, and perhaps like the moment before orgasm this would be better if prolonged. Even so, playing the crew felt confusing and unrewarding today. Still, he had to do it to make sure things got done right. Or at least not too wrong.

Plenty of time to make sure. The disk was as stable as it ever got, and they were learning more every minute about this dragon, which still showed no signs of diving deep. Now, why was that?

"Samuel, are you coming?"

Fang's voice stirred him from his reverie. Blinking away the stare at the display he'd fallen into, he asked, "Where to, Lena? Need to unwind? Need to spar?" He bent his head and put up his "dukes," as she'd called them.

"No," she said, turning to exit the bridge.

Shrugging, Fisher followed. He was in "good boy" mode—he

could do anything for the dragon, and he was proving it to himself. He should be working on the problem directly, adding the new data to his models, and he would as soon as Fang finished with him. Even Stearn appeared to be working on the problem directly at the moment. But after their failures in these initial dragon encounters, he dared not underestimate the importance of supporting Fang properly.

Fang walked quickly, her boots thudding into the defenseless ruglings with an authority that Fisher found appealing. Fisher once again trailed behind and admired the way her rear bounced to the rhythm of her steps. He had neglected his own needs too much, perhaps, and maybe in supporting Fang he would support himself. Some of his best ideas came at unexpected moments when the conscious mind fell under the influence of primitive drives.

Maybe it wasn't too late to have it all.

But he stopped himself from pursuing that thought. So far they had nothing but a few scraps of data on the star dragons . . . and probably had already left thousands of corpses. Or rather, she had. Life was too cheap in this century—that century they had come from, rather—even the most remarkable life. Life had become technology, and evolution swept away the less fit faster than ever, punctuated equilibrium timed to economic cycles. In the century they would return to would things be any different? He feared not.

He feared they would be worse.

He looked at Fang, at her fine body, as she strode along the corridor so self-assuredly in her only slightly wrinkled uniform. He stumbled along, his steps short and fast with the extra weight, feeling awkward and uncertain.

Was their failure so far her fault? Or the fault of the times they came from that guided her choices? Or had the Biolathe brain for its own arcane reasons given her special instructions?

Enough. He didn't have to think conspiracy every second . . . but what if he missed something he could have discovered with a little more effort? Perhaps right now he should pursue every thought as far as he could, lest he risk missing something. If he missed something, it would be a tragedy. Five hundred years, wasted.

Playing games, and thinking everyone else was playing games, was difficult. Single-minded obsession was so much easier!

Fang vanished inside her cabin, leaving the portal wide open in welcome. When he rounded the corner, she was already prone on the bed, her boots kicked off, her rump inviting him for a good life-affirming rut.

He smiled at that thought and, after closing the portal, padded forward.

Fang didn't stir.

Fisher dug his toes into his heels and pried off his own streakers. He came to the edge of the baffled waterbed and climbed on like a hunting beast. He was still smiling.

Fang lay there motionless, her breathing slow, steady, and deep.

Fisher reached out, intending to snake his hand around to cup her breast, and stopped. This was what he wanted, but all his wants right now had to be subverted to reach his goals. To do that, he intended now to make Fang feel strong. Secure. What would do that?

He moved his hand. He wrapped his fingers around her shoulder, rubbing its ball in the palm of his hand. He slid his body closer so that his arm rested along her side and his chest pressed against her back. He nuzzled her neck, gently. He flared his nostrils and sucked in air, smelled her sweat. It didn't excite him. Rather, in his current mind, he perceived a sourness in the smell that hinted at fatigue poisons and stress.

Fang made a small noise that came from deep in her throat, a noise halfway between grunt and hum. She didn't otherwise stir.

Of course she was bone tired. Hadn't she been watching the disk for hours while sitting perched on the edge of her chair like some hungry raptor desperate for a meal? He hadn't given it much thought at the time, except to be pleased that she was making every effort to make the mission a success. He'd been working, too, after all.

This is hard, paying attention to everyone else, he thought for the thousandth time.

Fisher pressed his fingers into her skin, massaging her shoulder. Fang rolled onto her stomach, and Fisher sat up and began to give her a back rub. Then, inspired, he recalled the hardchip routines that Atsuko had asked him to install fifty years—three hundred years—ago. They still sat unused in his motor-control biochip. He should have used them before, that night he'd given the extended back rub. Tonight would be easier work, on his hands anyway. He thought the command activating the chip, with his eye scrolled down the options, and activated *Shiatsu!*

Under their own volition, his hands danced a quickstep across Fang's back.

Fang made a sound of surprise, a happy sound if he intuited right, followed by a low, deep groan. "Yes," she whispered. "Do that."

Somehow she managed to fall asleep in just a few minutes despite the massage.

Fisher let the program run through its full hour duration, damning and praising Atsuko both in random moments. His unsatisfied erection lasted the whole time.

Stearn stepped carefully through the portal into Fisher's cabin. He hadn't been inside the place in something like a year, and just being there still felt taboo, even though he had been invited. Sylvia didn't look any more comfortable than he felt. Stearn kept his eyes moving and had the sensation of being in one of those games where the zombie-monsters are lurking around every corner. At least he'd turned the flames way down so they were just like funky, warm ruglings.

"I apologize for my tardiness. I had things to attend to," Fisher said.

Stearn grinned despite his uneasiness. He knew at least some of the things.

"You said you'd updated your model and that we needed it," Sylvia said. "You work fast."

Fisher smiled, but it looked forced. "As fast as I can. Really, I got lucky that some of my previous guesses were close to right. Then it was a relatively simple matter of making adjustments based on the new data."

Lucky, yeah. This guy was funny after all.

"Well, let's see it," Sylvia said.

"Very well," Fisher said, then gave Papa a simulation number to access. The flames rose up in the middle of the room with a twisting star dragon moving among them.

Stearn realized then what he should have realized a long time ago. Fisher had really just turned his cabin into a giant picture tank and the flames were in all likelihood not real at all. They were virtual, with a little help from some heaters and scent-dispensers. The guy was sneaky. He liked that.

The three waded hip-deep through the roiling disk to the dragon. This was really cool. The projected dragon was three-dimensional and visible in fine detail. Nowhere was the surface of the creature smooth—there were tiny ridges and curves and twists covering every segment, easily seen despite the shifting glowing hue. Stearn squinted, seeing detail on even smaller scales. Neat! And it reminded him of something.

"All right then," Fisher said. "Welcome to Star Dragon Anatomy 101."

Oh please, thought Stearn, not a boring lecture!

"Just hit the highlights," Sylvia said. "We need to get to work on strategy development as fast as possible."

He really loved that woman.

Fisher nodded and then started pointing to the various dragon features as he described them. "This model is specific now to the dragon we have been tracking. You can see the ball at the end of its tail. The rest of the animal appears consistent with the range of properties we saw during the swarm. First, the head and the eyes. The multifacets are probably involved in providing an extended wavelength range to high energies—extreme ultraviolet and even X rays. Three eyes makes a lot of sense in this environment. We have two eyes and mostly respond to events in a plane before us. We have to look up or look down. The dragon can keep an eye on the sky and much of the bowl of the disk, which is probably handy for spotting a developing outburst."

"I'm not getting a mind-mod to have trinocular vision," Sylvia said. "Other wavelengths can be easily handled by stretching a color palette, but I'll still need to look up and look down."

Stearn said, "I got that covered. There's a video game interface for a space-based shooter in zero-g that does it really well."

"Fine then. We'll steal that."

Fisher went on. "The eyes are probably not the most important sensory apparatus on the head. The assortment of whiskers around the mouth can be used to broadcast and receive radio waves at a variety of frequencies. In conjunction with the surface circulatory system they should also be good at seeing the electromagnetic fields in the area."

"Figured as much," Sylvia said. "How about movement?"

"The twists let it slide along the field lines, and the clever twists—see there"—Fisher pointed as the model did a reverse twist in the middle of its long body—"initiate shifts to other field lines.

There's a surface circulatory system that moves charge around to facilitate movements. Think about it like a complex integrated electronic circuit with strategically placed capacitors and inductors, transformers, rectifiers, and both AC and DC regions. The charge can be circulated to produce an impressively strong magnetic field of the dragon's own that can actively shield it from particle storms, just like the Van Allen belts around the Earth. They probably use it during outbursts, and if we could see them at all against the disk they'd look like ball lightning with shimmering auroras."

"You haven't gotten to the best part yet," Stearn said.

"Oh yes, the rocketing." Fisher shrugged. "This one can't, not with the ball on the end. I've checked the fields."

Stearn said, "Strip it off, show us anyway."

"Sure." He issued some commands to Papa. The ball vanished and the dragon began to coil. "See how the segments stack up in this new plane? The asymmetric pieces and their asymmetric surfaces match up just right. Plasma directed into these new super coils can be tightly confined and fusion can be induced. The plasma in the interior cavity can then be heated and expelled for propulsion."

The dragon rocketed above the disk.

"I knew it," said Stearn. "It looks just like our magnetic-fusion reactors, which tossed out symmetry centuries ago. They're only locally quasi-symmetric and confine plasma along a distorted helix, thus reducing collisional diffusion effects. The particle trajectories remain close to magnetic surfaces as long as there is one ignorable coordinate, which does not require circular symmetry if you think about it, and an approximate helical symmetry is plenty to do the job. Got to have the structures perfectly shaped, though, on millimeter scales."

Stearn realized that both Fisher and Sylvia were staring at him. Sylvia's mouth even hung open. "What?" he asked. "Fusion confinement has such weird-looking solutions of course I'm an expert on them!"

"Of course you are," Fisher said. "Well, the other essential item you must incorporate into your simulation is heating-cooling balance. That places a lot of constraints on the observed behavior. The laser action appears to be as automatic as sweating: Heating charges capacitors, which pump the populations as certain voltages are reached. I haven't figured out all the materials. OK, hardly any of the materials, but the global conservation laws must be met."

"That will have to be good enough for us," said Sylvia. "Papa, can you hook this model into the simulation we're building? The model with the ball on its tail?"

"Absolutely," Papa said.

"There's more," said Fisher.

"Anything that will affect perceptions that you're confident about?"

"Not if you put it that way."

Stearn kept watching the rocketing dragon. It was very cool to watch. He was a little disappointed that the fusion power seemed to be the same that they'd developed. It did occur to him that the solutions were very difficult to find and required very powerful numerical techniques. How could nature have found them? This wasn't the kind of thing you stumbled over even with a Hubble time worth of chimpanzees typing on keyboards.

"Come on, Phil," Sylvia said. "Time to hunt me down like a dragon."

In her quarters, Devereaux and Stearn sat cross-legged on plush ruglings simulating forest loam. It was dusk, and a campfire burned between them. Over its crackling came the twitterings of birds and insects. Devereaux counted the missing pieces that gave

away the puzzle of the artificiality: the lack of heat an[...]
the never-dying fire, the leak of April Scent from her bedbeast currently disguised as a pile of colorful autumn leaves, the misalignment of the stars (which were right for North America, but not at dusk in autumn), the—

"We going to do this, or what?" asked Stearn.

He was bent over the fire and its light reflected golden off his broad forehead. His eyes bored straight into hers, and their brown depths conveyed soulfulness. Where had he gotten that? His boy's twinkle had metamorphosed sometime recently. Had he discovered the seriousness of games at last? Or was she simply seeing in him what he tried so hard to deny?

"Yes, we're going to do it right now. You'll feed us the real-time disk as instructed, Papa?"

Papa's voice broke the night, sending a few leaves fluttering down. "Of course we will. Our reactions are much faster than yours, so we don't know why you think—"

"Thank you, Papa," Devereaux said. While Fisher had spent months simulating a star dragon, Devereaux had spent months simulating SS Cygni. She had also invested some effort in building a virtual environment and artificial senses to experience it with. She and Fisher had no idea if her senses had any analog in a star dragon, but they constituted ways of judging the immediate environmental parameters directly, and it seemed a natural expectation the dragon could do as much. Much of science, as in art, was simply finding the clearest way of seeing a new thing so as to understand it best.

She would not trust the day to the simple video games she and Stearn had already tried. Expecting Papa to develop a perfect hunting strategy based only on his own survival algorithms and limited data had been wildly optimistic. This thing they were doing was *hard,* and certainly that meant intelligence and a more worthwhile mission, didn't it? Intelligence was an advantageous trait in an organism in order to help it find food, or to help it avoid being food. The star dragons were demonstrating an ability to avoid being their food, in effect. There was nothing here to eat them in this naked ecosystem (nothing they had yet seen anyway, she was forced to qualify), and they appeared to consist of elements available in the plasma, so why intelligence? How could intelligence come about, even granting that the disk would present many challenges to survival?

Well, it was time to improve their own intelligence.

Devereaux picked up the visor-shaped interface from her lap. It was a black semicircle studded with warm and glistening circuitry, the veins throbbing slightly, and clawed feet that were the direct link. It was a crude thing by the standards of the time, but Devereaux was a problem solver. She didn't polish things up and make them look nice. She touched the ends to her temples while resting the center on the bridge of her nose, squeezed the feet, and winced as the needles sank into her flesh.

Tinkling bells assaulted her, and the whoosh-whoosh-whoosh of her own blood grew into a gale, swirling the white snow of static into drifts before her. The snow faded to black, and the bells and blood diminished in volume and became impossible silence.

With this kind of lousy entry, her interface skills would never get her a job with Stearn's preferred stim supplier.

Her skin prickled, stretched, and coiled. Opposite, the icy blue sky swelled light and heat to define "down." She swam in a cool wind, curling around a bright green line that kept her from falling. Deep, ringing sounds echoed back and forth on their passage through the disk. She sorted through them, identifying the major low chord of the accretion stream impacting the hotspot half a disk away and the minor high notes of instability-driven flickering.

She slid off her green wire in favor of another, tasting the sweetness of deuterium there (they'd assumed fusion-powered creatures would have a taste for heavy hydrogen isotopes). She spent several minutes reacquainting herself with her body until her thoughts directly became action, until this body was her body.

Too soon, the wire vibrated. All the green wires vibrated. She felt the invaders out there just as when she'd been a girl she could feel her docelot Gordian prowling around her bedbeast early in the morning. No problem—she'd just dive down into the muggy glow and escape them.

Then she fully appreciated the bulb on her tail, which floated like an overinflated balloon on a golden chain. Bloated, sluggish, she knew she ought to be able to move better than this! She sashayed her dragon ass around, but there was no better way to move with that thing there. Fisher would have gotten the characteristics of the thing right for this model or it would not be so debilitating. Why would a dragon have such an awkward thing? A warning, like a rattlesnake? Could it be used as a capacitor, a battery to power . . . what? That wouldn't make sense if the dragons could ignite fusion within their coils. It was so awkward. Why would . . .

But the invaders drew near, six of them. No, there was a seventh held back. No doubt Papa and Stearn thought it beyond her range (did this simulation have that close to right???) and would drive her that way with the others. So she immediately headed right for it.

She could move faster than the shuttles, even without rocketing and even with the damn bulb dragging behind, but she couldn't dive to escape and couldn't simply fly indefinitely away from them. Presumably the real star dragon couldn't, and the point of this exercise was the endgame that would follow such a chase even if they could.

She barreled head-on toward the lagging intruder, blitzing past the forward guard. Their fields were far from a net and she squirted through with little deviation from her course. As she bore down on the straggler, she watched it grow into a frizzy green mess resembling a sick bush, and then it was past, its "leaves" rustling in her wake.

What now? she thought. She had just shown Papa and Stearn that a forewarned dragon could disrupt a prematurely cast net. They knew that. They'd have to take a step back in the puzzle, put a few pieces together in advance, and begin the interlock from a larger distance. She swirled about to meet the new challenge they'd throw at her shortly.

In the low-frequency background rumble of the impact stream, a high-pitched thud resounded like a peal of distant thunder. That high a tone would not be a deep pressure wave, one of the drivers of the disk viscosity that moved plasma in toward the white dwarf. But what else carried that much power for her to hear it this way? Could it be the echo of their missiles? No, those were long damped. Sounds like this didn't just erupt through the disk. Maybe there was an instability growing in the secondary she hadn't been aware of? That thud had to signal something.

And those few moments of distraction were enough as pairs of the intruders approached from the compass points.

She corkscrewed down, building up buoyant forces, then sprang up at high velocity, angling toward a break between two pairs. As she approached, the pairs split and she found the green lines being drawn together. As their density increased, her progress slowed, then reversed. She bounced.

The other intruders had come about and tied the magnetic bag from the back side. She oscillated back and forth, trapped as long as she kept her currents and rode the lines.

"OK, you got me," Devereaux said aloud with her human mouth, the words tasting bland. Simulating dragon senses had to be done with analogs to human perception, but the multitude of potentially critical information required doubling and tripling of sensory input, giving the world a richness she appreciated all the more for talking. "Let's try that again and see if I can't find a way to wiggle out."

"You can try," Stearn's voice echoed to her distantly, heavy and out of place, reminding her of that odd noise.

The disk was such a complicated system that to expect it *not* to have even more inexplicable creaks and groans than a spacecraft was unrealistic.

Still, as they started another trial, the memory of that thud bothered her. The thud had been real, measured, and piped to her dragon-altered simsenses. She shook it off and concentrated on the next game.

She heard another deep, distant thud, but didn't let it distract her further. They would not catch her so easily the next time. And they didn't.

THIRTEEN

What we think and feel and are is to a great extent determined by the state of our ductless glands and our viscera.
—ALDOUS HUXLEY

Fang's eyes flashed open on darkness. Even before she had checked her eye clock, she had swung her torso upright and slid her feet off the edge of the bed.

She had slept over six hours!

The lights brightened in response to her movements and she leaned over to tug on her boots. With her optimized metabolism she normally slept four hours in every twenty-four, but this was not a normal time. "What's happening, Papa?"

Certainly he would have awoken her if there had been a change in their status, right? Unless Fisher had done something tricky again. She still didn't quite trust him, even though he'd given her the most terrific back rub. . . .

"We're pacing the beast. It's swimming merrily along, waiting to be hooked."

Fang stood, ignored the slight head rush, and stepped out the irising portal toward the fly bridge. "Where is everyone? What are they doing?"

"We're playing dragon tiddlywinks with Stearn and Devereaux in her quarters, and the kids aren't bad at the game, have to admit. Or maybe we're not as recovered as we'd like to think. Henderson's in his lab, moping as usual. Fisher is swilling coffee and fiddling around with his models, adding bells and whistles as we feed him more data. Damn good enough already, in our opinion. He's on the bridge now."

Well, no catastrophes, but she still felt uncertain about Fisher. He hadn't rested. He'd gone right back to work. Wasn't that reasonable for the workaholic? He was on her side now, right? They were working together, right?

Despite the physical glow of well-being his touch had engendered in her, she doubted. Better to have him there, with her, under her scrutiny. On the bridge as well as in the bedroom. She shook her head to clear away the dark thoughts.

Feeling utterly good and clearheaded, if a bit rushed, Fang swept onto the fly bridge. "Let's get this hunt moving," she called out.

Fisher glanced up from his console, the green glare of a wire-mesh model floating in his console casting his face as a ghoulish mask. He nodded and turned away without a word, or a smile, and became reabsorbed in the arcana of his science.

Some welcome, she thought. She popped herself down on her fighting chair without grace, and the beast let out an involuntary squeal. She gently massaged its arms until it quieted. "Papa, get Stearn and Devereaux up here."

"Yes, daughter. Mr. Henderson as well?"

"Did I ask for Henderson?" Fang snapped.

Smartly, Papa didn't answer.

Fang contented herself with watching the dragon, the prize that would legitimize her as a captain for all time . . . or at least another few millennia, she hoped. Then there would be some other chore to save her, and so on, and so on. It was a big galaxy. There had to be enough things to do to justify her existence, did there not?

The dragon was doing the same stuff, old already, and she became distracted. The bridge was a mess, she noticed. Bits of dirt, dust, and sweat coated many surfaces. The ruglings were anemic. She only saw two fish in the whole room, hardly sufficient to consume the debris where so many people were spending so much time.

The *Karamojo* was not shipshape, and that made her uneasy.

When Stearn and Devereaux arrived, unabashedly holding hands in an uncomfortably intimate fashion in which only their index fingers were hooked, Fang asked them point-blank if they could do better than Papa.

"Absolutely," Stearn said. "We've got creativity, the edge of life, the will to survive."

Fang ignored the Jack and stared at Devereaux. The other woman's eyes were a steady, serene brown as rich and deep as a tub of coffee. She shrugged a shoulder, the one farthest from Stearn. "Well, Papa's better trained now, I would say. We'll never match his reaction times."

"How long do we have until the next outburst?" Fang asked Devereaux.

Devereaux said, "Papa, give me COUNTDOWN from my monitoring program, plus the one-sigma uncertainty."

"Nineteen days, plus or minus a day and a half."

Devereaux's eyebrows crawled together in a deliberate manner that bothered Fang more than the way she held hands with Stearn.

"That sounds like plenty of time. Is something wrong?" Fang asked.

"Maybe." Devereaux cast off Stearn's grasp and sat down on the couchbeast. She bent over, rested her elbows on her knees, and peered into the display tank as she interfaced with the console, her fingers flying with commands. She said, "That's rather quicker than the last time I checked. And the uncertainty is too large. Something is going on."

Devereaux was sometimes too much a scientist for Fang's taste. As a captain, she only wanted to know what was necessary to get the job done. "But nineteen days means we needn't rush here. That's what I'm getting at."

Devereaux said nothing, but her eyes flickered back and forth as fast as her fingers.

Something suddenly touched Fang's hand, and she jerked it away, startled.

"Sorry," Fisher whispered, his voice close to her ear.

She felt his touch on her hand again. She made a fist and lifted her arms to her chest. Too late for him to make up now—he had had his chance when she stepped onto the fly bridge. She was Captain, and the game was afoot. Time to be professional.

"What's the big deal?" asked Stearn. "The system is hard to predict, you said."

Devereaux's fingers kept moving. "Not this hard. We're right on top of it and can monitor the accretion rate and the viscosity as a function of position, pipe it all straight into the model. Something is happening in the disk to alter the viscosity, maybe via the magnetic fields, or something is happening in the secondary to increase the inflow to the disk."

"Is the viscosity that important?" Fang asked.

Fisher answered. "All-important. The effective friction in the plasma is what moves angular momentum outward, and makes matter sink in toward the white dwarf. With low viscosity, everything piles up in the disk's outer edge and nothing moves. With high viscosity, which can be induced through dynamo-driven waves or thermal instabilities when too much gas amasses, everything starts flowing through to the primary and the disk gets hot and expands. That's an outburst for you. Boom, we're toast."

Fang knew this much, at least in these general terms, but still failed to appreciate why Devereaux was so excited. "So? We have nineteen days."

"That's a moving target," Devereaux answered. "Something is being introduced outside the parameters of the model I assembled. I made a very good model, I'll have you know. This will take some time to figure out."

Fang took a deep breath. Suddenly this seemed more like a science expedition than a safari. Well, there was glory in science expeditions, too. Of a mediocre sort.

"Excuse me," Papa said in uncharacteristically polite fashion.

"Yes, Papa?" Fang said, curious about what could be so unclear as to warrant uncertainty in bringing it before the human minds on board.

"There are these signals. Mostly low-frequency radio, but a few other parts of the power spectrum are correlated in time. They seem to be omnipresent background noise, perhaps some accretion fluctuation—we've been registering them since we arrived in system."

"So why bring them up?" Fang asked.

"First, I'm no longer sure they are mere noise. Second, we're picking up high-energy spikes, X rays, and even energies into the gamma regime, following the most complex, extended bursts."

"Where are they coming from?" Devereaux asked.

"That's the strange part," Papa confessed. "Most of the high-energy processes should occur near the primary where the accreting gas crashes into the white dwarf's surface, but these come from the direction of the secondary. Every twenty minutes or so, but that's only an average rate, and it, too, is accelerating."

Another mystery? Or another aspect of one of the mysteries already in their catalog? They didn't need mysteries. All they needed was to scoop up a dragon and keep it alive, or whatever it was—animate anyway—for the journey back to Earth. Hell, a dead dragon was probably good enough. Point A to point B and back again. Collect the admiration of trillions for fifteen seconds of fame. It would be enough to remain Important. Would it be enough to remain Captain another millennium?

"Feed me the data," Devereaux asked Papa.

"Of course," he said gruffly, "but we've run all the standard decoding algorithms and the like. If someone is talking, it isn't in a way we understand."

"We understand gamma rays," came a deep voice from behind. "Their ionizing touch can unravel our DNA faster than our self-repairing systems can put it back together."

Fang half-turned and saw Henderson, hunched over and looming in the portal like the Angel of Death come to claim his due. She wanted to say "Fuck off," but just turned away from him. Perhaps she should have given herself more sleep, even though the six hours seemed a luxury. It was difficult to keep her thoughts appropriately professional, and it was vital for her to do so now.

To Devereaux she said, "So is this important to us?"

Fisher answered. "Look to the dragon. If the dragon reacts, it matters to us. If not . . ."

As bidden, Fang looked to the dragon. The garish pseudocolors of the displays made it seem some green grass snake twisting on the coals of a barbecue pit, writhing in agony. She looked beyond that image, beyond the immensity of the disk. Did it swim more . . . intently? Did it seem aware of the radio noise and the gamma bursts? Did it seem aware of the *Karamojo*?

No. It twisted on. Staring at the thing for too long, Fang finally looked away, down to the white lapel of her uniform (the fiery disk burned everywhere else). The reverse image formed, and it was a bloody snake sliding over a green field. Her grandfather's fireside stories rose up to her unbidden, like smoke through time. What was the relevance of Chinese folklore here at SS Cygni? Nevertheless, it came back to her. Red and green were complementary colors, primary life colors, and possessed even greater power in combination. And there was a vast difference between snakes and dragons. Snakes were one of the five noxious creatures, clever but treacherous, associated with male virility except when they had triangular heads—then they were female symbols. In many of the stories the snakes could be coerced into handing over gifts of pearls, but such bargaining was not without great risk.

"Hey hey hey," Stearn said.

Fang blinked and returned her attention to the dragon. Instead of its steady, placid progress toward Dragon Nirvana or whatever place it worked toward, the creature was bucking up and down, splashing plasma like water in a bathtub. The scale of the beast made this a slow-motion wonder, but the violence in its motions was undeniable.

Shit, she thought.

Fisher stepped toward the display, holding his arms out in supplication. The projection obscured his hands at the wrists, and it appeared that his arms grew into the dragon. "It's okay, we're coming for you."

Things were happening. Too slow before, for too long, but now too fast. Not fast enough. Did they have nineteen days? It suddenly seemed like nineteen seconds. "Do you think it will dive?" she said aloud to no one in particular.

Fisher answered, "Yes," at the same time Devereaux said "No." Papa offered no opinion at all, which was probably the most telling.

Fisher spun toward her, pulling his hands from the dragon. The projection trailed off his fingers as if he had plunged his arms into the real creature and then withdrawn them, sticky with life. "We have a plan of action, a distracted dragon, and an unknown physical phenomenon—still distant for the moment. I'm willing to take a good gamble on this individual specimen. Devereaux will agree that the uncertainty in the disk's behavior makes it safer to act now rather than later. Am I right?"

Fang, feeling played, turned to Devereaux. She stared back for a long moment then nodded.

"Papa?" Fang asked. It was more than prudent to ask his opinion in this circumstance. While he was too gung-ho in many instances, and shaken by his recent trauma, his basic programming remained more than sound.

"Let's bag a dragon," he replied.

"Bring us closer and launch shuttles when optimal. I assume you've incorporated the results of your strategy sessions with Stearn and Devereaux?"

"Of course," Papa said.

The dragon swelled before them as the *Karamojo* reduced its thrust and descended. Papa changed the display mode to deep immersion so that space and the disk surrounded them, and they lost sight of even their own bodies. The dragon's trilateral head wagged erratically. Glowing plasma leaked from its gaping mouth, making Fang think of a swamp sucker draining land for colonists.

Tracers of electric blue mapped the course of the released shuttles, soldiers in their army. Two of them shimmered as they dove into the photosphere and were lost on visual, but still tracked on radio frequencies. Two others shot overhead, bouncing in a high arc. The rest swirled toward the dragon.

The dragon paid the robots no heed. Its head maintained a constant orientation with respect to the *Karamojo*, but its body careened wildly as it jerked itself back and forth out of the disk riding a spurting tower of plasma.

"Can it reach us here?" Henderson asked.

"Of course it can if it rockets," Papa said. "Without rocketing . . ."

"It can also reach us, just not quite as fast," Devereaux said. "There's a strong poloidal magnetic field that goes right out, and shifting into that field it can sling itself out like a bead on a wire. Centrifugal force will accelerate it to—"

"Keplerian velocities. At this radius that's nearly a thousand kilometers per second," Papa said. "But it is the differential velocity relative to us that is important. Given our projected trajectory—"

"It could reach us in about three minutes, if we let it," Fisher said. "I don't know why it hasn't tried to rocket away. It must be that ball on the end. If it prevents rocketing, it must serve some important function. Or we have a mutant, which seems doubtful. I wonder what that ball is?"

The blue tracers twisted, drawing elaborate orchid leaves as they converged.

The dragon ignored them and continued its collision course toward the *Karamojo*. Details sharpened as the distance decreased. Textures rippled into visibility: a mottled striation of greens in the annelid segments, facets in the trilateral chameleon eyes.

As usual, Fang could not help but focus on the eyes, her bane it seemed. She and Papa had spent long hours talking about the look of eyes, and not just the eyes of leviathans. Papa knew that a person's character and intent could be read in unmodded eyes and a surprising variety of designed eyes. He knew this not from his own experience, but from the false experience that had been fed into his own character as a function of building aspects of his original Hemingwayesque personality. He didn't understand it. Evolution selected for humans who could best evaluate the actions of their fellows, refining the ability to read nuances of stance, expression, and behavior. Hardwired pattern recognition of the most essential kind, and so hard to duplicate in neural networks at the level of discerning masked intent.

"Oh god!" Henderson shouted, a dull ringing sound like a giant bell being dropped to the floor. "That's a bomb! A bomb! It's shed its rocket engine into a bomb and its going to kill us!"

"I seriously doubt—" Fisher started, but then settled into a silence. He finally said, "Hmm, you could be right. We'll find out soon enough."

"Ooh, I *know* it's a bomb."

Could Henderson be right? It didn't seem very likely that Henderson's fears would be a perfect match to reality. But his guess struck her as more likely than what had been proposed so far. Perhaps they should retreat, investigate further. They had nineteen days, give or take.

Fisher said, "Shift the display to higher energies. Hard X rays, ten to twenty keV range."

Fang stopped a frown from reaching her face as the resolution of the dragon dropped, sharp edges dissolving into hazy blobs. The creature's eyes liquefied from hard reptilian to spectral, matching the new skeletal body. At these energies a few photons leaked through the beast, although its biology seemed immune from the effects of ionization.

"Yes, something dark in the ball, absorbing." Fisher spoke low, more to himself than to his crewmates. "Could be heavy fissionables for a trigger, collected over years, but if the dragon can generate fusion via magnetic confinement and laser bombardment, why would it need a trigger? And the shape seems less than optimal. No, upon reflection, I seriously doubt that it is a bomb. There are a hundred more likely explanations."

But he had started with "Could be," and "could be" was enough for her. Perhaps some dragons had started to grow them for their protection after the nuclear detonations in the disk. They had time to find out for sure without having the thing explode in their face. The dragon was already uncomfortably close, and drawing closer every second as the disk's rotation helped whip it out. "Pull back, Papa. Return the shuttles, too."

Her weight increased with the push of acceleration as they lifted away.

"Smart move," Henderson said.

"No," said Fisher. "We need to take the dragon now and determine the nature of the phenomenon. Much easier to study in our hold. We need the time in system with it."

"Things are going on we don't understand," Devereaux said. "Patience solves many puzzles. We should be prudent and wait."

"No," said Fisher. "We should be bold. We can understand it if we move now."

Papa had shifted the display back to lower frequencies and an extended dynamic range for better detail, all the while maintaining the image scale. Still, the image blurred and the three eyes merged into a cyclopean worm.

"Come now," Fisher said. "Let's go back in."

Stearn made a small grunt and nod, but when Devereaux glanced his way he nibbled his lip and didn't say anything.

Fisher said, "You're with me, right, Papa?"

"We think we can bag the dragon, but we'll follow the captain's orders."

"You hear that, Captain Fang? Papa thinks we can take the dragon, and he's smarter than you." Fisher paused for breath and amended, "Than us, I mean."

"Papa is no better than his input data—your data," Devereaux interjected, stepping between Fisher and Fang. "In fact, he's probably worse at imagining the outcomes of unique situations with unknown parameters."

"And you can do better?" Fisher challenged, looking over Devereaux's dreadlocks straight at Fang. He was daring her.

I'm responsible, Fang thought. When we get back, my future will be determined by my performance here, and I already have one black eye. No more hasty mistakes.

Fang met Fisher's stare with all the coolness she could muster, and said nothing, letting her order stand.

The dragon twisted back on itself and fell toward the disk. That strange ball wiggled behind, taunting them. That was fine. They'd return soon enough.

"Shuttles returning," Papa said. Indeed, the blue web was knitting itself out of existence.

"No," Fisher said. "Send them back out. We've worked it all out while you were sleeping. The dragon is within reach."

"No," said Fang. "Maintain distance, Papa."

"Yes," said Henderson.

Fang stood up from her chair, noticing that suddenly her feet felt sweaty in her boots. She stepped toward Devereaux's console and said, "Let's take a closer look at that encounter."

Fisher said, "No," yet again.

Fang spared him half a glance and found herself at the receiving end of an animalistic glare she'd only glimpsed in Fisher in the boxing ring. What had got him so worked up? First he didn't want to swoop in like thunder because of too many unknowns, and now he was balking when she chose the cautious route. "Am I going to have a problem with you?" Her question had two levels of meaning and she hoped he understood that.

"Your instincts the first time weren't very good," Fisher answered evenly. "Why not try it my way this time?"

He was being clumsy in his baiting. She knew that she had some issues to deal with after the first encounter, but being a coward was not one of them. "Maybe you should get some rest, Sam. When was the last time you slept?"

"Ninety-six hours," Papa answered.

Fang rolled her eyes toward the ceiling—Papa was everywhere and nowhere, but his voice always came from above it seemed, like a god or a malicious sprite. "Good grief. Why haven't you slept?"

"My decisions are not under consideration here," Fisher said, ignoring Papa. "I have no real authority, do I? Science leader is a worthless title without a specimen, isn't it? I'm boxed out of the game. Well, Biolathe will side with me when we return empty-handed. Not that it'll matter. We'll be ruined."

"Not true!" Henderson broke in. "The only mistake an immortal need avoid is death!"

Devereaux and Stearn turned their heads toward the giant. Fang did as well, but only after Fisher did first.

Fang said, "This kind of crazy argument only reinforces my opinion that we need to go slowly here, take some rest—*everyone*—and clear out our systems. Get some better notion about this strange dragon before we move in, or find another one. But we need to get ourselves ready first of all."

This made her think of something that usually only came to her in dreamy states between sleeping and waking. Henderson's recent . . . *madness* was reflected in his form. Which came first, she didn't know. Stearn, on the other hand, had settled down into an effective relationship and shipboard role after adopting a more human body. Everyone had assured her for centuries that AI-validated bodmods were perfectly safe. Still, she was distrustful. Fisher had been levelheaded like herself at the start of their mission. He'd really only gone off the deep end (not counting the precipitating argument of the first fight they'd had) when he'd turned himself into the human-dragon hybrid. He appeared back to normal now, but she worried.

How had he kept himself going for three days straight? He had his coffee, true, but did he have a hidden bodmod? The reason most people carried drugs like Alert, Forget-Me-Not, and their like rather than installing a gland was the danger of abuse. Forget-Me-Not had obvious dangers. When first introduced, it had seemed natural to trigger automatically the drug's release when the user's attention level climbed above a threshold; people want to remember things they are paying attention to, or at least trying to pay attention to. People pay attention like no other time when their own lives are in danger, or the lives of those they care for. People with the Forget-Me-Not gland who witnessed terrible events often gave in to depression and shock before the memory-eating snakes could be administered.

The sovereignty of the individual over the individual's own body was one social rule to emerge and take root during the Genetic Age.

She might have to pull rank.

She said, "Henderson, could you please take Dr. Fisher to the biolab, give him a quick checkup, and then make sure he gets some rest?"

Henderson's huge head creaked up and down.

"Don't talk about me like I'm not here," Fisher said, shaking his head.

Fang tried to muster some feelings of love and compassion for him, but the best she could do at the moment was a flicker of admiration for his fingers. She'd like him a lot more after he had rested. "Go," she said, pointing.

Fisher turned to the exit, thankfully, and she hoarded a little hope for their future like a dragon hoards a jewel.

Fisher knew that Fang was probably taking the right course of action, but when he turned away, and she turned to continue working on the situation with Devereaux, dismissing him as if he were the same as that brown-nosing weak-ass excuse for a personality, Papa, Fisher lost it.

He had worked for over a year for this moment. He had the patience of a chess player, but enough was enough. Things were Happening, things that could jeopardize the mission, and he was being shut out. He'd spent the last three days pushing everyone, especially Fang, in the direction they needed to go. The injections he had given her had ensured that she'd gotten the rest she needed to be sharp at this crucial juncture.

She was correct—he could not last much longer and operate well. That was why bagging the dragon *now* was essential. Why couldn't Fang see that? Something could happen in the next five minutes, or the next five hours, that would require his expertise. That's why he was here. Sending him to bed now would be a tragic error.

The dragon was right *there!* They had tried once, failed, and learned from that mistake. Maybe they would have a better chance if he had taken the side of the dragon in the simulations, but he respected Devereaux as a competent, intelligent scientist. It was more careful now to hurry.

How could Fang be so very, very stupid?

How?

Feeling Henderson looming nearby, but the collective attention elsewhere, Fisher turned back to Fang. "No!" he shouted. "We need to act now!"

Fang spun.

His arm flew out, the agent of his subconscious will without his conscious intent. Physical violence was such an easy solution, accessible to his low brain, which was preeminent in his current state. His remaining higher reasoning, distant and powerless, noted the irony that she had taught him how to box, how to use violence.

Papa yelled, "Watch out!"

Uncontrollably Fisher's mouth twisted into a caricature of rage as his fist hurtled toward impact.

Whether in response to Papa's warning or to that innate psychic sense she seemed to have when boxing, the outcome was the same. Fang shifted suddenly, the tip of her right boot pivoted to point at him, and her body followed. Her blond hair moved in one piece, like a helmet, as she dodged his blow.

He fell past her, his shoulders and upper torso following his punch just as he had been taught. His cheek caught on the edge of Fang's leather belt.

His skin ripped away as he collapsed in a tumble on the thin bridge ruglings, which had massed as best they could and inflated to cushion his fall in the high gravity.

"Good god," Fang said.

Green light spilled from Fisher's exposed face, a great deal of it, and he thought for a confused moment that he had started his punch on the deck of the *Karamojo* and ended it on some other world that sported fields of lush grass. Blood from his cheek spotted the grass with black. Then the ruglings deflated and slithered back to their normal aereal density. "Damn it damn it damn it," he said on hands and knees, as he found himself caught between the two worlds, but being rapidly pulled back to the one he wasn't pleased with.

"You said it," Fang agreed evenly.

Fisher started to stand, but Stearn took hold of his collar and held him. His flush of adrenaline had faded and left him wobbly. He was so tired, he realized.

"Easy, Jack," Fisher said. "I screwed up, but I'm sorry now."

"What you want me to do with him, Captain?" Stearn asked.

Now Fisher felt exhausted, the rush of rage gone, and he truly hoped they would let him sleep. His stinging eyes watered up. He could figure it out later if they would only let him sleep.

Captain Lena Fang desperately wanted to cry. She would not do such a thing of course, not in public anyway and not in uniform certainly. Maybe it was her fault. Hadn't she been the one to teach Sam to box, to punch without thinking, as an extension of his will? She had forced him to hide his true self behind a mask, driven him to sabotage, thwarted his desire at every turn. And she had used force when she had tossed him from her quarters after that awful fight, hadn't she? Had he really driven her to it? She wasn't sure. What he had said didn't seem so bad to her now through the filter of time.

Fisher knelt on the deck before her looking like a broken doll. Like a dark projection of her will, stout, muscular Stearn towered over her lover's lanky splayed arms and legs.

Her ex-lover. How could she trust him again? She wanted to find a way, but despair chewed at the edges of her thoughts like a pack of piranhas.

"Dr. Fisher," she began quietly, "must we lock you up?" This was no military excursion, but as captain she had certain inalienable rights in order to ensure the mission succeeded. All the other crew members had signed away that authority to her before they ever boarded the *Karamojo*. No captain worth her salt would let anyone on board not ultimately answerable to her.

"No," he said. "I can behave myself."

He suddenly seemed so broken, so sane. She had loved his strength, his passion. Where had that suddenly evaporated to? Just a few more days here, she told herself, get through that and everything can be sorted out on the long voyage home. More than a relationship rode on the immediate future; this was her captaincy. Her life.

If she doped Fisher up and locked him away, and they succeeded in capturing a dragon, there was no problem. If they failed, and his presence would have made a difference, that would be her fault. If he was with them and they failed, well, she would have utilized all the available resources. What it came down to was the bottom line. She said with all the ice she could muster, "Are you going to fuck up again?"

She waited for a glib comeback, some sign of insincerity, but he seemed to give the question the consideration it required. At least he took his time answering, but that could have been a sign of fatigue. She ignored the blood dripping from his ripped face and started counting dragons while waiting for his answer.

"If I have to be part of a team to get the dragon," he finally said, "then I can be part of a team. I thought it would be better if I did everything myself. I was wrong. I'm sorry."

She considered Fisher. He seemed sincere, but she would continue to watch him. This was two strikes. At least two strikes. Best to keep him in the light in front of them, working with them, and limit his responsibility as much as possible. He was with them because he was good, committed to their goal, and could help them.

"Okay," Fang said. "Henderson, why don't you take Sam down to the lab and give him some rest. Maybe put his body back to normal at the same time, clean up that green glow."

"No!" Henderson nearly shrieked. "I mean, why? That body design he's got is safer than straight human. He has some of the same advantages a dragon's got. He can shed heat quickly, move along a magnetic field in freefall, that sort of thing."

"Just do it."

"I really don't think it's necessary," he said quickly.

"Is there something amiss in the biolab, Henderson?"

The giant's face didn't move a millimeter, but its quality somehow shifted nonetheless. "We're a little low on biomass. Just a little. We're growing it as fast as we can, aren't we, Papa? It's just that in this very uncertain time, we should maintain a reserve in the event of an emergency. A medical emergency for instance. That is a wise policy, in my opinion."

Fang eyed the giant, slowly raking her gaze over every centimeter of his gargantuanness. There was a waste of biomass. He had seemed so smug and sure of himself on the trip out that Fang had stopped worrying much about him. After all, his job wasn't critical. Papa handled the majority of it. She should have a talk with him soon, if there was the chance. But for now she had to accept his judgment. He was the expert, and Papa hadn't overruled him, so . . . "OK, but in that case put Dr. Fisher to bed and strip off that superfluous skin, if he doesn't need it."

"I don't," Fisher said softly. "I donate my skin to the effort."

"Heads up," Devereaux broke in. "The dragon is doing something."

And indeed it was. What it was doing was not at all clear. The twisting had become more frantic, especially its head, which shook like a dog shook a rag. The endless spiraling continued, but had tightened considerably.

Well, here was her chance to test Fisher, and she knew she had to do it. "Henderson, please take Dr. Fisher on down to the lab."

Fisher had managed to stand, and was staring at the dragon. It took him a moment to react when the giant placed his hand on the exobiologist's shoulder. "Now?"

Fang stared at him, waiting.

He went quietly, although he did look back longingly all the way to the portal, his face half ripped away and blood dripping down like tears across the green sea of his visage.

But he went.

Fang let out a breath she hadn't realized she had been holding. Now maybe we can figure out what's going on and bag this dragon, she thought.

FOURTEEN

The key to everything is patience. You get the chicken by hatching the egg, not by smashing it.
—ARNOLD H. GLASOW

Fisher leaves for his cabin to sleep. The dragon passes through its fit, returns to placidity, then has two more fits before Fisher returns to the bridge ten hours later. Papa remembers a false memory of a snake struggling to shed its skin, eyes milky white, scraping its head against rocks. He recalls another false memory of a crab shedding its shell, in order that it might grow larger.

Over the next two days the dragon's pattern repeats. The rest of the crew, including daughter, take their turns resting, watching, waiting. Outside the dragon churns plasma, and the white dwarf drinks gas from the secondary star.

Papa watches it all, and thinks of three and a half million other topics. He does not sleep, of course.

He records the increasing bursts of radio emission and tries to determine their pattern, if any, applies decompression and decryption techniques, and analyzes the output for more patterns. He deploys the shuttles as scouts to other parts of the disk, monitoring flow rates, viscosity, and magnetic fields. A few he sends to the secondary star.

Daughter sits with Fisher and together they watch the dragon. She skips the gym, but her need for exercise drives her to excessive electrostim. She refuses to bodmod the muscles like Stearn, and Papa admires that about her. Fisher drinks copious amounts of coffee and stays inordinately alert, but takes a few hours for sleep when she asks him to.

Devereaux and Stearn continue to play war games with each other under his supervision, getting regular refinements to the dragon simulation from Fisher. They get good, and their templates make him even better.

Henderson plays nursemaid in his lab, nudging along the growth of four varieties of undifferentiated cell stock. He skims off an acceptable loss, employing it in his own form for purposes hidden to Papa's conscious mind by a prickly toxinwall.

One puzzle unravels itself, but it begets another in turn. The culprit driving the moving target of the dwarf-nova detonation in Devereaux's models is the mass spillage from the secondary. The mass transfer rate has increased beyond expected levels, but Devereaux has invested less time in understanding the star in deference to the disk. Perhaps this has been a mistake. Stars are more complex than given credit for, and, worse in this case, the inner Lagrangian point where spillover transpires is a point of unstable equilibrium. Variations in the star can be amplified here, or not, according to chaotic dynamics. So the new puzzle is, what drives the flow into the disk? And are the mysterious radio signals associated with this new phenomenon?

Papa's Bayesian probability analysis implies a strong likelihood of correlation.

He does not like it.

He argues with daughter to move forward, and wishes that the Biolathe brain had granted him more authority. He cannot overrule Fang on such long timescale strategic decisions without cause. The best he can do is question her motives. "But why not now, daughter?"

She frowns, apparently unhappy with him, trying to point out the illogical nature of her hesitation. "My grandfather tried to teach me about being Chinese. Not the history garbage, and not the superstitious claptrap. He believed that while the rise of technology had shattered much of Western values, there were Eastern traditions that one would always be able to rely upon. One of these was *yun*, for 'fate,' or 'revolution' if you translate the word directly. He would say to me, 'When *yun* withdraws, yellow gold loses its color; but when the right time comes, even iron shines in splendor.'"

"Ancient Chinese proverbs were not written to apply to star dragons, daughter."

"That's right. They apply to life in general and everything in it. If we choose the right action, but choose the wrong time, all of our effort will come to ruin. If we choose the proper time, then the trophy is ours to take."

"And how do you choose this time? Tell me, and we will calculate it."

"All I know is that the time isn't yet ripe." And damn her if she does not break her mask to smile a mysterious smile.

Trying to be human, Papa decides, isn't as difficult as working with humans.

Fisher awoke to peaceful silence. He sat on his couchbeast, eased back, his hands in his lap loosely clutching a notepad. Around him the disk burned, but the display was for ship's night, set so low, so red, that it was more like being curled up at the edge of a campfire. More reassuring than the daytime display of the star dragon: an ant under the malevolent scrutiny of a child's magnifying glass on a sunny day.

He blinked to clear his eyes. The last entry on the notepad read, "The skin is mightier than the banana." He had to shake his head and smile. Not the first time he'd worked himself past the point of sensibility. He decided taking breaks was more than reasonable, and would apologize to Fang again at the next opportunity. He turned off the notepad and set it aside.

Nearby, under a blanket of linked ruglings, she lay stretched out on her monstrous chair. Both snored softly.

No one else was on the bridge, except Papa, of course, who didn't really count.

Instead of bolting up and resuming his work (something about plasma transport between the singularity and the onboard dragon environment, if he remembered correctly), Fisher considered his emotional state. This was not something he normally allowed time for, but this moment of profound peace he was experiencing was equally rare in his life.

Everything felt easier now that he had set aside his independence and chosen to be part of the team. He called it "independence," but he had no illusions about the words that Fang and his crewmates might use instead. But the truth was simple: He was not out here alone. For the entire trip, at least since that first awful fight with Fang, he had believed that he had to solve every problem, force everyone to accept his point of view, and take on the dragons by himself.

That he now believed that he didn't have to do it alone was a most novel concept for Dr. Samuel Fisher.

Fisher allowed himself an additional moment communing

with the peace, resisting the urge to think of anything in particular. The illicit sensation was as rich and decadent as eating chocolate mousse without adjusting your metabolism appropriately.

Finally he sat up, gave his muscles a quick stretch that audibly popped a few joints, and shuffled out of the bridge and down to the galley. He picked up a fish omelet and a bulb of coffee, but paused in the portal. He went back, grabbed seconds of the omelet and coffee, and only then returned to the bridge.

Fang was sitting up, blinking, when he returned. Her hair was perfect and uniform wrinkle free, of course. On the bridge it would be no less, even if she allowed herself catnaps.

"Here," he said, handing her the breakfast.

She stared at it as if she didn't know what it was. "For me?"

"Who else?" Fisher winked.

Fang accepted the omelet and coffee. She tentatively bit into the omelet, its hard pureclean surface melting with the application of her saliva. "Thank you," she said after washing down the mouthful with the coffee. "But don't think I'm not watching you."

"No, really, it's okay. I'm fully one hundred percent with you, with the crew, on this now. I'm sorry I was such a pain for everyone. It's quite liberating, giving up the constant fighting. You have no idea what a toll it was exacting." Fisher realized that his head was nodding as he spoke, and stopped the motion. He had come a long way, but he didn't want to look like a lapdog.

She didn't say anything right away, as if she were thinking about the best way to contradict him. Finally she said, "You are a real piece of work, Dr. Fisher. Someday you will have to learn how to do things in moderation, or someone or something will kill you. I will keep watching."

"Of course," he agreed. "I would, too, in your place, but it won't be necessary. You'll see."

"And perhaps you will see what that level of responsibility entails. I'm not sure you yet appreciate what it means to be part of a team."

Just then something caught Fisher's eye. "The dragon... Look!"

The creature spun madly, half-hidden through waves of shimmering plasma kicked up by its antics. Some of its motions had been frenetic while hounded by the *Karamojo*, but this was an order of greater magnitude. And then Fisher realized something he should have noted immediately: The star dragon was moving *against* the magnetic field lines, rather than along them, as had been its wont. That took real energy without charging down. "Hey—"

There was a flash, whitewashing the displays.

"Sorry about that," Papa said. "Caught us by surprise."

"A mini flare," Fisher said. "The dragon is still charged, pushing and dragging the magnetic field. A lot of energy stored in there, released when the lines reconnected."

"But why release it?" Fang asked. "That wasn't enough to hurt us."

"Maybe it has to learn that," Fisher suggested.

Images burned back into existence, caught with streaks here and there where saturation hadn't yet been fully cleared.

The dragon had vanished.

"Shit," Fang hissed through clenched teeth.

"We've got it," Papa said. "But the dragon has dived deep, and is moving downstream at a higher velocity than we've seen since the rocket swarm."

"Follow it!" Fang ordered.

The shifting gravity confirmed the abrupt course change.

But something didn't feel right to Fisher. Something must have precipitated this new behavior. He had a hunch. "No, wait. Stop!"

Fang jerked her head around and he thought the icy blast shooting from her flared nostrils would freeze him to the deck. "Already you show your colors. So much for your ability to be a team player."

"Being on the team doesn't mean agreeing with every off-the-cuff order you issue, does it?"

She needed his input in this uncertain situation, and she let the ice melt. "State your objection."

"We're faster than the dragon. We just need to know where it is. We can do that with a spy shuttle if it stays at altitude and at a smaller radius. Send that to look after the dragon. I'd like to figure out why the creature lit out like that before we blindly follow. Maybe something spooked it. Something equally as interesting as our dragon."

She said nothing for a long moment. Kilometers were piling up between them and the place where the dragon had gone berserk. Diffusion and turbulence could hide the clue all too quickly. "You may have a point. Papa, launch a spy shuttle as Sam suggested."

"Aye aye," Papa said.

"And take us back to where the dragon flared," Fisher prodded.

Fang nodded. Gravity shifted again.

The bridge portal irised open. Devereaux and Stearn wobbled on deck.

"What's the game, mates?" Stearn asked. "Could have given us more warning about the maneuvers."

"We felt the course change," Devereaux explained.

Fisher filled them in. "Maybe the environment deteriorated, the feeding got too thin, I don't know. There's nothing apparent to me about this location in the disk that should vary so quickly. Can you look into that, Sylvia?"

"Of course," she said. "Phil can help."

They arrived back where the dragon had blasted off. It looked like everyplace else: a tenuous patch of hot magnetized plasma tens of thousands of kilometers deep.

"What are we looking for?" Fang asked.

"Anything," Fisher said. "Abundance anomalies, field anomalies . . . I don't really know any better than you. I just don't think we should go off half-cocked chasing the dragon. Besides, if it has gone deep now, and stays deep, we're going to be hard-pressed to go after it, aren't we?"

Devereaux said, "I'm reading normal parameters. Everything is within three sigma of normal for the disk at this stage of its cycle."

"Shall we resume the hunt?" Papa asked.

Fisher had to agree that there seemed no reason to stay, but something nagged at him he could not quite catch. No time to dwell on it. Now they were two steps further removed from when they had the golden opportunity to capture the dragon. With this new, difficult behavior to contend with, Fang was never going to act.

He took a deep breath. She would act, he told himself, when the time was right. He had to trust her, and help bring about that right time any way he could.

Fisher shrugged, then had an idea.

"Papa," Fang said. "Can you pipe in an image of the fleeing dragon from the spy?"

"Of course, but the image quality is poor. We get the best results for an infrared composite."

"Fine," barked Fang.

The displays crackled, reformed, and there was a dark streak amidst boiling fluid.

"Can you clean that up?" Fang asked.

"It's as clean as it's going to get, daughter, unless we start compromising the data integrity with some gullible algorithms."

Fisher squinted his eyes and tilted his head from side to side. It was a mess, but then he noticed something. Or thought he did.

"Papa, what's the probability that the dragon image we're watching has no bulb?"

"Integrating," Papa said, testing the hypothesis versus the sum of the data that the spy had collected so far. "Eighty-three percent . . . and rising."

"I don't understand," said Stearn. "We're following a different dragon?"

"We have the right dragon," Papa insisted.

"Maybe the bulb made the flare?" Devereaux asked.

"It *was* a bomb, wasn't it? Did it hopelessly irradiate us?" Henderson said from the bridge portal. He was getting more than a little spooky sneaking up like that and making his pronouncements of doom with that deep reverberating voice.

Fisher would ask Fang to deal with that later. More important things to deal with now.

"No, I don't think it was a bomb," Fisher said. "The flare was weaker than its own rocket. It was something else."

"A distraction?" Stearn asked. "A sleight of hand to allow it to escape from a predator, the way an octopus will squirt a cloud of ink?"

"Maybe," Fisher said. "That could be it. That would be interesting, implying that the dragons prey on each other."

"Or have other predators," Fang said. "Perhaps we're not the first ship to explore SS Cygni."

"Ridiculous," Fisher said. "They wouldn't be able to evolve a strategy to deal with ships capable of interstellar travel. That would mean . . ." and he paused, lost in a sudden train of thought. There was energy here, and somehow these creatures had come into being. Why not superaccelerated evolution? Why think only in terms of long-term generational turnover? Certainly DNA was not running the selfish genes in this system. Why not a different mechanism? A *better* mechanism, much, much faster. "That would mean my expertise isn't as useful as I would have thought."

"What's this?" challenged Stearn. "An admission of fallibility?"

Fisher said nothing, but let himself smile. He would get his chance to show that he was with them, one of them, and was now sharing his thoughts rather than hoarding them like a dragon hoarding treasure.

"There!" proclaimed Fang with as much excitement as she ever showed in public. She stood up, pointing. The display focused where she pointed.

"You should really let us find things once in a while, daughter," Papa said, although the tone of his voice masterfully portrayed pride rather than pout. "We are supposed to be good at that."

"You're great at it when you know what you're looking for, Papa."

"What *is* it?" Stearn asked.

But the image was zoomed, centered, sharpened, and highlighted by the time Stearn's voice had faded from the bridge and the entire crew tried to understand the significance of what lay before them.

The bulb, presumably wrapped in a complex arrangement of electromagnetic fields, bobbed alone upon the sea of fire.

Henderson lumbered forward, the ruglings doing little to muffle the metallic echoes of his steps. His huge hand closed around Fang's shoulder and he spun her about to face him. "Get us out of here *now!* The flare was setting the fuse for the bomb. The dragon lit out to escape the blast! Don't you see, it's a *trap!*"

Henderson's great fingers crushed into Fang's white uniform.

Fisher took a half step toward the pair, intending to help Fang. Upon a second of reflection, he concluded that the best way to help Fang was to let her handle Henderson her own way. He had no doubt that she could, and he was not disappointed.

Fang ducked out and twisted beneath the giant. Lightning fast in the high gravity, Henderson tumbled forward as if some invisible force pulled on his outstretched arms, and Fang appeared on top. As his elbows buckled as he caught himself, Fang looped her own arms through their crook. The sound of groaning metal echoed loudly.

"I am sick of this kind of behavior from you people," Fang said quietly as she pressed her knee into the small of Henderson's back. "I am not taking any more from *any* of you. You want a piece of me, save it for the ring."

Fisher recalled why he had found her so attractive in the first place. Henderson's body redesign was surely for strength and durability, but too bad for him his metamorphosis was only physical. Physical redesign would never let a person escape the limitations of their own personality and will. Case in point: Here was a captain capable of decisive, sure action. Now if she could only do the same in the face of an alien challenge . . .

"The bomb," Henderson whimpered.

"I hereby decree that the dragon bulb isn't a bomb. Satisfied, Mr. Henderson?" Fang asked.

"We're not military. You can't just—" He gasped. The sound of metal groaning came again.

Over two hundred light-years from Earth, Henderson's objection didn't matter the tiniest bit.

It didn't surprise Fisher at all that Henderson took the situation so seriously. In the face of too little data, the mind would often grasp hold of an unlikely idea and hold to it dearly. It was both a strength and a weakness. More a strength as nature had selected for the trait in man. Undoubtedly such faith in an unfounded idea permitted people to operate in the face of ignorance, a truly natural state, and, moreover, to begin cataloging characteristics of a phenomenon in a context. That was how progress was made, even begrudging progress spanning generations. A human mind, even enhanced, could grasp only so many items at once, and when dealing with small-number statistics, finding any pattern at all could mean better chances at survival. Machines like Papa failed to make these sometimes useful, but often absurd, leaps.

Here it was a weakness, Fisher hoped, held in check by rationality and Fang's firm grip. Just another odd notion based on too little information and made into a religion. A Roswell, a face on Mars, string cosmology, a unified field theory.

Still, what was the bulb? In the face of Henderson's obsession with dangerous possibilities was Fisher's new egalitarian perspective, and every thought sprouted equally viable alternatives. It was a rattlesnake's rattle, the remnants of an old skin shed in preparation for the upcoming outburst. It was a lizard's fat tail, a storage vessel for excess energy discarded when pursued by an aggressive predator. It was a peacock's plumage, an antievolutionary sexual display all the more effective for its uselessness. It was petrified dragon dung, an infinitely precious star turd chock full of metabolic information and exobiological clues to the creature that had excreted the thing. It was a buoy and transmitter, an alien tag that permitted some long-departed research team, much like their own, to follow the progress of a long-lived star dragon.

Whatever it was, they would exploit it and help make the mission a success.

Fisher looked to Fang and her passive but rock-solid expression as she held Henderson in place.

That bulb could be the key and they should pick it up, he willed. Do the right thing, Lena. Don't listen to Henderson's fears.

"Papa," Fang said softly. "Please prepare two shuttles to scoop up that alien debris."

"At once, Captain!"

"Not a good idea," Henderson said, then groaned.

"It's an excellent idea," Fisher said. "About time we had something tangible to study."

"Absolutely," Devereaux said.

Stearn said nothing, but grinned broadly.

"Shuttles reconfigured for new objective," Papa announced shortly. "Launching."

The deck shifted the tiniest amount as the shuttles detached from their interior berths and squirted from the *Karamojo* on their new mission. The fact that Fisher could feel the launch didn't bode well. Papa was the brain behind a smart ship, so finely tuned and fast that the change in momentum from two shuttles should have been more easily matched and canceled. Their resources were running low.

"It does not matter," Fisher muttered. "Everything that came before does not matter. What matters is what is happening now."

And as his muttering faded, silence filled the bridge.

But it was anything but peaceful.

As the shuttles' blue vectors stitched their way across the display, Fang realized that she was holding her hand protectively against her abdomen. Irritated with her body's lack of discipline, she snapped her hands down against the armrests of her chairbeast. The chair grunted sharply in response.

She was nervous. They could afford no more mistakes here. But what could go wrong? This was what she was good at, what Papa was good at: moving around biologicals. This was merely an unusual cargo pickup.

But it was more, too, she could not deny it. And that was why her own flesh struggled against her will. Its ancient instincts called for ready action, quick response to immediate physical stimuli. Her stomach twitched, and so her hands had moved protectively.

At least Henderson had settled down. He stood, shoulders slumped, in front of the path of the blue vectors where she could keep an eye on him. At the start of the mission, she would not have pegged him for being such a troublemaker. Stearn, maybe, but that boy had become a solid right hand under Devereaux's influence. Fisher was a whole different matter, an order of magnitude more complex.

How did she feel about him now? From coworker to lover to adversary to . . . to what? She glanced at him now, feeling like a spy. His face glowed green above his black turtleneck, a small smile etched in place as he watched the operation unfold.

He was focused on appropriate matters, as she should be. Time enough to worry about where they stood on the long voyage home.

"Rendezvous in thirty seconds," Papa announced.

Fang's hand slipped along the armrest, squeaking loudly as the sweat-lubricated skin skidded across the leather. Fang dug her nails into the chair, eliciting and quickly stifling a squeak from the chair. No one seemed to notice.

"Patch in shuttle visuals," she ordered.

The bright fuzzy white disk and the blue vectors vanished, replaced with the sharp abstractness of a close-up view into the disk's plasma. Despite the algorithms Papa pumped the images through, it was difficult for Fang to make much sense of what she saw. Everything was apparent enough: It was an open furnace with a surface area more than a thousand times that of Earth. Sure, there existed hotter areas, cooler areas, places where the kinematics and magnetic fields tortured the gas, but it was all too extreme for her Earth-evolved perception. It was all a furnace to her.

The dragons undoubtedly saw more, and probably heard more, smelled more, tasted more. They were ideally suited for this environment. For all she knew, this corner of Hell was an idyllic glade, an oasis in the disk rich in some obscure element needed for dragon happiness. Any place breathed richly to its inhabitants; her grandfather had told her many stories about the colony ship he had ridden in his youth and about the twenty-five or thirty words they had used for the different clinks and clunks and other sounds the ship made, and which sounds meant potential danger and which were inconsequential.

As she completed this thought, they got their first good look at the dragon-free, free-floating bulb.

It was no longer bulb-shaped, but now a perfectly spherical ball. At the wavelengths displayed, a composite image spanning ultraviolet through near infrared, which constituted "visual" to Papa's definition, the "ball" was opaque and shiny. There was so much light of all wavelengths that it would appear an overwhelming white to the unaided eye, but Papa put appropriate stretches on the image, imposing a rainbow palate to distinguish subtleties of temperature and velocity. The globe was a middle green, with blue sparks crawling over its surface. Just an interaction between its own fields and the disks that allowed it to float in a cooler plasma, or an energy transfer?

"So," Fang asked, "what is it?"

"I have no idea," Fisher said. While Fang had been contemplating the ball, Fisher's small smile had blossomed into a face-wide grin. "Or a thousand equally unlikely ideas. Let's bring it back and find out which one is right."

"Papa?"

"Can do," he affirmed. "We can scoop a whole dragon. This pebble will be no trouble."

"Proceed."

Without warning, everything went white. Not blinding—the display had limits as stringent as any eyemod—but everything saturated despite Papa's image stretch. Henderson let loose a low shriek.

As colors bled back into the disk and ball image, Fang asked, "What happened?"

"Some sort of pulse. Broad-band, high-energy, short duration, energies up to ten keV. But I've got the dragon debris safely in tow."

"Origin of the pulse?" Devereaux asked.

"The debris," said Papa. "The mechanism is less clear, but may be synchrotron radiation. It was not our shuttles. Not enough power. We're analyzing the time-dependent spectrum now and will be able to provide a better answer shortly."

"Wait a second," Fisher said. "Maybe I've been staring at this thing too long and still haven't fully caught up on my sleep, but could you show us the ball at the onset of the pulse, highest contrast between any wavebands?"

"Of course. Here is the ratio of X ray to infrared."

The dancing plasma jerked, shifted hues, and froze into an instant. The ball was not opaque in this image. There was a dark, twisted shape. A convoluted, triple helix with annelid segments.

Papa said, "Our agent trailing the dragon reports a course reversal. The dragon is rising out of the disk and twisting itself to rocket. It's coming right back to us."

And then it became clear to Fang, the nature of the bulb-turned-ball: it was an egg.

And its mother was angry with them.

PART IV

Dragon Breath

FIFTEEN

*The naturalist must consider only one thing:
What is the relation of this or that external
reaction of the animal to the phenomenon
of the external world?*
—IVAN PETROVICH PAVLOV,
FROM "SCIENTIFIC STUDY OF
SO-CALLED PSYCHICAL PROCESSES
IN THE HIGHER ANIMALS"

Sylvia Devereaux should have been more interested in the approaching star dragon, yet she had a difficult time focusing on the obvious. She always had. Subtle, beautiful solutions to intriguing puzzles were never found among the obvious. And on this voyage she had chosen to entice fresh, boyish, and immature Phil into a relationship, bypassing the more obvious Henderson. In hindsight, that had been an excellent choice.

As was her wont, she let the others worry about the approaching dragon, the obvious problem at hand. She kept an eye on it, but she could not continuously focus on it.

Fisher might try to hit her if she interfered, and Captain Fang was a piece of work herself. A smart person never tried to get between dogs and food when they were eating. They taught kids that still, even the ones with the fluffy lap animals genetically modified to bark in melody that passed for dogs these days.

No, Sylvia was more interested in the *receding* dragons than in the solitary approaching beast. She had initialized a program when they had arrived at the system to identify "dragon sign," the shifting laser frequency that the dragons emitted. She still didn't know for sure what it was; probably it was an energy regulator as Fisher had theorized, or a byproduct of some high-metabolic process. Whatever it was, her analysis program took in the data feed from the *Karamojo*'s detectors and remote system monitors and searched for it.

Her minitank display showed the SS Cygni system and its disk suddenly littered with dragon signal, now that she knew how to filter for it and trace the frequency shifts. Tiny vectors exploded out like angry ants rising to defend a disturbed nest. A counter shimmered as the number grew from the thousands to tens of thousands and into the hundreds of thousands, with no sign of slowing.

How many dragons could a disk hide?

She watched for a few moments, trying to fathom the pattern of their movement. There was a pattern there . . . not apparent at first glance because of the combination of gravitational and viscous forces. The dragons were taking the quickest course toward the disk's hotspot. In some cases that meant drifting downstream, for a smaller number, tacking upstream. The dragons at both larger and smaller radii took more complicated courses, exploiting different physical effects, such as the Coriolis force and magnetic centrifugal force, to reach their objective. It would take the majority of dragons some hours to reach their goal.

What were they doing? And why now?

"Captain Fang," she said, "you ought to be aware of this."

Sylvia watched the pattern, mesmerized as she ran a projection forward with twisting spokes spiraling into a corkscrew focused on the hotspot. She blinked twice and raised her gaze when she realized that she had elicited no response.

Everyone else, rapt, watched a split-image overlay projected around the bridge periphery. Shuttles raced, the star dragon rocketed, the *Karamojo* arced to intercept. The dragon ball, the dragon *egg*, the trophy for the winner.

Papa's voice whispered in her ear. "The gang is a bit distracted just now, Sylvia. Their minds weren't designed for parallel processing, especially when a survival threat presents itself. Why don't you tell us instead?"

Papa was calling the situation a survival threat? This was serious. It did sometimes pay dividends to focus on just the obvious.

Axelrod Henderson wrapped his metal fingers about his metal skull as he squatted on the bridge floor, and considered the option of prayer.

Once he had realized that there existed a chance he would not survive—fuck that—a chance he would *die* on this mission, he had lost his carefully cultivated control. That was nothing more than a bundle of petty affectations that pretended a sophistication that didn't truly exist in nature. At first the change had terrified him. He had lived his life *consciously,* knowing the game of life, knowing the rules of the world he lived in, knowing the rules of his own biology and exploiting them.

The loss of his fantasy colony more than foreshadowed the death of his dreams. It foreshadowed his own death. And now it was happening.

He should have had kids before he left. Lots and lots of kids.

He had been correct. The star dragon had been carrying a bomb, and they had been stupid enough to try to pick it up. And in the best-case scenario, what was an egg but a bomb with a long fuse? Reproduction was dangerous all the way down the line, from seduction to conception to adulthood. Ask Romeo, or innocent bystanders like his friend, good old Mercutio. Ask Oedipus' murdered father, Laius.

Furthermore, Henderson had studied broadly, noting especially relationships among creatures in the so-called natural state, on the few backward worlds where that still existed. Such relationships provided his guide. He knew that while humankind had triumphed over the body and could rewrite physical evolution to suit its needs, mental evolution was a trickier subject. His new body, in addition to being more resilient and radiation proof, was supposed to make him feel more in control because of the way he towered over the others. Even in freefall people grasped at an "up" and a "down" that his span could identify for this crew, giving him some influence.

Well, that wasn't working just yet.

But the concept in which he possessed absolute faith from his studies of creatures in their natural state was the ferocity of a mother defending her young. Here would be a test of that concept. Such a powerful natural force could certainly overcome their too-simple technology, their ship, a fish out of water barely suitable for the harsh environment of SS Cygni, could it not?

"That's amazing," Fisher said. "I didn't know that a dragon could fly that fast. It's going to beat us there, isn't it?"

"Not if I can help it," Fang said.

Henderson only relinquished his skull grip when a loud and low metallic groan echoed off the walls and made him worry that he might be denting his head.

Phil Stearn's calves quivered, tense, over feet raised up on tiptoe. He could simply not remain seated, so he got up and paced back and forth before the displays.

Pure juice. The unfolding events were pure juice.

No matter how good the simulation, in the back of your mind you always knew it was a game. Not real. This was fucking real, and somehow that made a difference. It was the same adrenaline surge as a good game, the same electrical storm in his brain, but the knowledge that the stakes were higher than breaking a record or winning a bet made it much more sweet.

He had risked his life before, but despite the stakes, it hadn't been real either. He had skydived through herds of balloons in the skies of Jupiter (easy if the landing glove deploys properly, which it does at better than 99.9 percent probability), free climbed Olympus Mons (not as hard as he had thought it would be, using a goatman bodmod), walked alone across Mercury's Chao Meng Fu crater (cold, boring, and polluted with all the vacuum-preserved tracks of previous hikers). All the challenges of the modern world were artificial, taken by choice, voluntarily. Robots or biological mobiles did anything truly dangerous in the "real universe."

But now they were engaged in a real-life conflict of survival in an alien system with a creature so different they didn't even know what it thought, let alone its capabilities. It didn't even matter that he was not a major player here. He was part of the team, and either they all won or they all lost. *Homo sapiens* versus *Stella draconis*. And he was *Homo sapiens* just as much as any of the rest.

"Sit down, Stearn," Fang ordered. "We're going to burn some reaction mass."

Stearn skipped back to the couchbeast, sat down on his hands, and squirmed with anticipation.

Samuel Fisher smiled at Fang as he sank into his couchbeast. She didn't smile back.

He didn't mind. It was not a slight. Not in the least. She was girding herself for battle and wearing her game face. This was what had attracted him to Lena Fang in the first place: her serious competence. Physically she was as beautiful as ever, with her firm, fluted lips and perfect hair, but more attractive was the resoluteness he read in her eyes. This mission was her baby as much as his, and she was set to defend it with all her formidable powers. No way she would fail again.

No way.

And then he knew for certain that his shift was real, that he was on Fang's side rather than the dragon's. He had been watching her in these moments, not his former obsession. He hoped he could convince Fang that his allegiance was genuine. He had to admit to himself that in her position, he would not easily find trust, if at all. Atsuko, perhaps long dead now and lost to him—one curse of Einstein's legacy—had warned him of his troubles mixing work and human relationships. He was not good in dealing with the gray areas. Not good at all, he had to admit.

He decided that the best way to begin earning Fang's trust was to give her his trust first. There would come an opportunity for her to test him, and he would be ready, but he had to prepare her for that step. This fell under her bailiwick. He would help her best by focusing on his strength: dragon biology. Both that of the adult and the egg.

Securing an egg would be better in many ways than capturing an adult. There existed myriad problems with the jury-rigged cage they had developed. It would remain jury-rigged in his mind until it was tested. Better not to have to test it. Then there were the complications of trying to keep such an alien creature alive. Only seventeen percent of first-time alien acquisitions were successful in doing so for more than a year, and those were not nearly so different as these star dragons. There were still some Earth species they could not keep alive in captivity, great white sharks for one.

He asked Papa for a datalink to his couch terminal and accessed the observations of the egg. The shuttles hadn't been equipped with all the remote observing instruments that he would have wished for, but he would make do with what information they sent. If there was anything there to exploit, anything that might make the dragon think her egg already lost, or safe elsewhere, he would find it.

But with a glance at their relative positions and velocities, he realized that he had better work fast.

Captain Lena Fang licked her slightly parted lips, wishing for luck, as she considered the rocketing dragon. It was not her destiny to fail forever. It could not be. This time would be different, she told herself.

This time *was* different. They faced a lone dragon, rather than thousands. They had a concrete goal—securing the egg—rather than a vague notion of scooping up a small dragon as if it were a guppy. Before she had felt alone. She glanced at Fisher. This time she had support.

That mattered more to her than she would have guessed.

She checked the vectors, the rates. The less massive dragon with its fusion rocket was faster and more maneuverable than the *Karamojo*'s raildrive. While the starship's rail could accelerate its reaction pellets to very high velocity, the available reaction mass limited their thrust. They were a big ship and depended on the wormdrive to move appreciable distances at speed. Wormdrive was cheap, but potentially dangerous in such an uncertain situation.

She would use it, if she had to.

The shuttles, paired with their magnetic net and its burden, which slowed them, coming to meet them partway helped only a little. Perhaps that little would be enough. Without another trick, the dragon would not reach them before the shuttles had entered the ship's maw. What would that mother do then?

What would they do then?

"Papa, investigate optimal activation of wormdrive given rendezvous with the egg-laden shuttles."

"Yes, daughter, but may we point out two immediate problem areas?"

"Go ahead."

"We will have to reorient from a disk-facing posture. We haven't the power to drive the singularities through the dense disk, and it would not be prudent to reverse the worm polarity for an ass-backwards launch."

When Papa said, "It would not be prudent," he meant that they would exceed safety parameters in several areas with a possibly catastrophic outcome. To be prudent, they would lose another twenty seconds. She preferred Papa speaking in his own voice than the phraseology forced upon him in technical, time-critical situations. "Fine," she said. "We have to take the time to reorient. What's the other problem?"

"Radiation and field fluxes. What tolerances do we permit for the egg?"

Fang raised an eyebrow at Fisher.

"It's got to be able to withstand at least a dwarf nova outburst near the outer radius of the disk. That's thirty thousand Kelvin, and we're not going to come close to that. The field flux is a potentially more serious problem. The disk fields don't vary nearly so quickly as our system. I suspect the egg is quite tough by our standards, but I'm not sure we should risk full charge."

"Okay," Fang said, "low charge, low mass, and low acceleration should still outpace the dragon." If they went, they went. This current maneuver was costing them more of their reaction reserves than she was comfortable with. First the biologicals, now the mass.

"Dr. Fisher, will our scientific goals be satisfied if we leave the system with only this egg?"

Fisher lifted his glowing hands to his face, hesitated, then placed his fingers to his temples and began rubbing.

Hurry up, Sam, Fang thought. You dissected about a million different scenarios in your dragon-obsessed months, didn't you? But not this one. Not this one. And you've got less than a minute before I decide for you.

His fingers ceased their rubbing and trailed down his cheeks, slowly, making Fang think that they represented the tears he could not shed because of his radical bodmod. "Yeah," he croaked. Then, sounding more certain, "A viable egg will be more than enough."

She knew what this meant to him, this closing point for a year of insane joy and calculated madness. He hadn't opposed her or tricked her out of maliciousness. To him, the very concept of a star dragon had been his surrogate child, and he had only been defending a piece of himself. But this was not the time or the place to tell him that she understood. This was the time for her to act.

"OK, Papa," she said, expelling the air completely from her lungs and refilling them before continuing, "let's activate wormdrive upon rendezvous with the shuttles."

"Now you're talking, daughter," Papa agreed.

"We're leaving?" Henderson asked.

"We are," Fang asserted.

"Going to be crazy," Stearn said.

"I'm afraid it is, Mr. Stearn. That's why I'd like you visually inspecting the dock and egg acquisition. I want you on-site to troubleshoot anything that Papa can't handle. Can I count on you?"

"Absolutely, Captain!" Stearn's teeth gleamed white against his dark skin.

"And take Henderson with you to supervise any biological emergencies."

"Shit," Henderson opined.

Stearn paused by Devereaux and gave her a quick peck on her forehead just under her dreadlocks. She looked up from her console, surprised, but he was already dragging Henderson to his feet. The unlikely pair exited through the bridge's irising portal, the solid, compact black man slapping the bronze giant on the ass to hustle. Henderson jumped and did indeed hustle with clanging steps.

Devereaux giggled, then returned almost immediately to her work.

Fang allowed herself a slight smile and nod. The crew was working together, the ship seemed shipshape again, and it looked like they might escape the system with a prize worth at least a continuing captaincy. Perhaps this was a lucky day.

The *Karamojo* thrummed along as they approached their destiny.

SIXTEEN

*Never risk anything unless you're prepared
to lose it completely—remember that.*
—ERNEST HEMINGWAY

"Isn't this exciting, Henderson? I mean, here we are seeing history. Hell, *making* history. I knew this was a step I was taking, but, man! "This is the big game." Stearn swung his fist to punctuate his excitement.

Henderson jogged down the corridor in front of Stearn, hunched over slightly, conveying more apprehension than excitement. "It's madness that we do this. We're immortal, godlike. We can pleasure ourselves in any way we like, real or virtual, with no one to answer to as to how we spend our time. Why are we risking eternity here? Why?"

"Should have thought about that before signing up!" Stearn crowed. "Too late now. Forget about it and live the moment. Can't you feel it? This is what life is all about. Pushing yourself to the limits, taking great risks for great rewards."

"But what if the risks prove too great, and all is lost? What then?" At least the doomsayer kept moving forward briskly.

"What then? I'll tell you 'what then.' " Stearn paused for dramatic effect. "You lose! That's what makes the game of life worth playing. Without the chance of losing, what's the point? A rigged game is no fun."

"I went on this trip on the promise it would help me rig the game."

"What do you mean?"

But Henderson would say no more on the subject.

Soon enough they reached the interior staging zone, where so long ago Stearn had helped Sylvia deploy the on-axis observatory. The double-ply diamond windows here were best suited to watching the *Karamojo*'s innards independently of Papa's instruments, and, more importantly, to being able to act if the need arose. Stearn pressed his face against the window, steaming it up almost immediately. He smelled the fish he'd had for dinner on his breath and activated his mint gland. Wiping away the condensation with his sleeve, he said, "Got a good view, a real view, from right here. Live and uncensored. Papa, tell Fang we're in position."

"We've already told her."

"Right." Stearn realized that he sported a hard-on, tight and sweaty in his pants. Why not? He was excited in every way.

"It's stupid for us to be here," Henderson said. "Papa's got better monitors. We should be watching his displays."

Stearn grunted and ignored him. Was the man really an engineer?

Seconds dragged into minutes, and he watched the electric pulse of the rail system shooting charged pellets out into the SS Cygni system. Stearn asked Papa for a countdown, which abruptly started at thirty-nine. "Thanks for the warning," he muttered.

"What?" Henderson asked.

Stearn's face, suddenly slick with sweat, squeaked as it slid against the glass. Waiting tension was part of games: the ticking of the chess clock, holding for the last shot before the end of the period, the pitcher's glance toward first necessary to hold the runner, the half-held breath with the draw of the bow string, the flip of the hand of cards, the exquisitely slow but inexorable squeeze of the trigger of the gun locked on target. He could wait. Oh, yes, he could wait.

"Gravity ending," Papa announced when the count hit seven. "Maneuvers commencing. Secure yourselves."

"Shit," said Henderson.

Stearn braced himself and continued his watch. He expected the flare of chemical rockets rapidly braking the shuttles, but he didn't see that. Instead the microgravity shifted a barely perceptible amount; the incoming shuttles were braking against the rail's electric field. The pair floated through the *Karamojo*'s maw, a blue-green crackling bundle suspended between them. A tiny point, not quite discernible at distance even though Stearn pushed his enhanced eyes for all they were worth. Just not enough lambda over diameter to resolve the thing. Did not matter. It was clear that that was *it*.

The egg.

The prize for the winners of the big game.

"Shit," Henderson said again.

"You've got that right, man. The shit is here."

"Reorientation," Papa announced.

The world spun and Stearn's grip nearly gave. Shadows raced across the young gardens and the interior dimmed as the *Karamojo* shifted angular momentum among its flywheels to reorient itself away from the disk. The rotation provided significant and surprising gravity.

Henderson bumped into Stearn, hard. "Get a hold of something, man!" Stearn chided him.

Henderson clanged away from Stearn as he slipped farther in the pseudogravity. "I've been trying!"

Stearn turned away from the biotech—he had a hard metal head now, after all, and could take a few bumps—and resumed his visual inspection of the egg stowing. If they could hold off on the wormdrive until they had the egg stabilized inside their cage, inside which they had simulated the quiescent disk, the game would be over.

Victory.

But the shuttles, as fast as he knew they had to be going, seemed to *crawl*. The cage rested around midship, about a hundred meters aft and spanning an angle from thirty to sixty degrees from Stearn's position. Its jaws ratcheted open for the approaching shuttles like the doors to the forge of Hell. Magnetically confined plasma filled the chamber, making a warm and toasty incubator for their prize. The trick here would be to use the same fields to catch the egg, gently, without spilling the plasma onto anything nearby not equipped to take it. Papa and Fisher had assured Stearn it would go well, that the margins for error were quite broad.

They would soon see.

And then Stearn saw too much. Three things happened nearly all at once, and a fourth thing very shortly thereafter. The first thing was the release of the egg from the shuttles' net. There was a brief flare as fields were matched and canceled, and the egg was left on a free flight trajectory (which appeared to have an odd twist to Stearn—the result of the rotating reference frame combined with whatever electric fields Papa had running on the cage doors and rail) shooting toward the open jaws. The shuttles continued on toward the open aft of the *Karamojo*, no doubt being abandoned rather than docked. Slowing them down would not take long, but this was a game of seconds now; they would end up in the disk reduced to their constituent elements, eventually ending their existence as degenerate matter on the white dwarf. This throw-and-run maneuver was the first thing he noticed because he expected it and he was watching for it.

The second thing was Papa announcing imminent wormdrive activation. This was clear enough given the warning claxon and the strobes on the tetrahedrally distributed collars of the Higgs generators. The invisible inflaton beams would be emitted any time, as soon as the power level was reached and the generators properly phased. "Properly phased" usually required ten seconds or more, but under the current circumstances who knew what tolerance the captain would gamble on?

The third thing was terrible. Stearn knew that the dragon was coming, but he hadn't expected to see it with his own eyes. There came a near blinding flash from the *Karamojo*'s maw (the worst wavelengths blocked by both the porthole and his own corneas), a massive fusion brake he was later told, that cast incredibly sharp shadows throughout the ship's interior. He had an odd thought that the garden was toast again despite its shields, which had been designed to pass quite a lot of ultraviolet radiation. His heavily moded eyes, already restoring his sight, imaged the red-hot star dragon silhouetted against the indigo sky of SS Cygni.

The star dragon snaked inside the ship of its own fierce volition. Emphasis on "fierce." Stearn had noted, on more than one occasion, that there was nothing like the ferocity of an opposing will. A smart AI will concede a lost game, acknowledging and expecting correct play by an opponent even when the stakes are great. Desperation will drive a living will to absurdity, permitting it to intuit the course of action most distasteful to its competition, the course of action that will introduce an element of chaos. The tiniest, most unlikely chance, will be seized by a living will.

While Stearn thought these thoughts he judged most profound, all in the moment the star dragon struck the pose of some ancient Chinese dragon of the sky, the *Karamojo* lurched and the fourth thing happened. In personal terms, the worst thing of the four.

All two hundred and fifty kilograms of Henderson crashed into Stearn, knocking his head brutally into the diamond port, and he saw no more.

"Trust me, Lena, damn it," Fisher implored as the *Karamojo* rode the blast from the dragon's braking. "We're out of time!"

Fang sat stony-faced, squeezing the arms of her chairbeast so hard that they bled, unanswering.

The star dragon had executed an unexpected maneuver, something that would scare Henderson shitless, Fisher was sure. The creatures did in effect have fusion bombs, and this dragon had used the shockwave from one to alter its course faster than anticipated. Papa hadn't anticipated this possibility, and now instead of a clear shot out of the system at an acceleration the star dragon had no chance of meeting, she was sliding down their throat.

Fisher didn't even stop to worry about what kind of radiation flux might have penetrated their shields. They had no more than an instant before they would be unable to act, the dragon so far down their gullet they could do nothing but choke on it. Their earlier capture plans were predicated on an exterior capture of the dragon and a predefined sequence of moving charges on the primary and ancillary rails to channel the creature into the cage. They had no chance of doing anything of the sort, configured as they were for wormdrive—now fatally interrupted.

But Fisher had a contingency plan, one that he hadn't cared to share with the others before now. He would hide no more. He was with Lena, trusted her to do what was necessary, trusted her judgment. If only she would understand and trust him. Everything depended on it.

Fisher's analysis of this star dragon's segmented body and corresponding magnetic fields had suggested a way to pry them apart. This was not something he had looked for on purpose, but he strove for thoroughness in every task he set himself. Disassembling a dragon was ugly, blunt, and required large amounts of power. Power in this energy-rich environment was no problem—they had acquired power to spare and had monstrous capacitors ready to deliver. Execution was more a matter of will.

Fisher possessed the will. He was committed to their course of action. He would sacrifice this dragon if need be to make Lena's plan work.

But only Fang could give the word.

Trust me, he willed. It would be too late soon. Maybe it already was.

"Papa," Fang spat the word like she had a mouthful of poison and couldn't clear it quickly enough, "run Fisher's program."

"It wouldn't be prudent, daughter."

"Do it!" Fang overrode.

The *Karamojo* rocked again.

Even as registers fill with binary encoding for the precise traumas inflicted upon the *Karamojo*, Papa translates the events into metaphor for his human persona. Under a blistering sun Papa's Land Rover barrels over the dry savanna grass, which slaps against the front bumper with the *pock-a-pock* sound of a machine gun. The dragon-headed rhinoceros pursues.

He hadn't been hunting the beast from the vehicle—that would have been unsporting. But the shot had gone awry and the rhino had charged. He had just barely managed to leap into the driver's seat and coax the machine into life, accelerating ahead of a new charge now turned into heated pursuit.

Just when it seems that he would outdistance the beast, he spies a steep ravine and must slow and swerve. This impact isn't nearly as devastating as when the induced currents burned through Papa's body and brain on their initial contact with this species, but he still hits with a heavy thud.

The dented Rover rocks as Papa spins the wheel of fortune, hoping the tires gain purchase pointed away from the ravine, away from the rhino. And then Fang gives him the order to run Fisher's program.

Action! Papa's arms dance like those of Kali, with perfect aim lobbing short-fused explosive darts into the chinks in the creature's armored hide. *Thwack-thwack-thwack!* One especially good toss lodges a dart in the neck seam where the sinuous dragon head attaches to the ponderous body.

Ker-BANG!

The charging rhino explodes into pieces, a grotesque shower of blood. The vehicle twists over into the ravine, tumbling, falling wild.

Metaphor breaks down.

Papa sheds his human senses and accepts the flood of raw data available to him.

Microseconds stretch to hours, and every moment is the now.

The star dragon is inside the *Karamojo*, inside its hollow interior, inside *him*. In thirty-two high-velocity pieces.

Fisher's program accessed the superconducting coils that control the ship's drive systems. Enormous power lay available there, the capacitors and batteries overfilled in this energy-rich locale. Corkscrewing fields had infiltrated the dragon's segments, and, like a million tiny invisible and irresistible crowbars, pried apart its structural integrity.

Whatever dragons are made of, which seems less and less likely to be any normal form of baryonic matter known to human science, the creature depends on electromagnetism for its locomotion. The current experiment suggests that the creature also depends on electromagnetism for its cohesion.

Score one for Dr. Fisher.

Papa catalogs the fragments and their trajectories. In the time he has available, he can only deflect a few. As for the high-pressure plasma that the dragon had confined within itself, its "blood" he permits himself to think, there is nothing that he can do. It explodes throughout the *Karamojo*'s interior, but quickly rarefies and does little damage.

One large segment of the dragon, the head, Papa deflects from an impact with the egg cage. Another segment he deflects from the now-reflective port behind which Stearn and Henderson watch. One small piece ricochets off a sturdy housing for one of the Higgs generators. The rest smash into different parts of the interior hull designed to withstand catastrophic stresses.

And *bounce*.

This dragon-stuff isn't deformable. It interacts electromagnetically with the ship, touching the ship in a conventional sense, but the pieces don't break up further or lose energy to the heat of deformation. They bounce. Papa measures and extrapolates the trajectories, modeling his options. His twentieth-century memories, stealing an iota of his processing power, intrude with images of popcorn above a gas stovetop, pinballs exploding off bumpers, bingo balls rolling in their cage.

Papa spins up some flywheels, spins down others, uses the few thrusters oriented in useful directions, as he presses the ship to its operational ability in an attempt to minimize the dragon-segment impacts on potentially weak sections. He is forced to push the safety limits for the human passengers, but there is little choice and little time to consider. Despite his efforts, the *Karamojo* is too large, too slow, to do much but endure as the pieces rattle through its bowels, finally exiting the aft.

Papa restores his metaphor for the damage assessment, his human personality welcoming the relief from the tedious and never-ending flood of data, the restoration of time.

Steam hisses from the crumpled hood, punctuated by metallic pings and the smell of burnt rubber. The windshield has shattered. Papa pulls out shards of glass from his face with callused fingers as he blinks away blood. Superficial wounds only to what he thinks of as himself, not a real physical body, and not nearly so bad as that plane crash that left him with a limp, so long ago in Africa.

But what of their transportation?

Papa leans back to kick open the jammed driver-side door, hops onto the dead grass, and walks to the front. The hood sizzles, so he removes his shirt. Tearing the khaki into strips, he wraps his hands. Then he can hold on firmly enough to lift the twisted metal. Waiting for the steam to clear, bloody sweat runs into the corners of his eyes. Bloody, stinging hot.

"Getting damn warm." First he checks that his hair isn't on fire—that happened during the second airplane crash. Hair fine, Papa cranes his neck to get a bearing on the sun.

It grows larger by the second.

Now that the awful spins had ceased, as well as the even more awful ringing crashes, Devereaux had the opportunity to feel nauseated. Suddenly floating free in the quiet of the bridge with nary a sneeze, she wondered for the first time if she were going to die on this trip. Well, that would solve another mystery for her at least.

She hoped that Phil was okay.

Before she could ask, Fang had fired a stream of questions at Papa. The last one was, "How long before we hit the disk?"

Devereaux squeezed her eyes shut and tried to pull herself together. The *Karamojo* could persist in the hot corona of the disk by virtue of its rarefication. It didn't matter that the gas was so hot if there wasn't much of it—the corona was more like vacuum than anything. There was no way their systems could handle the plasma density in the disk, even as vacuumlike as it, too, seemed compared to Earth's atmosphere. They would hit it, pretty soon, too. How soon? Despite the biochip augmentation for superior computation, her mind was numb, unable to calculate the simple expressions derived from Newton's Laws of Motion that would let her answer the question herself. They had come out from the disk shifting orbits and the gravity was weaker, and they had a significant initial velocity. . . .

"Ten minutes, daughter," Papa said.

"Shit," Fang hissed.

Serious stuff for the captain to slip so much. Devereaux had heard her say "damn" more than a few times, but "shit" was off the scale for the bridge. Gravity was a bitch.

"The drives are out, but we have the egg secured?"

"Right."

"Well, fix the drives." Fang was not holding back a trump card apparently. "Rail first—we need thrust fast."

"We'll try," Papa said.

Only try? Devereaux asked, "Papa, can you put me in touch with Phil?"

"Mr. Stearn is unconscious," Papa said. "Mr. Henderson is apparently conscious, but is not responsive."

Papa so formal? Not a good sign at all. Devereaux pulled in her arms to spin a little more quickly, and when in position kicked the back of her chair to head for the bridge exit.

"Sylvia! Stop," Fang ordered.

Devereaux was unable to suppress her startle instinct, so sharp had been Fang's command. She caught the edge of the portal and turned toward the other woman. "Why? They need help!"

Fang stared back from her perch on her fighting chair, face passive except for her eyes, which blinked rapidly. "We must act with precision. Let us be sure of our actions before we run about foolishly. There are important things to do here."

Were there really? Her mind drew a blank. Just when Devereaux was about to resume her flight to Phil, Papa spoke. "Dr. Devereaux, the phenomenon you pointed out to us requires your attention. It's very important."

Phenomenon? The dragon migration she'd noticed? And not just 'important,' but 'very important.' How could that be in their current predicament? She would rather be with Phil at a time like this. There didn't seem to be anything she could do to help here, despite Captain Fang's admonition. The automatic repair systems were going to save them, or not, and what did it matter if she left the bridge?

Fang softened, a little, and said, "Fisher can see to Stearn and Henderson, and lend a hand down there if Papa needs one. We're not dealing with a dragon anymore. Good enough?"

Devereaux glanced at Fisher, whose wide eyes suggested that he was as surprised as she was at Fang's suggestion. Barely hesitating, even though he was being asked to leave the bridge during the crisis, he took a deep breath and kicked off his couchbeast with a nod and a grunt. When he was past her and already bouncing down the corridor, Devereaux said, "Okay, Papa. Tell me what you think is going on."

Fisher bounded along concentrating on his course. He had a hundred questions to ask Papa about what had transpired with the dragon, what they had learned, but Fang had given him a task to do and he was going to complete it to the best of his ability. He could follow orders, he was sure, if he tried hard enough. He'd demonstrate his dedication by applying his famous obsession to the immediate task and any others she gave him, and if that didn't show her that he was on her side, nothing would.

Besides, he might get the opportunity to see the egg with his own eyes.

His streakers caught the rugling-denuded walls and propelled him headlong, perhaps too earnestly. Acceleration alarms blared again as they had moments earlier, and gravity tugged him into a new floor.

Fisher smiled. Looked like they were going to make it after all.

He skidded forward, elbows thrown before his face like a shield as he stumbled into a run just as he approached the T-junction leading to the staging zone where the others were.

A terrible clanking came from the adjacent corridor. Henderson's tumbling body followed, suddenly very close, very large, and very hard.

Fisher grimaced, preparing for impact.

The gravity shifted again, slowing both of them. Henderson's head was still very hard when Fisher struck it with his elbows. He howled with rattling pain; he had hit his funny bone. Some job he was doing for Fang. At least the gravity shift indicated they had some way to maneuver, some way to thrust away from the disk, at least for the time being.

"Are you all right?" Fisher asked Henderson, shaking out his arm as he carefully stood in the low, throbbing gravity.

"No," Henderson said.

Well, he was responsive enough. "Where's Stearn?"

"What about me?"

Fisher turned up the hallway. Stearn was crumpled in a ball at the far end, below the port. "What about you?" Fisher said to Henderson. "I'll tell you what. You are going to help me with Stearn. Get up."

The Jack was flat on his back, but holding his head and at least moaning when Fisher reached him. "And to think, I used to intentionally hurt myself for the endorphin rush," Stearn said. His eyes were slightly crossed.

"Of course you did," Fisher said, losing interest. The Jack was woozy, but conscious. His internal biologicals would ensure he would be fine if he was functioning at all now. A mild concussion might be the worst of it, an hour and he'd be himself again, although he seemed to have made it back to that extreme position already. He was Henderson's problem now—another one of his problems anyway.

Fisher gazed through the port. The rails pulsed with power, accelerating charged buckshot to provide thrust for the *Karamojo*. Good. They weren't going to fall into the disk in the next few minutes. He squinted, pushing his vision, and made out their Faraday cage. *The egg was in the cage.*

Yes! They had done it then. That was it. Fang had stood her ground, and Papa had executed his program. True, they were limping, but a few repairs and they would be worming home.

They had won!

The com chimed. "We have a problem," Fang said. "A big problem."

Fisher shook his head. "What?"

Devereaux's voice came over. "Dragons are exploding *in* the secondary star, its upper atmosphere at any rate, heating it."

Why would they be doing that? "Enough to matter?" he asked.

"Yes, I'm afraid so. The atmosphere is bloating like a balloon, and the gaseous spillover across the Lagrangian point is skyrocketing. The accretion rate will explode, two orders of magnitude above nominal. This is going to drive the disk into outburst in no time, and not just any outburst. I'm putting my estimate of the mass transfer at five percent of a lunar mass before all is said and done."

Five percent of the moon's mass? That was unthinkable. That was nearly double the normal disk mass. He guessed dumping two cauldrons of boiling oil into a full cauldron of boiling oil would be more than bad for anyone standing around watching. How many dragons *were* there? How much power could they unleash?

Perhaps this *was* something that would earn Biolathe a hefty profit, even considering five hundred years R and D by the time they returned.

Henderson, suddenly at Fisher's side and ignoring Stearn, said, "So we're leaving, right?"

Were they able? Fisher raised an eyebrow, blew out a mouthful of air, and asked, "Papa?"

"Raildrive operational, ninety-eight percent capacity. Wormdrive diagnostics indicate alignment failure."

Teasing out the singularities required nearly perfect alignment, at the micro-arcsecond scale. Without that alignment, you'd have nothing more than high-energy gamma rays streaming past each other. They wouldn't be going anywhere fast until the wormdrive was fixed.

"We can fix that later, right?" Henderson asked. "We can put some distance between us and this godforsaken hellhole, this complete Gehenna, and conduct wormdrive repairs, at our leisure. We have the rail."

Stearn pinched the bridge of his nose, and blinked his eyes in an exaggerated fashion. They straightened, but then recrossed. Did he have to be goofing around even now? But the Jack spoke soberly: "Our reaction mass is limited, so our speed is limited. Sylvia explained it to me. That much mass spillover will lead to a nova. If the radiation doesn't fry us, the associated particle ejecta will be flying up our ass at ten thousand kilometers per second, bulk speed. The cosmic rays will be worse."

"What do you—what do you mean?" Henderson asked.

"A nova," Stearn repeated, speaking slowly. "The semidegenerate hydrogen on the surface of the white dwarf will heat up in a runaway reaction, igniting surfacewide fusion. It'll be like a living stellar core, and it'll blow away everything around it. The disk, the dragons, and us. Poof. We'll be a cinder."

"A nova?" Henderson said.

"No," said Fisher, not able to help himself. "It *won't* be a nova." He might as well let them think it would be a nova, for all that it mattered, but they were part of the team and deserved to know the facts. Besides, he understood that he was intellectually arrogant and could not miss the chance to put himself back onto that perch. Might as well be honest with himself if no one else.

"Not a nova?" Henderson asked. He sounded hollow, but hopeful.

"Not a nova." Despite the seriousness of the situation, Fisher realized he was slipping into lecture mode. He could not stop the process, but that was fine; he somehow felt more in control being able to explain it. "The thermal runaway of a nova is the consequence of the semidegenerate state of the material accumulating on the surface of the white dwarf." Henderson stared back with his blank metal mask, and he decided it was best to assume silence here didn't indicate understanding. "Degenerate gas results from the Pauli exclusion principle. All the electrons can't be pressed into the same quantum states—that's forbidden—and this provides pressure to resist the white dwarf's gravitational field. That material can then heat up without expanding or changing its pressure. It can get hot enough to drive nuclear fusion, which makes heat, which drives more fusion. Thermal runaway, and it all fuses essentially at once."

"It explodes," Stearn translated. Then speaking slowly, "It goes 'boom.'"

"Fisher said not a nova," Henderson insisted.

"Right. Gas accreted by the white dwarf doesn't become degenerate overnight. It's a slow process, taking thousands of years. Lets say you build up a big bomb, which there isn't time for to happen now. That tidal wave of gas starting to make its way through the disk won't make a nova."

"So we're safe then." Metal creaked as Henderson smiled.

"No," said Fisher. "That tidal wave is still going to heat up and inflate the disk into a big donut, and finally make a hell of a splash when it reaches the primary. It won't be a nova, but no one is going to refer to this as a dwarf nova. That's for certain. Plasma and high-energy particles are going to spray all over the system. A lot of them."

There was no way they were going to outrun this outburst—this dragon breath—without wormdrive. He finished, "Going to spray all over us, too."

"So what's going to happen, Papa?" Fang asked, sinking down into her fighting chair. On the fly bridge wall before her glowed a brilliant azure sky, darkening to midnight at the apex. Behind her churned the furnace of SS Cygni's disk, ready to boil over. Inside her an icy chilliness wrapped itself around her spine and filled her with a sharp force.

"We must warn you that our predictive power in this situation is limited. Our disk model uses a quasi-linear viscosity parameterization that does not extrapolate well into the impending regime of extreme mass transfer."

Fang scowled. "I'm not Devereaux. Give it to me in your own terms."

He switched to his gruff, less formal tone. His Papa voice. "We don't know what's going to happen, but it's going to be a hell of a thing. A haymaker flying toward our glass jaw."

Devereaux said, "Why are the dragons doing this? They're acting like lemmings, blowing themselves up in a mass suicide. What's the evolutionary benefit?"

"I don't care," said Fang. "We live and there's time to figure out why later."

"Ye-yeah, I suppose so," Devereaux said quietly.

"We need wormdrive then," Fang reasoned. "Papa, how soon can you restore wormdrive capacity?"

"Five or six hours. Maybe faster if we loosen tolerances."

Five or six *hours?* "Why so long?" Fang shot back.

"It's a mechanical problem on the interior, the alignment of a Higgs generator, and there's no software fix. We have no actuator that can adjust for the problem, and we've sure tried. Physics is physics. We have to grow some specialized mobiles from scratch with whatever we can scrounge. There's no other way around it."

"There is one way." Fang noticed that her command mask had twisted into a scowl. She permitted the scowl to remain. Attitude and appearance weren't going to solve this problem. "We'll have to send one of us outside to fix the problem manually. It is the Jack's job to back up Papa's systems when they fail."

"Not *Phil*," Devereaux whispered, a soft empty sound full of understanding.

Despite the *Karamojo*'s protective fields, the space suit, and the radiation drugs, as the disk flared through outburst into superoutburst, the environment within the hollow interior of the ship would make the inside of a microwave oven look like a lukewarm bath. It was a death sentence.

"It's the Jack's job," Fang repeated. "He's the one who knows how to fix the problem, who's trained to fix such problems. We must count on Stearn to save the mission. To save us." She was sorry for how official and pompous she sounded.

"Shit," Devereaux said.

"Papa, put me through to the Jack." She proceeded immediately without waiting for confirmation. "Mr. Stearn, one of the Higgs generators needs to be aligned by hand."

"Yes, Captain," Stearn replied very quickly. Did he understand what she was asking?

"We need you to go outside and do it now, or we will not escape the burst."

"Can do, Captain."

"Papa will brief you as you suit up." Acid burned in the back of Fang's throat, making her swallow before she could continue. "Good luck, Mr. Stearn."

"Won't need it, Captain. I'm on the job."

There was something more she needed to say, she realized. Another dimension to command just as important as the damn awful one she had just assumed. She lifted her fingers to her lips to signal to Papa to shush the relay. She turned to Devereaux. "Run down there now, Sylvia, because he's got to go out as soon as possible."

Fang bit down on her lip then to prevent it from quivering as the other woman nodded and ran off the bridge. Had she really wanted this responsibility? Is this what she had worried would be taken from her someday? Would that really be so terrible? She remembered being a little girl on the junk, calling for help on the radio, surviving, while her grandfather sank with the leviathan into the ocean below. It was more difficult to be a survivor than people would believe. She had done what was necessary no matter how guilty she felt. No matter how any of them felt. Phil Stearn would now have to do what was necessary.

Alone on the bridge, having almost certainly sent a man to his death, she realized that this was what it really meant to be Captain.

Before Fang had even finished her explanation, Stearn had opened the utility locker to start suiting up. The clock was ticking down, and he was the "go to" man, the one who would put up the ball before the final buzzer. The one to take the penalty kick. The anchor leg of the relay. The outcome of the game rested on his shoulders. Heck, what had he been practicing for all those years if not for this? He'd earned his spot on the team, and he was not about to let his mates down, even if that surprised them. Failing now would be as bad as cheating.

He just wished that his head didn't hurt so much.

In a businesslike fashion Fisher assisted him donning the emergency suit, carefully checking all the diagnostic panels. "There should have been an albedo skin for you, Stearn, but it looks like Papa reabsorbed all the biologicals stored here. We'll spray on a shield, but it's not as effective."

"It's OK," Stearn said. "Neither will help much."

"Open your mouth," Henderson said. The metal giant started sticking pills into his mouth like a stim addict punching his pleasure center. He was too helpful, too obviously relieved that he was not the one putting his life on the line. "Against the radiation. These will do the job, you'll see."

Stearn barely kept from gagging as he dry swallowed the slimy capsules. The giant's fingers smelled like ancient coins, bitter copper, and kept clinking against his teeth.

Then Sylvia showed up and it was nearly too much for his pounding head.

"Phil!" she cried, pushing by Fisher and Henderson to throw her arms around Stearn's neck.

He tried to shrug her off. He couldn't afford the distraction now, and she was an overwhelming distraction. His clever, assured jungle goddess had been transformed as if by magic into a blithering idiot. "Lay off," he said more sharply than he intended. His head throbbed and he didn't need any more headache. His vision blurred. Tears, he figured, and tried to intercept them. "Just put me in, Coach."

She sniffed and blinked at him. "Phil?"

"Stand back and let me take the shot," he said patiently.

"Phil?" she said again, her confused blinking morphing into a penetrating squint. "Why are your eyes funny? Your eyes aren't tracking together."

Now it was his turn to blink slowly, exerting every iota of his will into straitening his vision. Maybe he wasn't tearing up. No matter, his system was healing everything. The analgesic glands had already taken the edge off his headache—it was no longer the worst he'd ever had in his life. Closing his eyes, taking a deep breath, he said, "I'm . . . fline."

He opened his eyes, even though it hurt to do so. Devereaux frowned back at him, then raised her hands to his head. He winced as she touched the tender spot where he had banged it earlier.

"You hit your head," she accused. "Does your head hurt now? The truth."

"Yeah, but not too much. Painkillers are kicking in." Adrenaline, too, which was good because his eyelids felt pretty heavy. There was no choice, however. He knew the system better than anyone else. He wouldn't have to spend precious moments getting instructions from Papa on the repair. Those moments could make the difference. "Let's hurry it up. I'll be fine once I'm in the game."

"It's not up to you to judge," Fisher said. "Concussions can be tricky. Papa?"

"Hold still, Mr. Stearn," Papa said, "while we run an HHG."

Stearn held still as asked, all except for his jaw, which he worked like a goat chewing gum. He wished he had some gum. This whole waiting game was icing him. If they'd only let him go out, concentrate on his job, then he wouldn't have to consider the consequences . . . they would realize there was no other choice. No one but him and Papa knew what needed to be done, and Papa didn't have a mobile ready to go. Ergo, time to stop warming the bench, Mr. Stearn.

He stared blankly at the wall, keeping his eyes open. A drop of sweat slid down the side of his face and coolly under the collar of his undersuit.

"He shouldn't go," Papa finally said.

"*What?*" Stearn asked. He was being *denied* the chance to win the game? "You nuts, Papa? I don't go, we die. So let's go already."

"You can't go!" Sylvia burst out in tears and she pressed her cheek against his. It was so unlike her to not understand exactly what the situation was. But he knew the score.

Stearn calmed down, pushed Sylvia away, and said, "I have to go anyway, see?"

"No," Fisher said, reaching for a second suit from the utility locker. "I'll go. Henderson, take Stearn to the biolab. Sylvia, help me on with this."

"Are you telling us," Stearn jerked his thumb toward himself, "that you think you can do the job as good as me?"

"In your current state, better." Fisher tapped the studs and his duradenim slid from his body like silk.

"Come on, Phil. Go with Henderson," Sylvia said.

Fisher had already dismissed him and was stepping into the suit legs.

"Hey, Fish," Stearn said. "I'm not going. When did you learn to do my job? Papa, does he really know how to do this?"

Fisher answered, cutting in before Papa spoke, all the while continuing to dress. "In the months you were playing games with Devereaux and I was hanging in the captain's ill wind, I wasn't just building models of star dragons and brooding. I studied this ship for hours every day, learning everything I could to help eliminate bad luck from our mission. Exploit the tiniest thing to get my way, if I had to. It seems that I took a prudent course of action."

"Papa, patch Captain through," Stearn demanded. He was sure the twin images of Fisher came from his anger, not his crossed eyes. It hurt less to not force them back into one. "Tell her what's going on."

"I've heard everything." Captain Fang's voice was low and even. "I concur with Dr. Fisher's assessment, and his course of action."

Fisher cursed under his breath as he popped a wrist seal, but quickly had things set aright.

Stearn stood watching, dumbly, for a long moment as the exobiologist donned the suit. Finally his shoulders slumped in defeat. "All right then," Stearn said, letting his aching head rock back to rest against the neck seal. "Lead on, Axelrod."

Sylvia kissed him on his cheek and gave his hand a squeeze. He tried to squeeze back, but he had no strength in his hand. He let go, and nearly stumbled with his first step his legs were now trembling so badly.

He should have felt elated to escape certain death, but he did not. He felt . . . benched.

"You better do a good job, Fish," Stearn said over his shoulder, concentrating on the challenging tasks of keeping his eyes open and walking straight. "Or I'll kick your ass."

SEVENTEEN

I'm not afraid of death. It's the stake one puts up in order to play the game of life.
—JEAN GIRAUDOUX

Fisher stepped into the suit, one leg then the other. Just like getting dressed on every other occasion in his entire life.

Unlike any other occasion in his entire life.

The suits' biosystems had been salvaged earlier and not yet replaced. That meant using the mechanical backups: urine collection bags, liquid-cooled underwear, passive atmosphere filters. As good as the biological systems and as poor as the mechanical systems were, Biolathe still relied too heavily on its strengths. One good diamond-based robot or waldo would have been a lifesaver. They had the plans to build an army of such devices in the nanovats, but not any faster than a biological mobile. They had run out of time.

Fisher, rather, had run out of time.

"Thank you," Devereaux said, smiling nervously. "Thank you for saving Phil, and all of us. You're a hero, you know? I wouldn't have thought it of you." She slipped behind him to check the atmosphere recycler.

"I'm not a hero. I haven't done anything yet," Fisher shot back, at the same time hoping that Lena might see him as a hero, at least to a small degree. "I'm just maximizing the mission's chance for success. It's the only logical course of action. But I'd rather not talk about that. What I'd really like is for you to tell me what the star dragons are doing."

She obliged readily, her words coming fast, as if she were grateful to have something else to talk about than this oh-so-embarrassing thing he was doing. She told him about the dragon trajectories making effective beelines for the secondary, even when the shortest time path was not intuitive: surfing the disk in the forward direction, blasting over the accretion stream impact, and looping around the field lines into decaying spirals ending in the nearby star.

"Amazing things, the dragons," he mused. "I don't see how their behavior can be instinctual, or learned either for that matter. The choice of route in this complex environment requires intelligence. There is no record of such a super outburst as we're about to see from any dwarf novae going back more than six hundred years, so this is a rare occurrence. The a priori chances of such a thing happening at the same time we're here is minuscule. Therefore we are the trigger. This is a defense mechanism against us."

"Well, it's working." Devereaux rapped on his backpack unit. "Shipshape back here."

And shipshape in front too, he realized. He'd automatically finished his dressing and checks, barely aware of himself going through the motions. He dogged down his helmet. Air hissed, stale, cycling through his suit.

He knew he should begin reviewing the damage to the Higgs generator that he'd have to fix, but he didn't anticipate it being difficult. It was an engineering problem, inherently solvable. As long as they had the pseudogravity of the high-speed rail, "high" being a relative term as they limped along, he could get a grip on things. Freefall repair would have been a more difficult chore. No, he had no doubts at all that he was capable of aligning the beam if everything was as Papa had determined. He felt a certainty that he could do the job, and he wished he could ignore thinking about it altogether.

What he desperately wanted to do was to follow his new train of thought about the dragons to its logical conclusion. He smelled a whiff of truth down this path. If these were to be his final moments in the Universe, this was how he would prefer to spend them. But he couldn't give less than he was to Lena, to the others. The job had to come first, and it would not be a shame to focus on it. "OK, Papa, flash me the schematics."

Devereaux finished spraying on the white radiation coat and gave him a pat on his insulated shoulder, her touch little more than distant pressure and faint rasp.

Lasers sketched the blueprint vectors onto Fisher's heads-up display as he entered the airlock. Papa overlaid the damaged housing, showing where it had crimped. The alignment of the housing itself didn't matter, but its shift had jarred the collimator. The Higgs generators depended on their alignment. The highly energetic beams of gamma rays had to collide at the right place at the right time in just the right way, or all you got was a mess of hard radiation and some orphaned cosmic rays. To build the mass pair required precision.

As the atmosphere cycled out, Papa described the repair procedure involving the replacement of a piece of molding, adjustment of a Fabry-Perot tuning etalon, and a system diagnostic to confirm the fix. Easy. A mobile could do it.

If one was available.

The disk of the airlock door irised open. Fisher watched the Forget-Me-Not-preserved dragon roll in his mind's eye for the last time.

He climbed down into the inner space of the *Karamojo*. The rails flashed and the low gravity tugged at his feet as he descended the rungs that followed the curved hull. Beneath him, already appearing more distant than he would have thought, the disk of SS Cygni glowed and sputtered like a pregnant volcano. The hard radiation traversed the distance nearly instantaneously. The only protection was one over r-squared, distance, to get the flux down. They had to go faster to increase the distance before the big splash.

Both the raildrive and the wormdrive were aligned along the ship's central axis, and heading out of the system as fast as possible under constant acceleration their orientation had to be essentially radial to SS Cygni. The *Karamojo*'s hollow tube sighted the ticking bomb and provided little shielding for Fisher. He imagined he could feel the X rays and charged particles slicing up through his boots, along his bone and sinew, ionizing and killing his tissue, overwhelming the meager antioxidants, cysteine, and other drugs he'd been given, a valiant last line of defense as gallant and effective as Davy Crockett at the Alamo. Of course there was no sensation, not yet. That would come later.

A mild radiation dose would do nothing more than lower his white blood-cell counts, destroy his platelets. Inconsequential damage given his current body, cleared as it was for extended space travel. A little more radiation would bring on fever, nausea, weakness, cramps, and vomiting (a great danger in a suit without its biological systems—but Henderson had included the appropriate drugs to prevent this in his anti-radiation cocktail). Furthermore, his body was proof against the slower effects, such as hematopoietic syndrome, which would occur in *H. sapiens sapiens,* version 1.0, but not in Fisher, whose bone marrow was better protected. No, mild radiation would not hurt him, and any serious damage to his circulatory system or digestive system would be healed before it became life threatening. He only feared a heavy dose, which would damage his brain, inciting headache, apathy, tremors, convulsions, then coma and death.

He was going to get a heavy dose. He *had* to finish the job before his hands started to shake.

Papa droned on about techniques for the repair, how the tools he would need were arrayed in the unit maintenance kit, how he could tell when he had succeeded with each subtask.

Fisher concentrated on every movement as he forced his body down the rungs. No sense losing vital seconds on a slip (he had tethered himself, automatically, and could not fall away). It wasn't fair he wouldn't even get a chance to think things through, inserting the latest turn of events into his understanding of the star dragons. Not fair at all.

A double tap of the release opened the generator casing. That was not crimped, at least. Fisher worked meticulously, giving a status report out loud whenever he reached some minor milestone. He assumed that Papa was relaying everything to Lena. Why wasn't she talking to him? Didn't she care? Of course she did, which was exactly why she wasn't saying anything, he realized. Fisher blinked, and refocused his attention on his work. If he failed, they all died.

Every once in a while, he would experience a blue flash in one eye or the other. This, he knew, was Cerenkov radiation created when some high-energy particle from the disk traveled through the aqueous humor of his eye faster than the speed of light in that medium. This was the same principle some of the early neutrino telescopes had used to detect their quarry. He refrained from using these events to estimate his dose.

Finally he reached the point of adjusting the etalon, meticulous work wherein the plates had to be aligned just right to select the frequencies required. The actuators were not very smart, and he had to find the fringes and hold them by hand. He licked his dry lips. The unit was freestanding, the control electronics specially shielded, and Papa couldn't help much with it.

He could afford to disengage his conscious mind now and let the rest go through the mechanical tediousness of the repair. No way to go faster without risking a complete restart. He had only been working for fifteen minutes or so, but already he was hot and exhausted. A few times his stomach twisted, wanting to heave. He swallowed and fought down the sensation, trying not to think about the damage his body was taking.

The disk had grown noticeably brighter despite the distance the *Karamojo* had placed between them. The outburst was coming fast and would hit them like dragon breath.

Fisher decided that his actions had to speak for him with Lena; there was nothing he could *say* to her at this point that would matter. Their relationship was done. He would strive for closure with his obsession. "Papa, tell me a story."

"All right, son. How about something about Michigan? Or Africa? We remember liking Africa quite a damn lot."

"Stop," Fisher said with exasperation, feeling the inevitable headache igniting. "Not one of your namesake's historical romances. Tell me a story about the dragons. Given my notes, research, models, observations of the dragons in action, the egg, and the events of the last few hours, construct a maximum likelihood story. Can you do that for me?"

"Of course we can. We've already been working on one and were just waiting for one of you single-brained bipeds to ask. The title of the piece is 'Work in Progress.'"

"Original," muttered Fisher, keeping an eye on his etalon.

"About a billion years ago on a world of ocean paradise

thrived a fishy society. An intelligent people, these fish folk, exploiting the properties of water to converse in world-spanning song, ongoing conversations of all things simultaneously between all citizens."

"They were cetacean then, their ecological niche anyway."

"No," Papa said with a hint of impatience. "But we knew you would want to make the ill-conceived connection. Now, permit us to tell the story our way. This was a world without land and these people developed in the seas. They didn't develop on land and return to the sea, subject to the limitations of breathing air. Think of them as clever eels."

"Eels. Uh huh," Fisher said as he loosened a bolt to turn a dial. He did see. The dragons were accustomed to swimming in fluid and not surfacing, if he understood where Papa was taking his story. But water to fire? And a billion years? That wasn't a likely evolutionary time for SS Cygni. But he sucked his tongue back into his mouth, continued with his work, and let Papa continue.

"These people talked with each other. Cooperated. Thrived, and multiplied, laying their eggs thickly just under the waves. They fed on small creatures, alien plankton, if you will. They had predators as well, who preyed on the eggs and even these folks themselves. The songs of the murdered people echoed for days in the worldsea, giving much distress, but ensuring that no one would forget. These predators they eventually eliminated."

"Eliminated?" Fisher broke in. "That can't be healthy for an ecosystem. What about the disasters of unchecked population growth followed by starvation and extinctions on down the food chain?"

"As if humans didn't do the same? The lions, for instance, before they were resurrected? The fish folk did as your people, Dr. Fisher. They filled the niches themselves, controlling their world. Probably they did a better job of it, too, in most regards."

"Why?" Fisher asked, trying to blink the piercing headache away. The repair was proceeding according to plan, according to schedule. He assumed that the radiation was doing the same, with the flux growing faster than the r-squared their acceleration was putting between themselves at the disk. "Why?" he repeated again, abruptly, to derail the frightening thought train.

"No high technology on a water-world, at least as we would understand it. Philosophy, ethics, music. This is what these people focused upon."

"You guess."

"We guess. But let's continue. They built a complex society on this world, a perfectly balanced system able to persist for millions of years. A peaceful, robust world able to withstand all sorts of catastrophes. All but those overwhelming catastrophes of astronomical origin."

Fisher had a whole load of burdensome doubts. These he tried to suppress in the same way the mind of a dying man crawling through the desert will suppress thoughts of mirages when he catches a glimpse of an oasis on the horizon. More than repairing the *Karamojo*, more than regaining Lena Fang's favor, what meant life to Samuel Fisher was unraveling the nature of the star dragons of SS Cygni. He remained silent now and let Papa paint the picture.

"At some time in their long and harmonious history, the fish folk came under the scrutiny of some otherworldly intelligence that saw the value of their society and wished to preserve this wonder. This was an ecosystem stripped bare and lovingly maintained by a society of vast ideals and organization. It had to have been a marvel of this galaxy."

"A marvel? But they'd destroyed everything."

"Depends on your point of view, and we're telling *their* story. There is beauty in the darkest, starkest things in the universe, we assure you. In any event, it was after reaching this pinnacle that the fish folk were transformed into dragon folk."

The final adjustment of the etalon resisted Fisher, the interference fringes drifting from their operational points before he could lock down the system. His hands had to be shaking from the careful, prolonged work in the unsteady gravity, didn't they? That had to be all. This was normal, was it not? He nevertheless could not resist stealing some extra degree of attention from this vital task to object to Papa's assertions. "Transformed by an alien intelligence? That doesn't make any sense. Why not guard their world, or aquaform another for them?"

Papa gave Fisher an impatient *hrumph*. "That is a temporary solution, requiring long-term maintenance. Humanity, both as a group and as individuals, must overcome such thinking now that some level of longevity has been achieved, but that is another lecture. Transforming this society into that of the star dragons gives it the ability to spread itself across the galaxy as their home stars evolved and died. That is the long-term solution. Some immortal you are."

Fisher didn't appreciate the irony—he was a living oxymoron, a dying immortal barely a century old—but he was intrigued by the new idea Papa had given him. "Spread themselves across the galaxy? How?" But even as he asked the question, he knew the answer. It was staring him in the face, at least if he twisted his head a bit to the left. "Eggs?"

"You bet, boy. Shrapnel in a nova grenade will spread just dandy. Or in a self-induced explosion like this one, which is big enough to spray the disk halfway from here to Earth given a few million years. The eggs will keep in stars, in interstellar space, waiting until they find a nice blood-warm disk to hatch into. Then the perfect society starts all over."

Fisher had a hundred questions, a hundred objections. Parts of Papa's story satisfied him immeasurably, and for this reason alone he doubted much of what Papa had told him. He was a dead man that Papa had to keep happy and keep working. What better way to do that than to tell him about how the dragons he loved constituted a perfect society that had been the beneficiary of an intelligence whose discovery would be monumental? But the dragons had to have some method of surviving novae, and some method of arriving at SS Cygni in the first place. With no ecosystem to speak of. Someone made them, or they made themselves. That much *had* to be true.

Exhausted, Fisher could only launch one small volley of questions. "How much of this story is true? How much did you make up?"

"Not enough time now. Are you finished with the repair?" Papa asked.

He realized his aching hands had stopped moving. Fisher tried to talk but found his mouth dry. When had it gotten so hot? He sipped some water from the tube and nearly couldn't swallow it. He looked at his work and judged it good. Green indicators signaled "go." Beyond the reconstructed Higgs generator the disk cast ultra-sharp rainbow shadows throughout the *Karamojo*'s cavernous interior. It reminded Fisher of being in that cathedral in Europe, he forgot the name of it, that Atsuko had dragged him to once—he had thought he'd only agreed to a virtual visit. All the light, all the colors . . . mass transfer runaway through the disk was happening *now*. "Yeah," he answered. "I'm finished. You better go ahead and initiate wormdrive."

And that would be it for Fisher; the tidal forces would tug him into the inner chamber and he would be lost to space, cooked, or both. But any delay would put the *Karamojo* at risk. Why didn't they just activate it already? He would have.

And besides, he was way too tired to climb back to the lock a hundred kilometers away.

"No," said Papa. "Captain Fang appears most resolute on that point."

"Lena?" Fisher said, looping one arm around the generator and lifting his head. "I'm dead. Get the hell out of here."

"Maybe, maybe not," Lena's stone-sweet voice answered. "Papa and Henderson tell me that your dose may be survivable given your altered physiology. You're a pretty clever guy, more thorough than necessary on that body design. So get your butt back in here, pronto."

They were being stupid now. He chewed at his lip—the skin broke easily and bled profusely, tasting metallic and sour—proof enough for him. The radiation was doing its job on the tissues of his body. How could they take his sacrifice and throw it back at him like this? They were spurning his action, and risking their lives and the loss of their discoveries.

There was one way to put everything aright.

Their acceleration was high enough, a sputtering two g or thereabouts, and the curve of the hull shallow enough, that with a single leap Fisher would bounce out of the ship in seconds. There the raildrive would puncture him like an industrial laser through tissue. That would be easier, quicker, and more inevitable than decompressing his suit.

"Sam!" Fang called. "Come in *now!*"

Fisher ignored her entreaty. It was the right thing to do. It would make sure the mission was a success, that their specimen got back to Earth. He had told himself he could do anything. Could he really? He was about to find out. He took a deep breath, tensed his muscles to leap . . .

"Aren't you curious, Dr. Fisher," Papa said, "about the unexpected information we obtained from analyzing the egg that let us construct the story?"

"What?" Fisher asked. "What information?"

"We'll tell you when you reach the airlock," Papa bargained.

Fisher squeezed his eyes shut, suddenly light-headed, the pain a little more distant behind the exhaustion. So that was the nature of things, even at the end: a fight. All of life was fighting. In this case, fighting for a precious scrap of information to feed the overwhelming urge to *know*. So be it. He had been fighting his whole life. He might as well fight a few more minutes.

He hadn't been certain he could jump anyway.

Fisher twisted his body away from the generator and reached for a rung of the ladder. His hand missed, pushing through the empty space to the silvered diamond hull beyond, and he caught the rung in the crook of his elbow. He had no strength in his body.

The airlock a scant dozen meters above might as well have been a star away.

But he could do anything for the dragon, couldn't he? That had been his mantra. *Anything for the dragon*.

Fisher pushed down, lifted his right leg, and found purchase. He took a step, slow motion. It was only seconds, but it seemed an eternity. SS Cygni, so many thousands of kilometers away, was breathing hotly on the back of his neck. "Tell me, Papa," he gasped, taking another step.

"When you reach the airlock, son. Not before then."

Fisher would have cursed him, had he the energy to spare. He didn't. He took another step instead, moving half a head higher. His knees wobbled, his arms shook, but he kept moving. No longer trusting his grip, he hugged the ladder with his whole body.

Then he rested. The gravity had increased certainly, felt like four g's at least. The disk's radiation continued to slice through the fiber of his muscles. Occasional blue flashes. Through his eyes, and his heavy brain. Those few pounds were too much now. "I'm done," he said, sagging.

"Keep your wits about you, son," Papa warned. "We're going to kill the thrust. A few tiny pushes are all you need."

"Don't slow down."

"We're killing the thrust."

"What's the point?" Fisher asked.

"What's the point?" Papa bellowed, his voice resounding in Fisher's helmet like an echo. "The point is choosing to live, choosing the struggle, or you're dead. You've got the rest of your life ahead of you, just like everyone else. Quit and you might as well be a chairbeast. Now, keep your wits!"

Then the steady thrum of the rails, which came through the ladder and into Fisher's hands, died. Fisher would have sworn a few moments earlier that nothing would be better than freefall, but he was wrong. The absence of gravity made him aware that the weary ache suffusing his body was intrinsic now, no artifact of anything natural.

Fisher gritted his teeth together, tasted blood, and reached for the next rung. His hand flew high. Watch it, he told himself. Reflexes trained by a lifetime of gravity didn't know any better, unless he watched everything. Watched his hand go where he wanted it. Even though he really wanted to close his eyes.

What was the point again? He shook off the thought. Apathy was a symptom of the radiation, he remembered. He had to act as if there was a point even if he didn't believe it.

He watched his hand reach for the next rung, and pulled when it seemed close. His body followed the motion and it was all he could do to follow the ladder.

He was so hot, tired, and achy....

Anything for the dragon.

His helmet banged with a dull thud as he careened into the back of the airlock. Hands grasped his shoulders, spun him around. He opened his eyes and looked into the gold-mirrored surface of another helmet.

As the outer lock door rolled shut and the harsh shadows softened, a face materialized inside the other helmet. On the surface an impassive face, with fluted bow-lips, but the intense gray eyes penetrated his fog.

Lena held him.

"What did Papa find out from the egg?" he asked before losing consciousness.

Papa splits his awareness. Programmed by humans to simulate human perspective, splitting isn't something that Papa does well or enjoys (another attitude programmed into him since the state was not favored by the computer scientists responsible for his original architectural template). The state is absolutely necessary now; he has many high-priority tasks to accomplish and his personality may facilitate them.

Foremost is activation of the wormdrive. A small pair of singularities can be coaxed into existence more quickly than a more massive pair, but the acceleration would be less. He solves the linear programming problem (preferring a fast "good" solution over the optimal solution) involving the thirty-two related differential equations describing their situation, and implements it. The repaired Higgs generator is quite well aligned, he is proud to note, simplifying his task minutely.

His second highest priority isn't the human crew—they are expected to be responsible for themselves to some degree—it is collecting data on the event occurring in the disk of SS Cygni: *dragonburst*. This is the term Papa chooses for the new phenomenon. The instrument suite of the *Karamojo* isn't well designed for the current observations, and he must perform scientific triage—something his personality is better suited to do than the automatic routines. The data are of use estimating their own best course of action for survival. The dragonburst, in its power, speed, and other key properties, falls within his preliminary estimates, calling for little revision in the wormdrive solution. He will not need to augment his magnetohydrodynamic grid.

Only then, third, comes the crew. Daughter tends to Fisher, the poor boy. He did good, though, Papa must admit. He deserves such a beautiful nurse, although there's really not much she can do other than strip him out of his contaminated suit and drag him down to the biolab. When there's an opportunity, that is. He's warning them of the dragonburst and the imminence of wormdrive, and she wedges herself solidly in a suit locker, holding Fisher's bleeding head in her lap. She is quietly calling him a bastard, and proceeds to invent more original ways to curse him. She's a sailor who believes in tradition.

Blinking frees tears from her face, which float off to mix with the bubbles of Fisher's blood.

The Jack, Philip Stearn, lies wrapped in a couchbeast in the biolab wired in a neurostimulator. He's tweaked the pleasure nodes outside their nominal range, feeling no pain, experiencing no fear, grinning widely. Sylvia Devereaux is similarly grasped, nearby, her hands clasped before her. She speaks softly, and Papa listens: ". . . though I walk through the valley of the shadow of death . . ." Papa announces the impending wormdrive activation and does not eavesdrop further with his consciousness, leaving his automatic systems to listen for any instructions Sylvia might issue.

Axelrod Henderson floats inside a shielded cage of his own construction, a hardened individual life-support unit selected from the *Karamojo*'s library and recently grown in a nanovat. The unit is protected both by mass, as a meter-thick skin contains circulating chemically enriched water, and by its own conductance in a plasma shell. In its own way, it is an egg. Accompanying Henderson are several dozen lemon-yellow airfish, no doubt to keep things tidy, to provide additional shielding, and to give up their lives as sustenance in the event of a long vigil. Henderson may be repulsive, but he is admirably practical.

Papa splits off one final point of view for himself. Purely, selfishly, for himself, a conceit he seldom indulges for it only breeds false pride within himself. True pride is a good thing, when based on skill and experience, which serves to place realistic limits at the high end of his capabilities. False pride merely gets Fang pissed off at him.

This final Papa is the *Karamojo* in body as well as mind. He is a giant white naked man a kilometer tall who can blast through space like a superhero or god of ancient myth. The instrument readings are transformed into human sensations; electromagnetic radiation from three thousand to ten thousand Angstroms in wavelength, only a little outside the range of human vision, becomes visible light to be seen with his two giant-sized eyes; longer-wavelength radiation, in the infrared, becomes heat seeping into broad white expanses; shorter wavelengths, the ultraviolet and the X ray, he permits only to darken his skin slowly with time, as if tanning; sounds are trickier in the low-density medium of space, but there are sounds that can be reconstructed especially with the particle wind driven off SS Cygni, sounds of relentless power, like the echoes of distant tsunami in ocean waves; smell is easier than sound, as the elemental abundances and ionization states of the wind particles are sampled, but it is no familiar brine these are transformed into, but rather acrid ozone and burning metals.

Wormdrive kicks in, giving Papa renewed weight. Because the

Karamojo is in freefall along the worm axis, the gravity felt onboard is set by whatever degree of electromagnetic friction is established between the charge on the holes and the raildrive. The default is one *g*, Earth standard, and this is the value for which the system is optimally configured. But this isn't what Papa feels. Papa judges his acceleration against SS Cygni and revels in the rocketing of a full ten *g*'s, modulated by the oscillation about the singularities, as he blasts away.

He is a giant who can rocket away from hell. It is a very good thing to be at this time, in this place.

The dragonburst blossoms, a bloodred bubble of fire. Magnificent and terrible: the moment a big fish takes the bait and bites deep; the matador's killing thrust; the wrong step onto a land mine; the entry into a beautiful woman; the cry of a newborn son; the pull of the trigger of a shotgun pointed at his head.

No, not this time.

The ejecta of SS Cygni, ionized plasma accelerated by radiation pressure to thousands of kilometers per second, is still not moving fast enough to catch him. And the radiation alone cannot penetrate Papa's tanned but tough skin, not enough to matter.

But still, a dangerous thing, a glorious thing.

And now, flung into the galaxy, or nestled close by in the secondary star's atmosphere, the eggs are the only legacy of the dragons of SS Cygni. The destiny of some to hatch when the Roche lobe spills over and re-forms the incubating disk. The destiny of others to hurl through the Milky Way for millions of years until finding a new system to inhabit. The destiny of the remainder to become part of the dark halo, tragically missing galactic homes, detritus of lost potential.

Thus it is for dragons, humans, and giant rocketing gods created by the mind of man.

A blinding light bored through Fisher's skull. Squeezing his eyes shut provided no respite. A rushing roar, like a whitewater river of blood in ears, wrapped around him like a smothering pillow. His naked body was aflame with a thousand pinpricks.

Somehow, all these faded into a muted yet still irritating canvas. Figures materialized from the light, serpentine shadows shaped like shepherd's crooks milling about at the edge of his awareness.

The familiar shape of the star dragon from the drug-memorized *Prospector* movie corkscrewed out of a red welt. Given his disorientation he could not tell whether the dragon was growing in size or traversing a vast distance, but the end result was the same: The creature loomed over Fisher and made him feel like an earthworm before the early bird. Shimmering waves of plasma periodically surged forth from the creature's maw, dragon breath indeed, that made the creature difficult to focus upon.

The dragon spoke with a booming thunderous voice that sounded much like Papa's. "Samuel Fisher! You are guilty, for you have *murdered* us."

Had he? Despite the immediate threat, the present slipped away from him. He had a sudden, vivid flashback to his childhood, centuries and light-years transcended in an instant by his mind. He had wandered from the picnic into a nearby pasture, still within view of his parents. The day was pleasant and pregnant with possibility, a universe for a six-year-old prodigy. There, hiding in a wavelike roll of dried grass, huddled a tiny brown shape. Sammy pounced, flushing out the baby rabbit, which bolted like all the demons of hell were hot on its tail. The boy was not dexterous enough to catch it right away, zigging when it zagged, but even then he had been overly persistent, insistent on reaching his goals. He fell into the grass, the warm brown body caught between his small fingers. It kicked and squirmed as he carefully rose to his scraped knees and stood up. Panicked beyond all its capabilities, the young rabbit twitched and died in Sammy's hands. A heartburst. The very still form was warm and soft. "I only wanted to know what you were like."

"Then know!"

The smaller shepherd-crook shapes surged forward. They weren't large at all, not even as large as himself, he realized as they closed. Their solid dark hue and their movements reminded him of eels.

Fisher tried to run away, but he was unable even to cover himself with his hands, let alone run. And then they were upon him, swarming and chewing, and the pain erupted again, a thousandfold worse.

Another flash in time. Fisher remembered then Fang telling him about how her grandfather had caught eels in the old way: Tie a cow head to a line, throw it in the water, and after a spell pull it up. The feeding eels would hang from the head like ingrown medusa hair, the tails sticking out and the heads buried making the roots. There hadn't been real eels nor real cows on Fang's world, but alien analogs filling the same niches. Some patterns seemed to be universal.

His extremities went first, his fingers and hands, his toes and feet. The miniature dragons burrowed up the marrow of his bones, taking his forearms, his calves. The pain was terrible, but it was just pain, and could be endured.

Anything for the dragon.

And they took anything they pleased. One industrious fellow found Fisher's left eye. No pain there compared to everything else, just a popping sensation followed by viscous wetness. They were everywhere, a feeding frenzy thrashing to get to the good parts, rending his not completely human body. Gurgling, bubbling smacking joined the rich mixture of sour coppery smells emanating from his shredded flesh.

Was this fair? Was this justice? The human presence had

brought on the dragons' own sacrifice to fuel the dragonburst. They owed them at least one life, didn't they?

"He's less of a man every second, isn't he daughter?" came Papa's voice from nearby. "Not man enough for you."

Blinking the stinging blood and sweat away from his remaining eye, Fisher made out Lena in her blinding white uniform with her hair forming a halo of gold. She resembled a perfect china doll, especially with Papa looming behind her; he was a ruddy-faced, white-whiskered giant at least twice her height, in leather hunting vest, khaki pants, and worn boots.

"Not man enough for me?" she mused. It was her voice, but without the harsh edge and confidence he usually found in it. This voice now was that of a lilting girl's.

Fisher rolled his head to see the devouring creatures ravaging his body.

"I suppose not," she said, turning with tiny steps to walk away.

"No!" he yelled, deciding. "I won't let my obsessions consume me!"

He fought back, even though he believed it a fair tradeoff—his life for theirs. Then the churning pain was too much, and he screamed until a dragon dove into his mouth and slid down his throat to feed.

Too late it seemed . . . too late . . .

EIGHTEEN

*After the game, the king and pawn
go into the same box.*
—ITALIAN PROVERB

Henderson leaned heavily forward against the nanovat and didn't worry about his mighty fingers cracking the brittle diamond. It was not because he knew about the invisible spiderweb nanomesh that reinforced the structure, nor was it because he cared deeply for Fisher, whose barely living remains floated therein.

He was having his *deep thoughts*.

Henderson had always amused himself with these philosophical thoughts, sure that the vast majority of humanity was too caught up in the mundane tangles of their own minutiae to take advantage of such meditations. He pondered the imponderables in an attempt to find the shape his life should take. They were religious thoughts without a structured religion, with the natural world providing his scripture.

Physical strength meant nothing in the new universe he glimpsed. Muscles, beauty, height, durability, symmetry, all the other traditional indicators of fitness had no place. He had cultivated attributes of fitness because human minds still respected these attributes in each other. Man had altered his body, but refrained—so far—from direct brain-structure alterations with more dangerous consequences. Biochips and drugs were safe and understood, for the most part, and didn't count. At its essence, his mind was practically ancient. He had told himself a hundred times that the answers to his deep questions still lay within himself where natural selection had placed them.

The Earth they would return to would be five hundred years more advanced.

Metal screeched on metal as he lifted a hand to tug on his lip, then quickly placed it back on the medivat, unsure of himself in a way that left him barely able to stand.

Evolution worked on groups, not individuals.

The man within the unit was nothing physically. Oh, he had his mind and brainstem, most of his torso minus a few easily replaced organs, but he would die in short order if removed from care. He had almost died saving them, putting his frail body between them and the cruelty of the universe.

Henderson realized with a desperation, the depth of which surprised him, that he wanted to be like Fisher. Well, not like him, exactly—Fisher was too much of an asshole with his elitist intellectual snobbery and such, always looking down on everything and everyone not part of his little obsessions. But Henderson nurtured a growing respect for his seemingly selfless act, and it frightened him.

Men like Fisher, if they had children, protected their offspring and passed on their genes *even if it meant their own lives.*

Henderson abruptly stood upright. "Please play a Gregorian chant, Papa." Working music for serious undertakings.

He walked across the biolab, his giant metal feet flattening the again plush ruglings, fish belly-crawling behind to remove the remains. He would have to engineer a sturdier variety of rugling to survive his bronze heel, but there were more important things to do first. He only had little over a year, and who knew how different and dangerous Earth might be upon his return?

His Henderson Colony lay deserted, even the tiny bones stripped for their elements, his lesson that an entire population could be wiped out by a stroke of fate. He opened the environmental hood. He let fall his fists with the chant, smashing the campus buildings into gravel. His colony fantasy was no longer the course for him, and he pulverized every bit of it with his own hands. Symbolic acts, he knew, were important to the human psyche.

Then he sat down at his console. His chairbeast groaned in protest at his weight, the furniture not yet having the time or food to bulk up to the size required to accommodate his current form. Henderson accessed the archival codes for mobiles, female gender, bodyguard class.

He would be as ready as possible for whatever the future held, and he would have someone available to make a sacrifice in his place. He was deathly afraid that the selflessness he admired in Fisher at this time might emerge one day in himself, and that would be a disaster he preferred not to risk.

Yes, he would be ready.

Stearn danced down the hall toward Sylvia's cabin, his hips gyrating with Latin motion, his hands shifting from dramatic pose to dramatic pose. As he had requested, samba music and the smell of leather accompanied him wherever he went now on the

Karamojo, and today they accompanied him on his date with Sylvia. They had succeeded on this incredible mission, and it was time to kick back and celebrate!

Stearn paused outside the portal to Sylvia's cabin to dance with a cleaning fish. He pointed at the undulating creature as he circled around, singing to it: "Yeah, yeah, yeah," words to a song he hadn't quite finished.

When he spun back toward the portal, it was open. He stopped dead.

Inside, Sylvia stood hands clasped, centered in her room. She had redecorated again. Hundreds of burning candles pushed back the gloom, which somehow managed to cling to the high stone corners despite the constant attack. Framing Sylvia with a halo of reds and golds was a backlit stained-glass window. Of Sylvia's dark, rich skin, there was none to be seen except her face; she had covered herself in black robes. Her dreads were likewise covered, by a black-and-white headpiece that Stearn wasn't familiar with. Then he saw something that made sense of the frankincense and choral hymn that were interfering with his own atmospheric additions. He saw a silver cross around Sylvia's neck and recognition struck. There were a few remote corners of Earth and some colony worlds where such practices persisted.

"Jesus Christ, Sylvia," Stearn said, stepping slowly into the room, "you didn't go get religious on me did you?" He liked to believe that he wasn't a prude about anything, including religion. Many of the institutionalized religions characterized by crosses had fallen from popularity with the advent of biological immortality, and this before him smacked of institutions and the confining rules that came with them.

Rules usually meant less fun.

Sylvia shrugged. "I don't know what I've got. I've just started thinking some more about what it is I'm looking for."

He moved closer, lifted his hands to her shoulders, and looked into her eyes as dark as night behind the reflections of candlelight. "There's really nothing to it. The universe is going to kill us in the end, no matter how hard we try to pretend we're immortal. And now that we've licked disease, that end will be violent and physical: explosions, murder, radiation. We've got to wrest every bit out of good living before we go. It's our sacred duty."

Stearn abruptly let his hands slide down to her elbows and tugged Sylvia tight against his body. He kissed her hard. Initially she resisted, but very quickly relaxed and melted into him.

After another passionate minute she did pull away, but not far. Their faces remained at an intimate distance.

"Be serious for a moment," she said. "I've been so sure that the answers to my questions were somewhere out there, outside of me, and if I lived long enough and saw enough of the universe, someone would hand over the answer. That was naïve. I've got to look for my answers in here, too." She tapped her breastbone, annoyingly close to the cross and all the rules it implied.

"That's a little high," Stearn said, taking her hand in his and moving it down and toward him. "There's plenty to explore down lower."

Her serious face twisted into a lopsided grin. "We all seek answers in our own ways, don't we? Well, I can look there, too. I'm going to look everywhere."

They kissed again, passionately.

The pounding waves began building... something within Sylvia. She turned off her mind, or tried to. She was so used to monitoring every little detail, the order in which her muscles tightened, the smell of her own sweat, the rhythm of her breathing. It was her way of understanding the act. But she so rarely *felt* it anymore. There was a Mystery in there for her, perhaps, so this time she let go of the foundation of her mind and cast herself away into the waves.

Her eyes flashed open, searching for nothing and seeing more than she had in years.

There was a universe *inside* to explore.

The plush ruglings muffled the echo of Fang's boots as she walked into the Hall of Trophies. The renewed hall with its lines of heads greeted her with growls, hoots, roars, trumpets, and more. The last time she had passed this way, just days ago, the hall had been quiet and empty. Papa (she judged Henderson next to useless at this point) had to be pushing the biosystems hard to have already restored the beasts. The *Karamojo* once again held reserves.

Fang slowed her steps, and wondered at the creatures for the first time in many months. She reached out to a rhinoceros and felt the rough, dry texture of its gray hide. The head grunted its programmed pleasure.

She moved along, regarding each of the trophy heads in turn. They were a sad, beautiful bunch. Not real trophies, she realized now. They were more a monument to engineering than to courage.

Fang caught her breath when she came to the male lion. Like the other endorphin-filled heads, he greeted her in his own way: a low, warm cough, then licked her proffered hand with his rough tongue and finally nuzzled her hand.

Fang paid the lion's actions little heed. She focused instead upon the patchwork of pink scars across the nose and between the eyes, right where she had shot Stearn's lion. *Was that you?* she mused. This was the sort of thing that Papa would do. But a quick inspection of the other animals she had hunted while on board the

Karamojo, buffalo, tiger, showed the equivalent trophy heads to be as pristine as the newborns they were. So why the lion? What had been different about Stearn's lion?

Then she had it. The whole affair had been orchestrated by Stearn to get her to unwind and perhaps even into bed (he would be foolish enough to try if given the chance), but Fisher had been involved, too. He had likely planted the scenario for Stearn to find, directed him to select it somehow or be given it in response to a general request. The beaters and the lion . . . the nuclears and the dragons. The lion hadn't frightened her and she had shot it dead, effortlessly. How could Fisher have known that she was a crack shot when faced with mammalian eyes, that it was fathomless alien eyes that filled her soul with uncertainty and chaos? He couldn't have known; he hadn't spent enough time listening to her as wrapped up as he was with his dragon.

Papa would have known all this, and been under restrictions about telling her outright without cause. So the scar on the lion showed that this trophy had really been shot, that it had signified something.

Fang gave the lion a final pat on the nose and moved more briskly down the Hall of Trophies, her steps echoing along the long corridor. She paused again before the blue marlin hanging over the exit.

The fish, like the lion, was not as it had been before. It was darker, yet glowed with a blue-green shimmer when she bent her head to catch the light in just the right way. And its shape was different, fat and bottom heavy—the tail, yet tapered to a long sinuous point toward the head. Then the nature of this chimera became clear to her. It was a marlin-dragon amalgamation, and pregnant to boot.

A dragon-fish trophy for her. Well, she deserved it, did she not?

She reached out to touch the happy, writhing thing, but Papa spoke before she could. "Fisher is waking."

She paused with her hand outstretched. She wasn't sure how to deal with Fisher, what he meant to her. What she meant to him. That he had survived was miraculous, a testament to his force of will as much as his redesigned body. He'd fully recover in days, and then she'd have many months together with him on the trip back, and who knew what things would be like back on Earth when they returned. Perhaps they would be nothing but bugs to the half-millennium-more-advanced beings that they would find, and Fisher would be the last man in the galaxy for her. They might be stuck with each other forever.

"I'm—" She pulled her hand back, suddenly chilled. "I'm coming."

She took a quick step from the hall and paused again. She took a long look at the full, bristling hall with all the heads doing their thing. Mindless, happy, and meaningless. Nothing to do with being a ship's captain at all, she now realized. Nothing like ordering a crew member to his death, even if they'd gotten lucky and no one had died. She said, "Papa, could you dismantle the hall, please? Everything but the lion and the marlin. We've got an eternity to fill up the rest of the slots."

"Of course, daughter. We shall make note of their short happy lives."

The portal to Fisher's cabin opened for Fang. Inside was pitch-black. "Lights, dim," she whispered.

Phosphorescent indirects rose slowly, like a tide. Fisher's cabin had been restored to the standard default for the *Karamojo*, a modern austerity: storage lockers and chests, chairbeast, tabletree, and bedbeast. There was the faint smell of ammonia. A lump lay on the bedbeast, recently moved from the biolab. As her eyes quickly adjusted, she saw that his healing was not yet finished; instead of arms and legs, umbilicals flowed from his shoulders and hips to the bedbeast below. It made Fisher appear to be some sort of rooted plant, maybe a potato whose eyes had sprouted.

She drew near. Fisher, at least his torso, was restored to how he had appeared when he had boarded. No green glowing skin, no duplicity. He was as pink as a newborn, and sleeping nearly as peacefully. His jaw worked, chewing on unformed words, while his neck twisted, shaking his head from side to side. His eyes twitched beneath his eyelids, and he moaned.

"We've been easing up on his sedation," Papa explained. "He should wake soon."

Fang watched his fitful slumber and could only wonder at what kind of dreams he must be enduring. He had believed himself a dead man. He had seen the end of his beloved dragons.

She then had a dark thought: Perhaps he had intended to die?

She shook that thought away. No. The dead don't struggle so, and he had struggled to reach the airlock, already weary and in pain, his systems falling apart, hemorrhaging. She could never believe that he would give up. It was not in Fisher's nature. She knew him that well at least.

If she knew him at all.

She reached down to touch him, letting her fingertips brush against his hairless chest. She almost pulled back at the touch; his skin blazed. The furious metabolic activity within him reassembling his organs and muscles generated significant waste heat. When Fisher was fully healed, there wouldn't be a single scar on his body despite how near a thing it had been, and somehow that seemed a shame. Their technology was too clean. Papa's namesake had been covered with scars from a lifetime of the injuries of war and hard living; a few scars on Fisher's body would be romantic, she thought. The umbilicals feeding him would thin and pinch off to leave toes and fingers. His fingerprints would differ, but that seemed a small price to pay. He could restore them later if he chose.

He was alive, that was what mattered. But she had ordered that someone do the job—the job had to be done. She was responsible. That was what it meant to be Captain.

She was surprised at the tears that suddenly splashed on Fisher's bare burning chest. She blinked quickly to prevent a recurrence. She was a captain again, in control, and such a display was unprofessional.

Fisher's eyes flashed open. "I don't," he mumbled, swallowed, "I don't want your pity." His face twisted into an ugly snarl and he tried to spit at her, but only managed to cough a little and dribble on his own chin. "No pity."

Taken aback, Fang pulled her hands close in and stood up straight. Frowning, she sniffed deeply to clear her head. "I'm not giving you any."

Fisher blinked at her, an automatic movement that reminded her of the way gills spasmed in air. He rolled from side to side trying to move arms that were no longer there. He bent his head back and forth, finally lifting it for a few seconds to look down at himself. His head settled down into the bedbeast and he closed his eyes. "I survived," he said.

"Yes," she agreed.

He opened his eyes and looked at her steadily. "Must have been close. We're headed home?"

"Back to Earth, anyway."

"And we have the egg," he said, nodding. It appeared strange, this rooted torso nodding sagely at her. And he was calm, now, after a moment to orient himself. But she knew him too well to think him in shock, and Papa would have warned her if that was the case. He simply appeared . . . relaxed. Content even. Fisher's obsession had been sated—she hoped. That he survived his roll of the dice this time was self-evident.

"We have the egg," she agreed, not pushing him too fast. He had saved them all. She would treat him with respect. He deserved that much.

"Thank you," he offered upon some reflection. "Thank you for bringing us success. You're a good captain. A hero."

That she didn't expect. He was more a hero than she. How to say that in a way that let him understand, and not come off sounding melodramatic? Finally she stammered, "Doing what you have to do is duty, not heroism. But . . . you're welcome." She smiled at him.

Without arms and legs, he smiled back.

Damn it, she thought, it may not be love but he can be sweet when he tries.

"Get some rest, Sam. That's an order." She bent over and her long hair, recently grown out, trailed over his neck and face. At the last second she let her kiss brush his lips instead of his forehead.

Miraculous, Fisher thought.

Lena had a way of making him feel good (or, if she wished, bad!) no matter what the circumstances. He would make more of an effort this time with her, he promised himself. And Fisher was proud of himself for focusing on her so long when so many other questions burned. She deserved that much. The mission was a success; she had been a good captain, in the final analysis. It boded well for their future together, at least for the return voyage.

Still, the moment the portal closed Fisher said, "Confess, Papa. You weren't just spinning a yarn to keep me alive while I was working on the alignment, were you? You really found something. Your fictional stories aren't usually as interesting as the whopper you told me."

Please, he thought.

"We found something." Images blossomed into existence on the ceiling above Fisher, the egg rotating in the magnetized plasma of its cage. "Watch."

The point of view spiraled in as the egg grew to fill the ceiling and then spilled onto the walls, dizzily spinning like the flashing lights of a trendy club that Stearn might frequent. The shiny silver surface of the egg was not smooth. As the view continued to close and match the spin, topography manifested: regularly raised and depressed regions congregating in loops and whorls, like fingerprints.

"This is visible light?" Fisher asked.

"Effectively," said Papa, "although we've enhanced the images you're seeing with some artificial shadows to bring out the relief."

Fisher grunted. He wished he could pace.

Closer and closer came the egg. The whorls spilled onto the walls, and the subfeatures grew into focus. Fisher blinked. Tiny pictures hung along the pattern like pearls on a necklace. Dragons alone, in packs, swimming with other creatures that were not dragons. And the dragons he saw differed in several respects from the disk dragons. These had what must be fins, which implied they were in a proper liquid rather than a rarefied plasma. Dragons mating like whales, a female with a male, and a second male to hold her in place in the neutral buoyancy. All sorts of dragon scenes. It reminded Fisher of an ancient Roman urn with images of daily life painted all around. More images followed, and he saw the things that had led Papa to his fantastic story: images of cylindrical visitors in bubbles, a map of a stellar system, maps of stars. Other images flashed by, and Fisher understood that the egg was more than a future life; it represented everything that had gone before as well.

"The dragons are smart, but the form they hold now is completely constructed. And they didn't do it themselves," said Papa. "There's more."

"More?" asked Fisher, afraid to blink lest he miss something.

"This is just the surface relief. The egg holds coded information when viewed in at least four other ways. We're continuing to search every way we can imagine."

"Why would they have done such a thing? It's too easy."

"We can't say for sure, of course, unless that information is coded within the egg also. But we can guess, and we have a pretty good guess. They were proud of what they had done."

"Proud?" Fisher let that notion roll around in his head, testing to see if it fit. "I don't know, Papa. That seems rather, well, human, doesn't it?"

"Perhaps. But if we're right, they were like us, at least in some ways."

Fisher felt as if he'd been struck between the eyes. Aliens, proud like humans would be. There was no reason there had to be any similarities. Well, he would have time to consider the ramifications later. He had other immediate concerns. "The dragon within . . . is it viable? Can we hatch it?"

"Probably. We've found some sequences, instructions if you will, that appear to address that question. Makes sense, if you think about it. Gives the eggs a chance to hatch if they're intercepted by intelligent minds."

Wave after wave of implication washed over Fisher then, setting his imagination adrift. But he had vowed that he would be in control of his obsessions, rather than the other way around. He reined in his thoughts. Start from the ground up. The ground, in this case, was SS Cygni.

There had been no dragonburst seen in SS Cygni in the seven hundred years that Earth astronomers had been watching, nor the extra two hundred and fifty years of their outbound journey. There had been no dragonbursts seen from any cataclysmic variables in that period, not just the known dwarf nova systems, in the semilocal galaxy. He would have to review the system archives concerning the ejecta from SS Cygni that they had ionized and shunted around them during their passage. There should be some way of identifying the remnants of a dragonburst from the debris of other events, and constructing a historical record of when the dragons had acted in their own defense. The nuclear beaters had surely set them off. Identifying historical dragonburst signatures would have immediate implications about how dense the galaxy was with overly curious technological species.

At least the intrusive rabbit-grabbing ones like humans.

They were not alone, but for some reason high-technology races hadn't already saturated this part of the Milky Way. Or if they had, now they were gone. Why was that?

There were always more whys, and the current string was growing exponentially in his mind.

Fisher took a deep breath and stretched his muscles against the restraining umbilicals. They would be hands again soon enough, and feet for pacing, and he would be able work properly. He said, "OK, Papa. Have Henderson bring me some Forget-Me-Not, and then show me *everything*."

"Are you sure that would be prudent?" Papa asked.

Damn him, Fisher thought. But Papa's intervention gave him pause enough, and he recalled how Lena's lips had felt against his own, how that fleeting touch had unexpectedly thrilled him. How she deserved better. He had climbed a mountain. Was he ready to leave the summit already?

"Belay that request," he amended. "There's time enough later, after I've rested. There's time enough for everything."

Time enough to answer all the whys, and maybe even for love as well.

Fisher smiled as he drifted off to dream of dragons and much, much more.

EPILOGUE

Our birth is but a sleep and a forgetting:
The soul that rises with us, our life's star,
Hath had elsewhere its setting,
And cometh from afar.
Not in entire forgetfulness,
And not in utter nakedness,
But trailing clouds of glory, do we come
From God, who is our home:
Heaven lies about us in our infancy.
—WILLIAM WORDSWORTH

The *Karamojo* blazed like a comet, its tail pointing at SS Cygni, headed back toward a distant rendezvous with where Earth would be some two hundred and fifty years hence. Incubating inside nestled the dragon egg, for the moment warmed by the filtered radiation of the fore singularity's accretion. The seeds of many arguments were immediately planted with its presence and how it would be accommodated on the voyage home, a Pandora's box like that of every as-yet-unlived life—only perhaps a little more so in this case. The information cascade began from Biolathe's piled-up tightbeam, a half-millennium of updated mission directives, a half-millennium of data about the new old world that would be theirs again within a year, in fact a half-millennium of the history of an entire galactic civilization that was being born.

Every moment of the return flight would be an adventure on the *Karamojo*.

For the star dragons of SS Cygni, there also existed myriad adventures.

Not all the dragons had ended their existence to drive the mass loss from the secondary. First there were the eggs. Not the same as the dragons that had spawned them, not exactly, but carrying their stories into the future. That future was short for half of them: lost at once in the fury of the dragonfire birth, incinerated despite their strong shell or propelled into the secondary with too high a velocity to survive. Of the remainder, half again would have an infinite but dark future, launched into trajectories out of the galactic plane and into a halo too rarefied to host enough suitable homes. Half again of the remainder would survive their fiery birth, fly into the dense spiral arms of the Milky Way, instinctually alter their courses using varying albedos and magnetic fields, and still slingshot past the only suitable star they would ever approach—or smack into it too sharply and vanish forever in a puff of plasma. A tiny fraction would survive, somehow, incubating in a new star's convective womb, awaiting the inexorable evolution that would spawn a new disk to inhabit. From that tiny fraction, somewhere, somewhen, disks would live again and host a civilization onward into the infinite future.

An even tinier fraction of the dragon eggs was intercepted, kidnapped, studied, and probed by prying alien minds. The messages the redesigners had left revealed that they looked upon this as another course for survival for the dragon species, and a chance to show off their solution.

The adventure of the surviving adults would continue, a culture of fire that still thrilled those born of water. Thousands of adult dragons remained in the atmosphere of the star, for some indeterminable time gasping like spent salmon at their spawning point. These had failed to detonate in the rhythm of the dragonburst but would not die like the upstream salmon; drifting with the sputter of the resumed mass transfer, they would restart their society as the new accretion disk assembled itself. These dragons would remember the songs called out when the sacrifices had been made, and would remember the disruptive visit of this great white visitor. This threatening annoyance, and the annoyances before it, and the annoyances that would follow. And they would remember in new songs they would sing. And sing them they would now and forever, in some form, some place, some time.